WAR HOUR

LAUREN LOSCIG

War Hour

Copyright © 2023 by Lauren Loscig

Published by LNL Publishing LLC

First Edition published November 2023

Cover Design © 2023 by Cover Dungeon Rabbit

Naked Hardcover Design © 2023 by Scribbubbles

Map Design © 2023 by Cartographybird Maps

Edited by Samantha Pico

Identifiers

ISBN: 979-8-9881018-0-2 (eBook)

ISBN:979-8-9881018-2-6 (paperback)

ISBN:979-8-9881018-1-9 (hardcover)

laurenloscig.com

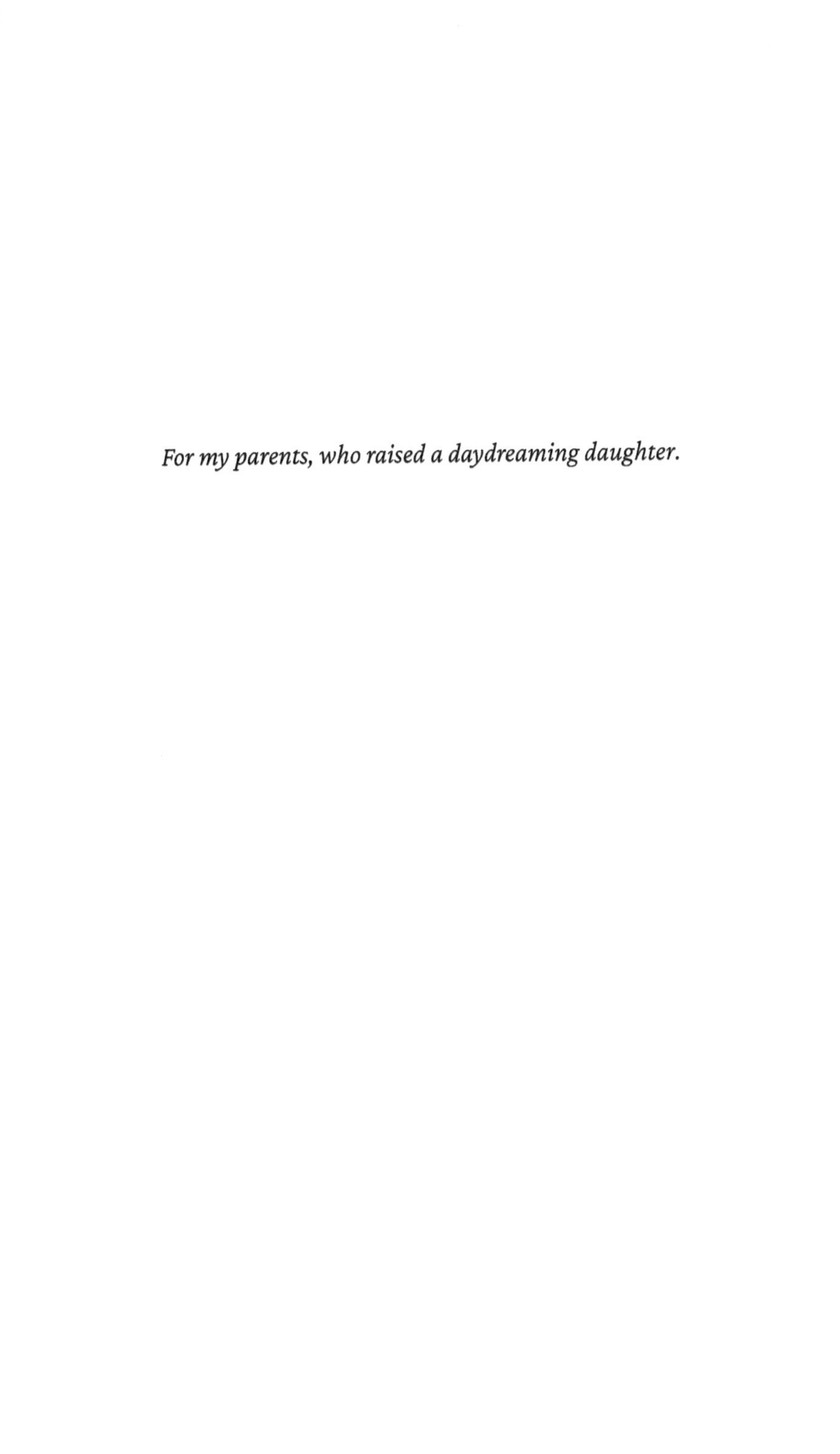

For my parents, who raised a daydreaming daughter.

THE COURTS OF
ALORIA
BROGAN
COURT OF WISDOM
FALLAND
COURT OF VALOR
CRIMSO
CAPITAL
THE BORDER FOREST
COURT OF TRUTH
ANDOLIN
TO SOUTHERN SEAS

TO UNCHARTED NORTHERN SEAS
TRATHE
KASTEAD
COURT OF
VIRTUE
COURT OF
SELF
ASS
COURT OF
CHANGE
COURT OF
WILL
BREYMORE
SEREECE

PRONUNCIATION GUIDE

<u>Names</u>

Thoman: TAH-mihn

Lysta: LIHS-tuh

Doireann: DOHR-ee-an

Ardis: ar-DIHS

Torryn: TOHR-ihn

Sarielle: SAR-ee-ehl

Gennady: GEHN-uh-dee

Bralas: BRAW-luhs

Ivianna: ihv-ee-AHN-a

Rhen: REHN

Nicaise: nih-KAY-see

Evander: eh-VAN-dehr

Neith: NEE-th

Visha: VEE-sha

Nennirea: neh-NEER-ee-uh

CHAPTER I

I don't make a habit of gambling with my life, but fifty-fifty odds are too compelling for even me to pass up.

It could always be a hundred.

The reassurance doesn't stop the breath from lodging in my throat as the decider of my fate flips above Thoman and I. No— *both* of our fates. Every muscle in my body turns to stone as it plummets.

It's been over a month since the last Trialing, and with each day that passes, the threat to Untrialed only grows. There's no doubt the Guard will be out in full force because of it, but that changes nothing.

One of us needs to brave the market to replenish our food supply.

Hence flipping a coin.

When the bronze coin ricochets off the rickety floorboards, I flinch as if each bounce threatens to sentence one of us to a cruel end. Spinning on its edge in a tight circle, it slows until it clinks to one side.

Crown side up.

I inhale sharply and allow myself a moment of self-pity. But the second my hands tremble, I clench them, tucking away my emotions for when Thoman's gaze isn't piercing me.

If I show even a hint of hesitation, he'll insist on being the one to go—my brother in every way but blood. Thoman's never been good at just keeping his head down.

It's better if I go.

"Trials, Lysta," Thoman curses under his breath, looking away from me. He takes a shaky breath, closing his eyes in a pained expression. "You went last time—just let me go."

Too predictable.

"And you went twice before that," I shoot back, already tugging my boots onto my feet. "It's my turn."

Thoman shakes his head, posture crumpling. "This isn't like other trips, and you know it." His voice is barely more than a whisper, making me pause.

He thinks today will be the day I don't come back.

Maybe he's right, but there is no convincing me it isn't my turn to face the streets.

"I'll be back before you know it." I'm out the door and hurrying down the street before he can make an argument against it.

THE THREAT of Trialing looms like a blade hung from a fraying rope. It isn't a matter of if the remaining threads will break free and send the weapon plunging, but of when—and the fearful anticipation is a greater torture than any killing blow the knife could deal.

It's days like these where uncertainty weighs especially heavy. Tension laces the fog-filled city of Falland, the feeling palpable as I cross through the Market Plaza.

Fewer people linger in the street than what is typical of the weekly affair. On most Sundays, they overcrowd the rows of stalls, packing them so tightly that weaving through ties your path in knots. Each person on their own mission of scrabbling together a pitiful amount of food before only the stale or turned items remain.

But, today, when the market vendors have just received their freshest stock from beyond the wall, there are only scattered handfuls of people.

It sets my teeth on edge.

People are lying low rather than risking the streets, even for the absolute necessities. It's been two weeks since I've braved the market for the same reason, but today would have to break that streak.

Tucking my head down as I dart through the stalls, I survey passing faces and shops for anything showing a need to cut my trip short—anyone dashing into an alley or signaling others with lingering looks—while listening for telltale shouts of the guard trying to rouse trouble.

The guards always make themselves known on Market Day. They flock to the streets, preying on the Untrialed at our most desperate, and put us under constant scrutiny. Punishment is swift in Falland but not fair. If the right person is watching, all it takes is one misstep, and anyone could face Trialing. They could handpick their desired flavor of justice for the day and ruin a life in one fell swoop.

It's exhausting. The unrelenting state of anticipation and fearfulness, but it's Falland's normal.

But today—is a new level of distressing.

The city is quiet. Quieter than I've ever heard it. Even the typical shouting matches between customer and vendor have subsided, haggling for a few coins saved not worth the attention it brings. It's unnerving to hear the boisterous district reduced to subdued grumbles and whispers.

Steeling my nerves, I hurry deeper into the plaza. I could be in and out of the market in ten minutes if I don't stumble into trouble. With only two stops in the maze of stalls, I'll have enough stale bread, potatoes, and dried meat to last Thoman and me a couple of weeks.

Stocked up on supplies, we won't have to risk the market until tensions ease.

At the end of the ninth row, tucked into the corner beneath the broken clock tower, is my first stop: Doireann. A friendly face—if there is such a thing in Falland.

Strolling up to her stall, head on a swivel, I watch people huddle around the older woman's cart before stepping up. When Doireann catches sight of me dawdling in her shrinking line, her face brightens. The beginnings of a smile chase away the frown permanently curving her lips.

"Anything new today, Doireann?" I ask, cringing at how awkward the pleasantry sounds coming from me.

She nods with a knowing gaze, a teasing smile growing in jest.

I'm no fan of small talk and its inconsequential conversation. The streets aren't the place to linger, but I indulge the elderly woman anyway, and she knows it.

"Same as usual, I suppose," Doireann says, a crease deepening between her brows. "It's been a while since you and Thoman have been around. Keeping out of trouble?"

Her voice is casual as she asks, but her strangling grip on the medallion hanging from her neck betrays her.

I reach out to still her twisting fingers. My gaze softens when I attempt to deliver a reassuring tone. "Not more than we can handle, but I'll be sure to tell Thoman he needs to take his turn coming here."

While the worry in her eyes doesn't ease, she nods stiffly in acceptance.

Trouble isn't avoidable on the streets, especially in times like these, but Doireann would single-handedly worry about every kid she knows of—probably even the ones she doesn't.

Most children on the streets are orphans because of Trialing, their parents taken and never returned. What makes it worse is not finding out if they'd died during the deadly test or if they'd succeeded and for whatever reason couldn't come back for them.

Neither is an easy truth to swallow. I think it's better off not knowing.

But Doireann, with her wrinkled skin and a few missing teeth, has been there for many of the street kids. Providing them with manageable tasks for food. Small jobs, such as sweeping around her cart or organizing the items lining her shelves.

I met Doireann as a starving twelve-year-old who nicked some bread from a vendor, and a member of the Guard was watching.

My older sister, Cenna, had been sick from lack of food. We'd gotten by just fine off pity scraps from passersby on the streets but then Lord Drytas had outlawed panhandling, and we couldn't risk it any longer.

Having seen me sprint down the street, Doireann had ushered me behind her stall, hiding me well after the guards had passed.

They couldn't have Trialed me yet, since the Trial doors won't open for anyone under fourteen, but that wouldn't have stopped them from finding another punishment for me.

For three years after, Doireann had given me meals for running her deliveries across the city. Her busted knee made it difficult for her to walk distances, so our arrangement worked for us. I didn't mind the work when my stomach was full at the end of the night, even if the exhaustion of the day always seeped into the next.

Eventually, I passed the job to someone who needed it more, and now Market Day is my only chance to check in on Doireann.

A crash down the street compels us to whip around, and I step in front of Doireann's tiny frame. I flinch toward my hip, where my dagger lay hidden beneath layers of cloth and leather. Fingers flexing in anticipation, I scan the plaza for the source of the commotion.

A wooden crate lay broken on the cobblestone, an array of vegetables rolling away from the scene. The owner of the cart stoops to pick up the scattered items, shaking his head, and the tension eases from my stiffened muscles.

I drop my hand from my side, the weight of the weapon comforting, despite the danger of possessing it.

Turning back to Doireann, I open my mouth to continue but stop when I see her gaze has landed on my hip. The clack of teeth is audible as my jaw snaps shut.

Weapons are forbidden for Untrialed in Falland.

Having stepped back, I force myself to regain the space I vacated. Doireann tilts her head to the side, a worried frown growing on her face.

If the Guard catches me with the weapon, it would mean certain Trialing.

Excuses and explanations flicker across the front of my mind, but my lips refuse to form words. I can't lie to her.

Shaking her head, Doireann avoids the topic, instead pushing a large bag into my hands, the contents shifting as I grip the burlap.

"Get headed home, Lysta. I have a bad feeling about today."

Feeling chastised, I juggle the bag over into the crook of one arm before fumbling with my coin purse. "How much for the—"

A wrinkled hand closes over mine and the purse. Doireann shakes her head. "Next time."

Any argument bubbling up dies at the shadow of fear crossing her face. Following her line of sight, I see two guards entering our block, and my heart forgets to beat.

Their gray suits with red trim stand out, even in the dreary street. Pinned to their chests shines the shield of our court—the Court of Valor.

The street freezes, unanimously holding their breath, as the guards saunter to where the vendor kneels, picking up his stock. When their figures loom over him, the vendor goes still, hand hovering over a potato. He retracts his reach, standing slowly, but his gaze never leaves the ground.

Just out of earshot, I can't hear what the guards say to him, but he pales and shakes his head. One guard steps closer, pushing a finger into his chest, nudging him backward, as he sneers into the vendor's terrified face.

Then the guard raises his hand, and several vegetables lift with it. The vendor watches silently as his livelihood swirls around him, as if caught in a windless tornado.

Doireann murmurs from behind me, "Maybe you should head out, Lysta." She gestures to the alley near her stand.

"Aren't you coming?"

She shakes her head, gaze not leaving the distressed vendor. "I need to stay with my cart. It'll only draw more attention if I leave it."

Vegetables thud as they rain down on the street. Wilted cabbages explode midair as the guard squeezes his fist. The other joins the chaos, knocking over the cart with a simple wave.

The vendor just watches, his spirit deflated, as the guards

destroy what remains of his stall. But he can't fight back, can't argue for them to stop. Because he would be disobeying a member of the Guard, and they would have reason to take him to Trial.

Instead, he stands there and takes the abuse, as we all have. Because if we don't crack, then they cannot take us. If we don't give them anything to use, then they have no control over us.

"Go, Lysta."

Clenching my fists, I fight the urge to intervene, my nails forming tiny crescents in my palms. This is why I didn't want Thoman to be the one to come. Because he would already be over there regardless of the consequences. He's better than me in that sense.

I'm brave in the easy ways. It's nothing to conceal an illegal weapon if it means protecting myself. But in moments like these, when it's safer to fall to the background, I'm reminded *that* kind of bravery is reserved for hero types.

No one would say Falland has a lot of those left alive.

Pushing down my frustration, I turn into the alley leading away from the market.

Part of me questions how this is worth it. The endless precautions and planning, the fear. The answer pulses like the heartbeat thrumming through my body.

It simply isn't.

CHAPTER 2

Navigating Falland's streets is second nature to those of us who have been surviving them our whole life. You build a map in your head. It starts out vague, with only general directions and street names, but over time, it fills in. Fills with the places that are dry when it storms and the nooks big enough to hide in when trouble comes calling. And when you're a kid on your own, trouble always comes calling.

I can still picture that determined little girl who fought with everything she had to survive. And today, I swear I'm looking right at her.

Just eleven or twelve, the girl who is now sprinting up the street toward me is a mirror image of my younger self. Her hair, a muddy mix between brown and blonde, with streaks of dirt across her face. Scuffs mar her skin, with a swollen cut on her lower lip. In her hands, she grips half a loaf of bread.

Feet pounding against the ground, she rips past me and into the adjacent alley. The alley I know leads to a dead end.

How you could live here for longer than a year and not know baffles me.

A few paces behind, three men stumble forward in chase,

one with blood dripping from his nose, coating his teeth with a red tinge. As they disappear into the alley, the pieces of the puzzle click, and I know how this will end.

I've found myself in the same position more times than I can count—outnumbered and unprepared.

I struggle to keep walking as I hover near the entrance to the alley. Getting involved would only put me in danger, especially if a fight breaks out with the guard just a few streets away.

Even if I know the kids of the street are tougher than they look, it's the one thing that never fails to turn my stomach. Surviving in Falland relies heavily on being selfish.

I think back to the vendor who'd stood silently at his stall and witnessed the destruction of his only means to support himself.

Maybe we all would fare better if we didn't just grit our teeth and keep our heads down. Or is the self-preservation ingrained in us too strong to overcome?

At the end of the alley, the girl stands with her back to the three men, staring at the wall blocking off her exit. When the men reach her, the shortest grips the girl's hair and yanks her.

I grit my teeth like I'm trying to sand them down flat.

They wouldn't continue if they knew the guard was so close —not over a lump of measly bread.

I don't know what makes me act. Maybe it's the girl's resemblance to me appealing to some selfish tendency, or the lingering shame at walking away from the defenseless vendor?

Either way, my feet march toward the alley before I make my decision.

～

THE STUBBORN LOOK on the girl's face wills me into action. Cornered by men who are twice her size and weight, the girl stares down her nose at them as if they are wasting her time.

I half expect her to roll her eyes.

In a smooth motion, she grabs the hand holding her hair, twisting it until it forces the man to let go or risk snapping it. She's out of their grip before I pass the alley entrance.

The three men opposite her look familiar, faces I've likely seen in passing, but nothing beyond vague recollection. Tracking any exposed skin, I see no sign of Trial tattoos, confirming my suspicions. They aren't of the Guard, or any other group of Trialed.

These men might be nuisances, but they would listen to reason. Everyone fears Trialing; thus, everyone avoids the Guard. It's the one thing you can trust on Falland's streets—what keeps people in line.

The man with the bloody, broken nose steps forward, growling in the girl's face. "Didn't think you'd really get away with it, did ya, girl?"

The girl really does roll her eyes, and even down the alley, I can hear her snort. I bite back the smile curling the corner of my mouth and slow my approach.

"Original," the girl scoffs as she leans back, resting her upper back on the brick wall and crossing her legs at the ankle. Confidence rolls off her in waves as she picks at her nails, bread tucked under her arm, completely unfazed by the men who look ready to rip her apart.

They falter at the girl's casual attitude. As they exchange a loaded glance, it's obvious they don't know how to respond. Faces reddening, in either anger or embarrassment, the men continue without acknowledging her retort.

"I've been itching for a fight, so maybe I should teach you a lesson."

The brutes on either side of the leader must be all muscle and no mouth because they've yet to say a word. But they step forward, cracking their thick necks and balling their hands into fists.

The girl smirks at the threat, reaching out to the side before waving toward herself. "I'm ready when you are."

My eyes nearly bulge out of my head at her audacity, practically begging the brutes to hit her. Who knows how she lasted on these streets with an ego like hers? Either way, stupidity doesn't mean she deserves a beating.

Clearing my throat, I pass the men, edging myself between them and the girl. My gaze meets hers, and her eyes widen.

For a moment, it's as if she recognizes me but then she shakes her head, muttering, "Stay out of this."

Furrowing my brows, I'm taken aback. I can understand her hesitancy. Even I would rarely trust a helping hand in Falland but not in a fight where I'm bound to lose.

Turning on my heel to face the men, I announce with a tremble of confidence, "Now I don't want to assume what was about to happen"—I cross my arms—"but I should warn you, the Guard was just in the market."

Even the two morons staring vacantly at me perk at the name of the guard, anxiety flaring across their faces as they look to their leader.

No one would pull anything as obvious as starting a fight when they risk being caught.

"That's a good point, Roebin. The market is only a few blocks—"

"No," the bleeding man, Roebin spats. "This brat broke my nose." His eyes narrow into slits as he peers past my shoulder to the girl standing behind me. "She's not getting off without punishment."

Before I have the time to regret stepping in, the two brutes rush forward, each latching onto one of my arms. Without hesitation, I try to throw them off balance, using the weight of my body to wrench my hands free. They lift me, grips bruising as they squeeze me. My toes skim the gravel near my feet.

I double over as a fist folds my stomach from the force of the hit.

Again.

Again.

Coughing, I gasp. Sharp pain stabs my chest as I try to reinsert the air into my lungs. A final blow to my jaw knocks me down. A metallic taste coats my tongue, and I spit to the side, blood landing on the ground next to me.

The seething men turn from me toward the young girl, and I panic.

When you're on your own, the only consequence of failing is on you. But here I am, thinking I could help for once and now someone else would pay for it. My heart squeezes from failure's sting, but desperation claws through me.

I know I'll regret this, but I can't stop the urge to do it anyway.

With a glance down the alley, I confirm there aren't any members of the Guard in sight—no one.

Hesitating, I tear the layer of fabric obscuring the metal hilt of my dagger. Pulling the blade from its concealed sheath, I push off the ground and get my feet under me.

I'm not afraid, with its blade poised as a protective barrier between me and them. Instead, my confidence surges, the thrill of the fight pulsing through my veins like lightning. Waking me up from a pacified neutrality.

Creeping up behind the men that crowd the young girl, I get my arm around the leader's neck and angle the dagger toward the delicate skin of his throat.

Roebin becomes stone beneath my hands, a strangled yelp

drawing the attention of the other two men. Circling me, they eye their friend's predicament, exchanging a worried glance.

With the upper hand, I position myself between them and the younger girl. Adrenaline thrums through my body, and I feel more awake—more alive than I ever have before.

Their faces reflect their stirring anxiety at my grasp on the weapon, but their expressions shift. Mouths drop, eyes widening—not at me but several inches above my head.

Sputtering intangible sentences, the men step backward, the first time they retreat since entering the narrow alley.

Inching forward, I knit my eyebrows as I watch them flee and knock over stacks of garbage lining the walls in their haste.

Real loyal friends, abandoning the man trying to pull my weapon away from him.

A weapon in the streets may warrant a double take but not enough to make threats just run away.

Turning my head, I hold my breath as I look to see what scared the men, as it certainly hadn't been me.

The brazen girl who startled me with her uncanny resemblance to a younger Lysta is no longer behind me.

Height climbing, shape morphing from a small girl to a teenage boy. Features shift in the blink of an eye. The darker blonde hair that had resembled mine has lightened into a fairer shade, and his gray eyes are swallowed in blue.

Panicking, I release the still struggling man, and he falls to the street in a heap. Roebin scrambles to his feet and runs, the smack of his shoes against the cobblestone echoing in the alley.

I don't understand. My mind whirls to catch up with the change of events, but it feels as if I'm leagues behind. Nothing about the boy in front of me soothes the fear billowing inside me, my inflated confidence shrinking into the hole it just dug itself out of.

It isn't one of the powers you can earn from the Court of

Valor's Trial, changing your appearance as if you were shedding a shirt.

Understanding pieces itself together, as rumors slot into place with what just happened—I realize he's a shifter.

I know so little about the other courts of Aloria, but I've heard of people from the Court of Change. It must be where he's from.

He takes a warning step in my direction, as if knowing what runs through my mind. When I back up, heart racing in my chest, he matches each stride before reaching out to grab hold of me.

"I really wish you hadn't done that."

The low timber of his voice, a drastic difference from the girl who stood here a minute ago, breaks me free from my paralysis like shock.

A scream for help catches deep in my throat as I tug, trying to rip my hand free from his steely grip. The more I pull, the tighter he squeezes until my fingers release the dagger. It hits the ground with a clatter of metal on stone.

Eyeing the dagger just out of reach, I focus on getting free. I twist, trying to move our position to my advantage, but his hand shifts. Pinning mine behind my back, he presses our chests together.

Head quirking to the side, he watches me with a dangerous glimmer in his eyes. He doesn't say a word but waits, as if expecting me to inevitably give up.

I slam my body into his, colliding his head and shoulder with the wall. But his grip doesn't loosen, nor does his gaze drift.

Craning my neck to see down the alleyway, I pray someone comes looking at the sound of our fight. As a shadow passes in front of the alley, I shout, "Hey! Help me out! Please!"

My distress obvious, I cannot keep the pleading out of my voice.

I don't expect anyone to come running to my aid. Whoever is passing by wouldn't double take at a cry for help. But maybe it would scare the shifter into fleeing at the risk of more people discovering his presence.

"Shut it," the boy hisses into my ear. "Wait, listen to me."

I ignore him, continuing to shout.

The shadow steps back into my line of sight—a member of the Guard.

It's hard to squash the ingratiated feeling of fear at the sight of the uniformed men, but they would help. The shifter gripping my wrists is an outsider. An intruder. Even if they have an issue with me, just a lowly Untrialed, they always hold the security of the court and the city as a top priority.

When the shifter curses under his breath, I take it as confirmation.

"Help! Someone has infiltrated the city. He's of another court!" I blurt out.

As the member of the Guard approaches, a look of recognition floods his face, and I stop breathing.

He *knows* the shifter.

"Ardis, I see you've hit the ground running," the guard says, nodding to the man in acknowledgment.

The floor all but drops from under my feet. Their words become fuzzy just as my tongue gets dry, feeling like it doesn't sit right in my mouth. My eyes flicker between them, my brain struggling to catch up to the surprising turn of events.

"Yeah, mind helping me get her to Drytas? She's a bit of a fighter."

Drytas. Lord Drytas. Lord of the Court of Valor and presider over the Trial.

Great.

CHAPTER 3

The walk to the grand hall where I'll face Trialing resembles my reoccurring nightmares. The ones where, when I finally wake up, I'm drenched in a cold sweat, hyperventilating. Not sure of where I am but begging not to be Trialed.

It's the same building I fought to follow my sister into, screaming my voice hoarse as they led her inside of her own free will. Choosing to leave me behind as I sobbed into the ground, wishing she would stay. Too young to follow her.

It's a conscious effort to keep up as I stumble forward. The two members of the Guard pull me along without faltering.

I try blinking away the memories like I would a few stray tears, but they haunt each step I take. Getting caught up in my emotions would only be a detriment to me now. I'd rather show indifference than weakness.

As we near the grand hall of the Court of Valor, anticipation vibrates inside me, with every instinct screaming for me to run in the opposite direction. Shifting, the steel chains containing my wrists bite into skin, metal clanking with each movement, announcing our approach to the street.

You can see the grand hall in practically every corner of the city. Its design resembles a shield, with layers of steel scaling its sides. I've gawked at it my whole life, first in curiosity and later contempt, as I felt the repercussions of Lord Drytas's power-crazed rule.

My accused crime wouldn't yield an arraignment or sentencing, no opportunity to defend myself. They will hold me strictly to the consequences of possessing a weapon.

It seems Falland will have its Trial after all.

Ardis, the shifter who so easily tricked me, walks ahead, examining the streets as we trek upward. Not a trace was left of the young girl who dashed past me in the market except for his lingering smirk.

The cheekiness is no longer cute now that it's on him.

I wish I could smack the expression from his face for even looking at my city, the one he is helping rip apart by aiding Lord Drytas.

The guards bordering me watch him, spines rigid, eyes narrowing. Following, I can feel them tensing at his every movement, and one thing becomes obvious. Despite their friendly greeting of the foreigner, they fear him, far more than they do me, as they have yet to spare me a glance.

Ironic, considering I'm the one in shackles.

When the member of the Guard had arrived at the opening of the alley, I had hoped they'd stumbled upon us by accident. Perhaps they would chain the outsider who had deceived me, but as the guard had greeted him with a faint air of recognition, my stomach had dropped. It was all part of some ruse. Using the image of a hurt girl to entrap an Untrialed into breaking the law.

How desperate they have gotten. How stupid I had been.

Guards mumble behind me, a sharp laugh drawing my attention.

"She's just a waste of a Trial. You think she'll actually pass it?"

The other guard chuckles in response. "She'll be ripped to shreds. I'm counting on one thing happening, getting one more Untrialed off the street—and that's it."

I can't help but stiffen. Even the guards know Drytas's plan to Trial everyone is pointless.

Eyes follow our path through Falland as they parade me along. Whispers burn through the streets as more people arrive to gawk at me and the foreign figure leading the way. They know where I am being taken, most likely feeling a rush of relief.

I don't blame them. I would be, too, if the roles were reversed.

If they Trial someone, pressure would die down for a time.

Panic seizes my heart and without hesitating I focus on anything but the guards who lead me forward. My chest heaves as my eyes dart around, settling on Gellmore Street. Barely more than an alley, the concrete walls are smothered in graffiti criticizing Lord Drytas, the court, and the Trial. Mostly abandoned shops, with broken windows and boarded doors.

My staggering breaths slow.

Peddler Street is the complete opposite despite being a block over, filled to the brim with people trading clothes and supplies. A hot spot for pickpockets but a lifesaver for many. There's even an underground tattoo shop where Untrialed can get fake Trial marks, for those hoping to sneak their way into the upper city. It would take years to save up enough for Thoman and I.

I can no longer hear the pound of my heart in my ears, instead focusing on the voices pouring from the street.

For every problem the Untrialed faced because of Lord Drytas's reign, there were ten solutions cleverly crafted to push back against it. But if Drytas is recruiting outside of our own court, I'm not sure if there is a way to solve that.

Composure regained, I look to the sky and thank the Trials that I didn't lose it here—in front of the shifter and guards and onlookers. I may not be choosing to Trial, but I'll walk into the grand hall head high like I did.

Grounded, I peer at the shifter who marches forward.

"You're from the Court of Change."

Ardis glances my way, giving me a glimpse at his profile. Jaw clenching, he twists his lips into a grimace and doesn't respond.

"How did you—are you a—"

I'm unable to settle on what I truly wish to know, unsure of his reaction should I ask the wrong thing. Everything about this man is uncharted territory.

"How is it you are here? Why work for the Guard?" I ask.

Ardis stops, and I nearly fall backward to avoid smacking into his stationary frame. Turning on his heel, the man leans over me, smirking, clear blue eyes piercing into mine. "What makes you think I work for them?"

A hint of amusement dances in his eyes, reminding me of a cat cornering its meal.

I guess it would make me the street rat.

"Am I wrong?"

Ardis considers me, eyes tracing down to the iron bracelets framing my wrists. His playful mirth falls to a blank stare, and he admits solemnly, "I suppose not."

Returning to his trek up the inclining street, he sweeps his gaze to his feet, no longer enraptured in the city unfolding around him. He shakes his head as if arguing with himself yet says nothing.

I wonder if he has just as much choice in this as the rest of us.

My heart stops when I catch sight of Thoman. My eyes almost pass over him, hidden just out of sight—part of me wishes I had. I should have known he'd discover what happened before I even made it to the grand hall. Or maybe he'd drawn suspicious when I'd taken too long to return.

His lips are drawn into a deep frown, eyebrows knitted, as he watches me walk with wrists bound toward my fate. Thoman's hands clench into fists at his sides, and when I think he is about to move forward—planning to do something he shouldn't—I shake my head.

He doesn't heed my warning, stepping out from the opening of the alley and moving toward us.

The only good thing that came out of losing Cenna was that, if I hadn't, I'd never have met Thoman.

Angry and spiteful from being left behind, I'd talked myself into more fights than I could finish. Just a scrappy kid who couldn't throw a punch to save her life.

Thoman saw past my biting words when I'd tried to pick a fight with him. He was a few years older and twice as large. I'd been practically asking to get pounded. Instead, he taught me how to land a killer right hook.

Letting him follow me to what could be my death would not be how I repay him now.

I have to stop him. If he gets to me . . . I know Thoman better than anyone else, and he would interfere with the guards. And then he'd end up Trialing right alongside of me.

Lurching forward, I slam my shoulder into the shifter's side as if trying to take him out and make a run for it. The guards are on me before I can step away, yanking me into their grip.

Ardis looks at me with narrowed eyes. "That was a pitiful excuse for an escape attempt." He wrinkles his nose at me. "I'm actually disappointed."

Twisting my mouth, I glare back at him.

Dragging me past Ardis, the guards mumble to each other.

Even if I know better, I can't help but sneak a last glance over my shoulder, finding Thoman shrinking in the distance. He curses, kicking the nearby wall.

My eyes cross Ardis's, and I know he sees Thoman. A look of understanding passes over his face, and he appraises me with renewed suspicion. A rush of panic surges through me, and for a moment, I worry what he will do. Instead, he shakes his head, following us.

Thoman can be mad at me all he wants, but I am saving his life.

CHAPTER 4

I t isn't until I step through the doors of the grand hall that I consider making a run for it—which is a ridiculous concept now that I've crossed the threshold into Trialed territory. Dozens of guards focus on my every breath, capable of blocking any attempt at escaping.

They wouldn't even need to *move* to stop me.

Maybe I might have stood a chance on the streets but then my common sense had been stronger than my fear.

Here—now, the same can't be said. When fear is in charge, common sense is only a minor inconvenience to be ignored.

I've always wondered how the other half lives—the Trialed. But as the cold reality of my situation seeps down to my core, my eyes glaze over my surroundings. All I let myself see is the floor—black-and-white mosaic, so utterly spotless that it shines even in shadows.

I don't move my gaze from it, willing for this all to slip away like another nightmare.

Dragged to a stop, I barely process the sound of Ardis and more guards grumbling to each other. They go silent, and every second only adds to the weight on my chest.

Towering doors screech open as a man steps through, guards perking to attention at the sight of him. He stands to the side, a smirk creasing his mouth when he sees me, before gesturing for me to be brought inside.

My slow pace spurns the members of the Guard, who walk behind me and shove me forward. I bite my tongue, worried an impulsive quip will leave me gutted on the pristine floor. Knees shaking, I pray my cowardice isn't as visible as it feels.

Surveying the room, I note the members of the Guard lingering at each entryway, including the one we just entered. They possess no obvious weapons, and I have to remind myself that the Trialed do not need them to be dangerous. I can't help but periodically glance between the stone-faced guards.

A massive chandelier hangs above, lit candles reflecting off its crystals. Similar gaudy ornaments fill the room, screaming of the wealth occupying its walls. My blood boils at the sight.

At the furthest side of the room sits an imposing male figure, dressed in bright crimson clothes. A gold crown rests atop cropped salt-and-pepper hair. The middle-aged man stands out in the monochromatic space.

I've never been in the man's presence before, only knowing what I've heard in hushed gossip, but his residence upon the gold throne leaves no question of who he is.

Drytas, Lord of the Court of Valor.

Head held high, Ardis drops my arm and strides to Lord Drytas, a liberty I'd imagine few would entertain. He bows his head, gaze pointed to the ground. "My lord." He moves to stand several feet from his side.

"Ardis, the first day of our agreement, and you have already yielded results."

Drytas's voice crackles as he speaks, and a shiver works its way down my spine. His eyes roam over me, a glint passing across his face as he does.

Did he speak with Cenna before her Trialing? I grit my teeth, pushing the thought away.

As I turn toward Ardis, his eyes meet mine when he answers his lord. "An honor to be of service."

Lord Drytas raises his arms. "Now you see why the Court of Valor has more Trialed than any other court. This is how I keep my court strong under my rule. If I continued with the tradition of only Trialing voluntary challengers, then we wouldn't be as formidable as we are. And with your abilities, Ardis, we can do so much more."

Abilities—plural?

Ardis steps back hesitantly. "As I have succeeded thus far in our arrangement, I hoped to inquire about the other part of our deal—"

Lord Drytas flicks a dismissive wave. "Yes, of course. You may face our Trial as promised, with your continued *assistance* in this matter," he says, sneering at me across the room.

Eyebrows furrowing, I look between the two men for any sign of what they aren't saying. Face our Trialing? Why would Ardis choose to confront the Court of Valor's Trial? Especially considering he's already beaten his own.

Doesn't he know what could happen? How he might end up?

I avoid thinking about the permanent effects of the Trial should I fail—terrified of becoming a ghost of myself. Those who failed but had made it out with their lives would stumble out. Minds fractured and abandoned by their court to wander the streets, permanently stuck in their own delusions and nightmares.

"And Ardis?" Drytas adds. "Remember, our deal still stands regardless of the outcome of your Trial. I'm sure you know your powers are useless when Trialing."

Ardis nods, swallowing thickly, throat bobbing.

"Bring the girl here," Drytas bellows across the room, igniting the members of the Guard into action.

They drag me until I'm ten feet from the base of the throne. My shoes squeak, trying to find purchase on the ground to halt my movement.

A shot of anger pierces my cloud of numbness, and I whip my head around to retort, pushed to my breaking point by their manhandling. No Trial tattoo nor shield of the court gives them the right to knock me about like a piece of furniture who keeps getting in the way.

My voice cracks as I try to say, "Keep your hands off—"

My half-hearted retort is silenced as I'm backhanded, the side of my face recoiling to the right from the force of the blow. Pins and needles erupt across my cheek from the impact.

Unable to use the pressure of my hand to relieve the sting, I stare at the member of the Guard who struck me. I lower my jaw, rolling it to ease the discomfort. I blink away the mist cresting my eyes, unwilling to let him see me cry. Stepping back from him, I can't help but shake my head in disbelief.

"My hands are literally tied."

Sarcasm drips off my voice to hide how affected I am.

His nose flares, eyes narrowing as he looks at me. In the breath of a second, the member of the Guard vanishes from his spot until he reappears, nearly stepping on my toes. Gripping my throat, he squeezes. "Tell me again—how you think you are on my level."

He looks like every other guard I've seen, same uniform, same Court of Valor tattoo swirling around the wrist of the hand cutting off my air. But this man couldn't be your average, low-level member of the Guard, his power allowing transportation across spaces, one of the lesser produced by the Trials. I've never witnessed it on the streets of Falland.

"Belthan, that's enough," Lord Drytas says, leaving no room for question.

The hand encircling my throat tightens for a beat before letting go, the force of which has me stumbling backward, coughing as I suck in air. A smug look crosses his face, making me clench my fists and flex my fingers.

Oh, how I wish my hands were free.

"Possessing a weapon in my court wasn't enough, but now you'll disrespect me and my head of the Guard." Drytas tilts his head to the side, eyeing me. "You are either extremely brave or very foolish."

Facing the lord who sits high on his throne, I'm unsure of what to say—if he expects me to say anything at all. Is one expected to apologize in this situation?

When I don't respond, Lord Drytas seems to take my silence as submission.

"Kneel. Kneel before your lord, and I shall be merciful. Should you pass your Trial, you may join the upper city or the Guard if I find you suited."

I swallow my scoff of disbelief. A lord who leaves some to starve while others get to live in luxury? A lord who amassed his power by condemning innocent people to Trialing. None of these were examples of any lord I owe loyalty to.

"You are no lord of the streets."

I push the words out between my teeth with little thought, having heard them muttered my whole life.

A wave of darkness crosses Drytas's face, and I swear if I weren't already likely to die in my Trial, I would be now.

My feet lift from the ground, my body stiffening as I rise. Drytas's hand sweeps across the room, and I move with it. Terror floods my body. Trying to shift, I feel as if I am attempting to mold stone. It is just like in the streets, when the guards tossed items and food around but on an infinitely larger scale. I hover above the ground until I'm mere feet from the foot of the throne.

I didn't know their powers were strong enough to do this.

Panicked, eyes wide, I look to Ardis, who doesn't meet my gaze.

"I. Said. Kneel."

With a force stronger than gravity, I slam into the tile floor, knees making impact. I'm held in place, breath rushing in and out of my body in short gasps. Pressure grips my chin, not unlike a hand, and wrenches my head up. From my kneeling position, I stare at Lord Drytas.

This is the face of my suffering and every other Untrialed in Falland. He is the reason I and so many others have grown up with no family. The reason we all starve. He may not have taken Cenna by the hand and dragged her into the Court of Valor's Trial, but he was the reason all the same.

Stepping toward me, face inches from mine, Lord Drytas snarls, "They all kneel. Eventually."

Spitting at the floor near his feet, I grin crookedly as he looks at me in disgust. "Willingly?"

CHAPTER 5

A member of the Guard leads me from the grand hall, pulling me along as I limp. I give up on concealing the grimaces permanently etched on my face but lock away each whimper begging to be released.

At first, I try to memorize the halls like I did the streets of Falland. A right turn. A long hall. Another right turn. A left down some stairs. But once we reach the bottom floor, there are too many changes, and I mentally curse when I lose track. It's unrealistic to think I can remember it all, but my heart still sinks as my method of escape evaporates like the memorized path in my head.

Footsteps sound behind us, and I try to look over my shoulders, but the guard yanks me forward.

"Hold up. Drytas wants me to take her."

I immediately recognize Ardis's voice, but the guard doesn't seem to. Sneering, he pulls me to a stop and turns. "And who do you think you—"

His face pales several shades when he sees the shifter behind him. Swallowing the rest of his sentence, he nods rapidly, holding my arm out to him.

Ardis, having yet to look at me, grips my arm, watching the guard. When he doesn't leave, Ardis says in a slow drawl, "Dismissed."

Muttering, the man speed walks away, but it goes unnoticed by Ardis. Once out of sight, the grip on my arm loosens, and we start forward.

Peering at him out of the corner of my eye, I wait for him to say something. A cruel joke at my situation or a snarky comment about what happened in the throne room. But he doesn't, and I welcome the silence.

Further down the hall, Ardis stops without warning. Opening the door closest to him, he pulls me to stand in the doorway. In front of him, I crane my neck to look him in the eye, refusing to waver my gaze.

"Turn around," Ardis says expectantly.

I blink slowly, trying to process his words. *Why?*

"Turn. Around," he says louder this time, his blue eyes looking insistently into my own.

When his fingers brush over mine, the binds slacken just as I hear them click unlocked.

The moment my wrists are free from the metal shackles, I try to soothe the irritated skin, running my fingers over the red indentations. Ardis nudges me forward into the small room.

Barely across the threshold, he shuts the door behind me, locking it with subsequent clicks. All without a word.

"Well then," I mutter to myself as I move further into the room.

Mostly empty, the room has a bed, a window, and a chair in the corner. Just a glorified prison where Drytas can keep the people he hasn't yet dealt with.

A waiting room for Trialing.

My first instinct is to go to the window, pulling with all my remaining strength to pry it open.

Locked.

Sagging, I abandon the useless endeavor. It would have been too easy if they had left it unlocked. When my eyes land on the chair, I rush to it, then pick it up and raise it above my head.

Opening the window isn't the only way to get through.

Stampeding forward, I ignore the protest of my knees; they ache and groan with every lurch of movement. Using the momentum, I swing the chair with my weight into the window, waiting for the telltale crash of glass to signal my victory. The wood splinters and breaks apart in my hands.

Irritated, I let out a strangled scream before throwing the remains of it at the wall.

How did I let this happen?

I slump to the floor, back pressed to the wall. Gripping the hem of my pants, I pull the fabric as far as I can up my leg and slide it until it rests on my lower thigh. Examining the damaged skin of my knee, I grimace as I do the same to my other leg.

The first shadows of blue paint my skin from where my knees smashed into the grand hall's tile floors.

A couple more cuts and bruises adorn my body than when I first entered the grand hall, but even I'm not ignorant enough to think mouthing off to the Lord of the Court of Valor would go unpunished.

Eyes drifting closed, I take a few deep breaths. When the locks on the door click, one after the other, I bolt up as the door opens.

At first, I think it's time to Trial already. Perhaps I fell asleep, and I can put an end to the anxiety and anticipation. But when Ardis steps in, food in hand, I feel no relief.

Stepping forward, Ardis holds out the plate, and I look at it, not moving to accept it or acknowledging him. Sighing, Ardis places it on the bed before looking at me, where I'm still sitting on the floor.

He scans the mangled chair on the far side of the room and shakes his head. For a moment, I think I catch the beginning of a smile before it's chased away by a warning look.

"You just can't help yourself, can you?"

Ardis leans against the wall, blocking off the door, arms folded across his chest; he reminds me of his demeanor in the alley from just this morning. Cocky. Confident.

"Are you saying I deserve it?" I snap back, a growl stirring in the back of my throat. "And whose fault is it I'm here?"

I've remained out of the Guard's reach, out of Lord Drytas's touch, for my entire life, learned their methods and warning signs, but they changed the rules. I would never have predicted someone who stood before me, a young girl with no Trial tattoos, could be the opposite in every way. Ardis is the only reason I'm in this situation, exactly as Drytas hoped.

Shaking his head, Ardis argues, "I told you to keep out of it back in the alleyway."

Frustration building, I stand, pointing right at him. "If I hadn't thought you were just a kid about to get beaten, then maybe I might have listened!"

"A kid you'd never seen before—in the small city of Falland. You didn't think any of it was suspicious?!"

His words penetrate my thoughts and refuse to leave. Why is he telling me this? To rub it in? I think about how the young girl ran down a dead end, and I thought it odd. To live here and not know. But I hadn't let it phase me. Blaming her mistake on panic and fear.

"It hadn't mattered."

The words come out in an exhale, airy and soft.

Ardis stares at me, eyes unmoving from my face. Not reacting to the quiet words except for the release of tension held in his jaw. He pivots, hands grasping the door handle to leave.

"I hope you sleep well tonight"—my sarcasm cuts the

tension—"knowing you've sentenced an innocent person to die for wanting to help a kid."

Ardis's hand tightens around the handle. "You won't die while Trialing because you won't even make it in the doors of the Trial."

The words linger like a threat in the air before he swings open the door and walks out. I hear the locks click again, and I sag, not having the strength to stand upright.

It ends up being me who doesn't sleep as I sit in the corner, watching for the door to open. I'm not sure if I'm waiting for them to come to collect me for my Trial or for someone to make good on Ardis's threat, but the fear stays with me the whole night.

CHAPTER 6

At dawn, I stand, expected to Trial; the reality sharpens with every passing second and frantic beat of my heart.

Members of the Guard line both sides of the hall, haloed in an ominous glow from the torches behind them. There isn't so much as a whisper released into the room as I'm escorted forward. Their gazes follow me in blatant curiosity, as if debating whether I'll walk back out in the end, comparing their perception of me to what they know lies beyond the Trial door.

Belthan stands at the head of the Guard, a disturbed smile plastered across his face, when his eyes land on my approaching figure. I flinch away at his look, remembering the feeling of his hand around my neck.

Ardis hovers nearby, arms crossed, head down, ignoring my presence. I find I prefer it to Belthan's unwavering attention.

At the very end of the hall, Lord Drytas lingers next to an ornate glass door, white etchings covering the face in intricate drawings. His bloodred cloak reflects in the mirror as if it's his own personal background.

The entrance to the Court of Valor's Trial.

A cold sweat beads at the nape of my neck, adding to the uncomfortable, clammy feeling of my palms. In the ultimate steps of my death march, I regret the few bites of food I managed to swallow. I'll need the energy to fuel me through this Trial, but now it only seems to fuel the urge to vomit down Lord Drytas's front.

Eyeing the drawings on the glass door, I find an empty area in the middle. A ring, absent of the swirling carvings, painting the expanse of its face.

"Okay, hurry it up!" Belthan pushes me toward the door, and I stumble forward, shooting him a glare over my shoulder.

Staring at the space in the center, I focus on a dull imprint on the reflective surface shaped like the outline of a human hand. Not jagged as if chipped away but smooth. Worn down. From countless people pressing their skin to the same spot.

Lord Drytas speaks as I'm nudged forward by Belthan.

"You'll enter the Trial alone, and once the door seals behind you, there is no getting out until it has ended."

"What do I need to do once inside?" I ask, voice cracking.

My mind races at all the possibilities beyond the door. There isn't any training to prepare me for this, but it still feels as if I'm being held under water and asked not to drown.

Drytas huffs in irritation, rolling his eyes. "We can only discuss details of what happens in the Trial with those who have successfully completed it. A rather annoying caveat, but alas, there is no workaround."

I shake my head. It explained why stories of what happened in the Trial never made its way to the streets.

"People die during Trialing," I say, more to myself than to Drytas.

I know he has little care for my life or any who came before me.

Drytas hums in agreement, unaffected. "Yes, but that would

not be nearly as interesting. I hope you live, or this will all have been such a waste of my time."

My stomach turns at his flippant dismissal. That's it? That is all I would get? I didn't expect an ounce of empathy from Lord Drytas, but no directions or explanation for what I would face?

The urge to throw up reappears.

Drytas nods to the door. "Hand. Now."

I step backward, but Belthan is there, gripping my hand so tightly I'm concerned he'll crush the small bones. My heart races as I fight against Belthan, and a few hot tears sneak out without my permission.

My fingers smooth out against the cool glass, pressed there relentlessly by Belthan.

Nothing happens for a beat, then another.

My heavy breathing fills the quiet space, accompanied only by my pounding heart. It crosses my mind it might be loud enough for them to hear.

Ardis, who has remained quiet, speaks up.

"The consent fail-safe. It won't open without her willingly taking part."

Confusion and relief swirl at his words. I wouldn't have to Trial? What did he mean, and why step in now?

I crane my neck around, narrowing my eyes at Ardis, whose face remains blank. "I don't—I don't consent. I don't want to do this."

The words tumble from my mouth as if they suddenly matter. As if it all has been a misunderstanding. Like in some mistaken order of events, it had been an accident I've ended up here at all.

But they knew I didn't want this.

A sharp edge presses against my neck, warm blood dripping down the center of my chest. I freeze, tensing every muscle, while I wait for someone to speak.

Lord Drytas steps forward out of the corner of my eye. "Ah, you have so much to learn here, Ardis."

Blinking my gaze to Ardis's, I can see confusion plastered across his face, with his eyebrows knitted in concentration.

He knew my sentence would be Trialing. He doesn't get to feign ignorance when faced with the consequences of his actions. If he hadn't deceived me in the first place, I wouldn't be here.

He could go to Trial for all I care.

Drytas waves about in a grandiose fashion. "Do you take on the honor of being Trialed here in the Court of Valor, or do you beckon death?"

It's quiet for a moment, and I realize they are waiting for an answer.

"What kind of question is that?" I huff, trying to hide my panic. My eyes flick between them all, watching for their faces to betray what they aren't telling me. "I just told you—"

Drytas drops his arms in irritation, his voice callous. "Let me rephrase for you. You can Trial, or you can die here and now, by Belthan's hand."

At this, Ardis inhales sharply and steps forward, but one deadly look from Drytas, and he stops in his tracks.

Drytas spits out, "Grow a backbone, Ardis. We both know you've killed for others. No need to take the moral high ground in my court now."

The knife at my throat stings in warning. Belthan's grip unfaltering on my arm. Hot breath spreads out across my cheek, curling around my ear, as he speaks.

"Give me a reason . . ."

My senses, already dialed to ten, are frantic. I have no advantage, no allies, and no clue what is truly waiting for me behind the door.

"I'll Trial."

It's nowhere near fifty-fifty odds, but a slight chance of surviving is better than none.

The second the thought crosses my mind, the white etchings in the glass door light up. With a soft click, the door cracks open.

CHAPTER 7

I vomit minutes after being thrown into the tunnel, anxiety and fear swirling in my stomach. Still dry heaving, I inch my fingers around the sealed opening, scrambling to pry it open. I pull at the door with my entire weight, but nothing. Taking deep breaths, I steady myself, wiping my mouth with the back of my hand.

Confronted with the reality that Trialing is no longer avoidable, I freeze, willing myself to do something other than stand here.

I don't know enough to beat this. Surviving in Falland is all about being smart. Knowing the who, what, where, and when for any eventuality. Running through scenarios of different problems I could stumble into is what prepared me every day on the streets.

But, for this, I know nothing.

Inhaling deeply, I toe my way forward into the dark abyss. Stomach settling, the only reminder of my moment of sheer panic is the vile taste still lingering in my mouth.

Time is immeasurable as I wander deeper toward a slowly growing light, but 742 steps and counting gives me some gauge.

Having spent the first half of the tunnel fumbling along the side walls, ears attuned to every reverberating sound, I'm grateful for the small beacon guiding me forward. Even now, I can still barely see the shape of my own hands.

Once the corridor is basked in enough light to see the rough walls I've been holding tight to, I stop, sucking in a deep breath to steady myself.

In crudely drawn letters, thousands of names coat the stone walls.

Names of people who had, like me, gone to Trial. I try not to dwell on how many made it to the end. Maybe they were living lives of luxury in the upper city, but I doubt it. The space in front of me contains more names than could fit in Falland.

I can't help but search the wall for hers--Cenna.

Walking along the slab, I read each name, flickering back a second time at every Cirin or Candyn. It's hard to believe she would indulge herself in the tradition, never having been one for sentimentality.

I squash the thought as I glimpse the five letters before me.

Hand trembling, I brush over the name with my fingers before bringing them to my mouth.

A sob breaks from my throat, emotions I've suppressed for ages reemerging with force. Even if I'd seen her enter the hall, even if I'd known she planned on Trialing, it's another thing seeing her name carved here as proof.

Leaning down, I pick up a rock from the tunnel floor. Rolling it in my hand, I find the marred white side. I drag the stone against the bumpy surface, spelling out my name, fingers still shaking.

Lysta. Right next to my sister's.

The anger swells in me, held at bay by the grief accompanying it.

For all I know, she is dead.

I stare at the wall before letting the rock fall from my hand. Continuing to the end of the tunnel, I'm unable to tell whether the shiver slithering down my spine is from the slight chill in the cave-like path or the implications of having written my name among so many others.

As I stand at the entrance of a deep pit, my eyes are drawn upward to an unimpeded view of the sky. No longer in a building or simply underground, the cave's ceiling is gone, leaving a crater-shaped hole to the outside. The early morning sky fills the space, and the first sun rays crest over the edge of the pit's opening.

A low growl rips my attention from the calming sky. Perched at the bottom of the pit is a massive black figure, camouflaged in shadows. Bright gold eyes pierce me, and as I step back, the creature stands. On all fours, it resembles a panther. Sleek midnight fur with a purple sheen where the light hits it—almost iridescent.

As it rises, wings unfurl across its shoulder blades. I can't stifle my gasp. They sweep open with a staggering span. Pushing off the ground, the beast launches upward, headed straight up before a golden chain latched around its neck yanks it back down.

Falland is remote from so much of the world, with its walls keeping us in and others out. Only rumors and folk legends made their way through the city, but this animal is one I remember hearing of.

Back when I joined a ragtag group of kids, where I first met Thoman, we had stayed up at night, sitting around a pitiful excuse of a fire and telling stories. Sometimes, blips of what we heard on the street that day, more than likely made up nonsense, never knowing which was which.

The beast in front of me is obviously no fable.

Kadaras were winged beasts, whose deadly, sharp talons and teeth could shred flesh into ribbons. Their fur is coated in a secreted substance, giving them their purple tinge. Any skin contact with it causes visions or hallucinations. The old tales never clarified that part, just that you would do anything to escape touching it.

I'm struck with a horrible realization. The people who have failed the Trial but made it out alive—we always said it was as if they were stuck in a nightmare. Is this how? Did they touch the Kadara and go insane?

People hoping to escape their past—and the fears the animal represents—worshipped these beasts as blessed creatures and wore medallions with the Kadaras engraved upon them.

Standing twenty feet from the majestic beast, I could understand why some thought them blessed. It's every bit as beautiful as it is terrifying.

Drawing my eyes away from the animal, I see a stone slab just inside the pit's entrance. With jagged edges, its surface is covered in a range of weapons. Swords and daggers, whips, and bows and arrows. Items so highly desired on the streets of Falland, the entire table is worth at least a year of food.

A gold plate adorns the center of the table, writing etched across its face.

Kill the fear to free the innocent.

Startled, I grip the slab, leaning my weight on my arms as I look up at the animal. As if I'm suddenly a threat, it hisses, curling its lip up over sharp teeth.

Kadara's are called fear incarnate.

My stomach drops, and I push away from the table, shaking

my head. By killing the fear, did it mean for me to kill the Kadara? Can that really be what the Trial requires?

If the riddle was referring to the one Trialing as innocent, it was rather ironic it was being used as a punishment for deemed criminals.

Staring at the beast that I have no hope of besting, I realize why so many people don't pass the test.

I've never killed before. There were few who grew up on the streets who haven't fought; the unhappiest people were always on edge and twitching for a brawl. But to be the one to take the life from something that breathed and feared just like us?

Tracing the weapons laid out before me, I reach for the only one I've held in the past. A dagger. My hand hesitates over the hilt, but I pick it up gently, as if squeezing it too hard would shatter it.

The Kadara lets out another growl, pacing the middle of the pit, and I freeze, eyes darting between the weapons and the animal.

The dagger is heavier than mine. Moving the blade through the air, I familiarize myself with its weight and grip before testing its sharpness, growing more comfortable with it the longer I hold it.

This is the Court of Valor's Trial. That must mean something. Valor means bravery and courage. Maybe that's what I need to have to pass and make it out alive.

I should be able to do this. I'd carried a dagger on the streets.

Even as the thought crosses my mind, I'm lying to myself. How did one come up with a strategy to kill a powerful beast without touching it in a room where there was nowhere to hide?

The perfectly circular cavern is empty other than the Kadara, and I would bet the chain will give the animal just enough reach to make it to all sides of the room, except for the hallway entrance I stand in. Nowhere would be safe.

Moving forward, I realize the Kadara follows each step I take, crouching as it hisses. I can't take it by surprise or get behind it. The layout of the room leaves no chance of an advantage, which leaves taking it head on as the only option.

I just need to think about this logically. Talk myself through it.

The fastest and most humane way would be straight to the heart. Make it quick—for me and the creature. It has the speed and the size, so the best bet would be to use its momentum against it. Have it do all the work for me.

A sob works its way up my throat as I try to shake the nerves vibrating through my body, but I swallow deeply, pushing the emotion back down.

Glancing back to the table where I took the dagger, my eyes rest on the sword. I grimace when I pick it up, staggering under its substantial weight, before moving to the empty wall just outside of the pit's entrance. Close, so I can easily duck inside but far enough away to draw the Kadara in.

Taking in a deep breath, I try to control my breathing. Freaking out would not win this battle for me. Lifting the sword, I raise the heavy blade above my head before letting it fall against the stone wall.

Again, I raise the sword and smack every surface with it. The sound pulses against my head, and I have to force myself to concentrate despite the distraction.

The Kadara lets out a string of growls, amping up in ferocity as I clang the metal. My rhythm stutters as I look at the growling animal, hesitating out of fear.

It paces, turning on its heel every five feet, but its eyes never move from me. A roar bursts from the beast, making me falter, taking me by surprise at the sudden vibration circling around the pit. The Kadara leaps, feet pounding as it bounds toward me. Its wings push back as air rushes over their protruding size.

I balance the sword in my dominant hand and the dagger in my other. All I need to do is get the blade behind the neck and the dagger in front of it. The Kadara's force should do all the work. I didn't have to truly attack it. It would be just defending myself.

My stomach lurches, panic sweeping through me as the distance between me and certain death shrinks rapidly.

Twenty feet. Fifteen. Ten.

Staring down the Kadara as it bounds toward me, I lock my knees to stop their slight wobble. My stomach drops as it launches into the air. I fall to my knees, ducking in surprise, not expecting it to take flight so close to the wall.

Instead of the attack I expect, the winged animal curves to the right, gliding in a circle around the room. As it does, I get a full view of the underside of the beast.

Covered in scars and gouges, with patches of fur missing from various spots, the Kadara looks like it's been through countless battles. The longer I look, the more I find.

Welts traverse its sides, as if the whip had wound its way around the body as it made contact. The end of its tail is jagged and uneven, like part of it had been cleaved off.

Of all the Trials, it was the same beast standing against tens of hundreds of people who tried to kill it.

I lower my weapons from my fighting position and watch the animal glide until it rests back in the middle of the pit. It lands on its feet, wings folding into its sides.

It doesn't make any sense.

There are different ways to beat the Trial. It was the reason those who successfully Trialed didn't all receive the same abil-ity. The way you completed the Trial determined the power you would be given.

But how is this beast living after having withstood centuries of torment? There is no way I'm the first to think of killing it.

Kill the fear to free the innocent.

The words echo in my head.

Laying down my weapons steadily, I eye the Kadara, trying not to make any sudden movements. Its lip curls as it bares its teeth at me, but the second the blades leave my hands it stops. It stares back at me, no longer growling or signaling an attack. I take one step forward, and the Kadara's ears angle toward me. It blinks slowly as it watches me, mirroring my stillness, save for the breath moving through both of us.

Another step and the next, all without reaction from the Kadara.

A crack of confidence breaks through the fear, and I smile to myself. Standing a few feet from the creature, I eye its collar. The golden chain hung from it would be difficult to break, but at the base of its neck was a buckle. It would allow for the metal ring to be opened. Maybe I could do it, but getting it off without touching the Kadara's fur would be another miracle.

Would it even satisfy the riddle's requirements? A part of me doubts it, but what is the worst that could happen—I fail the Trial? I came in here expecting to.

Holding my hands up, palms facing out, I close the distance. Slipping closer, the tip of my fingers brush the collar's cold metal. When the Kadara shifts, I flinch back, waiting for it to still once again.

Moving inch by inch, I slip my fingers just under the buckle. Nerves and fear thrum through my body. If it even rubbed against me by a hair, who knows how it could impact me.

Wincing, I pull the collar away from its fur to unlatch it. Spikes protrude from the ring, piercing the Kadara's neck, crusted blood covering the metal points.

The creature rips away from me, growling in pain. Instinctively, I grab onto the fleeing animal, trying to prevent it from hurting itself or—worse—me. Looping my arm around its neck as it bucks in agony, I try to finish taking off the collar.

My skin tingles where I touch the Kadara's coat, like when you hold snow and have to fight the urge to drop it to soothe the pins and needles it causes.

My head flings backward, eyes wide, as flashes of panic and fear flood my system, as pictures of my past fill my vision. I try to shut out the onset of images, but without letting go, the rush doesn't yield. Reality and nightmares merging. The overwhelming sadness and trepidation filter through my touch with the Kadara.

A nightmare of my younger self walking through an empty Falland. Buildings smoking and crumbling around me, the entire city having escaped—leaving me here.

Alone.

Hot tears pour down my face, filling my eyes and blurring my vision.

A flashback of when I'd raced through the streets, feet bleeding from running across broken glass. I'd been hiding from some older kids and ended up concealing myself in a dumpster of rotten food. I'd stayed hunkered among the trash for hours until I could no longer hear them shouting my name.

A wet, metallic taste fills my mouth. I've bitten my lip.

The Kadara lunges, trying to move away from my hand still fitted under its collar. As it leaps, I end up strewn across its back, my legs hanging as the creature uses its wings to barrel upward.

As more of my skin presses to her, the faster the images flicker through my mind. Tears, fights, and bruises, ones dredged up from a long time ago.

It gets harder to tell what is real as the Kadara fades to the background, and I question if it's all happening again.

At first, I think it's a memory. An image of Cenna walking toward the grand hall after volunteering for Trialing, but it's warped from what actually happened.

Steps from the door, Cenna turns with a malicious smirk I had never seen. "Really, Lysta?" the figure of my sister asked. "I'd rather risk death than suffer through another day with you leeching off me."

Words my sister had never said but that I'd feared following her departure.

I choke and hiccup between sobs, unable to shy away from the painful images.

Soaring in a circle above the pit, I squeeze the Kadara's body with my thighs, trying to free my hands from holding on so I can focus on the collar. I grit my teeth, eyebrows mashing together as I try to combat the voices haunting me. Once again, I pull on the buckle, begging it to release. It's almost impossible to see through the tears filling my vision.

Growls of anguish rip from the creature's throat as the points shift into its neck. Fresh blood pooling where the holes have reopened. The Kadara spins mid-flight, trying to fling me from its back. My legs wrap around its torso, desperately holding on.

My heart races, not fearing beyond the images in my head but the drop many feet below.

The Kadara turns its head, sinking its teeth into my arm. A scream bursts from my lips just as the clasp breaks off, and the tension holding the collar releases. I feel its jaw unclench.

The Kadara freezes beneath me, as if I've flipped a switch. Gently, it lowers to the ground. After lying across its back, I slowly sit up and reach for the collar. Each ragged breath the animal takes in rumbles under me. Taking a firm grip of the metal, I inch it toward me, and when I pull the spikes from the Kadara's skin, I wince sympathetically.

Once it is free, I toss the collar aside, the chain rattling as it skids across the floor.

Getting up from where I sat, perched between the creature's shoulder blades, the ghost of fear drips off my back with a sag of relief when my skin leaves its fur.

I turn and stand. The creature's gold eyes look back. Dragging the back of my hand across my cheeks, I wipe away the tears coating my skin. The Kadara watches before extending its wings. It lifts off gracefully, no longer bound by the chain. Soaring upward past the rim of the pit and up into the sky. Free.

I wave vacantly in its direction, sagging with a deep exhale, before muttering, "Yeah, good talk."

A burning sensation erupts on my arm, like fire is licking its way across the skin. I stumble to the ground in pain, my eyes blinking in what feels like slow motion.

The last thing I see before losing consciousness is the large-winged animal getting smaller and smaller in the distance.

CHAPTER 8

When the numbing effect of sleep dissipates, a stronger ache echoes through my body. Even when I still my movement, the pain radiates in my bones and muscles. It's a struggle not to listen to the part of me begging to keep my eyes closed. To just let myself succumb to the dreamless abyss and stay here where it's safe.

I can remember echoes of waking in the Trialing tunnel and stumbling my way back out, using the wall as a crutch. Delirious in pain as the skin where the Kadara had bitten me burned and itched like a new type of torture. The last thing I recall is slipping through the Trial door and falling into a pair of arms.

A groan bursts from my mouth as soreness ripples through me when I sit up. Pain lingers as if bruises cover every inch of my body. Bones shift and crack as I toss my feet over the side of the bed.

I push up on my arm, guarding the area where the Kadara had sunk its teeth. I have to will myself to look at it—expecting a chunk of flesh to be missing, but there are only two semicircles of red divots imprinted from the creature's teeth.

Brushing my fingers across the open skin, I knit my brows. Considering how raw and fresh the injury looked, I'd expect a great deal of pain from touching the wound, but there is none.

Catching a glimpse out of the corner of my eye of dark ink marking my opposite arm, I switch arms. I've seen glimpses of these exact ones my whole life, present on every member of the Guard in Falland.

Trial tattoos from the Court of Valor, signaling my completion of the rite.

No longer an Untrialed, I'm the opposite of everything I thought I was. Now I'm just another Trialed for Drytas to use as he deems fit.

Scoffing, I shake my head in frustration, looking up at the ceiling as if it is to blame for the injustice.

If the tattoo is any sign, I passed the Trial despite releasing the Kadara, meaning it must have been a valid solution. My mind wanders, disgusted at myself for immediately thinking of how simple things would be now—if I let them, that is.

I wouldn't ever have to go hungry again, but it would mean submitting to Lord Drytas. Something that contradicts every struggle I've experienced but very well may be powerless against.

My spine snaps to attention as the word crosses my mind. Powerless. No, I'm powerless no longer. I'm the very opposite.

I have a power of my own. One that I had earned.

Raising my hands, I examine them as if they are painted with what my new power would be.

While I doubt Drytas or Belthan would have set the Kadara free, I still imagine their powers in my mind and reach out as if I could summon the pillow across the room.

It doesn't move an inch.

A bitter smile curls my lips at the ounce of disappointment

that rolls off my chest. Less from not being able to move objects but from hoping maybe Lord Drytas secretly was a good lord who freed the innocent creature.

It's a minuscule part of me. The only optimism I can muster, even if temporarily.

I'm not sure if two people could even free the Kadara. How did the Trials even work? Had I truly freed the tortured animal, or would it all reset as if I'd never been there?

A ball forms in my throat. If it all resets, the Kadara would be right back there to fight every other Untrialed Drytas deigned to throw at it.

By clearing their throat, someone interrupts me, not having even heard the door open. Turning on my heel, I stumble backward in surprise. Belthan stands mere feet behind me.

Realization strikes me. He didn't *use* the door.

I don't let him see the horror threatening to cross my face at the implications of what he could do with his power. But there must be limits to what he could do, where he could go—right?

Arms crossed, Belthan smirks at me. "No one truly thought you'd survive, but here you stand."

Wrapping my arms around myself, I echo, "Here I stand."

A moment of silence lingers, and a wolfish grin grows on Belthan's face, widening as he takes in my disgruntled appearance. "Lord Drytas has some questions for you . . ." He glances at me, turning up his nose as he looks around the room.

I nod. "Okay, as soon as I—"

Belthan reaches forward, his hand wrapping around my upper arm. "Afraid not. My way's faster."

A MOMENT of weightlessness sweeps me off my feet, as if I'm falling. The floor rises to meet me and then I'm standing in the throne room. With no preparation, I stagger forward and try to find my balance in a whirl of dizziness.

Belthan mutters next to me as he releases his grip. "Please try not to vomit. I hate it when they do that."

I send a glare at him from my doubled-over position, too occupied settling my stomach to retort.

The world comes to a standstill when Lord Drytas acknowledges me from across the room. He sits on his throne, red robes spread out around him like a blanket of blood.

"You survived after all."

Suspicion glints in his gaze that wasn't there before, a sense of danger lingering in his tone.

Painful tension snaps through the air, and I know something has happened beyond my Trial.

"What's your name, girl?" Drytas asks, his face a cold mask.

He sentenced me to what could have been my death, and he didn't even know my name? Only deemed worthy of being more than another face now that I've passed the Trial. A pang pierces my heart as the names on the Trial walls carry new meaning. How else would they be remembered?

"Lysta," I tell him, strained, "my lord."

My stomach rolls at the words.

Searching the room for a hint at what has changed, I note the guards lingering in the doorways and beside the throne. The only difference is the sudden appraisal they give me. Before, their eyes didn't deem me worthy of a once-over, but now, they remain glued to me, waiting for an answer to a question I don't know yet.

"You will do well here, Lysta. Live easy, grow strong, have a purpose to your life." Crimson in Lord Drytas's cloak reflects like fire in his dark eyes, his gaze burning through me. "Try to remember that when you answer my next question."

I risk a glance at Belthan to see if his expression might give away what Lord Drytas speaks of. His face has darkened similarly to his lord's, a hard glare pinning me in place.

Drytas's voice is barely above a whisper when he asks, "Did you do anything during your Trial other than complete it as directed?"

I shake my head before I even fully process his question. Why is he asking that? Does he know about the Kadara? Did I truly release it?

"I-I did what I thought I was supposed to." I can't reign in the quiver in my voice.

"The passage to the Trial collapsed—the door you had your hand on, not a day ago, is now shattered into pieces." Drytas points a ringed finger at me, standing at the foot of his throne. "And you were the last one in there. Before you, I had Trialed no one in over a month. Then, the same day you Trial, it ends up destroyed!" Drytas's rage consumes his every word. "You did something, and you will tell me what."

Unable to string a coherent sentence that will convince him that I did nothing that he accuses, I shake my head.

"Tell. The. Truth." Venom drips from his lips, his eyes crazed as he reaches out to me.

My throat compressing, I scramble, fingers tearing at my neck as if able to pry his invisible grip from my windpipe. Air floods into my lungs when he lets go as I gasp.

"What. Did. You. DO?"

The force clamps around my throat again, my heels lifting off the ground as he moves his hand upward. Dark specks cross my vision, appearing one by one, before filling in.

Constriction forms in my chest, wrenching itself tighter and tighter into a compressed ball before it explodes. My terror and anxiety release in an instant, and through heavy-lidded eyes, I watch a barrier surge out from within me. Pushing out, hitting Belthan first, knocking him several feet backward.

The force field grows in a perfect circle around me, propelling back anything it comes into contact with. Guards from every corner of the room rush toward me, but like Belthan, they cannot stop the impending attack. They land haphazardly against the surrounding walls, Lord Drytas among the fallen.

CHAPTER 9

Doors at the far side of the room open with a bang, and Ardis strides through them, eyes looking anywhere but at me. Taking in his surroundings, he maneuvers past the fallen guards, heading straight for Lord Drytas. Broken glass crunches underfoot with each step, and I realize the chandelier didn't survive.

I fall to my knees, chest heaving as I'm struck by unbearable exhaustion. A wet trickle traces my upper lip, and I bring my hand up to catch it. Blood.

The shield collapses, cracking into pieces before disappearing. Leaving behind only the destruction it caused. That *I* caused.

Ardis helps Lord Drytas to his feet, leading him back to his throne. Lord Drytas orders Ardis in a strangled voice. "Take her to the dungeons. She has attacked the Crown. Who knows what she did to the Trial if all she utters are lies?"

Ardis's eyes meet mine, and I flinch, but it isn't fear that crosses his face. Just curiosity. "Perhaps, my lord, and I apologize if I overstep, but maybe she tells the truth," he drawls, looking me over. My skin prickles, hair raising as I feel him analyzing my arms, the bite and tattoo adorning them. "She doesn't seem capable of being responsible for what happened to the Trial."

Belthan chokes out a laugh, and I turn to see him standing from where he had been thrown. I shrink away from his accusing gaze. He looks at me as if I'm the monster here, but I only defended myself.

"She just gave us a perfect example of what she is capable of, and if you ask me, whatever she just did absolutely could have destroyed the tunnel." He steps forward, eyes narrowed in Ardis's direction. "And how did you know to come running?"

"I felt the shift of powers. Whether it be hers or the Trial itself. I thought to make myself useful to our lord." Ardis looks to Lord Drytas for confirmation, who nods. "Not to mention, I was the one to report the condition of the Trial."

Belthan twists his lips in agitation.

"If my lord wishes, I could settle this quickly. One look in her head, and I'll know exactly what happened during her Trial," Ardis adds.

Drytas hesitates, looking conflicted. "I have been looking forward to a demonstration of your other talents." After a moment, he nods. "Proceed."

Ardis navigates the bodies groaning on the floor. When he reaches me, he kneels in front of me, mirroring my position. When his blue eyes hold my gaze, I wince, an itch creeping along my mind. I don't look away, not willing to be the first to break. The itch grows stronger until it becomes a sharp pain.

Ardis's struggle mars his features as a bead of sweat rolls down his furrowed brow. The more anguished he looks, the stronger the pain gets—until it breaks, like an eggshell cracking against a pan, the yolk slipping out.

Lysta.

The voice saying my name doesn't sound like Ardis. It's

deeper, with a velvet quality to it. Although Ardis's lips have not moved from their pursed position, I know it is him.

Show me, Lysta.

Panic floods my body as the startling realization hits me. My feet fumble backward as I move away from Ardis, but he reaches forward, suddenly too close, and grips my wrist.

I clench my eyes shut, unsure of what allows him to speak directly to me. He's a shifter yet able to use another power.

That won't do anything to help.

Confused, I keep my eyes closed. There isn't a person in this room I trust, let alone the man who threatened my life just the night before.

Ardis speaks again. *You don't need to trust me. Just know that, right now, our interests are aligned. Show me. Show me what happened, and maybe he'll let you live.*

"What can you see?" Drytas asks, his frantic voice breaking through my daze. "What does she know? Is she responsible for the Trial breaking?"

"Almost, my lord. She's just walking down the tunnel now."

I struggle in Ardis's grip, but he makes it impossible to maneuver out of his hold. Steeling my neck, I whip my head forward, crushing it into his face. A sickening crunch accompanies the impact, and I know I broke his nose.

A curse bursts from his mouth, rushing past my ear in a sharp hiss.

Belthan barks out a laugh, but Ardis ignores him.

Easy there, fighter. Let me help, he pleads.

Memories flood my mind as it hits me. This is the only way I would get out of this alive.

So, I show him it all, and it breaks a part of me. To give him the weapon that could so easily end me.

I show him the Kadara and the weapons. Even a glimpse of when I was strewn across its back, sobbing from hallucinations as I tried to free the animal. His presence slinks from my mind, and I relish it.

Silence suspends between us. Both he and I breathe heavily, staring each other down, not even a foot standing between us.

"She did nothing, my lord. Seems she only passed the Trial out of sheer luck. Nothing related to the Trial collapsing."

Ardis isn't going to reveal my freeing the Kadara. Did that mean he didn't think it was related, or he just didn't care to share the information with Lord Drytas? For now, it doesn't matter.

I sag in relief, and wrench my wrist from Ardis's grasp.

Lord Drytas watches me warily. "It can't be a coincidence—she Trials, and everything implodes on itself."

Ardis steps away from me, wiping his bloody nose while nodding. "We can keep a close eye on her if it would soothe your worries, my lord. But I saw nothing to show a need for suspicion."

Leaning back on his throne, Drytas taps his mouth, deep in thought. "That is an acceptable solution, Ardis. But if she is loyal, as you say, then having her power at my side would serve me well."

My jaw slackens in surprise. His side?

Drytas stands, sweeping his robes out as he stalks to me. As he moves closer, I pull my arm with the Kadara bite behind my back.

It isn't a logical decision, but somehow, the injury feels like a sign of my weakness. Showing that I struggled through the Trial and nearly failed to make it out. Like I was barely Trialed.

"I haven't seen your power come out of the Trial before." Lord Drytas exchanges a look with Belthan that raises my guard. "How did you solve the Trial?"

Shifting under their gaze, I feel my heart rate accelerate at their questions. I should have expected it, but I didn't think about having to tell Drytas I'd freed the Kadara. The way they look at me like a deadly gift bestowed upon them makes me keep it to myself.

Drytas watches for a reaction from me when he asks, "Did you kill the beast or perhaps even scale the walls like Belthan here?"

Looking at Belthan in surprise, I try to imagine the difficulty of climbing the concaved, steep wall. The pit had been over fifty feet in height, which seemed impossible to ascend even in the best conditions, but the wall had been just dirt. Nothing to grab onto.

Seeing the surprise on my face, Belthan answers without prompt, chest puffing in pride. "Pierced the knives and swords into the walls and used them as footholds. The beastie was inches away the whole time, snapping at my back."

"Didn't ask," I mutter.

Belthan's answering scowl tells me he heard the whispered words but doesn't retaliate. His quick temper from a day ago lurks beneath the surface.

I wouldn't admit he'd been smart about it, *and* he didn't have to kill the Kadara.

"How did you pass the Trial?" Drytas asks again, agitated at my lack of answering.

Ardis shifts nearby, and I worry he'll tell Drytas the truth if I don't answer. But if I lie and don't have a power that matches, he'll be even more furious.

Blinking slowly, I give him an answer he won't be suspect of. "I didn't fight it, just the hallucinations it gave me."

Is it believable? I don't think it even fits with the riddle, but Drytas doesn't seem to notice.

He considers me for a moment but then turns toward Belthan. "It seems she will have more use than I thought. Better served in the Guard than wasted in the upper city." Addressing

Ardis suddenly, Lord Drytas tacks on, "Whether her abilities are a protective barrier or a force field, I want you, Ardis, to see if she can extend that protection to another."

The guard? For a moment, I contemplate whether I'm hallucinating once again, as a new fear rears its head. Because how could there be a world where I'm made a guard?

Ardis looks to me expectantly, as if I should be the one to protest, but I've faced Lord Drytas's wrath once already today, and I don't beckon the feel of his hands around my throat again anytime soon.

Even if I'm wary of Drytas, having control over my powers isn't something I can turn away from. If anything, it would give me time. Time to come up with a plan and to find Thoman.

If they are planning to use me, then I'll use them right back. And once I have control of my powers—they'll lose control of me.

Ardis nods at Drytas's request before bowing once again. "Of course, my lord." Without another word, he stalks from the room.

Lord Drytas turns to me, his eyes slimming into narrow slits like a snake.

"If it weren't for the fact you have given me such a gift, Lysta, I would raise you to the top of the wall and then let you drop." Drytas pauses, letting his threat sink in. When he speaks, venom laces his tone. "Do not use your powers against me again. I may not be able to take them away, but the same cannot be said for your life."

CHAPTER 10

A week has passed since my Trialing. I haven't once glimpsed Ardis . . . or Cenna. The latter of which hurts me more than I allow myself to admit. Save for the few hours of night, when the deathly silence pulls strangled sobs from me with no one to bear witness.

Pain festers like reopening a healing wound as I lose her all over again. The only thing keeping me from succumbing to my renewed grief are my hopeful reassurances.

She's in the upper city. I'll see her again.

Anything and everything that I do feels like a betrayal. A betrayal of who I am—or at least who I was.

I walk the halls of the compound, learning it like I did the streets—as if it could ever be my new home. Treated as an equal by guards who once terrorized me. I sleep in a nice bed, with a cushy mattress and soft sheets, provided with necessities that have always been luxuries to me. Even the untouched guard uniform in my dormitory feels expensive to the touch.

I'm ashamed of the fleeting moments when I don't hate it. Each time I taste another dessert I've never had, it sinks to my stomach like a lead weight, poisoned by guilt and anger.

Lord Drytas let Untrialed starve. People on the streets challenge themselves daily on how little they can eat. Yet, here, I could spend a whole day, from six in the morning to nine at night, feasting with no end.

I consider stashing some away and sneaking into the streets to hand out whatever I can carry. It's not like anyone here would notice, but as a freshly Trialed recruit of the Guard, I'm not allowed out without supervision. Not to the upper city, nor the lower streets.

I let my anger fuel me as I walk around, learning, memorizing everything. Directions, exits, how many guards are on duty at a time—information I'm not sure what to do with, but it makes me feel like I'm doing something other than what Lord Drytas wants.

His interest in my power taints any excitement I might have had.

With Ardis scarce to be found, I work on summoning the shield again, pressure only growing. Nothing. Not even a hint of the power at my fingertips. If I hadn't seen for myself the damage unfolding from me in the throne room, I wouldn't believe that I have one at all.

It's cruel—to have a power meant to protect myself locked away, out of reach, while defenseless behind enemy lines.

"Lysta."

A cold voice calls my name, breaking my trance as I walk the corridors of the grand hall.

I stop in my tracks, turning stiffly to Belthan, who smirks at me. "Belthan. Did you need something?" Hand lacing behind my back, I hide any hint of the fear that swirls at the head of the Guard's cruel grin.

Belthan studies me, quirking his head to one side as he drawls, "Nothing for me, but Lord Drytas was hoping for an update on your training. Any notable progress for me to report?"

He eyes me with amusement flickering in his stare, as if he already knows I haven't had any training, my power just as unrefined as a week ago. His gleam reminds me of a predator watching for its prey to make a fatal mistake.

Hopefully, I've yet to make mine.

With every morsel of respect I can muster in my tone, I conjure an answer that may pacify him temporarily. "Regretfully, none so far, but I'm hoping for more progress in the coming weeks."

Belthan chuffs a laugh, and I startle at the loud noise. Wide eyes flickering up and down the hall, I brace for what will follow.

"Weeks will not work for his lord. There have been some changes to our plans, and he will need you at his side and competent much sooner than expected."

My face goes blank, a mask for the flurry of thoughts racing behind it. Even if I don't have a hint as to Lord Drytas's plans, I can be sure they won't be good if he needs my power for them.

"We don't even know if it's possible for me to use the shield like he wants."

Belthan only smirks at my irritation, shrugging before adding, "Well, then, you better figure it out quickly, or heads will roll, Lysta." He turns away from me, walking down the hall, his voice echoing against the stone walls. "And it won't be mine."

Belthan's threat follows me to every corner of the grand hall, ringing in my ears as I search hastily for Ardis.

Maybe if I'd spent the last week actually looking for him

instead of trying to figure out my powers myself, I wouldn't be in this position.

With the places he could be dwindling, I check the last place I want to return to—the Trial hall. After all, Ardis's reward for bringing me in was to be allowed to be Trialed, at his request.

The torches lighting the way to the Trial entrance are extinguished, letting shadows overwhelm the space. The scuffing of my shoes on the floor echoes off the walls. The hall, now empty, is just as ominous as it had been the morning of my Trial.

A gasp escapes my mouth when the entrance comes into sight. The large circular glass door of the Trial is shattered. As I get closer, cracks all centering at the handprint in the center and streaming outwards becomes prominent.

When Lord Drytas had said the Trial was destroyed, I assumed it had caved in. This is something else altogether. Behind the rubble, the tunnel is filled in with a combination of stone and dirt.

Sifting among the destruction is Ardis. Standing with a growl of frustration, he runs a hand through the top of his hair, cursing.

"Looking for something?"

Ardis flinches at my voice, a piece of the door falling from his hand and shattering into shards at our feet. Before I can react, Ardis whips around, withdrawing his sword from the sheathe at his hip, and leveling it at my throat, all within a second.

I don't dare exhale as his wild eyes search my face, his arm lowering when he recognizes me. He steps back, tension draining from his body as he slouches against the wall. We breathe heavily for a moment before Ardis shakes his head at me.

"Do you have a death wish?" he asks, staring at me incredulously.

Opening and closing my mouth, I struggle for the right response. "How was I supposed to know you'd react like that?" Pointing into his chest, I glare back at him. "Why are you digging around the Trial entrance?"

When Ardis doesn't answer, I raise an eyebrow in his direction. Ducking around him, I shift to where I can see what he'd been working on.

Most of the larger shards have been placed into their original shape, outlining not only what was once the door, but the broken handprint at the center of it. He'd been putting them together on the floor.

Letting my gaze drift back to Ardis, I examine his nose. Despite the fact that I'd broken it only a week ago, there isn't a bump, scrape, or bruise anywhere on his face. I narrow my eyes, stepping forward to look closer.

I've seen a few broken noses in my day, and none of them looked the same again. But his looks exactly as before—not healed but as if it were never hurt in the first place.

Could his shifting abilities hide injuries? If Ardis notices my sudden attention, he ignores it, instead questioning me in a gruff voice.

"What do you want?"

"You're supposed to be training me." I cross my arms, a frown marring my face. "I haven't been able to track you down all week."

"And I will." Ardis brushes past me, leaving the glass pieces behind.

"No, you need to do it now."

He continues to shuffle down the hall, and I chase him.

I will not face Lord Drytas again without being able to protect myself.

Before, I barely escaped. I couldn't leave my life to someone who might try to strangle me on a whim because he was having a bad day.

"Why can't you figure it out on your own?" Ardis says over his shoulder. When we reach an intersection, he looks both ways before looking at me next to him. "You've already done it once."

My face burns, heat creeping over my ears and down my chest.

"You don't think I would've tried myself before coming to you?"

Ardis shrugs before continuing.

Of course he wouldn't care.

"I can't get anything to happen." The words come out quieter. My cheeks are surely a bright red now, as I admit my struggle—my weakness. "And Lord Drytas expects results sooner than I expected . . ."

At the mention of Lord Drytas, Ardis stops cold in his path.

"What did he say?"

Tension laces his tone, and a new wariness settles over him at the name of the Court of Valor's lord.

Pivoting where he stands, Ardis's eyes sear into me, and I blink slowly before averting my gaze.

Could he read my mind without me knowing?

Looking down the hall beyond him, I answer, "It wasn't him. It was Belthan."

He rolls his eyes, scoffing, and moves to start down the hall once again, but I grab his arm. His gaze darts to where my hand grips his forearm, and he shakes me off with a pointed look.

"Belthan says Lord Drytas's plans have changed. We don't have the months or weeks I thought we'd have."

Ardis's face pales. He chews his lip, deep in thought. "How long did he say we have?"

A spark of hope flickers to life in my chest, and I hurriedly answer, "He didn't say, but it sounded soon." Twisting my lip with my teeth, I wait silently for him to decide.

Even Ardis would face consequences if he fails to train me, and it seems he knows it, too.

Resolve settles over Ardis's face moments before he orders, "You will meet me at the front entrance at six in the morning. Training starts then, so do not be late. And you'll need to wear your guard uniform for them to let you out."

Before I can agree or question his directions, he stomps away, leaving me and the Trial behind him.

It's a quarter past six when Ardis strolls up to the entrance door. He doesn't greet me or make any comment on the gray uniform I wear but just nods in one direction, gesturing for me to follow him down the street.

I'd stood just inside the door since five-thirty, having been up for an hour before that. I can't remember the last time I've felt any sense of excitement, but standing here, I'm barely able to keep the bounce out of my step as I follow.

Tilting my head to the still dark sky, I let the morning mist coat my face, breathing in a large gulp of air that reeks of dirt and smog. The odor brings a corner of my mouth up in a half smile.

They hadn't allowed me outside since before being brought to Trial, and now, as the lungful of Falland's freshest air fills my lungs, I realize how much it had truly bothered me.

"What is your plan for training me?" I ask, peeking subtly at Ardis.

I had pondered it for much of the night, thrilled at the prospect of controlling the power inside me. The power to protect myself.

Ardis grunts, seemingly not going to answer, before he clears his throat and answers in a thicker morning voice. "You could summon the shield before out of fear. It was an emotionally charged moment, and you were trying to defend yourself . . ."

I look at him in surprise at his defensive words.

"We just need to trigger your power without your life being at risk."

I hum in agreement, letting the space between us fall silent.

His words don't answer why we are headed to the lower city. How would we test my powers in the streets?

As we travel further into Falland, the sun's glow creeps over the wall, hitting the buildings and chasing away the morning shadows. People emerge from their homes, walking the streets with a cautious air. When their eyes catch sight of us, they turn the corner or step into the next doorwell. Sneers plastered to their faces as we walk by.

That would have been me just a week ago, and now, I sit with guards for meals.

Things have changed so quickly.

I look at Ardis, expecting some reaction at their obvious distaste for him, when I realize he's several feet ahead. In my examination of the city, he'd overtaken my pace.

Meaning—their hateful stares were for me.

My face burns, eyes misting, as I quicken my step to catch up with Ardis. I try to swallow the emotion choking me. It all feels similar, walking the same streets I always have until a week ago.

But it isn't the same for *them*.

I'm not one of them anymore, at least not in their eyes. All they see is the uniform harassing them daily, not the person wearing it.

All the excitement of being on the streets deflates in an

instant. I fall back into step with Ardis and don't say a word when he glances at me.

"This is where we will train."

Ardis's voice breaks the silence between us.

Looking up at the Market Plaza, I shrink back, shaking my head in protest. "We couldn't just train back at the compound?"

No longer am I thrilled at being back on my side of the city.

Ardis stops, turning on his heel to look at me. I shift uncomfortably as his eyes meet mine. "For you to use your shield to protect someone else, we need to have people around who you'd actually want to protect from harm, at least to start. And something tells me we won't find someone like that back at the compound. Correct?"

My face gets hot as he stares at me expectantly, arms crossed against his chest tightly.

I mumble, "Correct."

He nods, satisfied, before turning back to the market in front of us.

A thought strikes me.

"How would I be able to practice protecting someone here? It's a quiet morning so far, and the guards are always more reasonable following a Trialing."

As he ruffles his blonde hair, Ardis winces. "I received some information from a guard"—he hesitates—"there will be a stronger guard presence today, as requested by Drytas."

Cataloging his forgoing of the word "lord" for later, I push him to elaborate.

"A stronger guard presence . . . Meaning?"

The answer finds me before I finish the question.

Shakedown conditions.

"They are looking to Trial more people."

CHAPTER 11

"That's not possible." I shake my head. "They said the Trial was broken. Why would they start finding more people with nowhere to Trial them?"

Ardis purses his lips before murmuring, "The city doesn't know that, though—only Drytas's inner counsel does."

Another power play. Making sure the Untrialed stay in line while they figure out how to fix the Trial. But what would keeping them in check really mean?

I pause, turning to scan our surroundings. "If they can't Trial them, what do they plan to do with the people they catch?"

Ardis looks away, and I brace myself for the worst.

"The dungeons . . . to be held for future Trialing."

My head draws back, a protest bubbling up in my chest. "It's only been a week since I've Trialed!" A large exhale rushes between my lips as I stare back at him with wide eyes, voice vibrating with frustration. "There's usually weeks!"

Ardis's face tightens, lips drawing into a tight line. He nods as if he knows what I'm trying to say, but he couldn't.

He isn't *from* here.

I chew my lip, glancing up and down the street we stand on.

He doesn't understand.

The week following a new Trialing was a brief reprieve for the people on the streets. With the pressure on the guards temporarily suspended, there were only a few out at a time.

It was the safest it got for Untrialed. You could shop, complete errands, anything you needed, without fear of being the target of their trouble.

The market. The first market since my Trialing.

Eyes nearly bulging out of my head, I stare at Ardis.

Did he even realize what it meant? What it would mean for the Untrialed?

"Half of the city will be in the market when it opens today."

Ardis nods again, and I want to smack him. Glaring at him, I stalk away from him, planning to warn the people gathering in the market.

A large hand wraps around my wrist, pulling me back.

Standing chest-to-chest with Ardis, I shove him away before smacking him across the face with my other hand.

He brought me here to use *their* misfortune as some training experiment, uncaring of the consequences they might encounter.

His face recoils to the right, and he holds it there, looking off to the side. Jaw ticking, he turns to me, eyes darker than before. "Don't start something you can't finish, which, without your powers, you can't."

Standing tall, I narrow my eyes at him. Ripping my hand out of his iron grip, I snarl in his face. "I don't have time for this."

"Do you really think any of the people will listen to you— freshly Trialed turned guard? They won't trust you!"

I look away from his growling face and back to the market, and my heart sinks into my stomach.

"But you can protect them in other ways." He pauses. "Can't you, Lysta?"

He isn't asking—no, he's reminding me I could do something.

Turning back to him, hands trembling at my sides, I ask, "What do I do?"

~

Ardis has to hold me in place when the guards arrive in the market, knocking over stands, smashing food. My muscles twitch, begging for me to run. A trained response from years of avoiding days like this.

"Calm down," Ardis hisses in my ear, and I still.

Staring him down, nose-to-nose, I snarl right back.

"Well, then, *tell* me what to do. If your form of training me is just pissing me off, you can just leave."

We stand in the middle of the Market. Before, every gaze had followed us, but now, guards were every ten feet, and we've become invisible.

Ardis nudges me as a passing guard bumps into him, but he doesn't move away and continues to talk into my ear, his voice prominent in the loud market.

"I can't tell you who to protect, but when you feel those same feelings from the grand hall, I want you to hold on to it. But you need to focus it away from you. Focus on how much you want to protect them, 'cause that seems to be where this power is rooted."

He's quiet for a moment, and I move to step away but stop when he continues.

"Just like with the Kadara."

My eyes flash to his, seeing only a neutral face. He hasn't

mentioned what he'd seen in my mind. I almost forgot all the things he knows from witnessing my Trial.

Hands balling in fists, I'm defensive of how I'd freed the Kadara and protective over the visions he'd seen.

Ardis shakes his head. "No, listen. You were protecting it. You didn't seek to control it or kill it. You didn't just try to escape it—you saved it. There's always a relation between how you solve the Trial and the gift you receive."

I get a glimpse of an impressed face before he tucks it away, reverting to his neutral mask.

"You just need to channel that."

He makes it sound easier than it is. Of course I want to protect them. What's happening isn't fair or just. It's another of Drytas's power highs, maneuvering his citizens around like pawns.

Anger surges through me at the destroyed food littering the ground that these people need desperately. It's followed quickly by frustration as I watch the people unsure of how to defend their knocked-over stalls. They stand there, staring, unable to argue or stop the madness as their livelihood is decimated in front of them.

It makes my blood boil, but it isn't enough to summon my shield.

Following the street, I can see a group gathered in a ring, three rows of people deep, shouting in protest at what unfolds inside.

"Leave her alone!"

It's Doireann's voice, piercing from the rowdy crowd.

I rush over, pushing to the center, before I even think about it. I just breach the line when Doireann, an elderly shop worker, is shoved back by a member of the Guard.

Doireann's cart lay in splinters beneath her feet. It's only when she pushes something further behind her do I see a young girl running off. When the guard moves to follow her, Doireann holds out her hands, trying to stop them.

"It was hers! She paid for it. I swear to it. She wasn't stealing."

Doireann's voice cracks as she insists, her face breaking in composure.

The young girl likely *had* been stealing, taking advantage of the chaotic market and hoping to swipe some food, while the vendors were concerned with protecting their stalls.

Doireann is backhanded, and I flinch.

When she turns her head back, a split mars her right cheek. Her lip trembles as she stares back at them, but she doesn't move.

"Hey! Don't touch her!"

While the words echo my thoughts, it isn't my voice.

Thoman.

Searching the crowd of bobbing heads, I look for my friend. My heart clenches at the thought he doesn't know what happened to me—that I'm now Trialed—that I survived.

My eyes land on him when he shoves who laid his hands on Doireann. Two more guards are on him before he can help Doireann up. All the air in my lungs forces out in a shuddering gasp as I watch the two pull his arms behind his back. The guard Thoman shoved cocks his fist and throws a solid punch, forcing his head to recoil to the side. When he looks up, his eyes are cold. A red cut mars the dark skin of his chin, already swelling.

Anger builds in my veins, pulsing with each beat.

Doireann tries to stand on shaky legs, as Thoman fights the guard's hold. Doireann cries, pleading with the guard, as she reaches out to Thoman, who groans as another fist plows into his stomach.

Panic rips through me as I feel the tightness in my chest

build, just like that day in the grand hall. What if it unfolded like last time? A shield of destruction rather than protection. My hands shake as I cling to the last of my control, but I can't stop chaos from unleashing from me. A culmination of every ounce of anger and fear.

The protective field blasts through the crowd, barreling over people on its path to Doireann. Just as I think it's about to knock Doireann off her feet, it stops as if hitting a wall and cascades over her in a dome.

The transparent shield fabricated around Doireann fades and blinks as I struggle to hold it. It takes everything I have to keep it from exploding outward.

When a guard's hand meets the protective layer, he flinches backward. His eyes are blown wide, staring at the shield in utter shock and horror.

"Trials, Lysta, you actually. . ." Ardis curses behind me, awe evident in his tone.

Gritting my teeth, I push for the field to grow. Expanding until it is just out of reach of Thoman. I can feel my hair crackle with static. My body is vibrating from the effort, arms shaking as I hold them in front of me as if physically grasping the shield.

"You're trying to do too much," Ardis warns. "If you push yourself too far before you know your limits, you could burn yourself out."

I tune him out. If I couldn't use my powers to do this, then what use were they?

The guards holding Thoman drop his arms in shock as they stare at the barrier in front of them.

The guard swivels, eyeing the crowd, when he shouts, "Who's doing this?!"

No one from the crowd answers, and I'm unsure whether it's because they truly don't know or if they refuse to answer.

Another guard comes running, pushing into the crowd to

the action unfolding inside, more headed our way in the distance.

Thoman stumbles toward the shield, eyes widening when his arm goes right through. Without hesitating, he dives in to help Doireann off the ground.

The guards argue from the other side of the shield, their words mumbled in the crowd's roar. They draw their swords, slamming the blade against it. With each strike, I get dizzier, and maintaining the force field becomes harder.

"I can't hold it much longer."

Ardis's hands startle me as they reach around me, gripping my forearms to hold them steady. "Trials, you're doing this. It's only as strong as you are, Lysta."

The space around me gets denser, people bunching in closer. I make eye contact with a woman who stands near me on my right. Despite her obvious fear, she steps closer to me. Concealing me from the guards, who are knocking through the crowd, trying to find out who's making the shield.

Pride swells in my chest. They were hiding me on purpose.

Encouraged, I manipulate the shield, inching it toward the closest alley. Doireann stands on shaky legs as Thoman holds her. They walk with the bubble encircling them, as the guards continue to rain blows against the barrier.

A guard catches sight of me, recognizing me from the grand hall, and shouts, alerting the others to my presence.

I push forward, separating from the masses, as the guard plunders through them, knocking over people left and right to get to me. When the shield slots in the alley's opening, I see Doireann looking at me from the other side of it with a sad look, the first time she has seen me since the market. She raises a shaky hand, tears escaping from her wrinkled eyes. Nudging Thoman, she draws his attention to me.

Thoman stumbles back when he finally sees me, a small

smile working its way onto his face. His eyebrows furrow when he sees the guard uniform I'm wearing. The smile drops, and for a moment, I worry he will hate me like the other Untrialed who had spurned my presence in the streets.

Thoman had kept me alive following Cenna's departure when I had given up all hope to continue on. In my mind, he was as much a brother as Cenna was my sister, if not more than. Having him hate me would be the last straw.

Go. I mouth the words, pushing the shield toward him as if to move him further into the alley.

Looking at the shield in surprise, he turns to me with realization dawning across his face. A small spark glints in his eyes, and a conspiring smile erupts. Steadying Doireann, he gives me a one-handed salute before moving down the alley. I watch until he disappears around the corner, not knowing when I will see him again.

With a bead of sweat dripping down my temple, I shift the shield to cover myself, blocking off the alleyway.

Ardis shoves inside next to me before it closes. We stand next to each other, my heavy breathing filling the space. Looking at him, I give him a small smile as the guards beat their weapons against the wall of the shield.

The Untrialed who fought to conceal me scatters while the guard focuses on us.

I look at Ardis. "Now what?"

Ardis shrugs, the ghost of a smile passing over his lips. "Well, fighter . . . I think that's up to you," he says, gesturing to the surrounding shield.

CHAPTER 12

No guard dares manhandle me as they escort us back to the grand hall. Forgone are the shackles I once wore. Instead, I'm gifted a wide berth and wary gazes. The tables have turned, and we no longer stand on uneven ground, and it seems I'm not the only one to realize it.

But that brash confidence withers away once we are before Lord Drytas.

Like a snake's, his eyes follow us, wide and unblinking. The haunting silence is unyielding, even when Ardis and I bow our heads, symbols of submission. Every second only adds to the tension building in the room, like a storm about to rain down in fury.

Lord Drytas leans forward atop his throne before speaking in an eerily calm voice. "I will hear no excuses. I will hear no lies. But I sure as Trial better hear a worthy explanation, or there will be *severe* consequences."

The room shifts at his lethal tone, exchanging worried glances out of the Lord of Valor's sight. Belthan stands beside Drytas unaffected, a growing smirk smeared across his face.

Ardis steps forward, bowing low, his blonde hair falling into his face. "My lord, we were training—"

Drytas snaps off his response in a booming voice, "And your training requires interfering with *my* members of the Guard? Who are carrying out MY orders?"

Ardis doesn't flinch as Lord Drytas reprimands him in front of a dozen guards, nor does he back away at the show of Drytas's deadly temper. But his hands clench and then unfurl at his sides several times, making Ardis's struggle obvious.

Lord Drytas stands, pacing in front of his throne, but his coal-like eyes never leave us.

Ardis tries again. "Please accept my apologies, my lord. I was only trying to produce your desired results in the only way I knew would work. We never meant to undermine your authority."

My stomach knots at his placating words that sound far more than just convincing. During our time on the streets, Ardis's loyalties faded to the background while he helped me harness my power. But now, it's like a slap in the face to be reminded he did so for Lord Drytas.

"And did you?" Drytas snarls the words, nose turning up at us. "Did you accomplish what I ordered?"

Ardis looks at me to answer, and I bite my tongue, staring back at him with hard eyes.

If he wanted to use what I accomplished to gain favor with Drytas, he could do so. I'd rather be punished for failing.

When I say nothing, Ardis answers, "We did."

My heart sinks.

Lord Drytas's pacing halts, frozen. His eyebrows raise toward his hairline as he looks between me and Ardis before sitting back on his throne. "You did?" Drytas asks, anger draining from his tone.

Ardis nods, bowing his head respectfully. Out of the corner

of my eye, I see Ardis gesture for me to do the same, and I do, lowering my gaze as if I'm remorseful for my actions.

Malicious compliance if there is such a thing.

"Well, then, that certainly changes things, doesn't it?" Lord Drytas looks between us, a hideous smile tugging at his lips.

I will forever regret the day I did anything to please this man.

"Show me, then."

My stomach drops at Lord Drytas's demand. Could I still summon the shield? I managed it in the streets, but I had wanted to protect Doireann and Thoman from a real threat.

Ardis steps in. "She already pushed herself further than I would advise. Perhaps we could delay—"

"Show me," Lord Drytas growls, some of his excitement giving way to anger.

Ardis backs away, giving me a short nod.

Preparing myself, I tug at the strings in my heart that vibrate in anger or fear, plucking them until my chest feels tight. Pride fills me when I realize I'll be able to bring it out.

The shield cascades, dripping at the top of Drytas's crown, surrounding him in a wide circle. It flickers as I struggle to hold it, but Lord Drytas doesn't seem to care or notice.

Eyes gleaming, he announces, "This will work perfectly."

As I let the shield fall, breathing heavily, Belthan mutters in Lord Drytas's ear, who nods before waving him away.

Locking in on Ardis, Lord Drytas continues, "Ardis, I will ignore your actions in the lower streets, as you have provided exceptional results. That will be *all*, Ardis."

Ardis bows before making his exit, and I move to follow.

"You have not been dismissed, Lysta."

Ardis exchanges a look with me as he passes by, and his concerned expression remains imprinted in my mind, even after the doors have closed after him.

Holding my hands together behind my back, my nails dig into my skin, leaving tiny crescents.

Standing, Drytas moves to walk the hall, circling me. "I owe you my gratitude, Lysta. Because of this development, my plan will move up to a more convenient timetable."

I risk a look at Belthan, hoping for some hint of what Drytas is going on about, but he gives me nothing, letting me squirm in anticipation.

"With our Trial, not *usable*," Drytas says, leveling a glance in my direction, "we need to explore other options immediately. Lest other courts feel we are vulnerable. All it would take is one whisper to get through our walls, and we'd be at war fighting for my court against all of Aloria."

My heart races, pulsing deep in my neck like a clock counting down. It's unsettling to hear Lord Drytas acknowledge the other courts, especially when sharing the same breath with the word war. Were they worse than Drytas? How could they not be if he feared them? Ardis must have had some reason for leaving his own to come to Valor.

"We leave in two days. My Generals have been scoping out our path ahead for the last month. We will head first for the Court of Virtue, as it's closest, then east from there. We'll bring every able Untrialed and an infantry of the Guard. With their Trial at our disposal, Valor will be the strongest court there is and ever will be."

Drytas comes to a stop in front of me, and I school my worried expression, stomach in knots. A cold sweat clings to my skin, and I swallow thickly.

"And you, Lysta, will be by my side to push the Untrialed forward and prevent anyone from leaving until I have what I want..."

～

My feet can't carry me far enough away from the throne room, where Lord Drytas and Belthan plan to round up Untrialed.

He's lost it. Drytas has lost all sense, and now I'm not sure if he had it to begin with. It no longer mattered if you'd committed any crime in Falland to legitimize your Trialing.

Drytas planned to Trial them all.

Everyone.

But not in the Court of Valor.

I turn corner after corner, trying to put as much distance between me and their plan as possible. He couldn't do this. I couldn't help him do this.

Thoman.

If I'm able to warn Thoman, he would believe me. Then maybe he could spread word, flood the message in the streets. At least they could put up a fight.

My heart races faster, sprinting for its life, and I stumble when it misses a beat as I brace myself against the stone wall.

We have rules, and Drytas was changing them—breaking them.

I lean my back against the wall, letting the cool stone press through my shirt into my skin. Closing my eyes, I take a few deep breaths, air rushing out between my teeth slowly. Someone mutters into my ear, and I push them away blindly.

I have no friends here, surrounded by guards and court members—they are all the same.

A hand grabs my chin, yanking my head to look upward. Opening my eyes, I stare at him. Ardis. He kneels in front of me, where I squat against the wall. Ringing echoes in my ears, and I feel another wave of nausea.

Ardis's lips are moving, but even when I focus on his mouth, I can't make out the exact words. His eyes lock with mine and then he's right there, whispering in my head.

Lysta.

It doesn't hurt like it had in the grand hall, when I'd first used my powers, when he searched my thoughts for what had happened, for if I were a liar.

Drytas is the liar.

What happened with Drytas?

A tear slips out as I stare back at him, shaking my head in disbelief. Ardis must have known. How could he be so close to Drytas and not know?

If I say the words, I might lose it completely. So, I show him.

Drytas's announcement of the infantry leaving in two days' time. The rounding up of the Untrialed. Taking on the other courts, all in the name of power and Drytas's paranoia. I don't show him the moments after. Where I'd stared blankly at Drytas as he and Belthan briefed me on details I shouldn't know.

Details a perpetrator would know, not a victim.

They said their plans in front of you?

Confusion breaks my spiraling thoughts at Ardis's question.

Why did it matter?

Do you want to stop him?

Ardis's voice is insistent in my mind, practically vibrating off the walls of my brain.

What kind of question is that?

Lysta, do you want to save them? The Untrialed.

A new hope shines in Ardis's stare. For a moment, I swear his pale blue eyes darken into a molten brown, light reflecting off them. When I lean forward to look closer, Ardis turns his face away, clearing his throat.

Was there really a way out of all this? For everyone?

"How?"

The one-worded question comes out, soft like a whisper.

A look of relief passes across Ardis's face, and he looks down the hall. "We can save them, but I'll need you with me to do it."

Hope ignites in my chest, but I struggle with whether to trust it. The only thing I've ever wished for, was for someone to look at the injustice we've suffered and say, "It's not right, and I'm not going to let it continue."

For a moment, it seems like Ardis is doing just that, but how do I know that he can be trusted any more than Drytas?

I debate it for a heartbeat before I've decided, although there isn't a decision to make. At least not one I could stomach. Even if working with Ardis opens Falland up to another enemy, nothing could be worse than what Drytas will do if left unchecked.

Ardis stands, bringing me up with him. "Be ready. Eat. Sleep. I need to contact someone, but as soon as I do, we'll need to leave." He fumbles with his shirt before pulling something out from the folds of cloth. At my first glimpse of a blade, I flinch backward on instinct until I recognize the hilt.

My dagger.

"Take this—don't let anyone see it, but keep it on you." He starts down the hall before turning back to me. "I'm going to stop this—we both will."

My heart leaps in my throat, and I shout, "Ardis. You bring Thoman. I'm not leaving him here."

Ardis's face tightens, and he gives me a stiff nod.

"Promise you'll bring him with us."

When Ardis turns on his heel to walk away from me, I panic for a moment. Was he refusing to bring Thoman?

But then his voice echoes in my head.

Just be ready.

CHAPTER 13

The grand hall is a war zone.

Guards run the halls in groups, headed down to the streets. Orders are shouted, and no one explains what's happening. I keep hearing them shout a protocol, but I don't know it.

Explosions sound in the distance, and when I look out the window from the higher floors, fires burn in various streets of the city.

Belthan comes for me within minutes of the chaos unfolding. Gripping my arm hard enough to bruise, he drags me behind him.

Worst-case scenarios fly through my head. Did Ardis go to Lord Drytas? Was his offering of help yesterday nothing more than a charade to convince me to reveal something? But this feels like something more than that.

I realize Belthan plans to transport us seconds too late. I barely have the time to cinch my eyes shut to avoid the whirling dizziness that accompanied the last trip.

The same weightlessness is followed by solid ground growing under my feet. We land in the throne room, steps from

Lord Drytas, who sits with his head in his hands. Belthan moves to stand beside him, announcing our arrival. "Lord Drytas, I have brought her, as you requested."

Scanning the room, Ardis is absent from the impromptu meeting. My stomach drops at the realization.

Silence fills the room like a heavy weight, adding to my anxiety with each second that goes by. When Drytas straightens, an angry vein protrudes from his forehead as he grimaces.

"Lysta, we have a problem." Drytas rubs his temples, drawing the skin in circles. "Do you know what that is?"

"Wh-What is that, Lord Drytas?"

My voice trembles when I speak, and trying to swallow the tension only serves to move the nerves to my throat. I try to clear it, but the thickness stays there.

"I'm sure you can understand. If we are to face the other courts, I need the Court of Valor to stand behind me." He levels a glance at me. "And that includes the Untrialed."

Not if I could help it.

I nod, waiting for him to continue.

"Even if the Untrialed dislike my rule, they choose to follow me as their lord."

I mentally snort at his statement. We follow him out of fear because there are no other options. There's no choice about it.

"But now . . . there is uncertainty in the streets following yesterday's events. They question my leadership, and thus they question my authority. And the reason traces back . . . to you."

My heart leaps to my throat.

"Your display in the market made them think they needed protecting—not from the outside forces at work trying to invade our court but from me."

The breath in my lungs freezes, my mouth dropping in surprise. A thrill runs through my veins at what he is insinuating, at what this could mean for Falland. Is this the plan Ardis had put into motion? To make the Untrialed turn against Drytas?

"I've snuffed out every whisper of rebellion since inheriting the throne from my father some thirty years ago. My rule has protected our court, strengthened our court."

My heart stutters at "rebellion."

There's never been even a whisper of uprising during my years. Is it possible that Untrialed have been fighting against the system the whole time and no one knew? The people of Falland stand isolated among one another, but maybe that served Drytas more than we considered.

Anger burns like fire through my veins. My shield flickers around me, only for a blink, but Drytas sees it, as does everyone else in the throne room.

"Problem, Lysta?" Lord Drytas questions with sharpness to his tone.

I shake my head, clenching my hands to regain my control.

Belthan steps forward, head cocked to the side as he levels a suspicious glare in my direction. "Did you disagree with something Lord Drytas said?"

Lord Drytas leans forward in interest, eyeing me dangerously.

I shake my head, mouth open, ready to say something, but my mind draws a blank.

"Answer him," Drytas growls.

"Maybe I should have looked into your little training incident in the lower city. I had Belthan look into the center of the fight yesterday. He'd led me to believe it was a young man and an old woman at the center of the insurgence, but perhaps more fault lies elsewhere."

Thoman and Doireann.

Drytas's eyes flicker with triumph as a flash of panic crosses my face before I can squash it.

"It will be dealt with, but in the meantime, you are an inconvenience. Normally I'd make a show of your execution to cut the rebellion at its roots, but unfortunately, I. Still. Need. You."

Drytas pauses, narrowing his eyes at me. "The moment my generals arrive with the map, we leave. You would do well to impress me, or I may find more reason to look into the other rebels from yesterday."

There's a sudden bang as both doors to the throne room are thrown open. Ardis enters with determination plain on his face.

The members of the Guard who stand on either side of the door startle at his sudden entrance. Across the room, their fists ball at their sides, eyebrows furrowing as they glare at the man moving toward us. One steps forward, mouth opening, but is silenced with a glance back from Ardis. Paling, the guard returns to his post, deflated.

"Ardis. I need you to look into her mind. Now!" Lord Drytas orders from his seat on the throne. "I feel she is hiding something about the events in the market yesterday. She may be working with another to ignite dissent in the streets."

Ardis ignores him, walking straight toward me.

Wide eyed, I try to communicate with him, wishing I knew what was happening in *his* head for once.

A shudder echoes through the floor. At first, it's a rumble until it builds and builds. Glass sconces from the grand hall's walls crash into pieces on the checker floor.

Drytas stands shakily, looking around his throne room in startled fear. Belthan moves to Drytas, the head of guard shouting across the space to the others.

Ardis reaches where I stand, moving toe to toe with me, eyes locked onto mine. "It's time." He slides his hand in mine, grip flexing around my own.

A gust of air barrels into us from behind, Ardis's body blocking most of the force.

Hair whipping uncontrollably, I turn my face into the wind, trying to see through the strands obstructing my view.

The blustering breeze comes not from a window but a small circle a few feet off the ground. The ring spins, the inside a portal to somewhere else. Somewhere greener than I've ever seen, certainly not Falland.

As it grows, a woman on the other side is revealed. Fiery red hair whips in the wind being sucked through the portal. Her hands are stretched out like she's controlling what's unfolding around us.

"Torryn, now!" the girl shouts across the blip in space.

Turning from her, I look to see if someone has stepped forward. Searching for a new player in this never-ending game, but no one does.

Ardis pulls me backward toward the glowing portal.

Drytas croaks from the other side of the room, hand pushing against the wind to block his eyes. "Torryn?"

Out of the corner of my eye, Belthan creeps toward us, just out of Ardis's vision.

"Ah, Torryn. How clever of you, infiltrating my court. Your father taught you well." Drytas sends a menacing glare behind me. "You shouldn't be here. You, of all people, should know the rules"—he pauses—"and their consequences."

Following his gaze, I look at Ardis as ice-cold shock floods my body, my jaw slackening.

He means Ardis.

As Ardis pulls me closer to the portal, Belthan mimics our approach, a hand reaching downward. Near his hip is a flash of a blade.

"Drytas, it isn't me you should be worried about." Ardis

says, causing me to freeze as he tosses a golden disc into the middle of the room.

"I, Torryn, lord of the Court of Self, testify for your judgment."

The disc glows before casting out a ring into the room.

Ardis drags me toward the portal despite my knees locking in protest. This hadn't been the deal—or at least not who I made it with.

Ardis is a lord of another court?

Standing at the mouth of the portal, Belthan bolts toward Ardis, knife poised to attack.

Without hesitation, I throw up a shield, blocking the blade from penetrating Ardis's torso, and we fall. Torryn's eyes meet mine as we disappear into another place—another world for all I know.

Dark brown swallows the bright blue irises staring back at me. Gold flecks shine in the warm, rich color as we are bathed in sunlight.

Falling through the portal is a dizzying experience, with a sudden overload of smells, sounds. My eyes shut on instinct when I land with a thud on the solid ground on the other side.

"Torryn, a little late! You had us worried."

Opening my eyes, I look at the people standing above me.

The redhead who had opened the portal is helping up Ardis . . . And beside her is Ardis?

The two men standing before me are identical, except for one has deep brown eyes. My mouth hangs open, trying to connect my eyes and brain to make sense of what it's seeing.

Just like the first day in the market, the Ardis who had come through the portal, my Ardis, shifts. Like water being poured over him, from head to toe, he transforms—shedding the identity I've come to know.

The blonde hair darkens into black, lengthening to rest just under the man's ears. His jaw widens, cheekbones resting higher—even his nose becomes more prominent. Staring at the man, I watch as his frame stretches out, the bulking figure leaning out as he grows several inches.

Torryn.

Understanding clicks into place as I look between them. The *what* becoming clear, drawing focus to the unanswered *why*.

My breathing quickens as the portal behind them cinches smaller until it closes like a blink of an eye, and I black out.

CHAPTER 14

"You found her."

A female voice jolts me awake, the soft tone mere feet from me. My eyelashes flutter against my upper cheeks as I struggle to keep them closed in a way I hope is natural. Grinding my teeth, I fight the urge to cinch them shut, which would surely give me away.

"I told you we weren't talking about that," a male voice retorts.

A moment of silence lingers before the woman sighs. "*She* wasn't a part of the plan, Torryn."

At his name, the last moments in the throne room flicker in my mind. Torryn. Torryn is Ardis, or is it technically the other way around?

I try to concentrate through the pounding radiating in my head.

Torryn answers back, "Well, now she is, Sar."

I hold my breath in their awkward beat of silence.

"She's Untrialed. How do you think it's going to go if we walk into the capital with her in tow?" Sar continues when he doesn't respond. "Torryn, she'll be eaten alive—"

"Sar! He wouldn't have brought her unless he had to."

The voice is familiar, and I realize it belongs to Ardis. Just not the Ardis I knew.

"Don't interrupt me, Ardis."

It's silent for a beat and then another. Just long enough for me to shift slightly, waiting for them to speak.

Had they walked away?

Torryn whispers in a foreboding tone, "She's not Untrialed." There is a pause once again before he continues. "If it was up to me . . . she still would be."

A nervous tremble echoes in my fingertips, and I slide them further into the corners of my body to hide it. The dagger concealed in my boot presses painfully against my ankle, but knowing it's within reach eases my growing anxiety.

Sar moves past what was the beginnings of an argument. "You'll have to explain . . . everything this time. We'll figure out a new plan, but we only have one shot at this."

Her voice gets softer as she speaks, and when Torryn responds, I realize they are moving away from where I'm crumpled up on the ground.

"Yeah, a new plan that involves her."

Their words become nothing more than mumbled mouthfuls.

My body screams for me to move. To stretch the limbs that have gone stiff in their curled-up positions. I sit still until I can't decide if it's their footsteps moving away in the distance or my heartbeat pounding in my ears.

If Torryn had lied about who he was, who's to say he hadn't concealed his true intentions about why he was in the Court of Valor in the first place? Would a lord of another court care to save Falland? Did he fabricate his promise about helping the Untrialed, too? And what of Thoman?

Cracking my eyes open when I've decided it's been long

enough, I wince at the sunlight flooding my vision, my hand coming up to break the beam.

We are not where we landed when we first fell through the portal. The grass under me might be the same I had stumbled onto, but I had seen a glimpse of great trees towering above, covering us in shade and letting only spots of light move between the clustered leaves.

Pushing up into a sitting position, I brace my weight behind me with my palms and examine the empty field around me. It strikes me I've never seen one before, my universe having centered on stone and metal, buildings and walls. Nothing so utterly . . . open.

White-flowered weeds sway under the whisper of a breeze. The field is not endless, with a line of woods spanning the expanse to my right like a wall without stone. On the opposite side of the forest, across the sweeping green, my eyes trace up a rising hill. It swells in size, surging into a mountain towering over the valley field. At its mount, a staggering structure that can be only described as a castle stands in its grandeur.

Trampled grasses trace a path from where I rest, moving toward the peaking monument.

The three individuals who stared back at me after falling through the portal huddle with their heads bowed, backs facing me.

I move my focus beyond Ardis and the redheaded female I assume is Sar, breath hitching when I lock eyes with Torryn. My lips part in surprise at his unwavering stare. Blinking softly, I maintain his gaze, nose tilting upward.

Torryn's eyes widen, arching one eyebrow. A glimpse of the same smirk he wore on Ardis's face sparks before it's gone.

He's the first to turn away, muttering to Sar and Ardis, who both peer over their shoulders at me. Sar rolls her eyes, whispering a retort before turning on her heel. The trio walks toward me, wading through the tall grass to approach me as if I'm a frightened child.

It's not until Torryn stands above me, extending a hand to help me up, that I decide how I feel.

It isn't fear that clenches my fists, although perhaps I should be afraid, considering I'm in a place I don't know, surrounded by three strangers.

Jaw tightly clenched, I take Torryn's offered hand.

No, I'm past being scared.

At the same moment Torryn's hand closes around mine, I yank hard, using my weight to pull him onto the ground beside me. He lands with a thud, and a gasp sounds from Sar.

Using his momentum, I haul myself on top of him, reaching to yank the dagger from my boot as I swing my leg over his torso. When the hilt is firmly in my hand, I lean down, holding the knife to Torryn's throat. My hair falls around my face from the motion.

Baring my teeth, I hiss into his face, "Explain."

Torryn doesn't seem surprised at the sudden change in events. His eyes darken when he looks at me.

Leaning forward, Torryn props himself up on his elbows even though it presses his skin tighter to the blade. "Trials, Lysta." With gritted teeth, Torryn forces out, "You're really making me regret giving you that back. And here, I thought we were allies."

"Torryn," Sar calls in a worried voice.

One of Torryn's hands raises from the grass, waving her off. "We're fine, Sar. Stay out of it. Both of you. Lysta and I need to clear the air."

"Answer me," I add, pressing the blade tighter against his skin, until a bead of blood pebbles at the tip.

"You haven't asked me a question," Torryn says with a raised eyebrow.

Frustration burns under my skin, and I can't help but let out a growl as I throw rapid-fire rambling at him like icy spears.

"Explain *is* a question, an open-ended one. One you have enough context to answer. But if you need me to break it down for you—" Releasing his shirt, I point at Ardis, who has the nerve to look sheepish under my angry focus. "You're not who you said you were, *Lord Torryn*. You used me. You manipulated me. Was there anything not a lie?"

"The only thing I lied about was who I was. It changes nothing else. I still plan to stop Drytas."

My hold on the dagger loosens at his words. Eyes searching his face, I look for a reason to not believe him. Furrowing my brows, I lean in tighter. "You left Thoman. You promised you wouldn't."

Torryn's hand reaches up slowly. "If we aren't able to convince the other courts to intercept Drytas, you won't be able to return. Going against him, against your court, is treason. He's safer there."

An angry laugh bursts from my mouth. "No, he's not. Someone told Drytas others were involved in the riot yesterday. He'll find him and execute him since he can't Trial him."

Torryn's eyes widen before he looks to the side.

He hadn't known.

When he looks at me once again, his eyes are hard.

"There are too many lives at stake for us to go back for your boyfriend. Even if Drytas thinks someone else was involved, he doesn't know who, and they would have to find him first. Maybe if you stop threatening me, we can get the courts to act before that happens."

I take a deep breath. "He's my friend, and he's saved my life more times than I can count."

Torryn rolls his eyes. "Well, I didn't need your friend. I needed you."

I can't help but growl at him, pressing the knife closer against his skin. "You were working for Drytas. You're the reason I'm Trialed in the first place."

A look of hurt crosses his face before it's tucked away, leaving a blank expression.

"I only ever planned to bring Drytas true criminals. The three men I was tricking when you showed up stole from a bunch of kids. It was you who got in the way. You forced my hand when you called over the guard."

My breath lodges in my throat.

If that was true . . .

"And why the ruse? You wanted to face the Trial?"

Torryn tilts his head, and his dark hair shifts across the sides of his face. He lets out a deep exhale. "That was only a small part of it."

My voice goes monotone as I look away from him. "You want the power. Just like Drytas."

In a flash, Torryn knocks me off him, grabbing the dagger from my hand, and flings it into the dirt. He hovers over where I lay, shocked, on the ground, before getting to his feet.

"Don't pretend you know me, Lysta. I've fought battles that have lasted longer than I've known you."

His eyes flash with unbridled anger, and I flinch, unwilling to be the fallout. At this, his face changes in an instant, back to his blank slate.

"We want the same thing, and once we get to the capital, they won't let Drytas"—he spits out the name with venom—"get away with it. The courts may seldom agree, but forcing citizens to Trial as punishment? Just so you can get as many Trialed as possible? It goes against every belief we have in protecting the Trials, what they stand for. It's supposed to be about choice. Choosing to test yourself—to face parts of yourself you normally wouldn't. It's an honor. Taking away that decision strips away the sanctity of it."

That's the plan, then? Appealing to the courts and hoping they will intervene? I know next to nothing of the other courts or the capital. But I don't have the power to change things back in Falland. I'd have to give Torryn an inch of trust and hope it doesn't screw me over in the end.

The group as a whole seems to take a deep breath as Torryn and I separate, exchanging glares. Torryn stands, leaning down to snatch my dagger off the ground. He shows it to me before making a point of stashing it in his belt. I grumble, prepared to fight for the weapon, until my thoughts are interrupted.

"How are you feeling?" Sar asks as she reaches to help me up, sweeping away the conflict as if we'd been debating the weather. "Portaling can be jarring the first time around."

I stumble on my feet. "Kinda like my entire world has been turned upside down, but I don't think it's from the portaling," I say, looking at Torryn.

He looks off in the distance, not acknowledging my pointed glance.

"Well, I'm Sar," she continues, smoothing her hands against her dress skirt repeatedly. The blue cloth contrasts with the red hair cascading to her waist, vibrant with color and energy.

She must be wealthy within her court to have such clothes —without stains or rips. In fact, nothing mars the fabric except white lace adorning the bodice.

I'm struck with a new sense of self consciousness as I examine her dress for the first time. I'd been offered extra clothes from the guard's supply, which had been perfectly acceptable before, but now, compared to Sar, I feel even further out of place.

Another part of me feels shame creeping up that I paid the

clothes I wore any mind when so many in Falland have much less. When *I* had much less, only just over a week ago.

Sar gestures to Ardis before adding, "And this is—"

"Ardis," I finish.

The three exchange a look before Ardis gives me a sheepish grin and nods. "Yeah, it's nice to meet you." Raising a hand to the back of his neck, Ardis fingers through his blonde hair.

Despite their, at one point, identical appearances, they carry distinguishable differences in their demeanor. Torryn, as Ardis, always wore a tight expression. Brows furrowed, lips pursed, and I can't recall if I've ever seen him smile. The same as Torryn wears now. But Ardis's face is relaxed, an easygoing air about him.

I nod back to him, and the tension eases.

What a fool I must've looked.

"Let's get moving," Torryn says, interrupting the awkward silence. He narrows his eyes at the line of trees across the field. "I don't like being this close to the Border Forest at dusk."

CHAPTER 15

There weren't any grasses or flowers in Falland, every inch covered in cracked stone and brick. Thinking back, I hadn't found it unusual, the city being so devoid of life. Fields and rivers were only in paintings or books of places I'd never go and had seemed every bit a fantasy as the creatures who filled them.

But now, feeling the soil compress beneath my boots, the grass skimming across the sides of my ankles, it speaks of more realness than anything in Falland. What surrounds me breathes, not with lungs that expand with air but in its movement as a flow of nature.

I imagined the world outside of Falland's walls to be the same as inside—bleak and struggling and wilting away.

Lord Drytas fed us this picture of war-torn courts, destitute in the aftermath of their endless battles. But he'd lied about so many things who's to say that wasn't another manipulation? Maybe some of us would have tried to leave if we'd known.

I'd like to think I might have.

The walk toward the capital is silent, Torryn and Ardis some feet ahead, whispering to each other.

I strain my ear for even a word of their conversation.

When Torryn peeks over his shoulder, catching my eyes, he straightens at my attention.

I wait for a snide retort, but he turns back to Ardis and speaks lower.

My mind is divided on Torryn and his deceit, attacking the other side's arguments but neither winning the war. He's the reason I was Trialed. But he's also my only hope of fixing Falland—if he's telling the truth about his plan.

Torryn didn't say why he'd been in Falland, leaving me to think he had, in fact, been hoping to face the Court of Valor's Trial but stumbled onto more than he expected.

Sar, walking next to me, says hesitantly, "You'll find, once we arrive in the capital, few people will care about fixing what's wrong in Valor as much as Torryn. Most would have turned a blind eye to it all."

Narrowing my eyes at her, I can't help but wonder if she'd heard my thoughts. If she was of Torryn's court, could she read minds, too?

"That does less to make me like *Torryn* and more to make me despise the capital."

Sar flashes me a small smile before tucking her lip between her teeth. "Not entirely unwise. The capital is"—she pauses—"not for everyone. It's supposed to be neutral ground for the seven courts to gather, but putting that many power-hungry, sword-happy people together—it's a recipe for war."

At "power hungry," my eyes find the edge of Torryn's sleeve, where I can just catch the beginning of his Trial tattoo. How many has he faced? At least two from the powers I know him to have.

I barely survived the one.

"Is Trialing more than once common in the capital?" I ask, turning to Sar.

At my question, Ardis and Torryn go silent in front of us. Torryn sends Sar a warning look, and my interest piques.

Obviously, I've stepped into a conversation not meant for me, but their hesitation only feeds my curiosity.

"No, it isn't."

When Sar doesn't continue, I summon the courage to ask, "I know so little . . . Drytas kept so much from the Untrialed. I don't want to head into this looking like a fool. Will you just tell me what you can?"

Sar's eyes brighten as she looks at me like I've passed a test I didn't know I was taking. In an instant, the rigidity in her posture relaxes. When she speaks again, the timidness that had laced her tone is gone.

"This is a mark of failure, or you can just call them your tally. We do." She extends her hand out to me, exposing the underside of her wrist. The beginning of a Trial tattoo sweeps under her sleeve, but she draws my attention to a single tally mark dashed across the protruding vein. "Did you see any of them in the Court of Valor?"

I think hard, scrutinizing every tattoo I'd seen in Falland, but shake my head. "You get them from failing a Trial?"

Sar nods, twisting a small braid between her fingers. "You can fail twice without consequences, but fail your third Trial, and that's the end. You don't come out. Even if you survived the test despite failing. It all just"—she lets out a shuddering breath—"ends."

My heart thumps.

"I barely survived my first one," I whisper.

For a moment, I don't think anyone has heard me. Sar says nothing but then Torryn and Ardis exchange a look. Torryn's face remains steely and unchanged, but Ardis purses his lips in a slight frown.

Sar answers back, just as quietly. "It's not for everyone." She inhales deeply, unwinding the braid, then braids it again. "That's half of the reason it isn't really done. You're already taking so much of a risk to Trial once—not to mention not all Trials are built the same. Some are easier than others. For some, if you fail, there is no walking out or second chances. You can't trust what happened in previous court's Trials to gauge what happens in another, and no one can warn you about what happens in it."

Noticing her careful wording, I push, "And the other half of the reason?"

Sar laughs half-heartedly. "The other half is just court politics. If you can convince each Crown to Trial in their court, then you could Trial in all seven courts if you truly wanted to. But there's a slim chance of convincing even one of them, let alone them—"

"Crown?"

My mind whirls with the onslaught of new information.

Ardis whips around, having had one ear leaned toward the conversation. Walking backward, his arms swinging at his side, he perks up. "The lords and ladies of each court"—he points a thumb at Torryn, mockingly whispering—"like Torryn over here."

Torryn rolls his eyes but doesn't engage, which only seems to encourage Ardis's antics.

He holds his hands a foot apart before lifting them above his head as if placing an imaginary crown atop. "They all have their own Crowns, and it's easier to just say 'Crowns' than 'the lords and ladies.' Such a mouthful." Ardis grins widely.

I'm taken aback at the expression, having never seen Torryn smile so free and unrestricted when pretending to be Ardis.

Sar argues back in an admonishing tone, "It's respectful—"

"It's utterly ridic—" Ardis barks mid-laugh.

"And where's his crown?" I gesture to Torryn.

No crown sits upon his dark hair despite being a lord.

Sar and Ardis's laugh settle, and they both look to Torryn.

Torryn answers stiffly, "I do wear one. When it is *socially required*."

His dry response stirs another round of chuckles from Sar and Ardis.

As I look between the three, a part of my heart winces at their obvious ease. The teasing and familiarity reminded me of Thoman.

"When we are in the capital, just don't address the *Crowns*," she taunts at Ardis, "as that to their face. They should all be referred to as 'lord' or 'lady.'" She tilts her head in thought. "You also will need to curtsy or bow if they address you, but I don't think it will be likely."

I sag in relief.

If they are anything like Drytas, then I'll avoid even being in the same room as them.

"And what are the courts again?" I ask, as if I've merely forgotten them, but from the pitying look in Sar's eyes, she knows it's because I don't know.

"There are seven courts in Aloria. You already know Valor, Lord Drytas's court, and Torryn's is the Court of Self. There's also the Court of Will, ruled by Lord Rhen, and the Court of Virtue, ruled by Lord Nicaise." Sar pauses, jaw clenching. "Then there's Lord Bralas's Court of Wisdom, and Lady Ivianna and the Court of Change, and Lord Gennady and the Court of Truth."

My eyes flicker back to Torryn. "The Court of Change? So, she let you Trial in her court. That's how you can shapeshift."

Realization coats my tone.

Torryn glowers at me over his shoulder before speaking in a low tone. "I cannot shapeshift. It's an entirely different ability."

Semantics.

I huff in irritation. "Then, what would you call it, my *lord?*"

Sarcasm drips off the title as I say it, but it doesn't create my desired reaction. Instead, Torryn's eyes darken, staring deeply at me, until Sar breaks the trance.

We both look away from each other.

"Torryn, can mirror-shift. He can transform into an identical replica of someone he has seen but only as they were when he last saw them. A mirror image. He can't make up a person or change specific features."

Frowning, I ponder the new information. "Why would any of the Crowns let another ruler Trial in their court? Don't they fear one becoming more powerful than the others?"

Ardis snickers. "Found someone who enjoys being lectured to, did ya, Sar? Our resident bookworm."

Even Torryn bites back a grin as Sar's face reddens.

"Oh, shut it, Ardis," Sar says without an ounce of anger behind it. "Ignore them. You are exactly right, which is why it's very rare for someone to Trial more than once. None of the courts want to give the others an advantage, so they only allow Trials from citizens within their court." Sar pauses before gesturing to Torryn. "Unless you have something to convince them otherwise . . ."

I catch her peeking to Torryn.

What did Torryn have over the other courts, making them amenable to him Trialing there?

"That's more than enough, Sar," Torryn interrupts, stopping in his tracks.

I'm ready to disagree, the words on the tip of my tongue. But then Torryn stiffens as he stares at the castle looming above us, far closer than it had been before. He clenches his teeth.

I'm not the only one who notices the sudden change in Torryn, as Ardis clamps a hand on the young lord's shoulder and pats it before leading the way. Sar leaves my side, brushing

Torryn as she passes. She gives him a single nod, following behind Ardis.

Glancing between the three, I'm unsure of what I seem to have missed. Not planning to be the last, I trail after Sar, stopped by a firm hand grabbing my wrist.

Suddenly far too close to Torryn, I hold my breath at the fierce frown settling across his features. Not planning to back down, I crane my neck to glare at him.

"You'll find while at the capital that the Court of Valor is very different from the other courts. Drytas used his power openly and encouraged others to do the same. You won't find that to be the case here."

I open my mouth to interrupt, but Torryn continues, tone leaving no room for question.

"Your ability is your strength. The more people who know your strength, the weaker you are. Until life depends on it, you do not reveal what you can do. Now I cannot stop you from telling whoever you want, but under no circumstances will you utter a word about Sar's. I'm hoping that, if you've trusted me to take you this far, you'll give me the same respect about my powers, but it isn't an option about Sar's."

Torryn's dark eyes search my own, letting silence follow his speech. I nod once, showing my understanding, and he relaxes.

"Then, it's time for your introduction to the capital."

CHAPTER 16

Crossing the threshold of the capital, we step through shining doors. Channeling the light of the dying sun, the glass refracts rainbows across our faces and onto the gleaming white floor. A grand staircase cascades at the back of the space, spreading out into the center of the room. White marble steps flow seamlessly into the surrounding tiles.

I can't help but rub the sides of my leather boots together, worried that, if I walk any further onto the clean floor, a dirt footprint path will follow me in.

It's hard to fathom—how the grand hall that stunned me a week ago is now so easily surpassed. But no one would dare compare the likes of this castle to Falland, and certainly not the streets.

The room hums with conversation, floating from the groups of people gathered in the entry hall. Everyone wears fine clothing made of silk, velvet, and other expensive-looking fabrics. My eyes lower to my grass-stained pants, and hot shame pinks my cheeks.

When Torryn steps ahead, a wave of silence moves down the room, heads turning in a chain reaction.

I sigh in relief when the stares barely skim my face, instead narrowing in on Torryn with startled looks.

My muscles tense as I catalog the fearful faces of those gathered in the room. They stare at Torryn with wide eyes, following his every movement, as if waiting for something to happen. A few reach for the swords hanging at their sides, but none of them move to unsheathe the blades.

Despite this, Torryn doesn't flinch as he stalks further into the room, head high with an air of importance.

Ardis and Sar a step behind him on either side.

I hesitate to follow them, shirking away from the attention they draw.

I whip around, body tensing for a fight, when someone screams, just in time to see a figure barreling out of the crowd toward us. Torryn stiffens in front of me, hands twitching, as if bracing for the hit.

A flash of metal shimmers, a blade. Heart racing, I raise my hands to bring up a shield, but Torryn grabs my wrists, yanking me behind him. He gives me a warning look before letting me go to move toward the attacker.

Torryn sweeps forward, grabbing the wrist of the man and maneuvering the knife away from him. Before I can blink, Torryn has the man unarmed and restrained on the ground, all without breaking his cool composure.

Looking up from his attacker, Torryn flicks his hair out of his face before calmly surveying the room. Ardis, without hesitation, comes up behind to take over restraining the man so Torryn can stand. When he does, it is almost as if I'm seeing him for the first time.

This is a man trained for battle, separate from what powers he may have. It's obvious he's a force without them.

Torryn calls out to a pair of guards standing nearby. "Would the two of you like to do your jobs, or shall I have you put in the dungeon next to his?"

The guards rush forward while I stand there, still in shock. Torryn turns on his heel, eyes sweeping over me and Sar to check if we are all right, before leaning in to whisper harshly to one guard. The color drains from the guard's face, a worried expression falling into place.

A voice carries across the room, echoing in the quiet from the top of the stairs. "Lord Torryn. We've been waiting for you."

I search across the figures standing on the next level for the person who's spoken. My breath hitches in my throat when I stumble over the multiple Crowns among them.

One steps forward, descending the staircase with a repetitive clank, as a cane meets the marble. It's an older man with tanned skin, white hair, and a matching beard, contrasting against the bright blue of his suit. Atop his head is a silver crown, similar to Drytas's but with a more understated quality.

As the older lord descends, Torryn gives the man a tilt of his head, bowing it in respect. "It seems you weren't the only one." Torryn gestures to the man being dragged from the room, a faint smile pulling at his lips. "Lord Gennady." When he looks up, he extends his hand. "It's been quite some time."

Lord Gennady takes Torryn's hand, giving it a long shake before patting it with his other. "Yes, since Lord Rhen and you nearly killed each other in the arena, I believe. I hope you have no plans for similar theatrics today, but looks as though the excitement seems to find you."

I nearly balk at the insinuation before Lord Gennady betrays his harsh words with the mirth dancing in his eyes, a soft chuckle escaping from his wrinkled lips. The crowned figures standing atop of the stairs exchange a look, none of them looking pleased at Torryn's presence.

Torryn doesn't even flinch. "I'm afraid we have much more

important things to attend to, and I'm sure Lord Rhen would agree," he says, looking at the top of the stairs where a wall of Crowns has formed. Each look at Torryn with distaste curling their upper lip.

A pair of women on my right whisper, oblivious to my attention to their words. Holding their fingers over their lips, they lean toward each other.

"I can't believe they even allow him to enter the capital after everything that happened."

"The Crowns are likely worried about how he'll retaliate if they didn't."

"I know, but it's like they're pretending the war never happened."

I don't turn to look at the gossiping ladies, but my stomach knots at their words. What had garnered such an apprehension toward Torryn?

At Torryn's foreboding words, any humor drains from Lord Gennady's face, his posture suddenly stiffening. He turns on his heel, gesturing for Torryn to follow him up the stairs.

"So, it is true? You've testified for judgment against Lord Drytas. I'd thought—well, 'hoped' is the better word—that it'd been a mistake. But it has been too long since we've seen anyone of the Court of Valor, Drytas included. And we haven't convened for judgment since . . ." Lord Gennady pauses before glancing at Torryn, who flinches.

"Yes. Not since my father," Torryn says, as if a foul taste lingers in his mouth.

My eyes widen at the admission.

Torryn's father? What had he done to be put under judgment? Sar had said they reserved that for issues going beyond just one court but impacting the nation. Was this what the women's whispers had been about?

"Yes, well. We'll need more details of what has happened before Lord Drytas arrives for the judgment hearing."

My stomach drops and tumbles across the floor.

Drytas is coming here?

A cold sweat covers my skin, leaving me feeling uncomfortable and sticky. I guess it would have been too good to be true to force change in Falland without facing him again. I could only hope the other courts would stop him from executing me on the spot for treason.

Torryn and Lord Gennady have nearly reached the top of the stairs when Torryn freezes, pivoting on the step. His eyes search the crowd standing at the base of the staircase, then stop when they rest on me.

"Lysta with us, please," Torryn proclaims, no question in his tone.

I freeze, paling, before I react. Around me, the people I've blended among look for who the lord calls for. Looking back at Torryn, I see he waves me on, seemingly oblivious to my hesitation. As I step forward, making my way to the foot of the stairs, whispers creep up again.

From behind Torryn and Lord Gennady, another lord steps forward to intercede. With burnt ginger hair and a gold crown of his own, the man speaks with an edge to his voice. "Lord Torryn, I know you've only been a lord for a short time, but you should know, only lords"—he pauses before sneering at the only crowned lady, Ivianna, standing beside him—"and *ladies* of courts may hear our inner speakings."

The lady rolls her eyes, glaring daggers at the back of the ginger-haired man who speaks.

Lord Gennady nods. "Yes, I'm afraid Lord Bralas is correct, Lord Torryn. The members of your court will have to wait with the rest of ours."

I stutter in my ascension, but Torryn looks back at me, only halfway up the stairs. Reaching out his hand, Torryn gives me a hard look, daring for me to go against him. His eyes leave no question to continue, as he'd asked. I can't help but freeze, gripping the railing.

Why couldn't he just let me be? I obviously am not needed, and now, he's only making a show of me. My cheeks burn with a fiery heat, and I look between Torryn and Lord Gennady, uncertain.

Torryn lets out a huff but doesn't move his eyes from mine. "I would agree, except she is not *of* my court."

Lord Bralas, the ginger lord who'd spoken out, shakes his head, shooting a look at the others standing beside him. "Then, who's court is she from?"

A chuckle echoes from the group.

Torryn walks down the steps between us, grabbing my hand from where it grips the railing. I fight his hold, trying to pull out of his grasp, but then he announces, "She's of the Court of Valor."

The whispers and rumbles of conversation dull once again. Gasps echo in the silence. The back of my neck prickles from the gaze of those watching me in renewed interest.

I am no longer someone so easily dismissed.

Torryn pulls me up to his step, giving me a warning glance, before leading me up to where the Crowns watch us from above. Trying to avoid eye contact, I stare at Torryn's grip on my hand and follow a thorn-like scar across his knuckles.

Standing before the Crowns, I bow as Torryn introduces me.

"Lysta here will be witness and evidence against Lord Drytas."

CHAPTER 17

Eyed with the level of distrust one would bestow upon thieves, regarded as if we have the reputation of murderers, Torryn and I are kept at a distance as we proceed to the meeting room.

Guards are staggered between the Crowns, with a few extra lingering near us in the rear of the procession. They stand stiffly in their uniforms—not unlike the guards in Falland—save for those carrying swords. In the middle of their chest, a seven-pointed star is embroidered with silver-and-gold thread.

Their gazes feel like shackles around my wrists, as if I'm the one with crimes facing punishment.

As we approach our destination, the Crowns are joined by others, most of which are about my age. They file into the room, their armed escorts remaining outside.

Torryn and I approach the doorway, ready to follow, when we are stopped. Without explanation, Torryn and I are pulled apart, and he is searched, their hands moving up his legs, torso, and arms.

"Torryn—"

"Everything's fine, Lysta. They are just checking me for weapons."

Despite how calm he sounds, his jaw clenches as he waits for them to finish.

Why was he the only one needing to be searched? The rest of the Crowns seemed just as dangerous if not more than Torryn.

Seemingly satisfied, they release him, and he brushes himself off as if dirtied. The guard who patted him down moves to me, and my eyes go wide, a protest on the tip of my tongue.

But Torryn grabs the guard's arm and locks it behind his back. "I allow you to search me out of my own generosity. She does not extend you the same courtesy." With fear obvious in the man's eyes, he nods tightly, and Torryn releases him. "We'll be heading in now."

Releasing a deep breath, Torryn gestures for me to enter the meeting room.

Blinking rapidly, I nod, unable to form words of gratitude. Without touching me, Torryn's hand hovers over the small of my back, leading me in.

A long oval table is centered in the room. Its surface is a sleek black, except for where the same star from the guards' uniforms is carved into the top. Fourteen high-back chairs are spaced around the table, and as everyone sits, I realize there are two for each court—one for its Crown and then a second.

Torryn is the last to move for his seat, and I follow reluctantly.

When I plop without a morsel of grace into the chair next to him, Torryn stills, his hand freezing its incessant tapping on the surface.

The mumbling of the room dissipates, with only a few coughs filling the silence.

Looking around, I realize I have captured their attention.

Some eye me with anger-filled eyes, while others look away and shift awkwardly.

Torryn nudges me, whispering in a strained voice, "Stand up."

I hesitate, leaning closer to question what he'd said, but Torryn repeats himself, his tone pitched. "Stand up. Now."

Standing in the sitting room, Torryn pushes in the chair I have sat in as soon as my legs clear the seat. When I send him a confused look, Torryn stares straight ahead, impassive, except for the tips of his ears reddening.

Lord Gennady, from the head of the table, saves me from the awkwardness.

"Lysta, perhaps you could stand at the end of the table. That seat is reserved for Lord Torryn's Heir, and unless this meeting is also an announcement of your engagement, it would be inappropriate for you to reside there, even if just for the day."

My face pales several shades, and a soft "Oh" escapes my lips. Pivoting on my heel, I look away from Torryn, who seems pained by the situation.

"I apologize. I was not aware."

From the end of the table, my knees shake from the scrutiny of the lords and lady staring back at me, many of which are not friendly gazes.

Glancing to the side, I see two empty seats reserved for the Court of Valor.

Lord Gennady clears his throat. "Lord Torryn, would you like to provide some backstory for us?"

When Torryn opens his mouth, Lord Bralas slams his hand down with a resounding thud.

Every head at the table turns to the red-haired lord, who levels a glare in Torryn's direction.

"If I may interject, perhaps Lord Torryn should start with why he felt he could invade another court." Bralas folds his hands over the table, leaning forward with a sneer. "Seeing as how no outsider has set foot in the Court of Valor for over a century, I'd assume it did not strike Lord Drytas with the sudden compulsion to make an allowance for you, of all courts."

Lord Gennady exchanges a tired look at the interruption but answers in a patient tone, "Lord Bralas, perhaps we ought to let Lord Torryn explain without first accusing him of such a crime."

Bralas leans back in his chair and crosses his leg. Lips pursed, he glares daggers across the room at Torryn and then me. When he speaks again, his voice is coated with lethal politeness.

"I'm sure Lord Torryn understands our *concern*," he says, gesturing to the others at the table, "considering his court's . . . history."

A look is exchanged across the table between Bralas and Torryn, and when the ginger lord smirks, Torryn's knuckles turn white.

It strikes me that the Crowns are much older than Torryn, the closest in age still likely decades apart from him.

"Lord Drytas sent a member of his court into my territory in order to recruit one of my own," Torryn answers with a steady voice.

Staring at him, I'm reminded of how little Torryn had given me of the story. It seems I'm only being offered bits and pieces and expected to understand the entire picture.

At the further end of the table, another lord leans forward in interest. "And whom did Lord Drytas attempt to recruit?"

"Ardis of Self." Torryn pauses as if expecting someone to interject, but the table remains silent. "I was well within my rights as a lord to pursue the matter, as I'm sure any of you would have if I had done the same as Lord Drytas."

His words are cold, and Torryn wields them like a weapon.

"Of course, Lord Torryn. We apologize for the accusation,"

Lord Gennady says, narrowing his eyes at Lord Bralas, who ignores the prompt. "We are just trying to get more of the picture. This is all with little precedent."

Torryn glances at me. "When invited by Drytas, I went in Ardis's stead to discern his motives. What I found was worse than I'd assumed."

The room stills as each person at the table waits with bated breath.

"Lord Drytas has been forcing his citizens to Trial by making it a punishment for crimes committed."

Eyes widen around the room, someone letting out a soft gasp at Torryn's revelation. The lords begin shouting across the table, mashing into a garble of words.

Lord Bralas stands, drawing the table's attention once again. "He can't force them—you know as well as we do. The consent requirement makes it impossible."

Arguments fling across the table, and I can't help but flinch at the cruel words being slung like mud, not only at me but at Torryn.

Feeling eyes piercing into me, I meet the gaze of a boy who sits quietly in the raucous room. He's younger than most people present but probably about my age. He's placed next to Lord Gennady, but a crown doesn't rest upon his head—his heir.

Watching him as the chaos unfolds around us, I notice his calm demeanor. He leans forward in his chair before bringing his elbow to rest upon the table, lowering his forehead into the tips of his fingers. Shaking his head, he rolls his eyes at the arguing match.

When he looks up, bright blue eyes meeting my own, I freeze, caught examining him. But he gives me a small curl of his lips before gesturing to his own sleeves. He motions for me to roll up mine. I can't stop the confused arch of my brows.

Torryn brings his hands down on the table, standing to

match Lord Bralas. "Drytas has found a way around it. He forced Lysta to Trial, and the door opened at her forced agreement with a knife to her throat."

The focus of the table moves to me again, their gazes searching me as if looking for evidence of Torryn's claim. I straighten my shoulders and head, trying to project any air but of a victim. My fingers intertwine and twist as if able to unknot my anxiety. Doing as the stranger suggests, I roll up my sleeve, revealing my Trial tattoo to the room.

"This is ridiculous. Having a Trial tattoo means nothing." Bralas starts again, but Torryn silences him with a deadly look.

"I have not finished!"

At the loud statement, the table goes silent.

"Following her Trialing, the tunnel collapsed." Torryn meets the eyes of each person in the room. "The door cracked into dozens of pieces."

For the first time since I've arrived, it is completely silent. No one speaks, each seeming to process the news with paling faces.

Torryn lets the information sink in. "There is currently no viable way to Trial in the Court of Valor, and I'm unsure if there ever will be again."

Of course, the one thing to break through and make the Crowns listen: a risk to their precious Trials.

Lord Gennady breaks the silence, his words but a whisper. "This is very alarming. I've never heard an event like this happening before. Do you know why?" He looks to Torryn.

"No, I don't," Torryn answers, leaning back in his chair now that the screaming interrogation has quieted. "Only guesses, but in our last days there, Lysta was able to reveal Lord Drytas's end game."

"And?"

Torryn looks to me, and I stare back with question in my eyes. He nods as if knowing the curiosity rooted in my mind.

Is this the best way?

My body shakes under the intense gazes of the room. If I tell them what I know, it would be my first real step of treason. My escape of Falland could be played easily as being coerced by Torryn, but in this moment, providing information against my court, I could never take it back.

When Drytas arrives, in what could be only days, he will have every reason to want my head. And depending on if these rulers believe me, they might let him.

Lord Gennady says softly into the room, "Lysta, you have no cause for fear from us. We only seek the truth."

I nod shakily, blinking away the mist smothering my eyes.

Even if telling them what I know makes it so I can never return home, it would still be worth it. To fix Falland. I have only spent a day outside the walls of the city, and I can easily say now—Falland is broken. But maybe these people would care enough to fix it.

Taking a deep breath, I focus on the center of the table. "He plans to bring all the Untrialed to invade the other courts." I pause, waiting for someone to question me. When no one does, I continue. "If he can't Trial them in Falland, then he said he'll Trial them all. In every court. Building an army to destroy any who stand in his way. He said he'd be the wielder of all courts' power."

The news goes over much as I expected, but I still flinch when the table stands in outrage. Even Torryn whips around to look at me with wide eyes, like I've said something he didn't expect.

Bralas lurches across its surface, hands pressed down as he snarls at me. "And why would he reveal this to you? Freshly Trialed, and he trusted you already? Drytas is no fool."

My gaze flickers to Torryn again, but I can't see him around the standing lords.

I hesitate before revealing, "He believed me an essential part of the plan. He wanted to use me to force the Untrialed—"

Bralas throws his hands in the air. Turning to Lord Gennady while pointing at me, he says, "Are we really believing this? Trusting the word of a barely Trialed girl over a lord? It's an outrage!"

"What would I gain from lying about this?!" I yell.

Bralas snarls as he stomps across the room to me before pressing his finger into my face. "You dare speak to a lord like that, you pitiful excuse of a Trialed."

The anger surges under my skin, and I feel the initial signs of my power emerging. He could not touch me. Not if I let the shield come out.

Not the time, fighter.

Torryn's voice shouts in my mind, and I wince in surprise.

Lord Bralas smirks, seemingly thinking I'm cowering in fear from his presence. He puffs out his chest.

Lord Gennady's voice cuts through the raised voices. "We will not decide on this today. Lord Drytas will arrive for his judgment hearing in a couple of days. We will hear more on this then and will give Drytas the opportunity to defend himself against these claims. Meeting adjourned."

TORRYN TRAILS as they lead me to my room, face hard and detached. A mile of difference compared to the man who had nearly cracked a smile among his own court earlier today.

Following the meeting, I tried to pull Torryn aside to ask him what happens now. I had expected things to go much easier. Expected them to hold some merit in what Torryn and I have said.

Had Torryn foreseen their reaction? He knows them better than I.

When directed to a room, I nod, entering without question. At least I'm being treated as a guest and not a prisoner within the capital.

Stepping into the room, I note its size above anything else. The farthest wall has wide windows showing nothing but a dark void in the dead of night. The space has more than I could ask for, and I turn to thank my escorts before noticing Torryn, whose body fills the doorway.

As he approaches me, he leans closer. "I'm giving you this back." He forces a heavy metal object into my hand.

I glimpse the hilt of my dagger. Even with my powers, the dagger offers a sense of relief. Stepping closer, I use Torryn's body to block me as I conceal the blade in my waistband. Looking up at him, I send him a grateful look.

Where had he kept it while being searched by the guards?

"Trusting me not to have it at your throat again?" I murmur in a teasing tone.

Torryn's lip twitches, and I take it as a victory.

"More like trusting you'll have a good reason if you do."

When a throat clears behind him, Torryn hurries out his last words. "Keep it with you, but keep it concealed. Don't speak of Valor with anyone. And, most of all, don't trust anyone."

Looking deeply into his dark-brown eyes, I ask, "Anyone?"

"Anyone."

He stands close. Close enough that I feel hot breath fan across my face. It reminds me of my panic attack in Falland.

How he had promised he could help.

Now I only hope I was right to believe him.

He pivots back, whispering, "Were those Lord Drytas's exact words? The wielder of all courts' power bit?"

Taken off guard by the question, I just nod, brows furrowed. "Why?"

Torryn shakes his head, waving off my question before stepping further into the hall, allowing me to see those who still stand just outside. The guards look away as if having caught us in a private moment, but Lord Gennady only watches with curiosity stirring in his gaze.

"Excellent. Well, Lysta, I will send someone in the morning to show you around. Get you acquainted with the capital. Do sleep well."

I nod before slowly closing the door. Stomping further into the room, I let my footfalls carry out to the hall. After a moment's pause, I sneak back to the door. Leaning in close, I focus, listening for retreating footsteps.

Several feet move away from the door, the hall growing quieter.

Until voices sound from just outside.

"Is there a reason she is being separated from my court?" Torryn asks, his voice a monotone drone. When no one responds for an awkward beat, Torryn continues, "I notice she's staying in the tower furthest from my own."

Someone sighs—Lord Gennady, who remains with Torryn outside of my quarters.

"Torryn, this is unprecedented for us. If what you say is true, then Lysta's testimony needs to stand on its own two feet. I will not assume you are oblivious to your court's reputation—or yours, for the matter. So, it is in our best interests if we maintain some separations. The argument she was coerced will be put on the table, and we must be able to negate that with what we can. I know you understand that."

"And that same testimony will make her a target for people in the capital. She should be where I can protect her."

I press my ear against the door.

Torryn had not warned me of enemies I could make here, only of the ones I would now have back in Falland. Now I know what he meant by him giving me my dagger and saying not to trust anyone.

"Well, then, it's good she has you among others to look out for her," Lord Gennady says with a tone of finality.

Their voices get quieter, accompanied by soft footsteps.

Leaning back against the wall near the door, I sag and run my hands across my face.

Tomorrow will be . . . something.

CHAPTER 18

I watch the sun crest the horizon and chase away the night from my curled-up position in bed. Tucked tightly between silk sheets and a soft down blanket, I stare blankly into the distance, ignoring the signs of morning's call to rise.

Sleep had taken me early in the night, exhaustion dragging me under with little fight. But the slumber was only restful for so long before Lord Drytas plagued my dreams, tormenting me with the decision I made and the lives at stake.

I hoped I'd feel reassured once sharing the war looming in the distance. By spreading the burden across more qualified hands, I wouldn't carry the crushing weight of what was at risk. Desiring some comfort, I chose the best path.

A fear lingers in my heart that I left Falland out of self-preservation, allowing myself to act under the guise of it being what was necessary to save the Untrialed. Deep down, all I wanted to hear from these people was that I had done the right thing.

But the Crowns had listened to my words with biased minds and incredulous stares, unwilling to hear the truth about one of their own. I don't fault them for wanting proof, but their indecision could cost people their lives.

It's like I'm Untrialed once again, starving on the streets, while members of the Guard look at us like rats in the sewer, mocking our desire to survive.

The hours I could have spent sleeping were instead filled with my anxiety playing out every scenario. What if Drytas never showed for the judgment hearing? For all we know, he's preparing the Guard and the Untrialed for an attack, using the absence of the court's rulers as opportunity for his invasion. The very thing meant to bring his actions under examination may prove to be what allows him to rise to greater power.

Dreary eyed and hopeless, I turn into my pillow, shoving my face deeper into the fabric, to scream into it. It muffles my anguish, but it can't conceal the tear stains soaked into its surface. I throw it across the room and hear it hit the wall before flopping to the floor.

A delicate knocking breaks me from my trance, and my heart leaps in my chest. I glance at the dagger resting on my nightstand, which glints in the sun's early rays.

Getting to my feet, I grab the knife and tuck it into my sleeve before creeping to the door.

Lord Gennady mentioned he would send someone to me in the morning, but I thought I'd have hours till they arrived. Either they came early, or the person at my door is not my escort. Torryn's warning words echo in my mind.

Not everyone in the capital can be trusted.

When the person knocks again, a soft voice accompanies it.

"Lysta, it's Sar."

I breathe a sigh of relief, pulling the door open, and concealing my body behind it at the sight of her perfectly styled hair and brand-new dress. I'd fallen asleep in my clothes after realizing I had no belongings, deeming it a problem for my future self.

Sar smiles at the sight of me before holding up a large stack of clothing. "I figured you might like to face the capital a little fresher than yesterday."

EVERY STEP we take is scrutinized in our trek toward the Court of Self's tower of the capital. By whom, I can only assume, are staff and court members flooding in and out of rooms we pass.

Sar interlocks my arm in hers as we walk, keeping my hands from smoothing out my dress for the umpteenth time.

The soft satin fabric gliding across my skin is a foreign sensation, and I desperately long for my pants. But even I understand the importance of blending in when our entrance yesterday already managed to single me out. I just can't shake the feeling that dressing like this only makes me stand out more. Like an impostor. As if I'm a fool who has donned a disguise, albeit a beautiful one, and made everyone believe I'm something I'm not.

Black satin comprises the majority of the dress, save for lace panels in the bodice. While the low neck leaves my upper arms and shoulders bare, the low sweeping sleeves cover not only my Trial marks but the Kadara's bite.

The capital doesn't deserve to see my struggle etched so plainly on my skin. Not after they denied it ever happening to my face.

The only remotely practical thing on me is the garter strapped to my leg, currently holding my dagger. Accessible from a slit that travels up the side of the skirt, landing mid-thigh, but hidden away in the fabric.

When Sar had initially mentioned Torryn suggested the

garter, I recoiled, incensed at its inappropriateness. But that was before Sar explained what it was for. My face had burned bright red for a few minutes after.

At the end of the labyrinth of halls, we reach what I can only assume is the tower's entrance. For a heartbeat, I hope that I'm wrong, that we'll pass the staff scrubbing off the words *Court of Monsters* painted across the double doors. But then Sar ducks through, nodding to the guards, who step aside for us.

I hesitate, gulping at the red paint dripping down the wall before hurrying after Sar. She doesn't acknowledge the smear against her court, but her hand clenches the railing as she ascends the tower's stone steps.

Sar exits the staircase at the first landing, leading me into a dark and moody living space.

A few couches sit to the left, a dining table and chairs to the right. Tucked into the corner is a colossal kitchen looking over the room. Tall bookshelves surround the space, save for a wall of windows spanning from floor to ceiling.

Hesitantly, I wander to the seating area and run my hand over the backs of the velvet pillows. From where I stand, the windows look out over the ocean. Humming to myself, I can't help my whisper of a smile.

I suppose one good thing about living on a peninsula is almost every room is an ocean view.

"Do you like the ocean?" Sar asks, seemingly having struggled to come up with a conversation topic.

She does that often. Thinking for a beat too long when interacting with me. Dancing between someone who desperately wants to be my friend and also someone who seems unsure of how to do that—not that I have any more experience with it.

I've had two—Thoman and Doireann. Not exactly a world of experience.

Turning away from the blue waves I desperately wish to see properly, I answer softly, "I think so."

Nothing has poisoned it for me yet. No negative emotions or memories. The ocean is a fresh slate to enjoy as I see fit. I only hope it stays that way.

"You think so?" Sar moves to sit in one of the armchairs. "I would think it'd be an easy question, one way or the other."

I shrug. "Considering it's the first time I've seen it . . ."

A look of realization dawns on Sar's face, and I no longer feel the need to explain.

"Oh," she says in a voice dripping with pity. "I'm sorry. I forgot with everything going on."

"Don't even worry about it."

The silence following is painfully awkward.

Falland's streets weren't exactly an environment that fosters conversational skills, but I'm saved by voices coming down the staircase—Ardis and Torryn.

"Tell Lord Rhen he is welcome to visit her—" Torryn appraises me from across the room.

Ardis gives me a smile in greeting, patting Torryn on the back as he passes him to sit on the arm of Sar's chair.

At his presence, Sar offers Ardis the smallest of smiles before crossing her legs, allowing for her knee to press against his thigh.

Ardis glances at her leg but says nothing.

"Joining us, Torryn? Or will you be conducting this meeting from the hall?" Sar asks, a teasing grin on her face.

Torryn begrudgingly sits on the couch, his face hard as he looks at me. "What is she doing here?"

My eyes flash to Sar. *She had said Torryn called for me.*

"You wanted to know how she was doing and make sure she knew the plan." Sar says, raising her chin at Torryn's glare.

"You knew what I meant. You were supposed to take care of it, not bring her here."

"Perhaps you should clarify next ti—"

Moving away from the windows and into the corral of seats, I ask, "Is there a problem with me being here? I'd just like to know what the plan is." When Torryn meets my eyes, his eyelids lower, peering at me beneath his long eyelashes. His lips purse as he chews his cheek, creating a dimple. "If you want me to leave, then tell me what I need to know, and I'll get out of your hair."

Ardis chirps in.

"There's nothing wrong with you being here, Lysta. How about you sit, and we'll go over everything?"

Was it a common duty for Sar and Ardis to have to soothe over Torryn's abrasive personality? How tiring of an endeavor.

Plopping in the seat across from Torryn, I smirk at him in silent victory.

Torryn raises an eyebrow at me.

My expression doesn't invoke the reaction I expect.

My mouth falls in confusion until Torryn drags his gaze down my body, hovering near my knees. He looks at me pointedly, and I follow his gesture to see the slit in my dress has shifted upward, revealing the tip of the dagger and a portion of my upper thigh.

I fling the skirt over my exposed leg, my cheeks burning. Refusing to meet his amused face, I rejoice nothing indecent had been showcased.

I'm used to trousers.

Torryn starts, "A judgment hearing is a big thing, and they are going to tear Lysta and my testimonies apart. We need allies right now, not enemies. We can't have any of us raising red flags that we can't be trusted."

"It seems like you already aren't trusted here."

The words tumble from my mouth before I can bite my tongue and shove the retort down. I internally wince, wishing I could reach out and take the accusation back.

Torryn's face gives nothing away. Instead, he leans back, propping his ankle up on his opposite knee casually, as if he had expected the strike. He glowers at me. "If you have a question, share. I may be able to read your mind, but I'd prefer to save it for emergencies. It's really an unpleasant experience."

Ignoring his attempted barb, I push, "Every step of the way, you've deceived me, lied to me, and now, when I'm literally in the lion's den, you are keeping information from me. Information that could cost me my life." I stare Torryn down, looking deeply into his eyes. "Information that risks everything I'm trying to do."

"If I told you everything, you'd be running for the hills, forgetting all about your little hero mission. I'm giving you the information you need, and beyond that, you'll just have to trust me."

I scoff. "Trust you? When most of the people in this place are scared to death if you look their way? Do you know what's being scrubbed off your entrance right now? I need more."

"Torryn"—Sar winces—"maybe you could—"

"No, Sarielle. Leave it alone," Torryn says, raising his voice. He stands, running his fingers through the top of his hair. Leaning in, his eyes dare me to continue. "Ask."

"Why do they fear you and your court? Why was your father sentenced to judgment?"

"Because they should, Lysta. They should fear me."

I recoil from him, surprised at his blunt statement.

"My father did terrible things to his people and then he got greedy and tried it against the other courts, too. They have every right to have some lingering concern about my presence here. Now, if you'll excuse me, I have bigger things on my plate than comforting *you*."

CHAPTER 19

Fleeing the Court of Self's tower, I try to keep my frustration at bay, afraid to say something I'll regret. Maybe I already have.

Turning another corner of the identical halls, I'm knocked backward as I collide with someone else. I land on the floor across from the casualty of my carelessness. I don't recognize her—which is a good sign, as it means she likely isn't a Crown or Heir.

Getting my feet under me, I hurry to help the fallen girl, offering her a hand. "Please forgive me. I've gotten lost and didn't see you when I took the corner."

She looks about my age, maybe a few years older. Her lavender dress pools on the floor around her, the pale color complementing her dark-bronze skin. Through the sheer sleeves, a glimpse of a Trial tattoo twists around her wrist, and I straighten instinctually.

The capital isn't like Falland. Not everyone who is Trialed is a threat to me.

My eyes meet her deep brown ones when she looks up for

the first time, and I'm taken aback by her disgruntled expression.

"You mean you didn't see me because you failed to actually look around the corner?"

Her tone is sharp as she smacks away my hand, then pulls herself to her feet.

Blinking a few times, I swear her eyes flash a purple hue. Realizing the girl is staring at me and expecting a response, I shake my head. "No! Well, yes, I truly didn't mean to!"

The girl straightens the skirts of her dress before rolling her eyes at me. "Mean to bowl me over? I would certainly hope so." The girl blinks rapidly, eyes transitioning between purple and brown. "Ugh, can you try to keep your guilt to yourself?"

Breath catching in my throat, I look at her in bewilderment.

Guilt? Would she rather I not apologize?

"Everything all right over here? I saw the collision. No casualties, I hope," a male voice calls over my shoulder.

Relief floods my body, and I'm grateful to be saved from the irritated girl ready to bite my head off.

Turning to look at him, I move to answer but am cut off by a sickeningly sweet tone.

"Oh, you're too funny, Evander. I am fine, just a little rumpled."

My heart stops when I see Evander, realizing I've already encountered this stranger before.

Sitting at Lord Gennady's side. His Heir.

With the same tan skin and blue eyes as his father, there's no mistaking him for anyone else. His hair is a warm brown that resembles honey where the light hits it.

Evander is handsome in every way that would make a young girl swoon. Except I'm not a young girl, nor do I swoon.

Evander gives her a wide smile, flashing two rows of

perfectly straight white teeth. "I'm glad, Visha. And, Lysta, right?" He looks at me.

I nod, muttering, "I'm good—"

"Evander, I don't suppose you have time for a walk. We have not talked nearly enough since we all arrived at the capital this session."

Evander tsks before answering in a charming voice, "Alas, I'm afraid I must be off with Miss Lysta here. My father has requested I show her around the capital. Duty calls, but I promise we will get together soon. At training, at the least." Evander takes my arm in his, already headed in the other direction, before Visha can respond.

Wide eyed, I look at him, surprised by his casual breach of my personal space. I yank myself free when we turn the corner but quickly offer a whispered "Thank you" to smooth over the abrasiveness of my instinctual move.

"For saving you from Visha, who looked ready to maul you right there, or for not reporting you ditched your escort?" He looks down at me, obviously teasing but still needing an answer.

Face warming, eyes wide, I shake my head. "I honestly didn't mean to slip you. Sar brought me clothes this morning and brought me over to the Self tower because Torryn wanted to check in with me, and—"

"And I completely understand. Going forward, the Crowns would like me to, uh"—he struggles to find the words—"escort you during your stay at the capital."

His kind words don't conceal what he's trying so valiantly not to say.

"You're in charge of supervising me. They don't trust me to roam the capital alone?"

Evander winces at my harsh words but nods. "Just for the

time being. This is all an unprecedented situation, and they are being cautious."

Groaning in irritation, I shake my head. "I really wish people would stop saying that word."

"And what word is that?"

"*Unprecedented.* It's infuriating and just an excuse for not having a plan in place for these types of situations!"

Evander lets out a deep chuckle, shaking his head. "I will endeavor to stop using it, then. But know it is the truth regardless, Lysta."

The way he says my name makes me look up at him. My eyes meet his blue ones, and he gives me a warm smile.

"Just no more disappearing acts, yeah?"

I nod, not wanting to anger one of the few people to be kind to me since arriving in the capital.

Evander comes to a stop, turning to me with sudden seriousness. "A bit of a heads-up—it's too easy to offend someone here. Enemies are made in an instant, so just be careful, yeah? Visha is a mild opponent to make, but even she has her connections."

"She's not an Heir like you, though, right? She wasn't at my inquisition."

Evander nods. "Yes, but her uncle is Lord Nicaise." When my face projects confusion, he continues. "Lord Nicaise of the Court of Virtue. Visha was wearing his colors today—purple."

"And should I be wary of Lord Nicaise?"

Evander lowers his mouth closer to me and mutters, "Nicaise is a good man, fair handed. His sister, Visha's mother Nennirea, on the other hand, can be—tricky. She's the one you want to steer clear of. I'll point her out if we come across her."

Cataloging the information, I nod.

The politics of this place is baffling. I haven't even learned the courts, their Crowns, and their Heirs. And now, there's more people I need to keep track of?

Back in Falland, all the power rested with Lord Drytas. I wasn't better off comparatively, but I had always known who to fear—who to trust. I can't say the same here.

Evander glances up and down the hall, eyebrows knitted in thought. "Well, originally, I planned to take you to breakfast before giving you a small tour. I don't suppose you feel like having it a few hours late?"

My stomach growls loudly in response, and he grins.

"Answer received."

"Any chance we can go somewhere less . . . busy than the dining hall? I passed by there with Sar, and I'm not sure I'm ready for the staring and whispers on such a mass scale."

A look of understanding passes over Evander's face.

"I know the feeling—I take most of my meals in my court's quarters. A bit of reprieve helps sometimes. I know a spot that should be pretty vacant at War Hour."

Evander continues ahead, while I'm stopped in my place, unsure if I heard him correctly.

"War Hour?"

Evander casts a glance back at me over his shoulder and grins.

"You can't just drop a bomb like 'War Hour' and then not explain it."

Evander frowns down at me. "I figured your people in Self would have given you a rundown of how things worked here. Wasn't trying to keep you in suspense."

I huff, shaking my head in disbelief. "Not as much as you'd probably think," I say in a sour tone.

How much did they not tell me?

Regardless of my reigniting frustration at Torryn, I give Evander what I hope is a convincing smile. I shouldn't be letting people on to the tension within our group. We need to at least look like a unified front.

So, I quickly add, "There's been a lot going on, and they've tried to give me a heads-up where they could."

Evander raises his chin, looking at me with disbelief, but I avoid his gaze, focusing on the tile floor in front of us.

"I planned to take you to the library for lunch. Perhaps you'd rather get a first look at War Hour. It'll give you some background on who you'll be dealing with here. I'll tell you more about the courts."

That would be more helpful than Evander probably even realized.

Peering at him from the corner of my eye, I watch for a reason to be wary of him. If everyone is so afraid of Torryn and his court, why Evander would work so diligently to help me?

But I can't turn away his offer.

If Torryn isn't going to prepare me, then I'll do it myself.

CHAPTER 20

At the heart of the capital is the arena, the stomping ground of War Hour.

Rings of seats encircle a battle field, separated by a cage of steel. Row after row of shouting spectators fill the stands, salivating at the action unfolding before them.

Perched above the crowd, Evander and I sit in the Court of Truth's viewing booth. It feels more like a glass cage, save for the luxuries trapped inside with us. Plush seats and a lit chandelier hang over a table of various foods and refreshments.

But Evander doesn't spare them a second glance, either too enraptured by the fight or blind to the extravagance.

Down on the sandy pitch, two men stand opposite of each other, swords crossed, feet sliding as they try to overpower their opponent. Locked with equal strength, one dodges to the side, barely escaping the blade's bloody promise.

"Who are they?" I ask, glued to the action.

"No one I know personally, but the taller one, wearing the purple, is from the Court of Virtue—ruled by Lord Nicaise. The other one, in gold, is from the Court of Change—Lady Ivianna's court. You can always tell by their colors. They're required to wear them in order to fight."

"Marking where they are from?" I ask, peeking at Evander out of my peripheral.

He tilts his head, pondering my question. "Not exactly. Most of the time, that ends up being true, but you wear the color that you've sworn loyalty to."

My confusion must be obvious, as Evander stifles a chuckle at my expression.

"Some renounce their birth court in favor of another. If you are powerful enough—or well trained—you can aim for a better position within a different court. That's another reason for War Hour being treated like a grand showcase—"

Looking at the battle with new realization, I speculate, "It's an audition."

Evander doesn't immediately confirm my hypothesis, but when I turn to him, he smiles, nodding. "Exactly." He leans toward me conspiratorially.

I wouldn't stand a chance of impressing anyone out there—not as I am now.

Shaking the line of thought from my mind, I change the subject.

"Why are they bothering with weapons? I can see their Trial tattoos, so they must have powers to use?"

"Most powers of the Trials don't give a physical advantage —or, at least not a significant one. That's why we train with weapons and combat. Powers work better when used complementary. But you're not watching close enough if you think they aren't using any abilities."

I frown, thinking his words are an insult, but his expression is light, teasing.

He nods to the field. "Look again."

I narrow my eyes, peering at Evander for a defiant heartbeat before returning to the battle.

The man from Change is on one knee, sword held high above his head, as his opponent attacks relentlessly. Arms shaking, I'm positive he'll falter, unable to withstand the unyielding attacks. But then I blink, and he's gone.

My eyes scan the pitch for where he's disappeared, but within a second, he materializes behind his opponent, mere feet from his previous position.

Eyes wide, I breathe out. "He's teleporting?"

Evander glances at me with furrowed brows. "Teleporting? No, he's momentarily turning invisible and moving out of reach. You know people who can teleport?"

Not wanting to open up a line of questioning into Falland, I quickly dismiss Evander's curiosity. "I thought I'd heard it was a possible power, but maybe not."

Evander looks at me for a beat too long, and I'm sure he has figured out something. But then he turns back to the field as if I never said it.

"What do you think the other is doing? The one from Virtue."

Following Evander's gaze, I see the man in purple cuts his attack off mid-strike. Without a beat of hesitation, he pivots on his heel as if already knowing where his opponent moved to. Seconds before the man from Change can raise his sword, he flinches out of the way as though expecting the move. Again and again, he dodges without a single hit landing.

"Is he—predicting where he will go?" I ask, uncertain of if my guess even makes sense.

Evander makes a clicking noise out of the corner of his cheek. "Close but not quite. He's reading his opponent's mind. Every move he even thinks of, the telepath will know before he even does it."

Like Torryn.

Torryn can read minds, too. Meaning Virtue is another court he has Trialed in. I note the revelation for later, knowing not to bring it up to Evander.

"Why doesn't the man from Change just stay invisible instead of just flickering in and out?"

Evander smiles, leaning toward me as if we are good friends.

I can't help but retreat as he advances, but Evander takes it in stride.

"Your level of strength with your ability varies based on the person. You can train and master it better, but each Trialed has a cap on their potential. So, he just can't hold it any longer than he is. If he did, he'd drain too much of his reserves."

The two adversaries swirl around each other, firmly gripping their swords as they heave them with alarming force. The man from Change disappears once again, flickering from random spots. The telepath keeps his head on a swivel, face contorted in deep concentration.

"What would happen then? If he used up his reserves."

"He'd be powerless for a while. Could be hours, days, weeks. It depends on the severity."

Before I can gasp, the telepath swings his blade out without looking in its direction, catching his opponent under the chin with his sword just as he comes back into view.

"Yield," he shouts, pressing the sword closer to the delicate skin.

Gritting his teeth, his opponent lowers a knee to the ground.

"Yield."

The battle has started and ended in mere minutes. It'd been exciting in a fight or flight, adrenaline pumping sort of way. But the stress of it all outweighed any exhilaration. Yet, I can't keep the awe out of my voice when I ask, "How often do they do this?"

Evander grins widely, pride settling in his posture as he leans back.

"Every day, at least when the capital is in session. Although, some days have bigger turn outs than others. Technically, you can use the arena whenever you want, but there's only an audience during War Hour. Saturdays are the best day because it's when the Crowns and Heirs battle each other."

My mouth gapes as I look at him. "You'll be doing that?" I ask, pointing at the battlefield where a new round has just started.

"If I get challenged or if I challenge someone." At my confused look, Evander continues. "Anyone can sign up to fight, and you can choose to either fight someone at random or challenge someone. Of course, you can abstain if challenged, but most don't out of pride."

Panic sweeps across me as I turn to him.

"I won't have to fight anyone, right?" I ask, the pitch of my voice raising.

Evander shrugs, not sensing my concern. "You might get challenged, but like I said, you can always bow out. But I have a feeling people will want to see what the girl from Valor can do. Most of the Heirs have never even met someone from your court since it's been so long."

"So, I have a target on my back."

Evander hums, tilting his head. "It's a compliment. They are interested enough to want to fight you."

Does he think that is something I want?

I lower my head, playing with my fingers in my lap. "There's nothing to be interested about."

Evander nudges his shoulder against mine until I look up at him. "I wholeheartedly disagree," he says, eyes locked onto mine.

Furrowing my brows, I scan Evander's face for a glimmer of deception.

Considering what I've come here to do and who I came here with, it would be unwise to trust someone with a sudden interest in me. But that doesn't stop my heart from falling out of rhythm for a beat.

Our gaze is broken by an explosive outcry, the crowd reacting to what is happening in the new battle before them.

A man with an emerald hood peeking out of his armor holds a woman in white by the throat, her feet dangling.

I'm brought back to Valor's throne room as she fights to get free. My chest gets heavy, and Evander is suddenly too close. I clutch my throat as if reminding myself that I'm fine—that I can breathe.

But then, in one fell swoop, the woman snatches the sword off the hip of her opponent, swinging it with no hesitation.

I gasp.

Blood swirls in the sand of the arena's pitch as the woman stands victorious. A severed hand is held above her head, while her adversary clutches his arm to his chest.

My breathing gallops, stuttering in my chest, and Evander turns to me with concern. I can hear him consoling me, explaining that there are healers that can fix it, that the man isn't disfigured.

I don't know how to explain to him that my reaction isn't from any concern for the competitors on the field, but from being reminded of what may very well be happening in Valor at this very instant.

In the chaos of the capital, I momentarily forgot what

brought me here. Even if the capital had battles for show, fights that were nothing more than a sporting match, the same can't be said for what Drytas threatens to rain down.

War is coming, and it will not confine itself to an hour.

CHAPTER 21

War Hour prompted multiple realizations in its aftermath. Like I've taken a dose of poison, I feel weaker than before. Seeing just a glimpse of what properly trained Trialed can do makes me question whether I could ever match up.

Even though I had a dagger in Falland, it had been more for in case someone decided I was an easy target. I never actually used it. Why would I, when flashing the weapon was enough to make thieves flee and brutes back down from a fight?

What I've always thought of as a blessing or just sheer luck is now my curse to bear. Without any practical training or experience, holding my own will be out of the question. And maybe my shield could protect me, but if I learned anything yesterday, it's that I've barely scratched the surface of what I'm up against.

And *these* were the people Lord Drytas would be setting the Untrialed up against. Untrained. Unprepared. Yet deemed fit to send off to fight Drytas's battles for him.

The harsh reality sets a dim outlook for the future. But the same poison that attacks the body also ignites a defensive response. And maybe yesterday was the poison I needed to decide I'm not going down without a fight.

Selfishly, I've been keeping isolated in the capital for my comfort, but I could be doing more. Torryn said we need allies, that people here need to trust me.

That is what makes me agree when Evander asks me to accompany him for Heir training.

Swords clashing together welcomes me to the arena before Evander leads me through the ground entrance. My stomach clenches at each resounding scrape and the shouts that follow. Stepping out from the tunnel onto the battlefield, rays stream in from the open ceiling and reflect off the sand. Momentarily blinded, I bring my hand up to block the sun until my vision adjusts.

From pitch level, the arena seems to stretch infinitely. Seats cascading upward away from the metal cage.

Peering at the seven glass viewing booths positioned around the pitch, I wonder briefly if the courts would ever see me fight down here.

Would they call me barely Trialed if they saw what I could do?

But today won't be that day, as there isn't a soul present, save for those on the field.

Evander had said Heir's training is closed to the public. Probably a smart idea, for I'm sure if it weren't, spectators would pack the house to the brim. Who wouldn't want to see the future of their court training?

Evander jogs ahead as I scope out my surroundings.

Visha squares off against a redheaded boy in a sword fight. It's obvious she's at a disadvantage, her movements slower than her opponent's. But he doesn't increase his attacks, backing off and motioning for her to start again.

Evander catches their attention and Visha beams, abandoning her practice to give the approaching Heir a side hug.

I try to mask my surprise at Visha's presence. I hadn't thought being a lord's niece made someone an Heir, but this camaraderie between them explains it. They're friends beyond just allies.

A shadow crosses my vision from above. I duck, craning to see what soars overhead. Finding the moving target, I swallow thickly when my breath lodges in my throat.

Four archer's peaks tower dozens of feet above me, positioned far apart in a square shape. Atop them, portaling from one stand to the next, is a red-haired boy, barely fourteen. Sword in hand, he holds the hilt with a tight grip, head on a constant swivel as he peers around for his target. The moment he looks to his right, a figure with large wings circles him, knocking the boy from the tower.

A scream echoes in the arena as the boy falls, arms flailing at his sides as he drops, plummeting toward the sandy pitch below him.

My heart thumps heavily in my chest as I watch, paralyzed at the thought of seeing this boy's body land broken in the sand.

I realize I'm the one who screamed.

The group surrounding Evander stares at me in startled confusion.

How could they not see gravity pulling the young boy to an early death?

Raising my hands, I plan to bring out a shield beneath him, hoping the impact will do less damage from a shorter distance, but freeze just before.

A portal opens beneath the boy in midair, closing as he falls through before disappearing in a quiet blip. Searching frantically, I pivot on my heel, breaths rushing from my lips.

Where had he gone?

Another portal opens above the furthest archer's stand, depositing the boy, who somersaults into a standing position. He looks around in confusion, zeroing in on my gobsmacked expression.

"Who's the newbie?" he asks, a childish grin plastering his face.

Chuckles ring out from the group, and my face heats. I debate whether to turn on my heel and leave, but Evander waves me over.

Walking toward them, I suck up the urge to run away. Leaving now would only make me look more weak than I already do.

Someone coughs out another laugh, but Evander sends them a silencing glare, and they quickly clear their throat.

The man who pushed the boy off the riser swoops down, his bird-like wings expanding as wind rushes past them, bristling through the white feathers. When he lands, they shrink, disappearing behind him as he strides in our direction. His skin is deeply tanned, hair blonder than the sun, as if he frequently flies as close to the rays as he can. His form is heavily muscled, arms flexing, as he leans into me, offering me his hand in greeting.

"Sebastian, but these idiots call me Bash," he says, flashing a look at the group. "I apologize if we gave you a fright. We were just training. Nothing we haven't done a hundred times."

This is their everyday type of training?

"Lysta." Shaking his hand, I force out a pathetic excuse of a fake laugh. "It's my fault. I should have expected—well, anything, I guess."

Bash chuckles, giving me a lopsided grin. "Not a bad philosophy when it comes to the capital."

Evander nudges between us, clapping a hand on Bash's

shoulder. "Bash here is Lady Ivianna's son from the Court of Change. Hence the shapeshifting."

I don't let my expression slip at Evander's explanation, but my mind races.

Why were the Heirs being so obvious about their powers? Torryn had warned me the importance of keeping tight-lipped, yet the same reservation is not held by the Heirs. I've only been here for a couple minutes, and I already could identify two of the Heirs' powers.

I'm dragged from my thoughts as the man who has been training with Visha steps up to me, sticking out his own hand. He smirks at me, eyes flashing with menace as he parrots back, "Lysta, is it?"

Evander makes introductions, ignorant of my growing unease. "Lysta, this is Neith, Lord Bralas's Heir."

I hesitate before taking his hand. "Court of Wisdom, right?" I ask, even though I know perfectly well.

Lord Bralas had not exactly been my biggest supporter.

"That would be the one," he says, chest puffing at the mention of his court. Neith looks every bit like his father, high horse and all. "No need for me to ask your court. I was there in the meeting when you first arrived."

I flinch at his reference, and he sees it, eyes glinting at my reaction. Half the people standing here had been present, I realize, now their faces aren't blending among the crowds.

Neith keeps pushing, latching onto my slip in composure. "Yes, we'd love to hear more about this *supposed* 'broken Trial,' Lysta."

My body freezes at his mocking words, and I tuck my chin in.

The way he says "supposed" tells me everything I need to know about how my presence and purpose here in the capital has been received.

Bash clears his throat, breaking the building tension. He sends Neith a cool warning glare. "Knock it off. You know we can't talk about it." Turning to me, he rests one hand on the hilt of his sword. "Please ignore his rudeness."

Neith laughs sharply, nodding with pursed lips. "Yeah, just ignore me. You'll be out of here soon enough." Before anyone can protest his word, Neith shouts without warning, "Conlen!"

The younger boy from earlier portals next to Neith, barely stumbling from the shift in location.

With them side by side, no one could mistake them for anything but siblings. The boy nods to me, lacking the same confidence his older brother oozes.

The portal Conlen had created looked so similar to what Sar had done only a few days ago, but the boy didn't appear to be struggling.

Did he have better mastery of the ability, or is it easier in shorter distances?

But that would mean that Sar Trialed in Wisdom—not in Self.

"You're with me next. Go grab your sword," Neith orders without taking his eyes off me.

A look of uneasiness passes over Conlen's face, but he nods, running to a rack of weapons where two other boys train together.

Seeing the focus of my attention, Evander interjects. "Those would be Lord Rhen's sons from the Court of Will. The sixteen-year-old is Jona, and the nine-year-old is Eiko."

Both boys have short black hair, narrow eyes, and a pale complexion.

Completely oblivious to the tension happening across the field, Jona shows his brother a maneuver with a thin sword before correcting how Eiko replicates it with a smaller wooden version.

Neither had been in my meeting with the Crowns and their Heirs, but I'm positive the only empty seats were Valor's and the one next to Torryn.

"Their older sister, Sora, is the Heir, but she wasn't able to join us for this capital session. Her mother has taken her spot in any official proceedings for the meantime."

Evander answers my unasked question.

It's obvious from the look on Evander's face there is more to the story, but I have too much going on to press the issue. Especially with Visha staring hot daggers at me from behind Evander.

"Heirs can be spouses, too?" I ask, shifting on my feet.

Evander nods. "Visha here is Lord Nicaise's niece, and since he doesn't currently have any children, his wife presides as his Heir. Which is typical until the Heir turns fourteen."

"And since I'm so close with my uncle, he offered me a spot in training with Evander"—Visha hesitates—"and the other Heirs."

Bash lets out a snort, and I struggle to not send a grin his way. Maybe my perception of Visha isn't as far off as I thought.

Visha ignores him, turning to Evander with a bright smile on her face.

I watch from the sidelines as the close group teases and bickers with each other, letting myself fall to the background.

Tension eases from my shoulders when I catch sight of Sar moving through the seats of the arena, perching in the front row. Giving her a small wave, I try to get her attention, but her focus is locked behind me. Her face is tight, a deep frown settling across it.

My first instinct is that Torryn sent her to keep an eye on me. Worried that I'll say the wrong thing to the Heirs.

Following her gaze, I survey around me for what has caught her attention, landing on Neith and Conlen, who are mid-fight.

As if feeling my attention, Neith jerks his head back and forth between me and his brother—watching for Conlen's attack with only half of his focus.

Conlen tries to use the distraction to his favor, swinging his sword, when Neith's eyes are on me. But Neith bends backward, avoiding the hit without even looking to his brother. Conlen groans at the missed hit, his brother's smugness rubbing salt in the wound.

The fight continues, Conlen unable to land a hit on the Heir. When Conlen takes an elbow to the face, I gasp, and Neith whips around to look at me. But his gaze moves past me to Sar, who stands at the metal cage, fingers clenching the barrier.

I think nothing of it until I see the wild look in Neith's eyes.

He gestures to me, leveling his sword at my face. "Would you like to get some fighting experience in? I promise I'd take it easy on you."

The smirk curling across his face tells me Neith would do anything but take it easy on me.

I shake my head. "As tempting as that is, I think I'll stay on the sidelines for today."

Disappointment clouds Neith's expression as his eyes flicker from me back to Sar. Flipping his sword in his hand, he circles me menacingly. "So, you'd make allies out of the usurper but discredit me because of a sibling rivalry? Doesn't seem quite fair."

Usurper? Was Neith calling Torryn a usurper?

My focus breaks, attention snapping from Torryn to the other part of what Neith had said.

Sibling rivalry? Who—

I peek over my shoulder at Sar.

It made complete sense once all the information was laid out for me. She had the same power as Conlen. Meaning she was of the Court of Wisdom. The three of them looked identical now that I was seeing them together.

Siblings.

When our gazes meet, Sar looks at me with a questioning glance.

Watching our interaction, Neith clicks his teeth, tsking. "Ah, Sarielle failed to mention that bit of information, did she?"

I ignore him, headed toward Sar, but it doesn't stop Neith from taunting me as I retreat.

"I hope they aren't keeping anything else from you. Dangerous waters you're navigating."

From the corner of my eye, I can see Neith switch gears, abandoning harassing me and instead picking up his sword and gesturing for his brother to start again.

I lean against the cage in front of where Sar sits, her eyes glued to the fight between Neith and Conlen. "They're your brothers?" I ask, even though Neith has done everything to spell it out for me.

Sar sighs heavily, as if the question holds the weight of the world, and she is cursed to bear the answer. "Yeah," she murmurs, tight-lipped.

"And Lord Bralas—"

"Also, yes."

The space between us gets quiet as we watch Neith and Conlen orbit each other, blades raised high.

Conlen portals behind Neith, only for his brother to have predicted the move, slamming his sword into Conlen's before the portal has even closed.

Neith pushes the younger boy harder, sweat dripping down his face. Conlen moves to tumble out of the way again, rewarded with a clean slice across his forearm. Neither of the redheads flinches at the injury. Neither of them moves to stop.

Now, standing above his kneeling brother, Neith levels his blade at his throat.

"I yield," Conlen cries out before dropping his sword, raising both hands.

Neith scoffs and bares his teeth at the boy. "We do not yield. Have I taught you nothing?" Turning from the boy, he steps away before gesturing for his brother to, once again, pick up the blade. "Again."

The metal gate whines open and slams shut, announcing Sar's entrance into the arena.

She marches to them, sand kicking up behind her. When Sar stomps right up to Neith, pointing into his chest, obviously snarling something at him, I tense. Waiting for the moment where I might be needed across the field.

As I stand on the sidelines, my fingers twitch as the two argue.

Sar bends to pull up Conlen. Neith grabs Sar's wrist as she pulls up the younger boy, squeezing until her face scrunches in pain. As her hand releases its grasp, Conlen lands back on the ground. Whipping to yell at Neith, Sar yanks free, knocking his sword from his grip.

Sar holds her hands up as if fed up with them before turning away.

My body sags in relief until a malicious glint flares up in Neith's eyes. I'm already moving across the field as he reaches up and wraps Sar's hair around his fist before yanking her down.

Sar falls, head smacking off of the sword discarded on the ground.

Neith's eyes widen before narrowing once again, glaring at her.

In the span of a breath, I am across the room, standing over Sar. Nose flared, chest heaving, I stare down Neith.

Neith grins as if he's won the battle and the war. "Well, look here. Valor's ready for some action in the arena, is she? Sign me up for the first round."

His words scrape my control, his taunting reminding me of Belthan. But when I glance at Sar, a small smear of blood trickles down the side of her face.

Reaching out for her hand, I pull her up with a grunt. She gestures to the exit, and I nod, following her when she moves to leave.

Neith gives me a mock salute as we pass him, and the urge to snap at him curls up again.

Not the time. Not the time, I tell myself.

The field watches us with rapt attention, and it sends a creeping sensation down my spine.

No one has stepped in. No one has even blinked.

CHAPTER 22

To Sar's credit, she doesn't pay much attention to the injury sitting at her temple nor the blood freshly dried along the side of her face. She floats through the capital halls as if the last fifteen minutes never happened, and I can see her mentally distancing herself as well as physically.

Son of Lord Bralas, the fact that Neith had been so bold as to strike his sister doesn't surprise me. What I found disturbing is that the other Heirs stood by and watched without doing a thing. Someone who stands by and lets injustice happen is not much better than the one committing the act itself.

I would know. I've been witness to more than my fair share of injustice, where I had done nothing.

Each time Sar's nervous ramble slows, I open my mouth, preparing to understand what happened. And each time, she beats me to the first syllable, sweeping my sentence under the rug with her enthusiastic observations.

I let her continue, knowing she likely cared as little as I do about how nice the decorations for the coming Peace Ball looked or if they'll be serving the glazed apple tarts she and Ardis love ardently.

Despite how desperately I want to know, to understand the relationship between them all. Understand what I have obviously not been told but still expected to navigate. I bite my tongue and let her continue to fill the silence. Because as buoyant as she seems, there is a slight quiver to her hands.

What happened shook her, and I don't think I have it in me to force anything out of her. She owes me nothing, and her truth is her own. To bury or not.

Safely in the Self tower, Sar sits heavily on an armchair, resting her head on the back. One hand comes up to touch her temple. She winces when her fingers meet the skin. Despite this, she continues the conversation, only half paying attention.

"Do you think you'll go to the Peace Ball? I'd imagine it would be an excellent opportunity to get some face time with the Crowns."

As I answer, I move to the kitchen to open drawers and cabinets. They had to have some sort of medical kit or bandages, especially if they trained and fought daily.

"I'd imagine it depends on if I'm allowed to go . . ." I shut the doors a little too hard in frustration.

"You won't find any medical supplies. The capital has healers. People from the Court of Change capable of regeneration. There's no need for any of us to keep that kind of stuff on hand."

Of course, Evander had mentioned that during War Hour. Why hadn't we gone to them then?

I sigh, settling on a white cloth. Taking the carafe of water sitting out, I dampen the cloth before wringing it out.

"I really am fine. Head wounds are dramatic when it comes to blood. It's not nearly as bad as it looks," Sar says when I hold out the towel for her.

Raising an eyebrow in her direction, I give her an unwavering stare. To which she gives me a half smile before taking the cloth and bringing it to her head.

Sitting on the couch adjacent to her, I watch as she cleans away the blood, the towel tinting pink with each swipe. The slice across her brow is thin and already clotting.

Sar was right. It had looked worse than it was.

I can't help but breathe a little easier.

"That'll hurt tomorrow," I said, stating the obvious just to fill the silence.

Sar nods but brushes off my concern.

Biting my lip, I try to decide whether the subject is open for discussion. I have few friends in the capital, but I would hope Sar is one. I don't want to ruin anything by digging through things she'd rather keep private, but at the same time, the people here are dangerous in ways I might not even realize.

I need to know if I'm making enemies without realizing it and, if so, who.

"Does it happen often?" I pry, ready for Sar to shut down the question.

Sar stifles a laugh before reaching forward to lay the towel on the glass table in front of us. "If you'd consider since we were kids often." Sar crosses her legs before looking at me with a blank expression.

A sad thought crosses my mind. Perhaps there is more anguish and pain under the capital's pretty dresses and luxurious lifestyle than I believed.

"I thought you were of Torryn's court?"

"I am *now*. Thankfully. But I was born to the Court of Wisdom. Just because you are born to a court doesn't mean you owe anything to it," Sar says with a knowing look.

I blink slowly at her, feeling much as if my brain is wading through thick mud. When I say nothing, she continues.

"Neithander and Conlen are my younger brothers. Conlen is innocent. He's just being molded by a bad influence."

"Lord Bralas or Neith?" I ask, having seen enough from both of them to know they each would fit.

Sar sends me a look as if the answer should be obvious. "Both."

A thought strikes me, and I hesitate to speak it to her. Tentatively, I broach the sensitive topic.

"But if they are your younger brothers, that would make you the Heir. Why is Neith?"

Sar grimaces. "You are right, but you are also wrong. I'm sure you could tell from the one female Crown out of the seven courts, but women aren't viewed as fit for power by many in the capital. Too emotional." Sar rolls her eyes. "It is within a Crown's *right* to skip over female Heirs."

Sounds about right.

Clenching my teeth, I nod. "So, because Lord Bralas designated him Heir, he can just act like that? Treat your brother like a punching bag? Treat you like that?"

Sar tucks in her lips, nodding. "I think Neith is trying to toughen Conlen up. He's always been a fairly soft boy, having been spared most of our father's wrath as the youngest. Neith is just going about it the wrong way." Sar curls her legs up under her on the couch, curving into herself.

"I wasn't trained with my brothers growing up. Wasn't allowed to learn combat or weapons training. And the only reason I could Trial is because it would be too embarrassing for Bralas if one of his kids hadn't. So, I taught myself everything I could, basically lived in the court library—not that it mattered. I was just a pretty daughter to control and show off." Sar turns her face from me, but she isn't fast enough to hide her glassy eyes. She mutters, "Ardis barely got me out."

My eyes widen, mouth dropping slightly.

It's obvious Sar didn't mean to give me this insight into her and Ardis's history.

She brings her hand to her temple as her eyebrows cinch together.

New questions itch at the back of my brain, begging to be asked at my new revelation. But I can't bring myself to ask, instead settling on something less personal.

"Why didn't any of the Heirs step in? They saw how tense it was getting."

"Tensions between courts are fickle. They can't do anything without fearing retribution from Lord Bralas."

Footsteps pound up the staircase, halting Sar's explanation. Torryn is the first to step around the corner, followed by Ardis, who silently rests against the wall.

"Bash let me know what happened. Are you all right?" Torryn asks as he comes to stand behind her, squeezing her shoulder in comfort or apology—I'm not sure.

Sar pats his hand with a slight smile. "More than all right. Lysta and I were just getting to know one another better."

Torryn hums at her response before moving to sit on the couch across from me, his eyes lingering on the damp pink towel. When he looks at me, I remember the last time we saw each other. It had not ended well. His face is guarded but not outright resentful.

"Ardis, are you planning on wallowing all day, or do you plan on joining us?" Sar asks without craning her head to look at him.

Ardis quips, "Do you plan on pulling any more stunts like you did today?"

His tone is hard, and I can't help but recoil from the disposition shift.

But Sar smirks, taunting him. "Oh, you didn't like that? Makes you think I'd be better off if someone wanted to train me so I *could* hold my own."

Ardis stalks past her into the living area before perching on the arm of a chair, crossing his arms as he leans back. "It would be *better off* if you stopped getting into fights you know you can't win."

Torryn clears his throat, leaning forward to rest his elbows on his thighs, hands clasped. "Ardis, enough."

Ardis twists his mouth angrily, looking off to the side.

Sar shifts higher in her seat, grinning in triumph.

Noticing, Torryn mutters to Sar, "I get it. You know I get it. But with everything going on right now, we can't be stepping over any court lines. You know how precarious of a situation it can put us in."

Sar frowns but nods once.

"I have a meeting with the Crowns, but I wanted to check on you first," Torryn announces as he stands abruptly. Turning to look at Sar and then Ardis, he adds, "I will see you both later."

In a moment's decision, I follow Torryn from the room, dress flaring around my ankles. I struggle to catch up with him, his paces far longer than my own.

"Torryn, can I have a minute?"

My voice echoes in the empty corridor, stopping Torryn in his tracks.

His shoulders sag, and I have to stomp down the flicker of hurt at his desire to avoid me.

Before he can dismiss me, I blurt, "I'd like to do some training while I'm here. My automatic defense is my shield, but I can't use it without giving away the only advantage I have. After what I saw these people do during War Hour—"

Torryn practically snaps his neck turning to look at me, a bite in his tone. "War Hour. You went to War Hour? Are you insane?"

My head rears back, Torryn's sudden shift giving me whiplash.

Shifting on my feet, I fold my arms in front of me. "Evander brought me. He thought it would teach me more about the other courts . . . and the capital. Why—what's wrong with that?"

"*Evander*." Torryn barks out a cold laugh, rolling his eyes. "Of course *he* did." Torryn runs a hand down his face, then brings a balled fist to his mouth as if forcing back what he wants to say.

I frown.

What does *that* mean? Evander seems harmless enough and nicer than anyone else has been—although I guess that could be a facade. My brows knot together.

"You—you seemed to trust Lord Gennady . . . I thought his son—"

"I told you not to trust anybody."

My eyes bulge, and I can't look at him, shaking my head. "That's *all* you told me. The only thing you felt the need to tell me before bringing me someplace where they literally fight like war for an hour, every freaking day."

Torryn opens his mouth but nothing comes out. His hand moves to rake through his hair as he stares at me in burning disbelief. Stalking toward me, Torryn closes the distance between us, pointing at my chest and whispering in a tight voice, "Entering the arena during War Hour means you are available for challenging. Even if we have healers, people have died on that field, and if you don't think Lord Drytas has friends in the capital . . ." Torryn trails off. "A lot of people's problems would disappear if you were to end up tragically killed in an ordinary Tuesday War Hour."

I choke on a gasp, staring at the dark look in Torryn's eyes.

How could he not have told me something that held so much risk?

"You should have told me."

Torryn laughs, backing up enough that I can safely breathe again. "You've been here a day. I didn't think the first place you'd go traipsing around would be a battle arena!"

Leaning on opposite walls of the hall, I glare at Torryn, and he reflects every bit of irritation back at me. I refuse to be the one to break the silence. For a moment, I think I catch the corner of his mouth curving, but it's gone before I blink.

"As endearing as this staring contest is, I do actually have a meeting that I'm now late for. There's nothing you can do about it now except, like you said, train. Perhaps your new ally, Evander, can help you."

Sniffing at the accusation in his tone, I cross my arms. "And what is that supposed to mean?"

Torryn sighs before heading down the stairs. "Nothing, Lysta. Now, if you would excuse me, I have a meeting."

I'm left standing there, contemplating everything Torryn isn't saying.

CHAPTER 23

I huff, muttering curses under my breath as I stomp down the stairs of the Court of Self's tower. It takes everything in me to not hurry after Torryn and keep arguing with him until I'm blue in the face—or until he apologizes, which would never come first.

How someone could be so utterly and unbearably frustrating is a curse to humankind. It's not like I think I know *more* than him—obviously, he's lived in this political landscape longer. But if you don't share any of it with me, providing only vague and ominous warnings, then what do you expect me to do?

I push open the doors with more force than necessary, but my anger is instantly forgotten at the sight of Evander in a heated discussion with the guards stationed at the tower entrance.

"I just want to check on them. Do you know—"

Whatever plea Evander had for the Guard is forgotten as he catches sight of me coming through the door. His shoulders deflate, and he takes a deep breath, a relieved smile crossing his face.

Despite my conversation with Torryn, my chest warms that Evander came to see if Sar is okay.

There's no hope of me surviving a week in this place without making an ally, and Evander seems willing to be that for me. If Torryn has a problem with Evander, despite seeming close with Lord Gennady, then he could tell me—blatantly. No more "trusting no one" nonsense. I can rely on Evander as a friendly face among enemies and not risk compromising myself or what we came here for.

Evander gestures for me to lead and follows me as we stroll the capital's hall.

Folding my hands in front of me, I examine the paintings adorning the walls.

"I'm assuming that Sarielle is all right?" Evander asks with a frown.

Lips tightening, I nod. "Sar's fine—or so she says." I shrug, not sure what else to tell him. "You all just stood there."

While I'm glad he's here now, I can't help but wish he'd cared this much when it was all happening.

Evander takes a shaky breath, knowing exactly what I'm talking about. "Interfering in other court relations is a political minefield. Aloria's peace treaty draws exact lines of where we can interfere with other courts' business, but when it comes to Sarielle, it's a gray area."

"Because she's of two courts?"

Evander nods tightly.

Even though Evander owes me nothing, I can't shove down how I wish he'd done more.

I stop in the middle of the hall, turning to him in disappointment. Lowering my voice, I stare into his bright blue eyes. "So, if Neith had tried to do worse, you would have, what, looked away?"

His body sags, a hand coming up to touch my arm. The heat

from his fingers spreads through the sleeve of my dress. I pull away to reduce the contact, face warming.

"Of course not. It's not the same thing, and it never would have gotten that far. Neith was just being a bully . . ."

Evander's tone sounds convincing, and I'm tempted to believe him. I find it unlikely the man who has been so kind in welcoming me here would allow anything truly grievous to occur.

My neck cranes up at Evander as he leans over me. My back presses into the wall behind me when I try to increase the space between us. "And if someone attacks me? If I yield, and they do not relent?" I whisper.

Evander's gaze softens when he looks at me. Licking his lips, he clears his throat. "You are under my protection, Lysta. I will defend you as if you are of my own court. No one will get the opportunity to hurt you. You have my word."

Evander's words offer some measure of relief, and I nod.

"I want—no. I need to train, Evander. But I can't do that at the risk of making more enemies than I've already got."

"Then, I will endeavor to make you some allies."

FALLAND HAD TAUGHT me more defensive moves than I'd thought, but even the streets could not prepare me for this. Here, in the capital, it's all a different game. These people were trained in combat with the intention of not just winning to get away but winning to defeat.

Upon arriving in the arena for the second day in a row, I'm greeted by what I assume is the Heir's version of a warm welcome.

A subtle nod in my direction without pausing in their training.

Evander leads me toward the weapons wall, pulling down a sword and stabbing it into the sand next to him.

I eye it cautiously, examining the silver blade with sapphires embedded into the hilt. The height of it reaches to my chest, meant for someone far larger than me.

Seeing my attention on the blade, Evander smiles at me as he searches the wall. "Don't worry. I plan on giving you a weapon you'll actually be able to lift."

I bite my cheek, holding back the snarky remark that I could lift it just fine, but my attention is pulled as Evander reaches up to dislodge a thin sword.

I can't help it when my gaze lingers over the flexing muscles in his shoulders as he lifts the blade before bringing it down.

A smirk plasters across Evander's face, eyebrow raising when he catches me staring. My cheeks heat, but I don't let myself turn away.

"See how this one feels," Evander says, offering me the sword. "It should be the right size for you."

Taking the hilt from him, Evander lets his fingers linger for a moment, making sure I've taken the weight before slipping his hand out under mine.

The sword is light, likely from the thinness of the long blade.

Silver ivy encircles the base, curving out to form a hand guard. It's a beautiful one, more intricate than any steel blade I've seen before. This is not a weapon meant to be slugged around with muscle and weight. No, this sword is meant to be wielded with finesse and skill.

Slipping my hand into the crown of ivy, I clutch the weapon.

Evander shines a bright smile at me as I lower the blade. "It fits you well." He picks up his sword from its place in the sand, flips it in his grip, then rests it on his shoulder. "Now let's see if we can get you using it."

Evander leads me to a clearing in the arena field, away from the other Heirs who fight.

With the Heirs at my back, I can't help but listen to every clang of metal and grunt of effort. Peering over my shoulder, I keep my attention on the distance between us.

Visha stands opposite a target as she pulls dozens of finger blades from her vest, each thrown with unfathomable speed and precision. I flinch at the thump it makes as the blades land.

"Lysta," Evander calls, breaking my focus. "Did you hear anything I said?"

With wide eyes, I whip my head back around to Evander, who stands with his sword at the ready. Before I can find the words to tell him I hadn't, his gaze flickers between me and the fights going on behind me.

"Switch places with me. I don't mind having my back to them."

My shock is written plainly across my face as Evander switches our positions, placing the arena battlefield in my view. It isn't a conscious decision to keep an eye on the other Heirs, yet Evander picks up on my motives right away.

My heart gives an awkward stutter in my chest as I watch him settle into where I had stood.

Blinking slowly, I force down the smile curving the corners of my lips.

"First lesson," Evander says as he guides my grip higher on the hilt of the sword. "There will always be someone stronger than you. Someone bigger than you. You will rarely have a strength advantage in the fights that actually matter. But—"

"You're really building my confidence here."

Evander shakes his head, a glint in his eyes. Leaning down, he kicks my right foot back, widening my stance. "If you'd let me finish, I was going to say you just need to learn how to make their advantage a weakness." Moving opposite me once again, he waits for me to respond but continues when I stay silent. "Bigger opponents are slower. They'll find it harder to dodge attacks. So, if you can be quicker than them, then you can get minor hits in. You just need to keep them from using their strength against you." Evander pauses, body bracing when he finishes. "Now attack me."

If Evander expects me to hesitate at the direction, he is sorely mistaken.

Shooting forward, I swing my sword toward Evander's legs. When he blocks, vibrations from the hit send an ache through my arms.

"You're focusing on power. If you can't out muscle me, Lysta, then you need to focus on speed and precision." Evander pushes back on my blade with his own.

My foot staggers backward before digging into the sand.

Heart racing, I follow his movements with keen eyes. Twisting my cheek between my teeth, I grip my sword's hilt with both hands. When Evander raises his arms, I step forward to swipe toward his revealed torso, but he brings his blade straight down, deflecting the attack.

"Better. Again."

Fire ignites in his eyes.

Sweat clings to my brow as I try repeatedly to land a hit against him.

It's obvious he's holding himself back, letting me get into the rhythm of parrying each attack. I get faster, slicing the air with a renewed ferocity.

Circling each other, we trade between the offense and defense, and I stumble as he smoothly transitions between them.

"You've never battled with a sword before?" Evander asks, showing the first signs of being winded.

I doubt he would consider my brief time holding the sword

as I prepared to fight the Kadara as experience, so I shake my head.

"Never. Just a dagger, but I didn't really use it."

Evander scoffs. "You've got the instincts for it. I'll give you that."

I grumble at his praise. "I haven't landed a hit against you." Frowning as I dodge a large swing, ducking under the sword, I tumble forward.

"I've been fighting since I could hold a wooden sword. If you could land a hit, I'd be insulted."

Another crash of our swords brings Evander's face close to mine, our blades crossing between us.

Chests rising and falling heavily, Evander smiles as he looks at me. "You're doing well. Don't rush your progress." His eyes flicker to my mouth for a split second, but the moment is all I need.

Locking my hand guard under the crossbars of Evander's sword, I thrust upward, knocking his blade from his grip. It flings into the sand.

The arena is silent for a moment. Evander blinks in the direction of his sword, mouth parted.

Taking a deep breath, he looks at me in bewilderment. "Okay, I'm insulted."

Nothing can stop the smile from breaking across my face. I'm barely able to keep the laugh out of my voice when I shoot his own words back at him.

"Don't be. *You're doing well.*"

Evander laughs with me, mirth shining in his eyes as he shakes his head, looking at the ceiling. Stepping away from me, Evander moves for his sword.

From across the arena, Bash hollers, cheering loudly, "I needed that desperately, Lysta. Finally, someone to keep Evander here on his toes."

Evander smiles, shouting back at Bash, "Well, if you spent more time on the ground with a sword in your hand than up there, maybe you'd be up for the challenge."

Bash snickers, encouraging laughs from some of the Heirs.

Turning to look at them from across the field, my eyes move to the quickly approaching Heir.

Neith.

Sword knocked back on his shoulder, Neith smirks as he makes his way to us.

Evander doesn't see the redheaded Heir approach, on the way to collect his sword.

Tension setting in my limbs, I raise my sword, preparing myself for any fight Neith might bring. Gritting my teeth, I call out Evander's name.

Whipping around, he sees Neith's approach, smile falling. Cutting off Neith, Evander moves to stand between us, putting me at his back.

"Lysta's just training with me today, Neith. She's only just begun."

Evander's voice has a warning edge to it, but Neith doesn't stand down.

"She needs to train against someone who won't go easy on her—or, better yet, someone who won't be so distracted as to let her win."

The tips of Evander's ears turn red as he gulps. "Going easy is exactly the type of training she needs."

"If you say so. But easy will not get her where she needs to be fast enough, and you know it."

As much as I hate to admit it, Neith is right.

"Evander, it's okay," I say, stepping out from behind him. "I can use all the training I can get, right?"

My words sound more confident than I feel, especially when Neith's eyes flicker with victory. But right now, I am fresh meat.

It's better I take a few hits now and have him lose interest than having him search me out for a fight later, when I'm not as prepared.

Evander grabs my wrist as I move to pass him, making my heart clench. Leaning to my ear, Evander speaks lowly, "I'm not sure this is wise."

I step past him, shaking his grip. "I never said I was wise. I'm from Valor . . . You know—bravery, and all that."

Neith barks out a laugh, grinning in Evander's direction, before moving opposite me.

Evander leans against the wall, watching us. His hands are in fists at his side, jaw ticking as he's forced to observe.

With no words exchanged, Neith lunges forward, his sword missing my arm by mere inches. Barreling to the side, I struggle to keep my feet under me at the sudden attack.

Sword up, Lysta. Sword up.

It is only once the battle has begun that I realize how drained I am from my fight with Evander. My movements are slowed, my blade heavier with every swing.

Perhaps this should've been a battle for another day, after all. But it's too late for me to stop, as Neith attacks again and again.

I'm barely able to block each attack, Neith not waiting for me to defend one hit before moving onto the next.

Evander really had been going easier on me than I thought.

My attention is pulled at the sound of a feminine giggle.

Turning my gaze for a moment, I catch sight of Visha, who's laughing as she rests a hand on Evander's forearm.

Hissing, I wince as Neith's sword slashes my upper arm, cutting through the fabric. I bring my hand to the stinging cut, warm blood coating my fingertips.

"Lysta," Evander shouts, stepping forward.

I hold out a hand to stop him and grunt out, "I'm fine."

Neith steps back, allowing me a moment to get my bearings before gesturing for me to attack.

Every blow I aim is diverted, ringing out the sound of metal against metal.

"I'd be careful of the usurper if I were you," Neith mutters as he pushes his sword against mine.

There it was again. Usurper. It's the second time Neith has used the name.

"If you have something you feel the need to share about Torryn, then just spit it out. I have no time for your games, Neith." I push off of him to put space between us.

Neith raises an eyebrow, smirking at me, as if I have just stepped into a trap he hadn't even had to place. "Interesting you assume I mean Lord Torryn."

Flinching at his words, I do a double take as my mind reels.

Then, who did he mean?

Neith uses the opportunity to strike at my feet, but I tumble to the side.

"I'm assuming you are aware of the young lord's controversial rise to power, then?" Neith asks, curiosity evident in his face.

I hold my tongue, debating whether I should reveal what I know.

Information is as much a weapon as any blade, and I don't want to be caught with a weak hand.

"I know his father was the last to face a judgment."

Neith hums at the information. "Ah, but do you know why?"

I keep silent.

"Torryn's father could influence people to the point of control. All he had to do was whisper in their ear, and he could convince them to believe anything. Say anything. DO anything. And he might have gotten away with it, but he became power hungry, and he tried to take over the other courts. Sounds familiar, doesn't it?"

It's what Drytas is trying to do. Take over the other courts to increase his power. If this is something they've dealt with before, then why had the Crowns been so unwilling to believe it?

Neith continues, tilting his chin at me. "Almost too familiar. Odd, you would come here claiming practically the same story. Makes you wonder if Torryn got his good ol' dad's powers, too."

My heart stutters at his words, sword faltering mid-flight. Is he suggesting—

"I mean, power hungry has got to be genetic. I mean, how he got that crown on his head so young? Fifteen is the youngest ever to ascend."

My eyes widen at the information.

Fifteen is far younger than I'd assumed.

"Seeing as how Torryn was the one to bring you as evidence against Lord Drytas, and he was the one to turn in his own father."

Stunned, I lower my sword. Torryn had turned in his own father?

Using my astonishment, Neith grips the hilt of my blade, yanking it from my loosening grip. Spinning the sword, he stands back with both blades raised.

"You're leaving yourself open to being blindsided."

CHAPTER 24

"I'd like to go outside, please."

My voice betrays me, cracking pathetically. I clear my throat, actively trying to shove my feelings behind the wall begging to crumble.

The guards blocking my exit of the castle are like mountains, hulking masses that don't flinch at my desperation.

I've been fumbling through the castle for the last hour, searching for a door outside. Panic hurtling through me and seconds away from just climbing out a ground-floor window, I glimpse glass doors at the end of the hall. The bright blue behind them screams my way to freedom.

Tilting my chin upward, I don't flinch under the gazes of the two guards. Neither move a muscle to open the door. Instead, they exchange a look at each other before staring into the distance behind my head.

Irritation claws its way through me.

With as much politeness as I can muster, I ask again, "Please, I would like to get some fresh air."

They can't keep me here. Locked inside until they decide I'm of use to them. That's what Lord Drytas has done by building that blasted wall that surrounded Falland. He kept Valor isolated and dependent, all the easier to mold to his will.

Rolling his eyes, one guard huffs out, "We've been given specific instructions. You aren't to be leavin' the premises, miss."

Nails digging into my palms, I try to take deep breaths, inhaling through my mouth. "Who said that? I'm here voluntarily. I'm not a prisoner." When my words stir no response, I raise my voice, agitation clear. "I just want to go outside!"

I go from nuisance to threat in a deadly instant. A dark look crosses the guards' faces as they tower over me menacingly. Before they carry through on the warning lurking in their eyes, a voice cuts them off.

"Open the doors. She's allowed out with an escort. I'll take her out."

Evander strides toward us. My momentary hero who looks equally disheveled, breathing heavily behind me. His eyes search mine before staring at the guards in my way. I'd left him in the arena, his voice echoing behind me as he called my name.

"You'll escort her?" the guard grumbles, scrutinizing me as if I would flee the second I stepped outside.

A featherlight touch ghosts over my spine as Evander guides me forward.

"I said I would, didn't I?"

The guards don't answer but begrudgingly open the doors for us to step past them.

Evander leads me out, his hand warming my skin through my dress. As soon as the door closes behind us, he removes his hand and steps away, giving me my space.

I gasp in the fresh air like I'd been drowning and have finally broken the surface.

The castle was stifling, and I just needed a break. This place brimmed to the edge with secrets and political pressures. It feels like I've come to fight with both hands tied behind my back and an extra punch to the gut for good luck.

Falland had been nothing like it. Then again, it was hard to contemplate the inner workings of the city when we devoted so much energy to surviving it.

Evander waits by my side as I neatly fold up my anxiety and panic, stuffing it through the cracks in my wall. Moderately put together, I nod to him in thanks.

Evander's eyes are kind as he appraises me before he nods for me to follow him. He makes his way down the castle steps without saying a word.

Curious, I trail him, unsure of where we could go.

Until I hear the crashing of waves.

The rocky path turns to sand beneath our shoes as we climb a dune. The grains squish under my weight, shifting with every step. Peeking over the tall grasses, I catch sight of the ocean hidden just behind. A brilliant blue that outshines the sky fizzles into white foam as it meets the shore.

I needed this.

My thoughts go blank, mind silenced as I stare in awe. The glimpse I've seen from Self's quarters is nothing compared to now. Not when I could feel the mist of the ocean breeze. Not when I could smell the salt.

"You like the ocean, I take it?" Evander inserts, breaking the period of silence.

I nod, humming. It's no longer a question without an answer.

We approach the ocean and sit where the water can barely reach. The mist is cool compared to the sun-warmed sand, but it feels nice as it coats my skin—soothing.

Once I've taken a moment to center myself, I look at Evander with grateful eyes. Watching as the breeze blows around his golden-brown hair. I rest my arms on my bent knees, settling my chin on my forearms.

"Thank you."

My voice is barely audible over the waves.

"You are welcome, Lysta. Anytime." Evander leans over, nudging his shoulder into mine. "You aren't a prisoner here."

Staring out into the water, I mumble into my sleeve, "Maybe not in name."

Evander takes a deep breath, rubbing his temple with one hand. "I'm sorry about Neith. I knew it wasn't a good idea for the two of you to spar."

I can't help but roll my eyes as I wave off his words. Of course he thinks I'm mad about losing to Neith. Not the secrets threatening my life being kept from me.

"He told me what everyone else wasn't. I'm grateful for it, even if his delivery was a tad aggressive."

After a pause, Evander shifts next to me.

"And how do you feel about what he said?"

"I don't know how I feel." I look away from him. "I think too much of the suspicion relies on reputation. Torryn's court, Torryn's father, but no one here seems to know Torryn."

At Torryn's name, Evander tenses. When he clenches his jaw, a muscle ticks in his cheek.

"You don't like him either," I murmur.

Evander responds through pursed lips. "Court politics isn't about whether you like someone. It's about who you can trust. Trust to back you up if something or someone were to threaten your court. Trust to do the right thing when lives are at stake. There are very few people in the court I like, but I trust some of them. I don't trust Torryn."

I inhale deeply.

Based on his characterization of the word, I don't trust many people.

"Do you distrust Torryn, or are you making a judgment based on his father's history?"

"I'll admit, what his father did has a lot to do with it, but some of it is Torryn. You know how he has Trialed in multiple courts, right?"

Freezing, I look to Evander with wide eyes. I didn't think that was common knowledge. I nod, pushing him to continue.

"He forged agreements with most of the courts. If we let him Trial, then we could send someone to the Court of Self to Trial. Torryn's father let no one Trial there, and now, we know what kind of power could be gained from what his father did. Everyone wanted the chance to Trial."

I sit patiently, letting him continue.

"My father didn't take the deal," Evander says spitefully. "He doesn't let many Trial in Truth—it has the highest death rate of the Trials, and he has some fascination with Torryn so he won't risk letting him die. But the other courts did. Even Bralas and Rhen and their feud with Torryn couldn't pass up the chance at that kind of power, but none of them successfully Trialed in Self. They came back shaken—and with a new tally mark. Obviously, they couldn't say what the Trial was—" Evander goes quiet, his gaze hardening as he looks forward.

Shifting beside him, I hug my knees tighter. "Sar said not every Trial is suited for everyone—"

"They said only a monster could complete it."

My stomach drops.

What could the Trial possibly require that made anyone call Torryn a monster? Sure, he was abrasive and brooding, but it was closer to a lack of social skills than that of humanity.

"So, no, I don't have any proof not to trust Torryn, but there are enough reasons for me not to either way."

Holding my head in my hands, I panic. "How am I supposed to convince all the courts to trust me when they don't trust the

Crown supporting what I say? If they don't believe me, what happens then? Do they give me to Drytas to be punished for treason?"

Evander reaches over, squeezing my hand in his. I flinch at the contact, but allow for him to hold it. "We'll convince them. I promise, Lysta. I'm on your side."

Stomach rolling, I meet Evander's gaze. "Can you successfully be on my side and not be on Torryn's, too?"

Evander's grip tightens, squeezing painfully, before he relaxes.

He looks down, nodding. "I get what you're saying."

Seeing an opportunity, I lean forward, catching his gaze. "Torryn got me out of Falland. He has vowed to stop Lord Drytas, just as you have to help me. If you stood with both of us, it would inspire a great deal of confidence."

Evander glances toward our hands, his thumb brushing against the back of my hand. "You think it would make a difference?"

I shrug. "To them, I am a fool blindly trusting Torryn. They know I have a limited perspective on his history. But you . . . You know everything. Maybe that would show there is validity in what he's saying."

Evander sighs, reaching forward to tuck a strand of my hair behind my ear. "For you, I will defend him."

CHAPTER 25

Torryn avoids me for several days before I even realize he's doing it.

Relationships are not my forte—nor maintaining them.

Thoman had been as blunt as they came, and his forthrightness never left me wondering what he was feeling or what was going on in his head.

Torryn, on the other hand, seems determined to be the very opposite. Holding onto every secret, every bit of information, like giving me even a crumb more than what is absolutely necessary will be his downfall.

At first, I blame his schedule, being rushed in and out of meetings and only catching a glimpse of him. I blame timing because, whenever I scope out the training room or find my way to his court's tower, Sar or Ardis gives me the runaround.

Just like today, Ardis says Torryn is in a meeting and isn't around.

I nod in understanding before making my way out of the tower.

Even if I'd sooner Trial again before trusting a word out of

Neith's mouth, that didn't mean Torryn and I didn't need to talk. Especially with the judgment hearing impending, we need to be on the same page. How could we expect to take down Lord Drytas if we are at odds with each other?

Then, not even twenty paces from the tower doors, I run into Ardis—again.

Freezing where I stand, I watch as Ardis walks by, offering a short "Good morning, Lysta."

Too flabbergasted to even process what I'm seeing, I wave and let him continue on his way as he enters the tower where the other Ardis had just been.

And it all makes sense. Torryn is using his mirror shifting to slip me whenever I come looking.

I let out a laugh, shaking my head at Torryn's trick.

So, he wants to play games?

Ready to face him head on, I recruit Evander into my plan, seeing as how Sar and Ardis seem content to leave Torryn to his own devices.

Evander greets Torryn just outside the room I wait in.

"Lord Torryn, good afternoon. I was hoping to speak with you on an important matter."

My stomach twists, praying my plan will work. Torryn is far from predictable, but Evander seemed confident he could say the right thing to get Torryn into the room with me. I only hope he is correct.

There's a scuffle of steps before Torryn responds, his tone hard and curt.

"A matter that shouldn't be between me and your father?" He doesn't bother hiding the smug tinge to his words, reveling in shoving the chain of command in Evander's face.

Evander's voice becomes stiff, but I'm grateful when he doesn't take the bait but instead continues with the plan without a hitch.

"No, this matter involves Lysta."

The hall goes quiet for a beat and I lean in.

"Is she all right? Why is she not with you?"

Panic seeps into Torryn's voice as he interrogates Evander.

I can't help but grumble to myself in frustration.

So, he cares enough to be worried, but not enough to talk to me?

Evander's voice gets louder as he steps closer to the door.

"She's fine, I promise. Can we discuss it in here?"

Evander had shown me to a small meeting room seldom in use, its location just past the other where Torryn was expected to exit.

Torryn steps through first, and I steel myself, waiting for the inevitable outburst. As his dark eyes meet my own, his face hardens, lips thinning into a line.

Evander meets my eyes before backing out of the room in a hurry, shutting the door behind Torryn.

Without a word, Torryn pivots on his heel, planning to flee from the room, but he growls when he meets my shield, an extra precaution Evander isn't aware of.

Torryn places a hand against my shield, and it buzzes under his touch. As he lowers his head, Torryn's hair covers his face, hiding it from me. His hand drops from the shield, clenching into a fist at his side.

We stand there in silence.

"Sorry for siccing Evander on you. I didn't like my chances of just trapping an Ardis and hoping that I'd caught you. The actual Ardis might have been offended."

My words land, and Torryn flinches.

"You've been avoiding me," I say, trying to keep the hurt, accusing tone out of my voice.

I fail.

Torryn moves his gaze to the window, his jaw set as he rolls it from side to side. I hope he is not so against my presence that he would consider the window as a viable option.

"I have not—"

"Don't lie, Torryn. We aren't children. You can spend as little or as much time with me as you so please, but I should at least get to know why."

He scoffs but doesn't budge on his vow of silence.

Irritation claws apart my plan to keep this from becoming an argument.

"You brought me here." My voice raises without my permission. "If you're angry at my presence, you only have yourself to blame."

Torryn's eyes flash to mine, ablaze with renewed frustration.

"You think I'm avoiding you because I don't want you here?"

"Why else would you be so suddenly upset? I know my being here hasn't made things easier between you and the other courts."

Torryn laughs darkly. "Don't flatter yourself. My relationship with the other courts has been hostile long before you came along."

"Then, why?"

"Because I have no reason to acquaint myself with someone who will just be used against me."

The retort on the tip of my tongue dies, and I swallow it down thickly.

Torryn looks deeply into my eyes, and for a moment, I see the crack in his wall. Mirrored so closely with how I grew up.

In Falland, everyone was so focused on surviving and making it through every day. You couldn't risk worrying about someone else. You couldn't risk trusting anyone else because, in the end, they would always look out for themselves.

Neith said Torryn had been a lord since he was fifteen years old. If that is accurate, he would have barely been a teenager, yet he was forced to stand among adults. No wonder he struggled so much, letting anyone into his inner circle.

I take one step closer to him, much like one would approach a wild animal bound to flee at the smallest movement.

"And how will I be used against you?" I whisper.

Torryn looks anywhere in the room except at me. I try to catch his eyes, but he closes them, breathing deeply through his nose. "They'll poison you against me. It's what they do. They'll tell you everything you need to know and then you'll see me as they do."

"And how is that?"

"A monster."

I pause, taken aback by his answer.

Is he telling me how the others see him or how he sees himself? For someone who has radiated confidence and certainty at every opportunity, it's unsettling to hear a rare moment of self-deprecation.

"You're callous and rude and not an entirely pleasant person to be around—" Torryn flinches as if I've attacked him. "But you have yet to show me anything to make me think you are a monster. I don't trust anyone, including you, but you're the closest I've gotten to it. So, trust me a little. What your father did has no bearing on what you may do, okay?"

Torryn meets my gaze, brown eyes locking on to my own.

A lengthy pause hangs, and I worry he won't take the truce I'm offering.

He raises his chin, crossing his arms. "It's still not a good idea for you to be seen around me."

I huff in irritation, shaking my head at him. "Why? We should show them a united front."

"I've known them far longer than you have, and I'm saying this way is better."

A hardness returns to Torryn's tone, and we've found our newest argument.

"Because why?"

"Their distrust of me is rubbing off on you. I've already heard whispers of it during our meetings." Torryn's jaw ticks as he continues. "They need to see you as someone they can trust, and they don't trust me."

"Or—and here's a revolutionary idea—you could show them you are human and are trying to do the right thing. Try earning their trust instead of powering on without it."

Torryn shakes his head dismissively, perching on the edge of the table. "It's not as easy as you make it seem. You're operating under the assumption that they will be fair in their judgment."

"Just try my way. What's the worst that could happen?"

CHAPTER 26

A thrum of excitement vibrates through the halls of the capital with the approach of the Peace Ball—the social event of the year, according to Evander. Not so coincidentally, it also falls on the eve of Lord Drytas's judgment hearing.

There isn't a corner of the castle that doesn't buzz with hopeful tales of the glittering night to come. It seems like topics of dresses and dancing find their way into every conversation. Even the capital staff gossip over the latest pairings who will accompany each other—Evander and Visha named several times as a hopeful possibility.

It grates against me with every giggle and whisper, but they don't know war looms on the horizon. Outside of the Crowns and Heirs, no one has been told what Lord Drytas did or what he threatens to do, only that Torryn testified for his judgment.

Despite knowing this, I can't help but hold their jovial spirits against them.

But the excited energy that has been building the entire week is not just for the upcoming festivities but for today's War Hour, as Crowns and Heirs take to the battlefield instead.

Even I can't deny an interest in learning more about what the rulers are capable of, regarded as the most powerful of their court as they are.

Few Trialed use their power in obvious ways, except during War Hour. Whether it's a strategic decision or just etiquette, I'm unsure. But it leaves me with a vested interest in getting to witness the battles.

When Evander escorts me to the Court of Truth's viewing box, Lord Gennady is already seated at the window, his ankle propped atop his knee, his cane across his lap. At our entrance, he waves in greeting before returning his gaze to the quickly filling seats of the arena.

I move to join him, but Evander stops me with a hand on my wrist. Looking back at him with furrowed brows, I hesitate in the doorway. "Aren't we going in?" I ask, scanning for what I must have missed.

Evander gives me a half smile, nodding at my question. "Yes, *you* are."

I balk at his words.

Evander doesn't need to finish for me to understand what he is saying. I don't know why I hadn't considered the possibility he might take part in War Hour, but I'm caught off guard.

Shoving my hand in my pockets, I look away from him, letting my gaze linger behind him on the battlefield.

"You're fighting today."

Evander nods, nudging me with his shoulder. "I am, but I'll be just fine. The Court of Change always has healers on standby, especially with Crown battles."

My stomach knots at the thought of him fighting with the Crowns—or needing a healer at all.

Wrinkling my brows, I nod. "I suppose I should wish you luck, then."

Ignoring what my mouth says, Evander reads my face. He

reaches a hand up to rub his thumb over the lines forming between my brows.

Yanking my head back, I scowl at him, but he only chuckles.

"This is how I represent my court. I've competed in War Hour with the other Heirs since I was twelve. It's nothing I can't handle, Lysta." Evander leans down to catch my eye. "You aren't angry I'm competing today, are you?"

What reason would I have to be upset?

I shake my head at the ridiculous notion. "Of course not. I'm still adjusting to the concept of the whole thing. Good luck, Evander," I say with renewed enthusiasm that sits only at face value.

Taking one last deep breath, Evander opens the door, preparing to leave the safety of the glass prison. "Will you be all right on your own?"

I straighten, giving him a forced smile. "Of course. I doubt Lord Gennady means me any harm."

Evander levels a look at me, adding softly, "That's not what I meant."

Looking away from his searching stare, I swallow thickly. "I'll be fine. Good luck."

"IF YOU'RE LOOKING for Lord Torryn on the field, I'm afraid you will be disappointed."

Lord Gennady's voice breaks my concentration, pulling my eyes from the line of Crowns and Heirs preparing to fight in today's War Hour.

Sending a guilty look at the older gentleman beside me, I open my mouth to explain, but Lord Gennady waves off any excuse I'd been prepared to offer. Warmth gathers in my face, and I turn away from him, hoping he won't push my embarrassment.

"Why is that?" I ask quietly, twisting my intertwined fingers in my lap.

"Fairness, I think. Many of the other Crowns might boast of their wins against the young lord in the past, but I doubt anyone would wish to take him on now, considering his Trial accomplishments."

Leaning toward Lord Gennady, I stay quiet, hoping my silence will prompt him to continue. Very few in the capital speak of Torryn's experience with the Trials, and even I have to admit that, knowing so little, I'm curious.

Tapping his hands against his thigh, Lord Gennady continues, "We can't even guess which abilities he's been gifted other than the couple we know. But the length of his Trial tattoo does not lie. He is far more powerful than they give him credit for, and he deserves their respect. He's earned every single Trial, but they act as if he stole them."

"I have a feeling it would mean a lot if he heard that from you, my lord."

When Lord Gennady's ice-blue eyes blink to mine, I'm afraid I have overstepped.

Freezing in place, I brace for a reprimand. It's too easy to relax in his presence, regardless of the silver crown propped on his salt-and-pepper hair.

But Lord Gennady's eyes are soft as he gazes at me deeply.

"I will take that under advisement. Thank you, Lysta."

Relief coaxes the tension from my upper body, and I sink into the soft cushion of the chair. I'm willing to let my focus latch onto the battle below.

Bash steps forward on the field, wings unfolding behind him as he brandishes two swords. When he crosses them in front of him menacingly, the crowd surges to their feet. The white smile he flashes them only incites a fresh round of cheers as his wings beat and he hovers just off the ground.

Opposite him, Lord Rhen swings a curved sword, flipping the weapon in his grip. Strung across his back is a quiver of arrows and a bow, and I lean forward in anticipation.

Without knowing Lord Rhen's ability, it's hard to predict how this matchup will go. Bash might have been able to avoid a ground assault with his wings, but any advantage he had is now lost if Lord Rhen can attack him long range. It all comes to if he's a decent shot.

Lord Rhen bows to Bash, holding the weapon parallel with his nose, then waits as Bash does the same.

The only warning Lord Rhen has is the bend of Bash's knees before his wings propel him upward.

Lord Rhen spins as he stabs his sword into the sand, eyes searching the sky for a glimpse of Bash's wings. Grabbing his bow, he knocks an arrow, pulling it taut.

I can't help but press myself closer to the window, even when my breath fogs up the glass. Searching the high roof of the arena, I, along with the rest of the arena, look for the pair of white wings.

A shadow passes over the window—Bash's figure blocking out the sun from above. Lord Rhen sees it as well, launching an arrow toward Bash.

Bash dodges, tucking his wings in as he spins into a roll out of the way of the onslaught of arrows. They zing past him, pelting the metal cage separating the battlefield from the arena seats. The crowd rumbles in their seats, not in fear for their lives but cheering at the action unfolding before them.

Bash swoops toward Lord Rhen, barreling down at top speed before pulling up at the last second.

He pulls the same maneuver over again, and I can't help but think he must not have a plan. Until Lord Rhen reaches for another arrow, fingers closing around air. He's fired every last one, defending himself from Bash's air dive attempts.

Leaning back, I bring a finger up to cover a small smile curving my lips.

Bash pulls his sword from its sheath, tosses it in his hand, and flips it, making the screaming crowd rise. Sending the crowd a winning smile, he dives once again. Grabbing Lord Rhen by the arms, Bash propels upward and drops him onto an archer's peak.

Furious, Lord Rhen snaps his bow in half, holding its pieces in two, the metal wire still connecting them. Spinning on his heel, Lord Rhen watches as Bash swerves toward him before swinging the mangled bow out. Lord Rhen leaps, wrapping the metal bowstring around Bash's neck.

The entire arena holds its breath as they both fall.

Bash's wings beat furiously, straining to carry the weight of two. His hands scramble to pull at the wire wrapped around his neck, his face reddening as he strains to breathe.

Lord Rhen grabs onto one of Bash's wings, trying to pull himself more firmly onto the flailing Heir. The wing snaps, bending out of its normal shape, and the two plummet to the sandy pit.

Lord Rhen crashes to the ground atop Bash.

I can't stifle my gasp at Lord Rhen's mangled leg, his foot turned in the opposite direction.

Despite how it turns my stomach, Lord Rhen stands as if nothing has happened.

Bash, whose face is contorted deeply in pain, flails against the bowstring still wrapped around his neck as he reaches for his broken wing.

It's completely opposite ends of the spectrum—Bash in utter agony while Lord Rhen looks as if he feels no pain at all.

Lord Rhen leans forward, pulling tightly against the bowstring, shouting, "Yield?"

Bash nods furiously, face redder than before.

Lord Rhen releases the bowstring, and Bash scrambles to remove it from around his throat, who gasps deeply when his airway opens. Leaning forward on his hands and knees, Bash sits before offering a hand in Lord Rhen's directions.

They shake hands, and it's an odd sight. One with a mangled leg, the other a broken wing. The crowd's cheers reach a deafening level.

As Lord Rhen turns, holding his hands up in victory for the arena to see, two people rush onto the field. A man and a woman, each with blonde hair.

They separate, each taking one opponent. Healers, I realize.

Bash's wing snaps into place, and he stands, opening and closing them. He nods a thanks to the healer before waving to the crowd as he treks off the sand.

Lord Rhen appears to argue with the healer before reluctantly allowing them to step forward to work on him. His leg returning from where it had been twisted 180 degrees in the wrong direction.

Lord Rhen waves on the cheers before shouting, "I challenge Evander. Heir of the Court of Truth."

My body stiffens entirely at the sound of Evander's name, and I look quickly to Lord Gennady. His calm face and eased composure do nothing to console my pounding heart.

Evander is going against Lord Rhen? Who beat Bash in the most brutal way—completely unfazed by his own pain?

Anxiety whirls in my stomach.

At the sight of Evander's golden-brown hair making his way out onto the field, I grip my hands in front of me as if praying the battle will be over quick.

The healers run off the field as Evander struts over to where

Lord Rhen stands. His gaze searches the seats, immediately locking in on the viewing booth where Lord Gennady and I sit. His stare not even hesitating over his father, Evander finds me.

When our eyes meet, he grins, showing off his perfect white teeth gleaming at me from across the arena.

I can barely bring myself to give him a half smile, worry clouding my excitement.

Evander takes it in stride, raising his sword in my direction before nodding. *I'll be okay,* Evander mouths to me.

The crowd claps as the opponents face each other.

Rendering his bow and arrow useless, Lord Rhen reaches for the sword still stuck in the sand before bowing to Evander just as he did Bash.

Evander mimics his motion.

It's hard to imagine a fight being more intense than the one between Lord Rhen and Bash—every moment someone else having the upper hand. But within seconds of the fight beginning, I already know I'm wrong.

While the previous battle had taken over the entire battlefield, each move unpredictable leaving me and the crowd in anticipation, this one was solely based on skill and mastery.

Each equipped with a sword, Lord Rhen and Evander circle each other on the field. It's much like my training with Evander but on a different level. Each clash of swords bears the weight of true intention behind it.

After defending a low hit from Evander, Lord Rhen slams his shoulder into Evander's chest, knocking him back several feet. Without giving Evander a moment to catch his bearings, Lord Rhen rains hits with his sword. But Evander keeps up with cool composure. He sidesteps each swipe, blocking Lord Rhen from landing any attacks.

I watch closely as Evander taught me, trying to catch even a hint of what powers might be practiced before me. Evander never talked about if he has Trialed or any ability he may have received. But, then again, part of me doubts he has—he did say that Lord Gennady rarely let people Trial in Truth since it has the highest death rate.

Turning to Lord Gennady, I expect to see my anticipation mirrored in him, but he watches with a blank face, mentally distanced from what takes place on the arena field.

"Have they fought before?" I ask, wondering if he knows something I don't.

But Lord Gennady shakes his head, eyes not leaving the battle taking place before us. "No, I don't think we have seen this particular match as of yet. The Heirs are only just being of an age where the fight would be even worth it."

The arena seems to gasp when Evander dodges a hit, surely to land deep in his torso. As he swings out to the side, he brings up his blade, swiping across Lord Rhen's shoulder. It leaves behind a gaping wound, blood pouring from the cut.

I lean back as Lord Rhen growls in pain. The wound is not what surprises me but the reaction. While the gash is deep, it surely can't be worse than a leg being dislocated and twisted in its socket. Yet Lord Rhen hadn't shown a wince of pain then, but he's obviously hurting now.

Narrowing my eyes at the fight, I lean forward with renewed interest. I'd thought for a moment Lord Rhen had some resistance or immunity to the pain he experienced, but that suspicion is disproven now.

What has changed between this fight and the last?

Pausing in his relentless attacks, Lord Rhen looks at his arm before examining Evander with a new apprehension in his eyes. More critical in his appraisal of Evander, Lord Rhen switches to a slower, more calculated attack style.

Evander does the opposite, launching into a quick flurry of well-aimed strikes pushing Lord Rhen backward in retreat.

Lord Gennady stands next to me, and I recoil in surprise.

Pushing forward on a shaky cane, Lord Gennady stares through the window at the battle before turning to walk away.

"Sir?" I call after him, standing. "You're leaving before Evander's done?"

Lord Gennady turns to look at me, a sad expression forming in his eyes. "I find watching only makes me anxious. Better I finish some work before the Peace Ball anyway."

I nod, turning to find Evander once again on the field.

He holds his sword up defensively as Lord Rhen presses his own against it with his weight. Despite the blades resting so close to his throat, Evander's eyes are on me.

Did he see his father leave? Is that what has him distracted?

In a flash, Lord Rhen kicks Evander's ankle out from under him, making him fall backward. Lord Rhen presses a foot to the center of his chest, leveling the blade at Evander's neck.

Evander doesn't wait for Lord Rhen to prompt him before he yields. But his eyes don't leave mine until a crease forms between his brows as his gaze bounces from me to Lord Gennady's vacated spot.

CHAPTER 27

I'd like to think in my time at the capital, the people here have begun to palate my presence. Keeping my head down is instinct after living under the guard's terror in Falland, and it works just as well here. I blend in until I'm just another invisible among the rest.

But as hard as I work to fall to the background, Evander draws focus like a beacon in the night. As my constant escort, he pulls me under scrutiny with him.

Today, following the Crowns' War Hour and hours before the highly anticipated Peace Ball, I get a taste of freedom. Not a single person spares me even a glance.

Court citizens and capital staff alike hurry up and down the halls. Women rush past with a plethora of dresses draped across their arms, all a range of colors and fabrics. Staff cart around trays of covered food and glass chalices.

And, in their preparation, no one is concerned with my presence.

I'm nearly back to the Court of Truth's tower, where my quiet room awaits me when a woman's voice hisses in the hall I must enter. The venom in her tone stops me before I turn the corner, instead pressing myself against the wall.

"It is too late!" the woman says in a shrill voice. "Now the ball is upon us, and there will be no Heir on your arm. You've had weeks."

Turning my head back toward the hall I just came from, I hesitate. I've learned to navigate parts of the capital, and this is the only way I know to get to my room. But I can't just continue on by an obviously tense conversation.

A girl's voice sounds down the hall.

"I'm confident I can make tonight work for your plans, Mother. I have not failed you yet."

In the beat of silence, I hold my breath, praying the two women will not come my way. I've obviously stumbled upon a tense conversation, not meant to be overheard.

"Have you sensed a change in his feelings?" the older woman asks, voice tight with frustration. "Anything at all?"

"He's hard to read. It's like I see a glimpse and then it's gone. From what I catch, he enjoys my company. That has not changed, but I have had so little time with him. It's as if he spends every waking moment with her. Meals, training—there's never a chance to get him alone."

"I expect so much more from you, Visha. You will not have my brother's favor indefinitely. And then what?"

I freeze, air escaping my lungs in a quiet gasp.

Nothing could stop me from leaning forward to peek around the corner, confirming what I've just heard.

Visha stands crowded against the wall, her mother gripping her wrist. While Visha is at least a head taller than her mother, she shrinks under her cold gaze.

"Can't you feel my disappointment, Visha? I know it weighs heavily on me. Don't you wish to relieve us both of this burden?"

Visha looks away, face void of emotion. "Of course, Mother. I'll do better."

The older woman steps away from Visha, patting the girl's hair as she responds. "Good. Now, go get ready. You have an Heir to impress."

Her mother slinks away, leaving Visha standing in the hall alone, staring blankly at the wall.

Part of me considers going to her, offering her morsels of sympathy. I'm no stranger to being manipulated. but then her head whips in my direction, and I hide behind the wall.

My heart races, praying she didn't see me watching from the shadows. I wait for the sound of her footsteps to signal her departure, but they never come.

I lean to peer down the hall once more but stumble back in shock. Visha stands not a foot away, frowning down at me.

Pulling a small knife from beneath the cloth at her sternum, she pushes me until my back hits the wall. One hand pins my shoulder while the other holds her knife. She doesn't wield the blade like a weapon but as an extension of her finger as she points the tip at me.

"If you have the guts to eavesdrop on my conversations, at least have the stomach to not pity me." Visha snarls in my face.

"I didn't mean to—"

She scoffs, rolling her eyes. "Speak of anything you heard, and I'll kill you myself. One minor accident during training, and you won't be my problem anymore. So, don't make yourself a problem for me."

I flinch at the threat, nodding slowly when she glares at me.

Pushing off the wall, Visha stows away her knife before stalking down the hall. Her purple dress floats behind her.

~

RUSHING UP the tower to my room, taking the stairs two at a time, I decide I won't tell anyone what I'd heard in the hallway.

Whoever Visha had set her sights on would have to figure out her motives on his own. I push away the thought that it more than likely is Evander.

Even if I know I should tell him, I can't have Visha working against me in the capital right now. If her plan was something more than just harmless flirting, I would, but no one is in danger. But surely, I would be if Visha's threat holds weight.

I will, however, be storing the revelation of Visha's power away for later. It's obvious from her mother's words and even Visha's own. She must be an empath of sorts—able to feel other's emotions to some degree. Suddenly, our first meeting makes a world of sense.

When I arrive at my room, I stutter, heart swooping.

The door is already slightly ajar.

Fumbling in my layers of skirt for the slit, I pull my dagger from its holster, brandishing the weapon before creeping into the room.

I push the door open with one hand, grateful when it doesn't make a noise. Stepping through the entryway, I hold my breath as I peer in.

"Sar!" I sag in relief when I recognize the figure flitting about my room.

The redheaded girl whirls around, hair whipping over her shoulder. Hand to her chest, she gasps. "Don't scare me like that!"

"You're the one who snuck into my room."

"Yes, but I come bearing gifts," Sar sings, gesturing to the bed behind her.

The surface is littered with jewelry, ribbons, and shoes. A large white box sits in the middle with a blue bow at its center.

Sar turns to pick something up from the bed and holds out a

red dress when she turns to face me. It's sleek and far more revealing than I would like. I try not to cringe when she shows it to me.

"I brought a dress for you to wear, the only red one that I own, but this was in front of your door when I arrived." Sar gestures to the white box.

Leaning past her, I caress the silk dress before grabbing the box. Slipping my fingers under the bow, I pull the ribbon loose.

"I thought it might be strategic to dress you in the colors of your court, remind them of your connection to your home to curry some favor. But if you've gotten in someone's good graces enough for them to send you a dress—perhaps that would be the better move."

I don't like the idea of wearing a dress a stranger picked out for me. Like I'm a puppet they can control. But the idea of wearing Lord Drytas's colors sits even worse with me. It makes me hate the color red.

Inside is a breathtaking dress. It's a pale blue, like the color of waves as they mix with sea foam. Silver crystals are beaded in swirling designs across the entirety of the dress, making it shine like the moon over the ocean. Gripping the dress, I lift it out of the box and hold it to my body to show Sar.

Her eyes sparkle. A smile grows on her face, obviously pleased with the gown.

After convincing me to step into the dress, Sar fusses with my hair before painting my face with small pots of color. She dabs at my cheeks and eyelids, refusing to let me see her work before she's finished.

With every second ticking away and every minute bringing us closer to the ball, a knot in my stomach clenches tighter and tighter. My chest gets heavy, panic setting in.

"Sar, I'm still not convinced I should go tonight," I say for what must be the tenth time since arriving in the room. "I've been able to stay under the radar of most of the Crowns while here. Maybe it's better to keep it that way."

Sar sighs as she smears a thin layer of something across my lips. "We've discussed this, Lysta. Right now, all the Crowns see is a young girl making a wild accusation against one of their own. They don't trust you."

"Even more reason for me not to go!"

Sar shakes her head, dismissing any hopes I have of convincing her to let me stay behind. "It is the very opposite. Socializing among them, showing them who you are, will humanize you. They need to see you as one of them, not one of us."

"And making a fool of myself in front of them is worth humanizing me?" I ask, pitch rising.

"Frankly, yes," Sar says, laughing. "It's funny. Ardis used to call it the same thing."

I tilt my head, unsure of what she means.

"Dancing." All the mirth leaves her eyes, and a frown takes its place. "Back in the Court of Wisdom, my only use to my father was for appearance purposes. So, he'd drag me out for every ball and celebration. I put on the perfect show, except Ardis always saw through it."

It's obvious then, even if our struggles were worlds apart—Sar had grown up bathed in as much trauma and struggle as I had, only a different kind.

"You mentioned he helped you escape?" I ask when she seems to lose herself in her thoughts.

Sar inhales deeply. "Lord Bralas, my father, found him fighting in an illegal battle ring and, instead of punishing him . . . hired him. Ardis became my personal guard by title and my warden by practice."

I can't stifle my gasp. "He worked for your father?"

Sar nods with a grimace. "Not willingly. You can't exactly say no to a lord."

It's impossible to reconcile the Ardis I have witnessed with any version who would align himself with Bralas. From the snippets I've seen of the two together, there isn't a world where Ardis would ever harm Sar.

"How did he end up helping you?"

"We became friends. He tried to shield me from my father as much as he could, but we both reached our last straw. For me, it was when I caught wind of an arranged marriage in the works. I decided right then I was done being controlled—by anybody."

"So, you escaped?"

Sar gives me a half smile, nodding. "I escaped. I couldn't portal a fraction of what I can now, but I got us out of the fortress, and Ardis got us out of the court. And he took me to Torryn."

I take in what Sar has revealed. The story is obviously one that pains her greatly, yet she chose to tell me. Maybe it is that she is starting to trust me or wants to give me a glimpse of a reason to have faith in them. Either way, my panic at what comes tomorrow eases a little, knowing that, no matter what happens, I have people I can depend on. Trusting them to do what they say they will.

CHAPTER 28

Delicate music floats down the halls like clouds in the sky, gentle and welcoming, as it announces our nearing of the ballroom. A sound that would otherwise be a soothing melody sounds foreboding, a warning of the night ahead.

My hands tremble with every uncertain step. I grip the fabric of my dress, bunching it until it wrinkles, just for the sake of occupying my hands.

Tonight's Peace Ball holds more weight than just the dancing or the feast awaiting us inside. While all attention would be on the frivolity and spectacle, I would make my way through enemy lines, trying to gain allies. So much could go wrong within these next few hours.

Sar reaches over, startling me, and pulls one of my arms to twist with her own. She gives me a tight-lipped smile, and I sag into her for a second.

"It'll be over before you know it," she assures me.

I nod, letting her lead us forward despite my reluctance.

"Torryn better be ready," Sar mutters as she flicks a tendril of her sleek red hair out of her face. "I can guarantee he is hiding out somewhere, hoping I won't find him before the procession, so I can't drag him here."

I wish I had thought to. I can hardly blame him if he was, for these people like him even less than me.

We round the corner of the ballroom's entrance and stand atop the marble staircase where a few guests trickle into the sea of people below.

Sar turns to me, eyes still surveilling the crowd. "I need to retrieve our lord to make sure he is ready for his entrance in the procession. I pray he'll save me the tantrum—you two are so much alike." Sar shoots me a teasing glare.

My jaw drops at the realization that she plans to abandon me atop the staircase just as more and more eyes find me, pinning me in place.

When she sees my gaping expression, she nudges me forward. "Find Ardis, and I'll be back in ten minutes."

Wiping away my fearful expression, I turn back to descend the stairs, and all I allow them to see is a blank, neutral one. The more uncomfortable I look, the more it will emphasize I do not belong here. Instead of showing the anxiety swirling below the surface, I raise my gaze, letting my eyes meet several in the crowd.

Circling the room, I do as Sar had suggested. Each time I near someone, I peel my lips back, trying to give them my best smile. But from the way they turn away quickly, I worry it looks more like a grimace. Catching sight of Ardis tucked away at a table in the corner, I abandon the pointless mission.

In his hand is a dark drink, which he nurses as he surveys the room. The hair that normally grazes his ears is slicked back, revealing the clipped hair underneath. Shaved symbols and lines mark the short hair.

Beelining across the room, I grab a drink off a passing tray before coming to stand next to him.

His eyes sweep over me quickly before he nods in greeting, muttering, "You look good."

I bite back a laugh with a sarcastic smile. "I'll let Sar know you appreciate her work."

He snorts as I take a long drink from the glass. Startled, I cough at the burning sensation creeping down my throat. Narrowing my eyes at the drink swirling around in my cup with new suspicion.

Ardis looks at me with a curved brow.

"Alcohol. I've never had it."

Without a word, Ardis nods and leans over, swiping a drink from a passing tray, this one a milky, iridescent white. "No need for any more new experiences today, wouldn't you agree?" he asks as he hands me the fresh beverage. He then swipes the one I'm holding and glugs it down.

I nod, chuckling as he nudges me.

Examining the room, I easily differentiate the court members from the staff flocking about toting food and drink trays. Donning simple black dress clothes, they blend into the swirling sea of sparkles and silk, velvet and lace, like how the darkness of the night sky highlights the stars among it. A part of me wishes I were among them tonight—fading into the background.

I crane my neck to glimpse the group of musicians sitting on the balcony, playing their instruments. When a song ends, they pick up another without so much as a glance from the crowd.

"How long does the ball last?" I ask, turning to Ardis.

He snickers, shaking his head. "Had your fill already?"

"Absolutely." I nod before leaning toward him with a conspiring smile. "I want to be able to count down the minutes until I can ditch these pointy shoes and head back to my room."

Ardis chuckles, his shoulders shaking, which coaxes a broader smile from my lips. "You'll probably be in the clear in a couple hours, but it's a night that never ends. People stay here—"

When I look at Ardis, his eyes shine as he looks at the entrance to the ballroom.

Following his gaze, I find Sar stepping through the doors and hovering at the staircase's landing.

Sar holds herself like a Crown. Head tall, back straight, always with a gentle smile on her face. All the beauty but with every morsel of modesty and dignity. She deserves to be an Heir, walking in the procession instead of Neith.

"Perhaps you could escort her," I say, nudging Ardis.

His eyes flick to me in surprise before moving back to Sar. Lips pursing, he turns to grab another passing drink. "She's an Heir. It would be inappropriate."

Watching him swallow a gulp of the drink with wide eyes, I can't help but wonder if it's the reason the two seem to ignore how drawn they are to each other despite everything they've been through. Every time I see them, they are touching in some small way.

Were there rules for relationships between courts and the different statuses?

"All I meant was escort her down the stairs," I tease as a flush creeps across Ardis's cheeks.

I'm positive that, if I pointed it out to him, he would blame it on the drinks, but I know better.

Ardis hesitates, finger swirling across the rim of his glass in deep contemplation.

"I'll be fine on my own. Go," I assure him, taking his glass and pushing him in her direction.

Ardis strides across the room, dodging anyone who walks

into his path. He takes the stairs two at a time before stopping at the step below Sar's.

At the sight of him, Sar smiles, her face a rosy glow, before stepping forward to encircle her hand through his arm.

As they descend the stairs, Ardis leans toward her ear, whispering something to make Sar burst into giggles. She throws her head back, laughing, lightly shoving at Ardis, who smirks at her reaction.

Staring at them, I can't help but smile until I realize I'm not the only one who watches them.

For a moment, it's as if the procession of Crowns has already started as people turn to watch the two descend the staircase.

It's obvious when Sar and Ardis realize the attention lies on them. Their shared smiles go stiff, their conversation halting. Ardis pulls away, putting distance between them, as he guides Sar. She flashes a hurt look at Ardis when he does, but it goes unanswered by Ardis as he looks off in the opposite direction.

Eyebrows knitted, I examine them.

They had more practice than anyone under people's gaze. Why did it matter now?

It isn't until I look at the crowd, finding disgruntled expressions and frowning lips, that I understand. Ardis's hesitation makes sense now.

The warmth from Sar's face vanishes, replaced with a neutral mask hiding the turmoil swirling in her eyes.

When the pair reaches the floor of the ballroom, they separate, Ardis taking two healthy steps away as Sar drops her hand from his arm. She gives him one last look before steeling her gaze and turning her back to him.

Ardis knocks his head back, sighing as he stares at the ceiling before following her.

I meet her halfway, grabbing her hand and squeezing it

once. She gives me a watery smile but doesn't acknowledge what has just played out on the steps for all to watch.

The soothing melody floating from the orchestra halts, and a new one takes its place. This one builds anticipation, the sounding percussion making the room shift their gazes toward the top of the staircase, spines straightening.

People move aside, parting a path down the center of the ballroom from the last step to the head table.

Lady Ivianna is the first of the Crowns to step through the entrance, her husband on her arm. She smiles graciously as she descends the stairs, waving to the crowd watching her below.

Bash follows a few paces behind with a wide grin, just as he did this afternoon during War Hour.

When they reach the bottom of the stairs, the crowd bows like a wave. As they approach our side of the ballroom, Sar and Ardis do the same, gesturing for me to mirror their movements.

Once they've passed, we rise to see Lord Rhen descending the stairs, his wife walking with him. A stern glower darkens his face, eyes narrow, as he peers out over the crowd surrounding him.

Jona and Eiko follow, both of whom look less than pleased to be dressed up and paraded through everyone.

The pattern continues as each court debuts their Crowns and Heirs through the ballroom, the crowd bowing as they pass.

When Lord Nicaise and his wife pass, with no Heir to trail them, I search the crowd for Visha. Surprised she didn't find herself in the procession, as she acted almost as if she were an honorary Heir.

Visha stands among the people, a distant expression on her face. Her mother presses to her side, whispering harshly into Visha's ear. The same purple glaze crosses Visha's eyes, and the corners of her mouth turn downward.

I'm jolted from my thoughts as Sar yanks me into another bow.

Lord Bralas has already made his way down the steps, Neith and Conlen strutting behind.

I bow but turn my head to Sar. Her face betrays nothing except for the tight line her lips are pulled into.

I anticipate Lord Gennady is the next to proceed in, just from the sound of his cane clanking against the marble floor. But when I turn to watch his arrival, my eyes move past him without my consent, landing on Evander, who follows.

Evander's eyes surf the onlookers as I examine him. His cobalt blue dress coat isn't the best color for him. It makes him look pale, makes the gold brown of his hair fade. But then his gaze locks onto me. A wide smile curves his lips, and my heart stutters. His eyes only leave me when he reaches the bottom and people drift in the way.

A startling silence settles over the ballroom, and for a moment, I think that even the orchestra has stuttered.

Standing at the staircase's landing, Torryn steps forward, and his persona shifts into place. The persona of a feared lord.

Torryn's pale skin stands out against the black of his hair and dress clothes. Embroidered into the cloth of his dress suit's jacket are silver swirls.

He looks good, but the part lodging my breath and making the crowd whisper is the silver crown sitting atop his wavy hair.

It's easy to forget Torryn's position as a lord. Decades younger than the other Crowns, he fit better among the Heirs, but now there is no denying his status—his power.

The crowd hesitates when Torryn reaches the bottom of the stairs, and for a moment, I worry they won't bow to him as they did the other Crowns. It's no secret the fear held for Torryn and the Court of Self, but would they go so far as to publicly deny him? But then the first person bows, and I sag in relief as everyone else follows suit, eager to avoid the gaze of the young lord.

When Torryn passes, I try to catch his attention, but his gaze doesn't waver, staring forward as he follows the procession. Every step he takes is rigid, like a snake coiled up tight before it attacks. Ready to attack any who dare tread near it, friend or foe alike.

CHAPTER 29

As the procession ends, the Crowns and Heirs stand in front of the head table. Lord Gennady raises a glass, mirrored by the rest of the room.

He makes a grand speech containing the word "peace" more times than I deem acceptable, but it evokes the reaction he's aiming for. The crowd watches with rapt attention, latching onto his every word, holding their breath at every pause.

Maybe my perception is jaded, but it all just sounds like a bunch of pretty words. Easy to say, harder to mean.

After a thunderous applause for Lord Gennady, the music kicks back up, and the crowd disperses. I take the opportunity to sink into the wall, blending into the background.

It isn't hard to disappear in the superficial frivolity. Everyone is focused on the Crowns and the Heirs. Once the dancing starts, graceful steps on the ballroom floor enrapture the room.

Even I can't deny how entrancing it all is. The way dresses fan out around their wearers as they spin away from their dance partners. How every movement seems to have been written for that exact moment's melody.

Without trying, my gaze wanders to Evander, as if every time I look away, he seems to move into my sight. He makes his rounds beside his father, greeting people with a charming smile that disarms. Every time he scans the room, I freeze, waiting for his eyes to beckon me from my safety zone.

But the clash of blue and gray is inevitable, and I couldn't end my stare if I wanted to. And, for some odd reason, I don't.

A small smile curls Evander's lips as he scans my dress, and I shrink under his examination. I rub my sweaty hands up and down the fabric, unsure of my appearance.

Evander waves me over, and I shake my head, letting out a small laugh that startles me. When I don't move to join him, Evander starts toward me.

Until someone steps in his way.

Visha.

Her hand slides along his arms, and I grit my teeth. She says something to make Evander give her a tight smile, but he shakes his head. His face flushes a deep red as he rubs the back of his neck.

Watching him, I can't decide if he's flattered or embarrassed. I blink slowly, eyes wide as I watch the interaction. A fleeting moment of triumph flashes when Evander finds me in the crowd once again but then she pulls him toward the dance floor. He shoots me an apologetic look over his shoulder as he follows.

If I needed confirmation of who Visha has set her sights on, I have it now.

Stepping into the middle of the crowded ballroom floor, Evander bows to Visha, and she curtsies before moving in closer.

I can't name the reason it bothers me, but now isn't the time for it. Evander is kind to me, and I don't need to read into it more than that.

Even so, I can't pull my fixation from Evander's hand on her waist. I don't even notice when someone slips up beside me on the wall. It isn't until a voice sounds next to me that I tear my eyes from the dancing couple.

"I see Visha's found her mark for tonight."

My head jerks to the right, landing on Bash, who stands beside me, one leg kicked up behind him to rest on the wall.

"You know about that?" I ask with wide eyes.

I assumed what I stumbled onto between Visha and her mother was secret, but obviously, I'm not the first to catch on.

Bash frowns down at me. "Of course I do. I've known Visha since we were children—she told me. The question is, how do you know?"

Eavesdropping. But I won't tell him that.

"I stumbled upon a conversation between her and her mother."

Bash winces and groans. "Ouch, I'm sure Visha handled that well."

I can't stop my snort. Exaggeration of the century.

"If you would consider well to be putting a knife to my throat."

Bash grins, a sparkle in his eye. He shakes his head, looking at Visha fondly. "Sounds like Visha." When the smile falls from Bash's face, I follow his gaze. "It's torture watching her do it. Reducing herself to this person who giggles to get their attention." He looks at me with a serious face. "Visha doesn't giggle."

"Then why does she do it?"

Bash inhales sharply. "Let's just say her mom, Nennirea, never got over being Lord Nicaise's spare. She wants her daughter to have the power she never had, even if she has to sacrifice her to do it."

"Why Evander, then? There are plenty of male Heirs. She gets on well with Neith"—I hesitate—"or you?"

Bash laughs loudly, drawing the attention of passersby. He covers the laugh with a cough, bringing a fist to his mouth as if forcing down the noise. Smiling, he explains in a low voice, "I'm not an option for what her mother wants. Visha knows that."

His answer confuses me, but Lady Ivianna waves him over before I can push the conversation. Bash gives me a reluctant look, as if I will single-handedly tell his mother, a Crown, to leave him alone.

I shake my head, holding back a smile as I gesture for him to go.

Left to meander through the crowd, I can't shake the stiffness from my shoulders. Passing smiles drop when their eyes meet mine. Searching across the room for a friendly face is an arduous task, and I lost Ardis and Sar among the crowd.

Maybe it's time to call it. I obviously am only alienating myself here.

Torryn hasn't left the head table since the procession, his eyes prevailing the sea of silk and velvet. A burgundy drink swirls in the glass chalice he grips onto like a lifeline. Each time his head dips to take a sip, he winces, swallowing the bitter liquid with a frown.

Is he really drinking *tonight* of all nights? This is supposed to be an opportunity to convince the Crowns. How can he do that drunk?

Then again, I was just debating abandoning the endeavor as well.

As if able to feel my eyes on him, Torryn glances in my direction. He gives me an appraising look, lingering at the sleeves of my dress. When our gazes meet, he raises a brow, arching it in my direction.

I mock curtsy, pulling my dress out around me. How ridiculous I must look trying to fit in among these people?

Once a street rat—always a street rat, no matter how you dress it up.

Without realizing, I step back, bumping into someone walking behind me.

Whirling on my heels, I'm a flurry of apologies. "My apologies, I hadn't—"

Lord Bralas sneers at me, nose wrinkled with distaste. "Ugh, *you*. Your presence is relentless."

Stepping back, I catch sight of Sar and Ardis on the other side of the room, both watching me. Unable to flag them down for assistance, I swallow the words itching to flay Lord Bralas alive, even more so knowing what he'd done to his own daughter.

But I'm supposed to be making allies, and anything other than begging for forgiveness wouldn't do that. This is what Torryn had called unwanted attention. So, even though Torryn would sooner burst into flames than apologize to Lord Bralas, that is exactly what I do.

"Lord Bralas. Please forgive me," I say, curtsying in subservience.

Lord Bralas looks around the room with narrowed eyes. His nostrils flare as he breathes in heavily. Then, with a fake smile, he mutters through gritted teeth, "Enjoy your glimpse of the finer life while you can, Valor. You will not have it for long."

A presence comes to rest behind me, a chest pressing against my back. Peering over my shoulder, I sag in relief at the sight of Evander.

Bralas stiffens, painting a passive expression across his face.

Evander stands strong behind me, his chest brushing my shoulder as he leans past me to cut Lord Bralas off, just loud enough for the three of us to hear.

"I'm afraid I must interrupt, as I had reserved this dance for Lysta. Likely for the better, though, isn't it, Lord Bralas?"

Halting my plans to slip away, Evander slips his fingers around my wrist. His eyes implore me to listen, his grip tightening.

Whipping my head to look at Evander, I open my mouth in protest but stop short when Lord Bralas rolls his eyes.

He sneers at me before saying, "If you can get her to stumble through a few beats of the song, it would surprise me to see it."

Evander nods as if he hadn't even heard Lord Bralas's word but pulls me away.

Out of Lord Bralas's earshot, I speak through a forced smile, aware of every set of eyes glued to us.

"He's right. I haven't danced in my life, let alone something choreographed like this. It would take me weeks to learn even one of these dances."

Evander smiles at me, using every ounce of his charm. "I thought you were going to trust me."

I grit my teeth, nodding tightly. "Yes, but—"

"Follow my lead, and I will not let you down."

Evander doesn't waver, waiting patiently for me to decide.

When I give him a small nod, he leads me further into the sea of dancing bodies.

Standing in the middle of the dance floor, pairs swirling to the surrounding music, I look up at Evander with wide eyes, heart pounding in my ears.

Evander watches me, moving slowly, waiting for me to protest again.

But I don't.

He takes my right hand, raising it until my palm faces him at shoulder height. He then places his palm to mirror my own, the heat of his hand warming my own. "Keep your hand here." I let him maneuver my position. "Use your other hand to grasp your skirts so you don't trip on them."

When I've done as he says, he nods. His other hand slides around the curve of my waist without warning, and I startle, stepping in closer to move away from the hand. But his hand stays on the small of my back, but now our chests breathe a few inches from each other.

Evander looks at me with an arched brow, making sure I'm ready to continue. He moves backward, pulling me with him.

The feeling of being so close to someone else is foreign in a way that feels like an uncomfortable itch I can't shrug. Like I'm going against everything I'd learned on Falland's streets, every survival instinct. The instinctual hyperawareness I've gained to combat passing pickpockets in crowded street corners screaming for me to break away.

Being within reaching distance left you vulnerable, and by standing so close to Evander, I can see the gold flecks in his blue eyes--I'm too close.

Each time he tugs me in a new direction, I go with him, and we circle the room.

It is entirely to Evander's credit I make it through one step into the next without making a fool of myself.

Unable to stand his focus for any longer, I move my gaze to the lapel of his suit, focusing on its gold decorative pieces. The weight of dozens of eyes following my every move becomes more obvious when snickers ring out after I step in the wrong direction.

Wincing, I open my mouth to apologize, but Evander only pulls me an inch closer. My cheeks get hot as I realize my palms are likely drenched in the same clammy sweat creeping down my spine.

How is this something people enjoyed?

What makes it worse is I'm not sure if the stares bother me more or the prolonged touch of someone else.

We fall into an easy rhythm, and I tear my eyes from my feet. Evander breaks our silence, just loud enough for me to hear, his mouth brushing the hair by my ear.

"What did my father say to you? While I was fighting during War Hour?"

Pulling my head back, my eyebrows furrow at his question. Of all the things he could ask, why is he concerned about my nonexistent conversation with his father?

Meeting his gaze, I notice a new rigidity in Evander's shoulders and jaw. His lips are pursed, eyes flickering between my own with an underlying sense of urgency.

When I hesitate, Evander prompts me again, hand tightening on my waist. Shaking my head in confusion at Evander's insistence, I think back to the discussion he is referring to. It had been mostly niceties.

"Nothing. Well, he mentioned it was your first time against Lord Rhen, and that he had things to get done before the Peace Ball as he was leaving."

Evander relaxes, letting out a deep breath, fanning warm heat across my flushed cheek. Flushed from the dancing— nothing to do with being in Evander's arms.

"What did you think he had told me?"

Evander lets out an awkward chuckle before muttering, "Nothing." At my unrelenting gaze, Evander continues, "You seemed confused and anxious all of a sudden. I thought perhaps he'd discussed the judgment hearing tomorrow."

Realization hit me. I had been rather anxious but less from Lord Gennady and more from Evander's place on the battlefield. I'd only just seen what could happen in these battles from Lord Rhen's fight with Bash—it hadn't been pretty.

Eyes drifting toward my feet, I reluctantly admit, "I find War Hour unsettling still." I shift under Evander's gaze. "You all fight each other with such ferocity—it feels as if one of you won't make it out of the battle alive." When Evander says nothing, I risk a glance in his direction. The blue of his eyes has turned stormy. "It's hard for me to remember everyone walks away in the end."

My throat tightens as I think of my Trial. How sure I had been I wouldn't walk away.

Evander nods, not letting his gaze move from mine, and it is as if he is trying to convey every ounce of understanding and comfort he has into one look.

"Spin," he says in a low tone, gripping my hand to whirl me out away from him.

My skirt fans around my ankles, and the crowd *ooohs* at the sight, swooning over the smooth move. Looking around, I see we are the only pair on the floor to have fallen out of rhythm, and it is all Evander and not just another part to the dance.

Evander pulls me back in, and my breath lodges in my throat. Looking away, I scramble for something to ease the tension clouding the space between us.

"You dance well," I say, mentally groaning at my lack of subtlety. "You're making a complete beginner look competent. Visha and you looked like the perfect couple out there, obviously because you both know how to dance and are comfortable with each other—"

I notice the mirthful glint in Evander's eyes. "What? I'm just curious. Do all the Heirs receive dance classes?" I try to smile, hoping my question will land as teasing.

He doesn't need to know how closely I watched him dance with Visha.

Evander doesn't take the bait.

A grin splits across his face, his hand tightening around my own. "Do I sense a bit of jealousy? I'm more honored than I can convey."

I force a laugh. "Of course not. Why would I be . . . ?"

His smile only grows.

I pull back slightly, only to be pulled forward by Evander. "I'm not," I say indignantly. "I was merely curious if Bash was also a good enough dancer to take me for a spin about the room and make it look like I can dance."

Evander arches an eyebrow, a smirk replacing his smile. He lowers his head to speak in my ear, and his lips brush against my hair. "There's a compliment in there somewhere, but I can't get past you trying to use Bash to make me jealous."

Nose turned upward I answer stiffly, "I don't know what you are talking about. Bash and I had an interesting conversation earlier, and I merely wish to continue."

Evander smiles, glancing over my shoulder. "Yeah, I saw you. But I wouldn't get your hopes too high on that front."

Narrowing my eyes and scrunching my nose, I pull away from him, but Evander only pulls me closer. "What is that supposed to mean? You don't think anyone would be interested in me?"

Evander looks to the ceiling as he chuckles, shaking his head. "Oh, anyone could, and many will, just not Bash."

"And why not?" I ask, trying to push down the hurt.

"Because regardless of how stunning you look right now, Bash is not interested in women."

Oh.

My conversation with Bash rings in my ears, and I realize what he had been trying to say earlier. It had gone completely over my head. Now it makes sense why he isn't an option for Visha.

"I was not aware," I say, blushing.

"I assumed from how offended you were."

I can't meet his eyes. I laugh awkwardly, trying to blow off the uneven ground between us, but Evander doesn't let me.

The music slows, signaling its coming end, and I'm ready to make a less than dignified exit.

But then Evander spins me, before dipping me low. Our faces are a whisper apart, and he stares deeply into my eyes.

"I can't imagine a world where you would need to feel less than compared to someone else, because I am entirely and unequivocally entranced by you, Lysta."

CHAPTER 30

Evander bows when the music ceases, taking my hand in his and brushing his lips against my knuckles. My cheeks flame and I look away, squirming under the gazes scrutinizing us. I open my mouth trying to find the words to respond to him, but I'm saved when someone steps in asking to borrow the Heir. Evander spares me an apologetic look and murmurs he'll find me before following one of his father's generals.

My heart races like I'm fighting for my life, and Evander is to blame. I had only set out to make allies in the capital, but with every moment spent in Evander's company that boundary seems to fade.

Still in a daze, I barely make it off the dance floor when someone grabs my arm in an iron grip, nails biting into my skin. I gasp, trying to wrench myself from their hold, but they stay locked on.

"Don't make a scene, dear," a sickeningly sweet voice says in my ear.

She pulls me along, wrapping her arm around me so that, to others, it looks like we are enraptured in a friendly conversation. Glancing at her with wide eyes, I recognize the shorter woman.

Visha's mother. Nennirea.

The middle-aged woman gives me a smile that makes my stomach drop. It tells me everything her words do not. "We haven't had the pleasure of meeting. I'm Nennirea. The Lord of Virtue's sister. You know my daughter, Visha."

She pulls me further from the center of the room until we hover on the outskirts. Out of direct sight or earshot of the majority of the party.

"I'll be direct with you, dear. My daughter is positioning herself to be the next wife of the Lord of Truth. For that to happen, I need you to give him . . . a wide berth."

My jaw drops, and I look around.

Is this really happening?

I laugh in disbelief.

Pain shoots through my face as my teeth pierce my lower lip, followed by the metallic taste of blood. My head recoils back, flinching away from the woman who backhanded me. Bringing my fingers to my mouth, I wince as I touch the raw skin—a split lip.

She actually *struck* me.

Without my permission, she brings my head to where she stands. Under the guise of examining my lip, she hisses in my face. "You laugh now. But you need my brother, Lord Nicaise, on your side in your endeavors against Lord Drytas. I have his ear. Remember that next time you feel like throwing yourself at Truth's Heir."

Ripping out of her grip, I bolt away, planning to put as much distance between me and the woman as possible. Peering back over my shoulder, the woman waves at me before disappearing into the crowd around her.

These people—do they really think that this is why I'm

here? I want no part in their self-absorbed dramatics and political maneuvers.

Slipping out onto the balcony from the stifling ball room, I can't help but sigh as the cool salt air whispers through the fabric of my skirts and across my sweaty skin. The ocean breeze sings as it rushes up the sandy dunes, kicking up onto the stonework of the capital's walls.

In this moment, I want nothing more than to feel the water rushing past me, soaking through my dress, and cooling my heated skin.

But I can't swim, and I have no desire to drown.

Headed for the balcony, I stumble when my heel catches a raised stone. I kick the shoe off, flinging it from my foot, until it hits the balcony with a satisfying smack. The other quickly follows as I shout.

A deep chuckle sounds behind me, and I jump backward, bumping into the edge of the balcony. My heart races, my hand coming up to smother it through my chest.

Torryn perches atop the stone ledge, resting his back against the castle with his feet kicked up in front of him. An empty chalice lays knocked over on the ground. Whatever alcohol it held now drained. His head rolls around as he looks between me and the ocean.

It would seem he succeeded in drinking himself into a stupor.

Swinging his feet off the ledge, Torryn faces me, giving me a wide, unbridled smile that catches me off guard. "You lasted longer than I thought you would," he says, as if it is his own personal achievement.

I don't move to close the distance between us, eyeing Torryn with a renewed suspicion, but can't stop myself from scolding him. "I'm not sure you should be that close to the edge with how much you've had to drink."

Torryn's grin only stretches wider.

It isn't a bad smile. In fact, it seems to void his otherwise brooding, angry aura. I wish he would smile like that more—not at me, of course. Just in general.

"Worried about me?" he teases, shifting onto his feet with a slight stumble. Moving toward me, Torryn walks in far from what I consider a straight line.

"Do I need to be?" I ask, letting out a deep sigh.

As angry as I am with him, there's something sad about his quiet somberness. So, instead of yelling, I quietly add, "You only had to play nice with the other courts for one night, Torryn. One night. And you are drunk and absent an hour into the ball."

"I am not drunk, but Trials, I wish I were," Torryn mumbles, completely unconvincing of the former statement.

The declaration throws me off guard, and I can't help but let a snort of air rush through my nose. It's barely a laugh. But Torryn latches onto it, turning to look at me as if I'm the one behaving oddly.

Now much closer than he was a minute ago, Torryn stares at my lips, narrowing his eyes as if they've personally attacked him. His softened glare seems to flicker with the moonlight before they darken, a storm raging behind them. A frown curls his lips.

"Who did this?" Torryn growls, bringing a hand to my face.

My split lip. Courtesy of Visha's mother.

I flinch before his skin can touch mine, and a stab of hurt crosses his face.

It's not as if I thought he planned to hurt me. It's just a reflex to someone being so close, to someone reaching for my face. But before I can assure him as much, he moves back, giving me space.

Torryn's jaw clenches as he looks toward the party floating

on without us. His gaze is unfocused, and from this close, I can see the rosy tint to his cheeks.

"Tell me who did this, and I will take care of it. Anyone who thought they could lay a hand on you should fear for their life."

My eyes widen at his words, and I can't help but blink back at him.

There is no way he is truly this defensive of me after how he has been acting the past week. It must be the alcohol, I rationalize. There is no other reason for it.

When Torryn turns to march toward the ballroom, I pull him back. "It was an accident. It's just a split lip, and it doesn't even hurt."

A small lie to prevent Torryn from going in there to start the next war. Not a bad plan for if tomorrow goes awry, but perhaps a decision that should be made *sober*.

Torryn stumbles, unsteady on his feet, when I pull him, and his hip knocks into the balcony.

Now that he's even closer to me, I can feel his breath against my forehead. I don't smell the alcohol, having expected it to be oozing from his pores and coating his breath. Instead, sea water, amber, and a deeper woodsy scent overwhelms my senses.

Torryn's lips purse into a thin line, as if holding them tight will keep him from ever having to divulge what's running through his mind.

He leans in closer, ducking so our noses are nearly touching.

He's drunk, I remind myself. *He wouldn't be doing this if he were sober.*

I place my palm over the center of his chest. Nudging him back, I increase the space between us.

"Stop. I'll make it better," he whispers, eyes heavy lidded. "You've hurt enough."

Is he truly planning on kissing me? What, did he think I'm

so pitiful out here during the ball that I need some pity attention?

But then there's a rush of air across my lips, and I freeze. Torryn's breath caresses my lips, bathing the sensitive skin with warm heat.

And then the pain is gone.

I blink at him, processing the shift before the realization hits me. Could he heal? But he already has a power from the Court of Change. . .

I bring my hand to my split lip, and the slice is still there. When I pull my hand away, tiny specs of blood tint my finger.

He hadn't healed me. But any lingering pain has vanished. Before, my mouth stung with just a salty breeze, but now, it's gone.

He took away my pain.

Torryn looks down the bridge of his nose at me, obviously pleased with what he has done. In his drunken state, Torryn revealed another one of his powers. Something he had insisted upon avoiding from the beginning.

"You know, he's probably so proud of himself—dressing you in his court's colors." Torryn leans towards me conspiratorially. "Little does he know that pale blue is my favorite color."

I look down at my dress and then back at him. "Who—the dress—"

My mental spiral is broken when Sar opens the door, popping her head through.

A question is apparent on her face, but I ignore it. Leaving Torryn at the edge of the balcony, I move to slip past her, but she stops me with a hand at my wrist.

"Is everything okay?"

"No, he's drunk. It is not okay."

Sar's face darkens, looking at Torryn with a searching gaze. She shakes her head before glaring at me. "That's not possible."

I huff out an irritated laugh. "I assure you it is. He just accidentally outted one of his powers to me."

"No, Lysta. It's not possible. Torryn *doesn't* drink."

Torryn rubs his thumb across his lower lip, wincing and groaning. "You lied, Lysta. It did hurt." At the sight of Sar, his eyes widen before he shouts her name.

I turn to Sar, gesturing at Torryn pointedly. "You were saying?" I chance one last look at Torryn before slipping out the door back into the ball.

CHAPTER 31

Consciousness is fleeting come morning despite how much I battle the drugged like drowsiness. In the lulls between nightmares, at my closest to being awake, I remember I'm supposed to be somewhere. That I shouldn't be wrapped up in bed with the sun beating on me through the windows.

But the call to sleep beckons me into its embrace, pulling me further into the endless chasm of nothingness.

Awareness returns to me as a splitting ache bisects my brain. Pressing my fingertips to my forehead, I try to relieve the pressure built in my head to no avail.

Something is wrong. And someone is pounding at my door.

Groaning into my pillow, I ignore the sound until it breaks through my half-conscious state. The room spins as I sit up. Bracing my head against the heel of my hand, I close my eyes to ease the sensation. I have no such luck because, as I stand from the bed, my room tilts sideways.

Trying to remember how my night ended, I catch swirls of memories that don't make any sense. Like a heavy fog has settled in my mind, clouding me from remembering things clearly. I hadn't drunk any alcohol, other than the one sip by accident. Ardis had pointed out a safe drink for the night, and I had stuck to it.

Something is wrong, and the banging won't stop—inside my head and on the door.

It isn't until I look out the window, noting the sun's high position in the sky that I remember the judgment hearing. Hopping into action, I flitter around the room, tossing on the first clothes I find. When my name accompanies the next round of pounding, I throw open the door.

Evander stands with flushed cheeks and wide eyes. He pants and gestures down the hall. "Just ran—from meeting—you're late." His words come out raspy. "Lord Drytas. He's here."

"LYSTA, you've deigned to grace us with your presence," Drytas says from his seat at the table. "At last."

His tone bites like a lethal strike.

How late am I? Have I missed my chance to say my piece?

My racing heart stammers in my chest, as if it clenched alongside my fists at the sight of Valor's reigning ruler. It doesn't matter that I knew I would face Drytas once again. I still feel a chill move down my spine at his crooked smile.

When Drytas leans back in his chair, opening his arms wide to gesture to the group, I try to pull my gaze from him. But his eyes crackle with excitement and anticipation. He can't hide how he takes pleasure in this moment. He turns to the rest of the table. "I can only apologize for any inconvenience Lysta's presence here may have caused . . . or her *lies*."

"I have lied about nothing—" I start to say, eyes searching, pleading, with those sitting at the table.

"You have not been given permission to speak!" Lord Bralas

growls from further down the table. "Considering the allegations you have made against your lord, I'd have imagined today would be a priority for you. If we were in as much danger as you claim."

My face burns at Lord Bralas's insinuation, and I open my mouth to argue, to explain.

But Lord Gennady catches my eye from the end of the table where he gives two quick shakes of his head.

Fight the battles you can win. End the battles you can't.

At least I still have an ally among the group. I bite my tongue. Maybe now is not the moment to stand against the two lords, but I *will* say my piece before this hearing finishes.

Drytas looks me up and down with a sneer. "You should be ashamed of yourself. Betraying your own court. You treasonous—"

"What did you just say to her?" Torryn growls from behind me.

Looking over my shoulder, I can't help but let out a deep breath at the sight of Torryn behind me, Evander a few steps behind him.

Evander went to get Torryn after me. If it were any other moment, I would have allowed the smile threatening to curl my lips. Evander had helped Torryn—retrieving someone he didn't even trust. Because he knew I needed him.

My stomach drops.

Why wasn't Torryn here in the first place? If this meeting is as important as he led me to believe—he should have been here. He should have been the one to come for me.

Coming to stand next to me, Torryn looks just as ragged as I do, as if he had too only just woken up.

Thinking back to the night before, I can't remember anything past being on the balcony. I'd wanted some fresh air after my interaction with Nennirea. And Torryn had been there, drunk.

My heart rate picks up in speed as my mind races to put together what had happened. Sar had insisted Torryn didn't drink, yet he had been completely out of it—acting nothing like himself from the way he reacted to me on the balcony.

I specifically didn't drink any alcohol, yet I can't remember anything of how the night ended. The only lingering impression of the evening is the split on my lip and the raging headache seeming to wreak havoc inside my skull.

Had someone done something to us? By drug or by power?

Lord Bralas claps mockingly as he stands to walk the room. "Ah, Torryn. I see you managed to tear yourself from your lover long enough to grace us with your presence. I think we can all safely assume why you both arrived equally late and"—Lord Bralas pointedly looks us up and down—"disheveled."

I pale as blood drains from my face. The people sitting at the table shuffle awkwardly, and Neith chuckles. My expression falls as I realize what is happening.

This hearing relies on reputation and credibility, and someone has set us up to destroy mine.

I look at Torryn, eyes pleading for him to say something. His jaw clenches, muscles tensing as he levels a hard glare in Drytas's direction. But he says nothing.

I find Evander's gaze over Torryn's shoulder and his eyes are blank. Nothing in his expression tells me what to do or what he is thinking. Instead, he walks past Torryn and down the length of the table, then settles in his chair beside Lord Gennady.

What is wrong with him? He himself had found me alone in my room. Why did his walk across the room feel like a shifting of sides?

I stumble through an explanation. "We weren't—I'm not —" But no one can hear me over their own voices.

Lord Bralas comes to a stop in front of me, hands clasped behind his back. He leans forward, hissing at me. "Oh, save it, girl. You're only piecing the story together for us all. Lord Drytas has already provided his account of what happened in Falland, and to think we almost believed your scheme." He peers around the table, a hideous smirk forming. "Just the manipulations of a lord's whore."

In the time a chorus of gasps echoes around the room, Torryn pushes past me, grabbing Lord Bralas's throat in his hand. Shoving the man back until his legs hit the end of the table, Torryn bares his teeth in Bralas's face.

"Treaty or not, Bralas. Call her that again, and I will bring war upon you myself."

No one in the room does as much as breathe, all waiting in anticipation of how this will play out. As much as they discredit him, they all fear Torryn. Trialing more than once is not something they take lightly, and it's the only thing keeping Bralas from starting something right here.

Lord Bralas's face pales several shades but does not falter under Torryn's grip. "Sore spot, Lord Torryn?"

Before Torryn can react to Bralas's jab, Lord Gennady interrupts with a commanding tone. "Lord Torryn."

Torryn flinches but does not let go. Glaring at Lord Bralas as if his gaze could rip him in half. Torryn leans forward, his knuckles whitening as he squeezes Bralas's throat. He hisses something in Bralas's ear before shoving him backward.

Lord Bralas catches himself on the table, coughing as he rubs at his throat. "Well, I would say that confirms what Lord Drytas explained."

I glance between the Crowns, some who nod at Lord Bralas's words.

What had Drytas said in our absence? What tale had he spun to make himself out to be the victim and Torryn and I to be the aggressors? Did Torryn's defense of me just sentence us to the wrong outcome?

Lord Rhen answers with a pensive glare. "Does that mean we end the inquisition here?"

The words bubble out of my chest, erupting into the room before anyone can answer. "You have not heard me speak. After all I have been through so I could warn you—so you could help Falland, and you'll rule without hearing both sides?"

Lord Drytas scoffs at my words, but Lady Ivianna sends him a withering scowl. Her face pinched the moment Lord Bralas accused me of having been seduced by Lord Torryn. Solutions and compromises echo across the table, but her eyes never leave mine. After a moment of hesitation, she stands, drawing the room's attention.

"I say we bring in the Truthsayer. What does it hurt to hear the same thing twice if we are confident in Lord Drytas's words?" Lady Ivianna turns to Lord Gennady. "With your blessing, Lord Gennady, as he is of your court."

The *Truthsayer*?

Several faces in the room pale at her suggestion, sending concerned expressions between Heir and Crown.

"Of course," Lord Gennady says. "As with my court's name, I want nothing more than us to find the truth in all this." At this, Lord Gennady levels a look in Lord Drytas's direction.

When the table discusses Lady Ivianna's suggestion, Torryn pulls me to look at him. "I didn't know the Truthsayer was here, or I would have prepped you for meeting him."

I can't even listen to what he is saying.

In a shaking voice, I ask, "What are they talking about? What did Drytas tell them?"

Torryn's face hardens, and he looks to the ceiling in frustration. Moving to sweep his fingers through the top of his hair, Torryn sighs. "I don't know what he said, but I have no doubt he is spinning it to look like we violated the treaty. But if they bring the Truthsayer, then he can't get away with it."

His words do nothing to comfort me. A crease forms in between my eyebrows as I look over his shoulder at the table. Evander sits, his face passive as the chaos unravels around him.

"Lysta, listen to me," Torryn insists, pulling back my attention. "The Truthsayer can make it so no one can question what is truth or lies."

Of all the powers that I've seen in the capital, I have yet to hear of one from the Court of Truth. But this must be one of them. But why would just another power have its own title? Truthsayer sounds ominous and official.

My eyes search the table, landing on Lord Drytas. Sitting with his hands clasped on the table in front of him, Drytas leans back in his chair. Nothing about him portrays anything but cool composure. As if sensing my attention, Drytas turns his head, meeting my gaze. He gives me a grin, nodding to me, before turning away.

If Torryn is right about the Truthsayer, this will not end well for Lord Drytas. But if it is true, why isn't he more worried than he is? Shouldn't he be fighting tooth and nail against bringing in the Truthsayer?

CHAPTER 32

The Truthsayer does not bow. Not to Lord Gennady, whose court he belongs, nor any other Crown. Instead, he offers a half-hearted tilt of his head as he passes each court—acknowledging them but not submitting. It is a new dynamic I've yet to encounter in the capital, but the Crowns don't blink twice at the behavior.

In fact, the Crowns don't make eye contact with him at all. As if carved from ice, the room is frozen in place, tension weighing heavily.

I've seen the man before, always at Lord Gennady's side. He's younger than most of the Crown's—maybe thirty or so. His black hair is longer, dangling in limp strands around his features. He'd stood to the side of the viewing booth during War Hour with a scowl the entire time. Watching me like, at any moment, I planned to attack his lord.

I had thought he was a guard.

The man strides across the silent room with the same sneer, and I fidget in the chair I've been given. Placed front and center for all the Crowns and Heirs to watch as I meet with the Truthsayer for the first time.

No one explains how this man will pull the truth from me. Could he see into my mind like Torryn? Discover my lies from within. Did he torture secrets out of you?

Just as I finish asking the question in my mind, Torryn answers.

Once he touches your skin, you will only be able to tell the truth. It will not hurt, but most find it a disconcerting feeling. The Crowns are terrified of him.

My eyes flick to Torryn, who has taken his seat as the Court of Self's lord. Just as before, the seat next to him is vacant.

I consider scolding him for skimming my thoughts without my permission, but I'm too worried about how this will play out. I need every bit of help I can get.

Wrinkling my brows, I frown.

It didn't explain how the Truthsayer did it. Would it make my thoughts just flow out of me? I already planned to tell the truth.

Lysta, I mean, it will be impossible for you to tell a lie.

Oh.

It explains the room's apprehension of the man. Wielding the truth is a weapon that could start and end wars without ever setting foot on a battlefield.

The older man stops in front of me, blocking Torryn from my view. He doesn't greet me, but from the way he shoots disdain over his shoulder, I think it has more to do with his dislike of the Crowns rather than me.

Lord Gennady chirps in when the Truthsayer does nothing to introduce himself. "Lysta, this is Severin, my second in command—besides Evander, of course. He is the last remaining Truthsayer and has been for the last few decades. A rare gift of the Trials indeed."

Meeting Severin's dark eyes, I tilt my head in greeting, murmuring a soft, "Thank you for coming to help."

The Truthsayer's eyes widen at my gratitude, the corner of his mouth twitching, before his eyebrows furrow deeper. Severin pulls a black leather glove off one hand slowly, bunching it in his other fist. "Where—may I—" he asks, gesturing to my body, and I realize he is asking for permission on where to touch me.

I offer him my hand, and he hesitates in taking it. His eyes flick to the table of Crowns and Heirs before reluctantly sliding his hand into my own. Looking at me with sad eyes, he offers a whispered, "I'm sorry."

Despite the anxiety swirling in me, I offer him a small smile, squeezing his hand. What has his power done in his lifetime to make him fear using it so?

Turning back to the Crowns, the Truthsayer nods, and the interrogation begins. One by one, the Crowns take their turns asking me a question.

"Why did you come to the capital?"

"To stop Lord Drytas from harming Falland any further. I was told I would find help here."

"You were told by who?"

"Lord Torryn."

"And what did Lord Torryn do or say to convince you to testify against Lord Drytas?"

I look to Torryn with cinched brows, frowning. "He promised me he could help the people of Falland. That he knew how to stop what Lord Drytas was doing."

Ask it, I repeat to myself. Begging for them to ask what will tell them what they need to know.

"And what was Lord Drytas doing?"

I sigh, letting out the pressure hovering over me since I first stepped into the grand hall of the Court of Valor.

"He forces Untrialed citizens to Trial against their will. He manipulated the consent requirement by putting a knife to my throat. And when the Trial collapsed, he made plans to attack the other courts in order to use their Trials to build an army."

The room is still. No one turns to look at Drytas for a moment. Not until his outraged shouts fill the room.

"That is not possible. She is lying."

Lady Ivianna turns to Drytas slowly. "Even you know she can't under the influence of the Truthsayer."

"Then, she must be manipulating it somehow." Seemingly shocked, Drytas gives the room a contemplative look. "Her power—from the Court of Valor's Trial. It was a protective shield of sorts. She must be able to use it to block the Truthsayer."

When all eyes move to me, I freeze. Suddenly being analyzed at the revelation of my power. All this time, everything I did to keep it a secret, and Drytas has just negated it.

"It doesn't work like that," I insist, but none of the faces looking back at me seem convinced. "He's trying to worm his way out now he's been caught."

"Then prove it." Lord Drytas leans in, pointing his ringed finger at me. "Make. Her. Lie."

I wait for someone to deny his outrageous request, but the other Crowns don't dismiss it as quickly. Instead, waving for the questioning to continue.

"Lysta, please repeat the following sentences. 'My name is Lysta. I am from the Court of Valor. I am Untrialed.'"

I repeat it without thought.

The room goes silent. My heart stops in my chest.

"Lysta, do you understand what just happened?" Lord Gennady asks in a deathly whisper.

"I'm able to lie—" Panic creaks into my tone, and I look at him with wide eyes. "I swear my power isn't capable of this. I'm not even using it."

"You have just shown you can manipulate the Truthsayer's influ—"

"This is outrageous." Torryn moves to stand beside me. "You know she's telling the truth, Lord Gennady."

Lord Gennady shakes his head. "Regardless of what I think, we need evidence."

Lord Nicaise stands. "Use the Truthsayer on Lord Drytas. If he's telling the truth, and Lysta can manipulate its impact on her, then he can tell us again what happened and then also try to tell us a lie."

Lord Drytas stands, strides sweeping across the room. Approaching the Truthsayer, he takes his hand before turning to the group. "Lord Torryn has reached out to me many times before, wishing to face the Court of Valors Trial. As within my rights as lord, I have denied him. And now we've learned he does not take no for an answer. It seems Lysta is how he planned to dethrone me. After finding his way into my court, he poisoned her against me, hoping by removing me from power, he would have access to Valor's Trial. Lord Torryn infiltrated my court, seduced one of my citizens into committing treason. We have every reason to believe Lord Torryn is trying to disrupt the power balance."

Shock floods my body, and I freeze where I sit only inches from Torryn. He tenses next to me.

Had it all been a lie? Or is Lord Drytas able to lie for the same anomaly that I can?

Then, as if sensing what would be asked next, Lord Drytas continues. "My name is Drytas, and I am the Lord of the Court of Valor, and I am—" He chokes as if trying to force out the lie. "I can't say it. I can't lie."

This sparks an argument among the Crowns, but it all fades into the background. The only sound I can hear is my heartbeat in my ears.

Injustice had been happening in Falland long before I'd been born, but I never questioned Torryn's sudden desire to help.

He'd been prodding my anger all along, stirring up feelings that eventually led me right to his plan.

My stomach swoops with each realization.

He'd been so upset the day I found him sorting through the remaining shards of the Trial's entrance. He'd been piecing it together and had led me away when I started asking questions. Distracting me from what he was doing.

I thought I had been annoying him.

"Who knows what length Lord Torryn will go to in order to garner more power? He testified against his own father for his crown. Do any of us really think he wouldn't do ten times worse to us?"

When I look at Torryn, he stares back at me with dark dead eyes. There is no anger or guilt in them—not a single emotion passes.

I can't stop the quiver in my lip as I look at him. Waiting for him to argue against them or explain that Drytas is wrong.

Lord Gennady speaks, a quiet whisper from the end of the table. "What of Lysta? Even if the things you accuse Lord Torryn of are true, which I am not entirely certain we have all the information, I do not believe Lysta has culpability in this."

"I believe as a citizen of my court, her punishment is up to my sole discretion, is it not, Lord Gennady?" Drytas sneers.

"Which would be?"

"A punishment fitting this level of treason."

"Execution?" Lady Ivianna gasps, eyes wide.

My heart races as I swallow a cry of outburst. The room falls silent. Hands shaking, I fist them in my dress's skirts. My vision goes blurry, and I blink, trying to clear my line of sight only for tears to escape. Chasing down the flushed skin of my cheeks.

Execution. I'll be sentenced to be killed?

How could they let Drytas get away with this? They were so focused in on what role Torryn has in this. They were completely ignoring what Drytas has done. No one noticed Drytas left out all the details of his own wrongdoing, instead pointing all the blame on Torryn.

They are just assuming that if Torryn had manipulated things, everything else we said is automatically untrue.

"That's outrageous—" Lord Gennady begins, slamming a fist into the table.

Evander stands, and my heart thumps in my chest. He has been silent the entire hearing, avoiding eye contact with me. "Lord Drytas, your right to sole discretionary punishments was rendered obsolete the moment Lysta stepped into the capital. She has lived in these walls and communed among us all as if a citizen of the capital. Not of the Court of Valor."

"And what is your point, boy?" Lord Drytas spews, eyeing Evander with pinched brows and a curled lip.

Evander addresses the table. "By the treaty, any punishments must be voted and sealed by the majority of the Crowns. It isn't just up to you."

Understanding the meaning of Evander's words, my stomach swoops with the early fluttering of hope. A political loophole.

Lord Bralas steps in. "That law is meant to concern when crimes have been committed while capital is in session, not when the crime has occurred within a lord's Cour—"

Evander shakes his head. "Yes, but the exact wording covers any punishments delivered while capital is in session."

Lord Gennady quickly grasps onto my only chance. "So, it is up to a vote, then?"

Evander gives his father a hard stare before sitting. When I finally catch his eyes, I mouth a thank you.

He nods, turning back to the table.

"I hardly think it appropriate for Lord Torryn to be voting on such an occasion," Lord Bralas adds.

"And unless you would like to render the treaty void, you cannot stop me from doing so," Torryn growls out, snapping at Lord Bralas.

Drytas stands, circling the table with one finger pressed to his lips. "How about a compromise? If Lysta steps foot in Falland again, I may pass judgment as I see fit. Otherwise, she is banished from Valor. Would my fellow lords and lady agree to that?"

CHAPTER 33

My eyes mist over, forewarning the hot, heavy tears threatening to fall with my every blink. Storming from the room, I twist my lower lip between my teeth, pulling on a blank mask, hoping if I deny my emotions, the brimming tears won't betray me now.

I will not give them my tears as their victory.

"Lysta, dear. You've forgotten something."

Drytas's voice stops me dead in my tracks.

Turning slowly, I face the cruel lord, who follows after me.

"You left something *important* in Falland before you left. I figured you might want it now, since you'll never step foot there again . . . alive at least."

If he expected his threat to shock me, he's sorely mistaken. There's nothing more he can do to me . . . nothing more he can take from me. He is right about one thing . . . because of him, I have my power, and now, he'll never have control over me again.

Or so I think—until he reaches out, a chain hanging from between his fingers.

I furrow my brows, confused by the object he dangles in front of me. Then I catch sight of the pendant, and my mouth drops. My heart shatters, and Drytas practically dances on the pieces as he sees my heartbroken reaction.

Reaching out, I snatch the necklace from his fingers, searching the face to confirm it's whose I think it is. *Doireann.*

"It may be a little worse for wear than you left it. Maybe if you hadn't abandoned *it,* it would still be with you."

He isn't talking about the necklace.

The rest of the Crowns and Heirs file out of the meeting room, stopping when they see Drytas standing before me.

Drytas doesn't pay them any mind, leaning toward me conspiratorially. With a smirk, he whispers, "I hung it on Falland's wall in case you came back looking for it but looks like you've been too preoccupied."

A moan of agony escapes my lips, and I stagger, almost falling to my knees. Doireann.

He's killed Doireann.

Drytas catches me against him, and I start to fight him off until he hisses, "Stop. You're going to turn around, walk away, and I better not hear even a whisper of your name near my plans again, or the old lady's friend. Thoman, I believe it was. He'll be next."

Falling to the ground, I stare up at Lord Drytas with wide eyes. Footsteps approach from behind him, Torryn and Evander moving toward me, but I hold up a hand, waving them off.

The crowd of Crowns and Heirs watch as I stand on shaky legs, before turning and walking away. They don't see the sobs that shake my shoulders, or the tears I blink back.

No one calls after me. No one rushes to follow me as I flee. I try to swallow the storm swirling inside.

Outside. I need to get outside.

I need to leave.

My breath shudders through my chest, feeling much as if someone is gripping my heart in their hands and squeezing. Out of their sight, I stumble into a wall. I clutch my throat, clenching my eyes shut as tears slide down my cheeks, like fire melting ice.

My mind races, and I can't help but bring my fists to press against my temples, trying to stop the onslaught of questions circling in my head.

Everything I had done. Everything I came here to do—all meant nothing. And while I was here, playing dress up and dancing with Heirs, Doireann has been dead.

None of the guards manning the entrance dare stop me when I flee the capital, but then again, do I really serve any use to them now?

More so, is there anything left here for me?

I'm not so naïve as to think the games they played here in the capital were black and white. Everyone was looking out for their own interests, playing along with the others when it bene-fited themselves. But when is the shade of morally gray too murky for me to wade through?

Torryn had obviously had more to gain from helping than I assumed. Here, I thought he was interested in rooting out the corruption within the courts, and in reality, he'd been only clearing out a space for him to dig in even deeper.

He hadn't cared what I'd risked in this—who I'd risked. Regardless of what happened in the judgment hearing, Falland is still in as much danger as they were before I'd left, if not more. And part of me blames Torryn right along with Drytas.

Here, I'd left in some misguided belief I could make things better, and now, I could never go back under fear of execution. My only friend, I've left behind. And now he's left to the whim of Lord Drytas, to be used as a pawn in a war no one saw coming.

The sob I've been suffocating myself holding back bursts from my throat, echoing into the empty air around me.

I am hopelessly, and entirely, alone. If I'm forced to return to Falland, I will not survive long enough to beg for my life. Drytas played his part so well. Feigning the merciful leader who would allow for banishment to be sufficient punishment for treason, all while using it to hide his true plan.

I didn't know to look for those who would play me the fool.

I trudge away from the capital until I have nothing left to cry. And when the last of my tears have dried on my cheeks and my breathing has evened from my hiccuping sobs, I sit, letting my hair fall into my face.

Sitting in the grassy field where I'd woken up only a couple weeks ago, I breathe in the smell of dead leaves and dirt. I like the aroma more than the odorless scent of the capital.

Palming Doireann's necklace, I flip it over, reading the words that surround its edge.

No bravery without fear. No strength without struggle.

Lying back, I trace the wall of trees separating me from the rest of the continent. My eyelids droop just as the last tear falls, trickling into my ear. The only thing on my mind when I drift off—what do I do now?

I stare at the sword levitating in the air above my head for a couple of heartbeats before I realize I'm no longer dreaming.

Mind no longer muddled in the space between sleep and reality, a new terror races through me at the threat looming above.

My sleep-groggy eyes are now wide awake, watching with

fearful anticipation for the blade to move even a hair's width closer to where the pulse beats in my neck. The silver blade shines as it catches the light of the dying sun and the early arrival of the moon. Trembling in midair like a weapon wielded in the hand of an unresolved attacker.

My fingers twitch at my sides, ready to throw up a shield between my skin and the tip of the weapon.

Listening earnestly, there's no way to tell how many attackers stand nearby, poised to kill. Or maybe one is all it would take? One assassin who is levitating a sword above me, ready to end it all. It isn't hard to recognize this power as I've seen it my whole life as one of the gifts of the Court of Valor's Trial.

As much as I'm certain Lord Drytas would salivate at the opportunity to be the one to execute me, I know he wouldn't jeopardize the rest of his plan to do it.

I can't stay like this. It will only be a short time before the attacker realizes I am awake and is pushed to act. Freezing up is only prolonging the inevitable fight.

The second I raise my hands, spreading a disc of shield in between me and the sword, the blade is moving toward me, attacking the shield with renewed vengeance. While before it had sat hesitantly, it now flourishes in its siege against me.

Rolling out of its direct path, I stumble, pivoting to scan the horizon for my attacker. Without yielding in my defensive shield, I search for the assassin.

A figure stands in the distance, merely a dark outline in the sunset's glow. From the height and muscular physique, I assume a man but can't guarantee it.

I walk forward. Steps hasten into a jog before surging to a full out sprint. Barreling toward the man who tried to kill me. They had seen my power anyway, so there is no point in cowering now.

I halve the distance between us, protecting myself with my shield. It's still impossible to make out the features or the identity of the man.

And then my shield drops.

I stumble, gasping as the sword nearly lands a hit, grazing a strand of my hair where a few pieces float to the ground.

When I try to pull the shield out again, it's as if a piece of myself has been locked away. I can feel it thrumming inside me, waiting to be released, but it is out of my reach.

My power is gone.

Reaching for my dagger, my hand smooths over my thigh where it is normally tucked away in my garter. I curse under my breath. "Trials, Lysta." In my frantic rush to the judgment hearing, I had left it behind under my pillow.

Across the field, the assassin steps forward, which makes me stagger backward automatically.

Breathing heavily, I wait for a moment before turning on my heel and running in the other direction. Directly toward the Border Forest.

The sword follows, its wielder not far behind.

When I approach the boundary separating the forest from the field, I feel my power thrum to life. Relief courses through me, a strangled sob making its way out of my throat.

I don't have the time to bask in it, immediately whipping around to bring the shield up just as the assassin's swords swings toward my throat.

A satisfied smile twists at my lips until the assassin moves closer, still at least one hundred paces from me, and the shield slips away.

Horror slinks down my spine.

Could this shadow-covered man take away my powers?

Again and again, I try to pull out my shield with no success. The sword lashes out at me, and I block it with my arm, hissing in pain as the blade slices through my sleeves and skin.

How can I pursue a man or defend myself against someone I can't get close to? I look to the left and right, desperate for a way out.

My only escape, the forest behind me.

Without hesitating, I pivot and sprint into the canopy of the trees.

CHAPTER 34

Dusk chases me in the forest, stealing every bit of light that guides me through the endless, winding trees. The evening haze makes it impossible to see if the assassin still follows me, but as my chest heaves with rasping breaths, I have to stop.

Falling into the shadows of a tree with cascading branches, I use my quick break to listen for someone pursuing me. There's a shuffle of leaves as wind swirls through the fallen piles accumulating on the forest floor. But no footsteps or voices.

I collapse at the base of the tree to collect myself, adrenaline pumping through my body. My ankle throbs an aching pain, twisted from stepping on a rotted through log that caved under my weight. I'm lucky I didn't break my leg, but I still curse as I touch the swollen area.

Why would someone try to kill me now? I could see before the judgment meeting, keeping me from talking, but they already ruled in Drytas's favor now.

It has to be about revenge.

I'm out of Drytas's way. The Crowns will never take

anything I say at face value again. I'm no longer a threat, if he ever considered me one to begin with.

Maybe if I'd made enough of an impact, the ink of my words would stain his reputation for the foreseeable future. But he won—what do I know that would threaten him enough to kill me?

Leaning back against the tree, I close my eyes, body and mind exhausted. The trauma and weight of everything that I've experienced in one day weighs heavy on me, and I haven't even had the time to truly process it—to grieve.

My throat tightens.

Spending the night on the forest floor isn't favorable, but for all I know, the assassin could just be waiting for me to retreat to the capital.

I freeze when a thud echoes through the ground, not moving a muscle until the tremble sounds again. Flying to my feet, I crouch, surveying the surrounding area for the disturbance.

But the shakes continue without revealing its origin, becoming louder and heavier.

I stumble to the right, gasping when a flock of birds burst from a nearby tree, their cries sounding as they flood the sky, disappearing into the darkness.

From behind the towering trees, where the birds have just flown from, steps out a creature. Its body is as green as the surrounding trees. Patches of moss and flowers grow on the skin of its back and hang from its large, protruding antlers.

A stag. Sort of like the ones Doireann used to get in occasionally for meat, but this one is impossibly massive. Its antlers tangling in the thicket as it pushes forward.

It's a creature like nothing I've ever heard of, and I breathe shallowly in its presence, unsure of how dangerous it may be. Unlike the Kadara I faced in Valor's Trial, I haven't heard tales of this creature. Whether it is so rare, they never passed the stories of it on, or it is commonly ordinary enough it isn't mentioned, I'm unsure.

It steps forward again, and the ground shakes from the impact. Mirroring its movement, I retreat silently into the shadows, stumbling over a gnarled tree root.

Landing on my back, I try to push backward, feet scrambling against the forest floor, trying to find purchase. My ankle screams. I hold my hands out to summon a shield, but nothing comes. Panic flashes through me.

The assassin is nearby.

I tuck my head to the side, not wanting to watch as the stag sees me and moves closer.

But nothing happens.

Looking back, the stag lowers its head, neck stretching out as it reaches for a large branch covered in red berries. Its mouth closes around a leafy bundle and pulls. Leaves fall from the jostled bunch and drift downward, raining over me in a red-and-orange storm.

A rush of air pushes out of my mouth as I sag in relief.

The stag stares into my soul, the orbs of its eyes a mix between green and blue—like a swirl of land and water. It blinks slowly, as if taking me in as I do the same.

A moment passes between us, and the stag starts to bow its head.

A smothered shriek escapes my mouth as a shadowed beast appears over the trees to my left, leaping through the air and snapping its jaw around the stag's leg. The stag squeals in pain, rearing up on its hind legs to buck off the wolf. When the kicking motion fails to pry the beast's teeth from its hind quarter, I try to summon a shield but can't.

My body shakes as I watch the stag fight, trying to maneuver its antlers as a divider between them, but the animal doesn't let go. A hand slips over my mouth from behind me, and the scream cowering just under the surface is swallowed.

"Get to your feet. Now, quickly," a male voice mutters into my ear.

The relief spreading through my body is an automatic response. Evander. He's come after me.

I sag against him. My back pressed to his chest.

"Hurry, Lysta. We only have until the Lunacade finishes with the Gradeneer before it notices us."

His voice heightens in urgency. From behind me, Evander hooks his arms under my own, getting me on my feet. I hiss as my ankle protests at the movement.

"Why are you here?" I ask, looking at Evander wide eyed. "You followed me out?"

"You're hurt?"

I don't have time to answer before I'm caught around the waist. My arm pulled up over his muscled shoulder.

"You followed me? Why?" I ask. I hadn't even hoped Evander would follow me after everything. I just assumed the worst.

"My question takes priority, Lysta! Where. Are. You. Hurt?" Evander looks at me fiercely, something flickering in his bright eyes, highlighted by the moon's light. Seeing my stubbornness only growing, he answers, albeit reluctantly.

"I started looking for you the moment you ran from the hall. I came out just in time to see you duck into the woods—which might I add is insane at this time of night. Do you know how dangerous that is? The Lunacade is nothing compared to some of the things you could stumble upon in this place. Let alone while you're hurt. So, once again, where are you *hurt*?"

"I'm fine," I whisper. "I just twisted it running."

As we move away, the stag groans.

No longer directly in the fight's underground, I turn back, letting my arm slip from Evander's shoulder.

It's difficult to keep myself from turning away, my eyes misting as I watch the animal I had feared only minutes ago, force to kneel until its legs collapse. Its body falls with a resounding thud, like a tree falling over. Its face lay on the smooth grass, the bright green stained red.

Without imminent danger looming over my head, using Evander for support becomes uncomfortably intimate—considering everything from the last twenty-four hours. My arm hooked around his neck brings his face much closer to mine, making it impossible to look anywhere off to the left without ending up locked in his misty blue eyes. An ache spreads in my neck from keeping my gaze turned in the opposite direction of him.

Our feet find a rhythm that minimizes the limp in my step, but our hips brush with each movement. The arm curled around my waist is faint, only a ghost of fingers whispered against my side. Save for the moments where I stumble over the rougher terrain, climbing over fallen trees blocking our path— then his hand tightens, holding me against him securely.

A hot flush creeps up my neck, pooling in my cheeks as I think about the last time Evander's hands had held me this close. Everything has changed since the night before, when we'd danced, and I'd been able to tune out everything but his smile and kind words.

I can't help but wonder if his presence now means perhaps the way things unfolded at Drytas's judgment hearing hadn't ruined things between us as I thought.

I know his position as Heir complicated things, and I

shouldn't have expected him to defend me when all he had to stand on was my word. Evander had seen nothing of Falland or what Drytas had done. Torryn had.

"Where were you going?" Evander asks, breaking the tense silence.

I sigh. "Nowhere I just—"

"You left! You had to have some destination in mind, Lysta."

"I wasn't going anywhere. I don't have anywhere *to* go."

Evander looks over his shoulder at me. Pity swims in his eyes as he meets my own.

My eyes get hot, and I turn away, trying to keep Evander from seeing the tears welling. "I was suffocating." My voice cracks. "I was suffocating, and I just needed to get out of there."

Evander says nothing. Only furrowing his brows as he peers at me. I look at him when he stops. He moves closer, and with every inch closer he gets, words tumble from my mouth as if they will give me the space slowly being taken from me.

"I have nothing. No court to call home. No friends left to trust. And this whole time, Torryn . . ." I pause as a sob bubbles up. "I just barely escaped with my life—a fact I'm sure Drytas is regretting very much based on how he just tried to have me killed."

Evander leans back suddenly, eyes blown wide. "He what —" Evander growls, sending a threatening look over his shoulder toward the capital.

"Obviously, he wasn't successful, so it's not even like we can use it to convince the Crowns to act against him."

Evander frowns at me.

"Your life is not some bargaining chip worth trading. Not to stop Lord Drytas. Not for anything."

I go silent. Looking to the ground.

"You were wrong before," Evander says, stepping into my space. He towers over me, his stare unflinching, unwavering, refusing to grant me a reprieve, even for a moment. "You aren't alone."

Raising my chin as he stares me down, I snap back, "Yes, I am. Until you are right next to me, receiving banishment from the only home you've ever known, the home you were trying to save. And are left to find sanctuary in another court, none of which trust you, and they all believe you are some lord's whore whom he used like a pawn." My chest heaves as I pause in my rant. "Then," I continue breathily, "you can say I'm not alone. For you are an Heir to a court, with an entire future ahead of him, and I am nothing."

Evander sighs, a frown still etched on his face. "And you never considered as Heir of a court, I could help you. Convince my father to bring you into our court."

My heart skips a beat—a terrible feeling, really.

"I hadn't thought you would—the way you looked at me, Evander. It was as if you believed everything they were saying."

A look of hurt flashes across his face. He stares past me, jaw clenching. After collecting himself, Evander looks at me again. Reaching out, he grabs my chin in his fingers, lifting my head toward his own.

Briefly, I'm reminded of Torryn. The night before on the balcony. When Torryn had done the same thing, and I had thought he planned to kiss me.

"It took everything in me to not strike them down where they stood, and if I could do it again, I think I'd forgo that restraint."

My heart leaps into my throat at his words, eyes widening, lips parting.

"Stand beside me, and I will give you everything they have taken from you."

And then his head dips lower, bringing his lips closer to mine. His breath warms my face, and my hand trembles as I bring it to the one at his side. At first, it is just a brush of skin. Our knuckles rubbing against each other, before I slide my palm till it touches his, entangling our fingers.

His eyes never leave mine as he squeezes my hand, lightly pulling me in to close the distance between our bodies.

I take a shaky breath, allowing his scent, a mixture of sandalwood and leather, to fill my nose. His gaze darts between my eyes and lips, and I realize he is asking for permission. Permission to close the distance.

As soon as I move forward, he is on me. Lips caressing mine with a firmness that pulls me further, deeper, into the kiss. I'm drowning and Evander is pulling me to the surface.

It is a kiss that promises safety and hope that I have some future in this, and with it, I have control over my life once again.

CHAPTER 35

Shouting welcomes us when we open the capital doors. The culprits, Torryn and Sar, go quiet at the sight of Evander and I.

I'm sure we look a sight. My dress sleeve torn and soaked with blood from where the assassin managed to get in a swipe. Not to mention I'm limping along, supported by Evander.

Shifting where I stand, I drop my arm from around Evander's neck to hide the limp from my hurt ankle.

I wouldn't let them see me as weak and vulnerable. Not anymore.

Torryn sits on the marble steps, arms resting on his raised knees. His hair is more chaotic than usual, as if he has run his fingers through it a hundred times—a telling sign. When he looks at me, his face is blank, not revealing what's beneath the surface, save for the hard set of his jaw. His crown lies discarded on the step near him.

Sar, on the other hand, lets every one of her emotions flicker across her face. Relief, followed by confusion, before morphing into concern. She stands in front of Torryn, hands on her hips as she looks at him, lips pursed. She glances between us as if waiting for one of us to be the first to speak.

It won't be me.

Evander tenses next to me, and the hand wrapped around my waist tightens. Looking up at him, his eyes are locked onto Torryn, glaring daggers.

Sar sucks in a sharp breath when her eyes lower to the blood dripping down my arm and onto the floor. She rushes toward me, pulling my injury up to her face. "What happened?"

I pull out of her grip, taking a step back. My heart wrenches at the hurt expression passing over her face. In a split second, I decide not to tell them about the assassin. Even if I doubt they are connected to the attempt on my life, I still can't look at them without feeling like a fool.

"It doesn't matter," I say, hoping she'll drop it. "I'm fine."

Before Sar can push the issue, Evander says, "What are you doing here?"

His question is open for anyone to answer, but his glare is directed toward the young lord of Self.

Torryn stands from his seat on the stairs, leaning against the railing. He doesn't dignify Evander's question with an answer. Merely crossing his arms in response.

Speaking louder now, Evander growls out, "Haven't you done enough?"

Torryn looks up at the ceiling as if in disbelief, a sarcastic smile curling at his lips. "Because *you've* done so much for her." He lets out a cruel laugh before looking at me. "She knows who tried to save things during the hearing."

"After you ruined them in the first place!" Evander yells, pointing at Torryn. "I at least tried to stop her from being executed."

"And *I* tried to help her save her people—what she came here to do."

"Well, that worked out well—didn't it?" I ask, cutting off the fight building between the two men.

Torryn twists his lips between his teeth, staring at me. Not a sliver of remorse twinkles in his eyes, and I can't help but wonder if Torryn even realizes what I've lost tonight.

Without breaking from Torryn's gaze, I step away from Evander. "I'll see you in the morning, Evander. Let me settle things here."

He hesitates beside me, giving me a questioning look. I nod to signal that I'm sure, and he steps in the direction of the Court of Truth's tower.

Evander out of the way, Sar turns to me with hopeful eyes. Like we are part of a team.

A part of me wishes there is some chance Sar had been unaware of the game Torryn had been playing. That like me, she too had been blind to Torryn's ulterior motives. But I know that wish can't be granted, regardless of what hopeful utterances I release into the universe.

"You and Torryn were both drugged during the Peace Ball," Sar says as if expecting me to balk at her revelation. "I figured it out because you said Torryn was drunk. But he *doesn't drink.*"

I chance a look at Torryn, who shifts his feet.

Sar continues, "Ardis says you only took a sip of alcohol, nothing to make you act like you did last night before I took you back to your room."

My eyes flick to her, searching for any sign of deceit. I hadn't known Sar had extradited me from the situation. The memory is missing, along with most of how my night had ended.

"I already figured out someone drugged us," I tell her, glancing at Torryn.

Did he remember the night before? When he had stepped into my space, saying things he had no business telling me as merely a reluctant ally. Even less now that I know the wider scope of his plan.

Trials, I hope he didn't.

Sar looks at me as if she expected a different reaction. What did she want me to say? That confirming Torryn and I were drugged explained everything that happened in the judgment hearing? That it's the answer I'm looking for, and all will be forgiven?

"Sar, why don't you let me talk to Lysta? Alone." Torryn nods for her to leave.

She scrunches her nose, but bites her tongue, turning on her heel to leave. Before she exits, she gives me one last half smile. "I'm glad you're safe. We—I was worried."

Left with just Torryn, I brace for what he has to say. Even though Torryn comes to stand in front of me, I angle my body, lowering my eyes. I tell myself it's so he can't skim the thoughts floating on the surface of my mind. But even I can't deny how much it will hurt to hear his excuses while meeting his eyes.

"Things aren't the way it seems," Torryn starts, tilting his head to catch my gaze.

More excuses. More manipulation. When would he learn I just want the truth?

Pursing my lips, I nod tightly, anger rushing through me. "I'm seeing that now, Lord Torryn," I say, keeping my voice just on the icy side of polite.

Torryn does a double take, peering down his nose at me. His jaw clenches. "Why are you calling me that?" he asks, voice lowering.

"What? Your title? I find it is the appropriate thing to call you." I tilt my head in his direction. "Lord Torryn."

"Yes, but you've never cared to do so before."

"Well, I'm sure you'd prefer it to what I want to call you."

Torryn backs away from me, both hands held up in defense.

"Obviously, you aren't ready to talk about this yet. When you're ready to hear my side, you know where to find me, Lysta."

My jaw drops.

"Your side? Your side is you used me. You manipulated me. Worst of all, you gave me hope you could fix everything."

"I didn't come to Falland to fix everything!" Torryn shouts, voice echoing off the marble of the entry hall. Torryn looks to the side before speaking again, this time in a whisper. "But that doesn't mean I haven't been trying to since I met you."

I want to believe him. I want to trust that he didn't bring me here for selfish purposes. But every lie, every misdirection, the kept secrets and manipulations—they outweigh any hope I have.

"You need to leave me out of whatever game you're trying to play here. I can't lose much more Torryn—I can't be the one to pay the price for whatever you're angling for."

CHAPTER 36

In the morning, Evander isn't the only one waiting outside my door.

Next to Evander's lean figure, the guard posted to the side of my door seems massive, with hulking shoulders and trunk like limbs. He grips the hilt of the sword hanging at his hip when I appear and watches me.

I freeze for a moment, pausing in the doorway as I glance between the two figures. My heart rate doubles in speed. Why is a guard outside of my room, where there never had been before? Evander had said nothing about what happens the day after you are banished from your court. However, I assumed he would warn me if I'm to be carted out of the capital premises.

Evander doesn't acknowledge the guard as he greets me good morning, quickly leading us on our way. Nor does he concede anything different about this morning until we are well out of earshot.

"Sorry about that," he mutters with a sigh.

"Am I a prisoner now?" I ask, glancing back at the guard shrinking with our increasing distance. "'Cause this doesn't feel like I'm a guest anymore, Evander."

Anxiety seeps into my tone as I look at him with wide, panicked eyes.

Am I now such a threat I require an armed guard to watch my movement in the dead of night? They hadn't feared the freshly Trialed girl who had walked up their steps only a few weeks ago.

Evander rubs my upper arms, shushing me before pulling me into a hug. I tense, then relax in his embrace. His voice is low and soothing in my ear.

"You're technically not a part of any court, at least right now. That's why they added precautions. As soon as we talk to my father, it'll go away."

He doesn't mention his father may deny our request, but I appreciate the optimism from him. All I have to contribute is the worst-case scenario, so I will take his hope gladly.

I nod into his chest before pulling back. "Let's go. I'm ready," I sigh.

It isn't hard to like Lord Gennady, who is kind even when difficult. But it doesn't make it easier to ask for such a monumental favor. I'm the poisoned fruit he'd be willingly bringing into protection, and who knows the potential ramifications of that.

Evander tucks my hand into his arm, helping me along as I limp, ankle more swollen than the day before. I decide to let him.

"Actually, I'm trying to schedule us a meeting with Lord Gennady, but he seems to have limited availability. But we will soon. I promise."

I nod, not even questioning he will, but my heart still sinks. After standing with me during the judgment hearing, did Lord Gennady still feel the same after the result? The sooner I could talk to him, the better.

The guards systematically placed throughout the capital

watch me as I pass. Their eyes following as if they expect me to start the next war if I even so much as breathe the wrong way. It bothers me at first. But then I remind myself it'll be harder for someone to kill me with so many attentive witnesses.

Evander looks at me with a bright smile. "I figured I'd take you to a healer to get your ankle and that gash looked at," he says, nodding to my arm.

"And you think Lady Ivianna will have her healers work on someone she thinks committed treason?"

"Maybe not," he says, and my shoulders fall. But then he nudges me. "But I know where there are two capital healers right now that she has no control over."

VISHA THROWS her finger blades across the pitch of the arena with honed velocity and guaranteed destruction. In smooth, practically unnoticeable movements, she pulls each blade from the sheaths on her vest, before twisting them in her fingers. Her narrowed eyes survey the moving target in front of her, before lashing out.

I hold my breath as she throws them, grateful for the metal cage that separates us.

The moving target of mention—Neith—climbs the wooden framing of an archer's peak. He leaps from beam to beam, narrowly missing Visha's attacks as her blades hit the wood will a dull thunk.

"I'm almost there!" Neith shouts, grinning over his shoulder. "You're not losing your touch, are you, V?"

How could they joke and tease, knowing with one misstep, their lives could be at stake? As if having healers on standby is a free pass to throwing all caution out the window. Having come from a court who didn't even know healers existed, I couldn't imagine so easily taking the same risk.

Visha, from her spot on the sand, rolls her eyes before throwing another blade that catches the hem of Neith's pant leg. She bites her cheek, hiding away the beginnings of a smile.

I no longer feel safe behind the cage. With Visha's pinpoint accuracy, she's skilled enough to make it through the small squares of the fence without trouble.

Neith, on the other hand, doesn't flinch as the blade pins the fabric to the wood. Easily thirty feet in the air, hanging only by his arms.

Neith laughs, throwing his head back at his unfortunate position. He drops until he can sit on one of the wooden cross-beams before reaching for the knife impaled in the wood. Once in his grip, he flips the knife, sending a cheeky grin at Visha.

Evander opens the cage door, stepping through as it creaks loudly. Neith's attention flicks to us, his eyes hardening as he stares me down. "Target on your six, V."

Visha spins on her heel, flinging a blade in our direction before she even sees us. Unlike her offensive attack against Neith, she doesn't aim to miss.

There isn't the time to look at Evander for his reaction. As the blade soars toward my head, nothing can stop it from hitting its mark.

With only a breath to decide, I raise my shield, adrenaline pumping through me. The force field hums in my bones as it solidifies, feeling stronger than I do myself. The blade hits the shield with a pathetic *thwack* before falling into the sand.

Immediate threat diverted. My gaze shifts from the blade to Neith and Visha. Both of them examine me with renewed suspicion, blinking when I release the shield.

Evander doesn't seem fazed by his first glimpse at my

power. He quickly checks me over for injuries before leaning in to mutter, "Go see the healer. I'll handle this here." Before I can respond, he's stomping across the pitch. "Trials, Visha." Evander curses. "What was that? It was headed straight for her."

Neith swings down from the riser, landing in the sand. He rubs his hands together, dispelling any sand from his palms before resting his fists on his hips. "Valor shouldn't be here. Not in the capital, but even more so at Heir training." Neith sends a burning glare in my direction, cocking his head with something akin to curiosity. "Although I suppose I can't call her that anymore—being exiled, and all that."

"Plus, I wanted to see this shield that Drytas mentioned," Visha adds.

I try to pretend I don't hear them as I walk to the underground arena's waiting area, where Evander said we'd find the healers.

Gritting my teeth, I put every effort into walking without a limp, even when my ankle threatens to give out. I already have enough people aiming for my throat. I don't need to show them a single ounce more of weakness—more than they've already seen, at least.

Even as I pass the other Heirs, I keep my gaze locked forward. Bash calls out to me when I pass him and Jona engaged in a fist fight. I just tuck my head in and continue with what I came here for.

When I step into the shadows of the arena dug out, I find one of the healers that I'd seen during War Hour. She looks at me expectantly, waiting for me to be the one to break the silence.

The healer is younger than most of the staff I've seen here at the capital—not much older than me. Her midnight-colored hair is tied in a braid, hanging over her shoulder and landing by her knees. Bright pinks and oranges of her dress stand out against her amber skin. She doesn't wear a capital uniform, nor a color of any court.

"My name is Lysta." I pull the sleeve of my dress, flashing the scab on my arm before pulling up my skirts to flash my bruised ankle. "I was told that you could help me."

After a few slow blinks, she nods, "I'm Surya. Take a seat." The corner of her mouth tightens as I sit, and I try not to flinch when she reaches out to touch me.

"Oh," she murmurs when she examines my arm.

I'd imagine a healer who frequented War Hour would have seen more gruesome things than I could fathom. Which makes it even odder she would have a reaction at all to the slice on my arm. Until I realize it isn't the gash across my arm that stuns her but the shiny white scars of the Kadara bite.

It hits me. She's the first person to ever see the marks. I always wear long sleeves, both here and back in Falland. Not wanting to leave room for discussion where they had come from. But now the healer had . . .

"I can heal both for you. If you'd like?" she offers, not moving her eyes from the marred skin.

I look between the marks and her with wide eyes. "Both— Both? This one's already healed."

She runs the tips of her fingers over the Kadara's bite, sending goose bumps up my arms and a chill racing along my spine. "I can still heal the damaged skin. The scars I mean." Her eyes rise to meet mine, and it's like she can see straight through me.

I blink at her before shaking my head slowly. "No. It stays with me."

Nodding, she pays no mind to the decision. It obviously

isn't an odd request, considering the scars I've seen in this place. She presses a cool hand to the scabbed over cut, and I get to see close up as the skin mends back together. When she pulls away, it's as if the assassin had never touched me at all.

She moves to work on my ankle, and I hold my breath in anticipation. It's as if the purples and blues of the bruise drain through her fingers as my skin returns to its normal color.

The healer stands from her kneeling position, moving back before looking at me expectantly. Hurrying to my feet, I hesitate before putting any weight on the injured foot. No pain comes, though. I shift easily between my feet, twisting my ankle underneath me.

I send her a reserved smile. "I know you did not have to help me, but thank you for doing it anyway."

At the sound of echoed shouting, I rush out of the dugout. Running past Jona and Eiko, who stand to the side and watch the fight unraveling in the center.

Evander has Neith's shirt in one fist, yanking him until they are nose-to-nose. If looks could kill, Lord Bralas would be naming his new Heir. Evander growls in Neith's face, spitting out harsh, inaudible words. Bash locks his arms around Evander's, trying to yank him away from the ginger Heir.

Neith only smirks, leaning back from Evander, and when his eyes lock on to me, it only stretches. He says something to Evander while looking at me that makes my cool, collected Heir launch into a frenzy. Evander shoves Neith back, knocking him to the ground, tearing his shirt.

Rushing forward, sand kicking up from my feet, I slam into Evander, pushing him off of Neith. Evander tenses, rearing for a fight until he sees me, then all at once, he relaxes. He curls a hand around my waist, leaning his forehead up against mine as he let out a shuddering breath.

"Hey. Hey." I repeat over and over, trying to get Evander to look at me. "What was that, Evander? What happened to Mr. Protect the treaty?" When he doesn't answer, I grab his chin, turning his head toward my own. "What's going on?"

When gray meets blue, his jaw relaxes, and he lets out a deep breath. "Nothing." Evander reaches for my hand, pulling me away from where Bash and Visha help Neith up from the ground. "Can we please just go?"

Seeing the ache and worry in his eyes, I nod, letting him pull me away. But I can't help but glance back at the Heirs watching us leave.

Neith pulls his shirt together, made difficult by the rip extending from his neck down his sleeve. I get a flash of his Trial tattoo, eyes widening. Seeing my gaze, Neith covers his arm.

Evander's hand tightens around my own, and I trip, stumbling after him. He doesn't answer as he leads me from the arena. But what had only taken a few moments lingers in my mind.

Neith's Trial tattoos extended beyond where my single one did, creeping past his wrist and moving up his forearm. Meaning he has secured two Trials. Why hadn't I known that? It hadn't seemed like something he wanted known from the way he quickly hid the inked skin away.

Neith and Lord Bralas have been against me since I first got here. Shutting down my stories of what had happened and standing firm in support. During the judgment meeting, Lord Bralas seemed to argue Drytas's side at every opportunity. And then Neith, who is believed to have only been Trialed once by everyone, is revealed to have two?

Not to mention, the assassin had the power of a Valor Trialed. Yet, the only person from the court here in the capital has been me and Lord Drytas. The figure hadn't looked like him, though.

A new realization strikes me, and my stomach ties in knots.

If Drytas has allies in other courts . . . and let them Trial in Valor prior to its collapse. Then maybe the assassin could be any of the people here. I couldn't accuse Neith based solely off his hatred of me and having a second Trial tattoo. But the fear in his eyes when I'd seen it meant something—I'm sure of it.

CHAPTER 37

Nearly a week has passed since Lord Drytas's judgment hearing—or maybe for how it turned out, I could call it my own.

And since then, it has been increasingly obvious how unwelcome my presence is in the capital. My only hope of sanctuary within the courts lies in Truth, even if I have yet to confirm that with Lord Gennady.

At every meal, every moment I spend outside the walls of my rooms, I am watched. Watched with hatred and fear, suspicion and concern. Whether for what I actually did or what they've heard I did, doesn't matter. They take the intriguing bits and pieces and stretch them just enough that the next person latches on.

Rumors and gossip surround me like air, burning as I inhale it into my lungs.

I tried to overthrow my lord, seduced another. I planned to assassinate Lord Drytas, organized an Untrialed rebellion. I infiltrated the capital to attack the Crowns. They never end, only getting more distorted and further from the truth.

Except that I'm banished from my own court. That part is true.

One can only take so many plates of meals knocked to the ground and shoves into stone walls. Eventually, I just stick to my room, grateful for when Evander brings me food, offering to escort me anywhere. He won't let it happen in his presence, not that anyone would dare to.

That's how I agreed to go to the next War Hour, even when every ounce of me warns against it. Why would I want to be in a place where my enemies could be weaponized against me for sport? But Evander says it may be our only chance to speak to his father.

In the Court of Truth viewing booth, I think it a curse until I realize who sits inside already.

"Lysta, you're a hard person to get an audience with," Lord Gennady says, his ocean eyes twinkling at me from his chair centered at the windowed wall.

My body stills, tensing for a fight after the week I just had. Even though I acknowledge Lord Gennady had fought for me during the judgment hearing, I want to be far from every Trialed in this building. But then Lord Gennady's words hit me, and I frown, eyebrows cinching. "I hadn't realized you were trying to, my lord. I've actually come to speak with you as well."

The smile on Lord Gennady's face drops before he gestures for me to take a seat next to him. "I'd hoped to speak with you immediately following the judgment decision, but Evander mentioned you were having a difficult time, and you were not up to such conversations yet."

I nod, realizing what Evander had done for me. "I needed some time to get my bearings. It felt as if for a while all hope was lost, and I wasn't sure what to do next. Evander helped me figure out my next steps, which is why I've come to speak with you."

Lord Gennady leans back, eyes wide. "My son helped you come up with a plan? I'm relieved to hear it, as it was why I'd wanted to speak to you—about what we shall do next, about Lord Drytas and Valor. I promise you we will not give up just yet, regardless of the other Crowns." Eyes sparkling with excitement, Lord Gennady clasps his hands together. "What plan have you come up with?"

My heartbeat stutters as I look up to Lord Gennady in surprise. With the wind knocked out of me, I fumble for what to say.

"I thought we'd exhausted all options with the judgment hearing. I didn't think there was anything left for us to do." Rubbing my chest over my heart, I take a deep breath. The first hum of excitement runs through me, and I wish to tell Evander.

All is not lost. I can still do more for the Untrialed.

Lord Gennady frowns. "If you did not have a plan for Drytas, what plan did you come up with?"

My stomach drops as I remember what I'd come to ask Lord Gennady.

Praying he won't turn me away, I straighten in my seat. "Since I cannot return to Falland, and the capital will end its session soon, I was hoping to convince you to let me become a citizen of Truth."

I shift under Lord Gennady's intense stare, waiting with bated breath as to his answer.

"This comes at my son's prompting, I assume?" Lord Gennady examines me. He brings a finger to rest against the seam of his lips as he thinks, tapping his cane in a slow rhythm against the floor. "And this is your desire separate from Evander's wishes?"

Jerking my head back, I fumble, not sure of his question. My hands tremble in my grip. Is he against the idea of my joining his court? My eyes flick to the door as I pray that, any second, Evander will rush through. He should be here for this.

Seeing my anxiety, Lord Gennady covers my hands with his. "Take a breath, Lysta. I have no intention of denying you citizenship in my court."

I sag, sighing in relief. A small sob chases out of my throat, strangled, as I try to force it down. Looking away from Gennady, I blink rapidly, trying to dispel the tears gathering in my eyes. When a single tear swims along my cheek before dripping off my chin, Lord Gennady reaches forward, wiping it.

I startle at the caring gesture from the older man. Steadying myself, I nod that I'm fine, waving off his concern. "I'm sorry, this is not the reaction I meant to have." Dropping my hands in my lap, I sag. "It's been a long week."

"Let me share with you why I think you should think further about your decision." Lord Gennady pauses, letting me regain my composure. "Once you are a citizen of Truth, you will be under my protection. None of the other courts can conspire against you without it being a move against myself. This includes Lord Drytas."

If anything can fix my situation, it would be that.

Shuddering, I inhale. Not only giving me a new place to make home, but removing the target that Drytas has painted on my back in bright red.

Lord Gennady hesitates, taking my shaking hand in his. "But there are sacrifices as well. While I believe your testimony against Lord Drytas, I cannot make any moves against him without the support of the other Crowns. Not without bringing the two of our court's to War."

I nod. It makes sense. They have a treaty for a reason. It's not like I could expect Lord Gennady to stop Lord Drytas on his own. He would end up an outsider among the Crowns instead. "Of course, my lord. I wouldn't expect—"

"That is not all, Lysta," Lord Gennady says, firm. "If you were a citizen of my court, they would see any actions you were to take as following the wishes of your lord. For the same reason I cannot take action against him, you could no longer pursue Lord Drytas. You would not be able to continue in your fight for your people."

My head draws back as if Lord Gennady has backhanded me. I can't help but look away from his piercing gaze that sees as the revelation hits me. I press a hand to my mouth before rubbing my face.

Trials. A roll of anger goes through me. That he is asking me to let Drytas win. That he is making me choose between my safety and that of those I'd left behind. But the frustration fades like the tide.

Lord Gennady is giving me a choice, which no one has afforded me thus far. Always adjusting to the consequence of others' decisions and the aftermath. Never giving me the opportunity to dictate my path.

No one can expect to move mountains without sacrificing something first.

Lord Gennady continues. "Perhaps, I do convince the other courts of my suspicions of what Drytas has done. I want nothing more than for him to pay for the injustices he has committed. But if it is impossible, you would need to stand down. Indefinitely."

Pinned by the weight of the decision placed in my hands, I don't respond right away, but Lord Gennady offers a sympathetic gaze. "We do not leave the capital for a few days. Decide before then, and I shall honor your wishes, no matter the answer."

I manage a small "Thank you, Lord Gennady."

～

Lost in thought, I distance myself from the bloody battles taking place on the field below. Fingers picking at the skin of my lip my teeth had torn to pieces, the roars of the arena dull in the background. Each well-aimed hit stirring equal cheers and boos. When an opponent rises above the other, the crowd stomps, sending vibrations all the way to my seat in Truth's viewing box.

Despite the resounding activity enfolding, my focus lingers on Lord Gennady's words. Every few minutes, I glance around to see if Evander has arrived. I suddenly have a choice to make.

Silence cracks through my focus, making me stiffen. Spine straightening, I sit up to peer around the arena that has gone still. The crowd shuffles in silence, eyes wide, staring at the middle of the arena where a new challenger steps forward.

Torryn.

Looking back and forth between him and Lord Gennady, my mouth gapes. Today isn't a Crown's War Hour. Even if it were, Torryn doesn't usually participate in the battles—Lord Gennady informed me the last War Hour.

"What is he doing?" I breathe.

Torryn's eyes search the crowd as if he is looking for someone. With every moment, the crowd squirms under his gaze, praying they will not be the sacrifice given to the feared lord to battle.

I lean away from the window after Torryn's gaze locks onto me. His expression is cold, brusque, lacking the sliver of warmth he'd shown me an eternity ago. Raising an eyebrow at me, Torryn dares me to look elsewhere. When I refuse, he sends me a devilish grin. The persona he puts on for the capital and the Crowns.

"I challenge Lysta, of the Court of Valor."

My heartbeat pounds in my ears as the arena roars. I shake

my head at him, mentally begging Torryn to take his words back.

Why is he doing this? Hasn't he interfered in my life enough?

Lord Gennady grips my shoulder, leaning in to speak, but his words dull as the crowd cheers. "You do not have to fight him, Lysta. You can choose to abstain."

Looking up at the older man, I see his eyes shine with worry.

If I accept Lord Gennady's offer of citizenship, I could never stand against Lord Drytas. But at this moment, I'm being offered the chance to contend with someone who holds culpability in how it all fell apart. Not nearly to the level that Drytas is responsible, but reason has no place in my mind as adrenaline spikes in me.

I clench my fists in my lap before standing, tension thrumming in my spine. If Torryn is offering himself up for a fight, I'll take it. Win or lose.

CHAPTER 38

It doesn't matter I arrived at War Hour with no intention of fighting. The crowd will not be denied once they are offered the battle of a lifetime. The young lord with more Trials under his belt than any other, against the court, who has been isolated from the capital along with any of Valor's powers. If it weren't for the healers—it would be a slaughter.

I'm given fifteen minutes before I need to be out on the sand, armed, and ready to fight, or else it will be considered abstaining. Which, according to Gennady, there is no shame in, even though it never happens.

I trade my dress for spare training clothes that are shoved into my hands when a War Hour staff member spots me, headed toward the pitch in a dress. Leather pants that hug my skin, tall boots, and a sleeveless top to go under a leather vest. Easily something I would have worn in Falland on the streets, although much nicer quality. Except now I'll be displayed in front of the entire capital, Trial tattoo and Kadara bite scars out for anyone to see.

Torryn makes his way into the waiting area of the arena. Sar chases at his heels, arguing with him as Ardis follows behind.

Sar's expression darkens several shades until the red color rivals her hair. Pushing at Torryn, he snaps at her, making her halt. The anger on her face seeps away, replaced with utter disappointment.

It's been almost a week since I last spoke to either of them. Since that night, where I limped into the capital. Nothing could quell my anger at Torryn, but Sar—it hurt to ignore her and a part of me wants to reach out. To break the silence I forced between us. But I can't push aside she had played some role in it all.

When I turn away from her, she huffs, turning on her heel and stomping away. Her voice rings out as she shouts, "You both are impossible!"

Focusing on Torryn, I notice his longer black hair is tied up in a knot at the back of his head, shorter pieces falling around his face. When his eyes meet mine, they darken, sending a chill up my spine.

As I stomp to him, he crosses his arms across his chest, drawing attention to the tattoos entirely exposed for the first time. The sleeves are cut off his top, revealing that his Trial tattoos circle from his wrist, up past his bicep until it dips in toward his shoulder. There isn't any doubt it's the longest one I've seen.

"Is this what you want?" I ask, shoving Torryn backward. Fury fuels me as I press on, but he doesn't budge an inch. "You want me to show you how I really feel, *my lord.*"

Locking his knees, Torryn holds me firm when I try to push him again. His eyes flicker to life, a fire burning in them as he smirks at me. He grabs my chin in his grip, not relenting as I try to tear my head away. Torryn leans in before speaking softly. "No. I want you to show *them* how you really feel." He nods toward the arena, emphasizing who "them" is.

My breath lodges in my throat at his words, eyebrows knitting, as I search his face for a hint to his meaning. I'm about to ask him just that when we are interrupted.

My name echoes down the entrance to the waiting area, shouting at the top of his lungs—Evander. When he turns the corner, the worry and anxiety he feels aren't hidden on his face. His eyes soften as they take me in, cataloging the distance between me and Torryn.

Looking at Torryn, I realize how close we stand as I push him away from me, knocking his hand from my face. He backs up, hands mockingly held in the air, as he smirks in satisfaction. As if our closeness is his own personal victory against Evander.

"Don't you touch her," Evander growls as he slams his fist into Torryn's face without warning.

Blood flows from Torryn's nose when his head recoils back, and I suppress the urge to go to him.

He is the enemy, Lysta.

"Like hell you're battling him." Evander pulls me to the side away from Torryn, glaring at him the entire time. "Over my dead body."

"That can be arranged," Torryn jibes from behind us.

I have to yank Evander back as he lunges toward Torryn again.

I shake my head at Evander, completely lost at the person slowly being revealed to me. Where is the collected man who has steadied me ever since arriving in the capital? He certainly isn't around based on the two fights in the last week I've had to pull him away from.

A part of me warms at his protectiveness of me. But he needs to let me fight my own battles.

"He's just getting even for how the judgment hearing went down," Evander says, taking my upper arms in his hands. Almost as if he doesn't realize he's doing it, Evander rubs my arms, trying to soothe me.

But *I'm* not the one who needs to be soothed.

Evander continues. "He's the one who lost out when the hearing went bad. Who knows what he is up to? Making a spectacle or getting revenge—it's the last thing the Crowns need to see right now. Especially if we are going to convince Lord Gennady still."

Why is he so against me fighting Torryn?

I shrug off his hands. "This isn't your decision, Evander." Leaning over, I pick up my sword, which lay propped up against the wall. "And I already talked to Lord Gennady."

What happens between Torryn and me is just that—between us. He can't stand in the way now when he isn't the one hurt by Torryn.

Anger seems to deflate out of Evander, Torryn completely forgotten.

With wide eyes, he turns to me, body frozen. "You already have?"

"I got to the viewing booth early, and he was there. I planned on waiting for you, but then he beat me to it." I can tell from the look in his eyes that he has a barrage of questions ready to hurl at me, but I silence him with a single hand. "I need you to stand back while I do this, because it's what I need, Evander. We'll talk about what happens next after, okay?"

My tone leaves no words for question. He steps back, and I take it as my signal to head out. Almost in the arena's view, I brace myself before stepping out. The crowd cheers and boos as I step out onto the sandy pitch. Only surging more when Torryn comes to stand beside me.

War Hour will have its encore, after all.

Sword in hand, I follow Torryn out onto the sandy battlefield with false bravado fueling every step. As we emerge from the tunnel, the crowd roars at the sight of us, thrilled at the prospect of witnessing a fight unlike any other. My spine stiffens under the gaze of thousands. It doesn't matter how loudly they cheer—they will celebrate just the same when I fail.

I'm sure they expect a swift, brutal fight. All I want is for it to not be embarrassingly quick.

Trials, let me get in a few swings first.

While there's no way Lord Gennady would rescind his offer if I make a fool of myself, I'd still like to hold my head high afterward.

Today would showcase just how powerful Torryn is, and while everyone certainly fears him, they would not turn away from the opportunity to watch him fight and bleed like the rest of them.

The arena stomps in sync, pounding a haunting rhythm like a war drum, forewarning our fight. It builds the anticipation as we draw closer to the center. As we pass each court's viewing boxes, it doesn't escape my notice—or Torryn's, from the glare he pins in their direction—that the Crowns and Heirs watch us with bated breath.

Standing in the windows of their boxes, their faces are drawn tight, eyes narrowed. They glance across the pitch to the other Crowns, too far away to communicate their worries— unable to decide if they should stop what's unfolding before them.

My shoulders raise as their attention falls on me. They'll see me now.

Torryn brandishes his sword, turning toward me in one smooth motion. My hand flinches for my own, fingers brushing the silver guard cresting the hilt, as I think the battle has already started. But then Torryn's molten eyes meet mine, sparking with a fire I can't unsee. Arms out to the side, Torryn leans forward and down, sweeping into a low bow. His loose strands fall into his face.

A thunder of gasps echoes around the arena, watching as the young lord bows to his opponent, one who is neither a Crown nor an Heir.

Anger quells the anxious trembling of my hands. My grip is firm as I mirror him. Torryn looks up at me through his thick lashes, eyeing me as I swoop into a similar bow. Sticking one foot out behind me, I raise my arms, bowing to Torryn and never letting my eyes fall from his. His lips curl into a smirk, showcasing his bright white teeth.

It's now or never.

I flinch back at Torryn's voice in my mind, before steeling my face.

Looking around at the surrounding crowd, they have no idea what Torryn is capable of. But they will after today. Tired of always being on the defensive in every aspect of my life, I leap to strike with my sword, which Torryn blocks with his.

Swords crossed, I push against Torryn, whose face is one of complete composure. Knocking me backward with sudden strength, I stumble, barely keeping my footing. We skirt around each other, watching for the other's next move with narrowed eyes.

I aim for his torso, and he sidesteps, locking his cross guard with mine as he pushes it away from him. Our swords lock, and my arms shake, trying to not crumple under his strength.

Torryn doesn't seem affected at all by my efforts, barely straining, as he holds his weapon tight against mine. While I can already feel a trickle of sweat follow my brow, Torryn looks like he could do this all day—he probably could, considering he's been training at this his whole life.

When he looks at me with a tilt of his head and a quirk of

his eyebrow, my face heats. Is he taking this battle seriously—taking me seriously? I know why I wanted this fight to happen, but why challenge me in the first place?

"Why did you do it?" I growl, my face inches from Torryn's.

Torryn pulls his lip between his teeth, then smiles. He snorts before chuckling. "Do what? Come to Valor to Trial in the first place, or bother trying to help you?"

I recoil at his words, and my foot slips in the sand. Torryn's sword pushes forward at my stutter, scraping down my own with a piercing screech. Knocked backward, I land on the ground. Fingers fumbling through the sand, I feel for my sword. I roll to the side when he attacks again in quick succession.

Torryn edges forward, leaning in till his shadow blocks my face from the sunlight. He tilts his head mockingly. "I know it's so hard to believe, coming from a place that fears the Trials, but most of us want that power. To prove we possess the virtues worthy of such gifts. Most of us want to become stronger versions of ourselves. Instead of staying the same—going through the motions every day. Waiting for someone else to fix our problems."

Fiery red anger surges through me. I reach for the dagger strapped to my thigh, kicking out Torryn's feet. He falls to one knee, still a head taller from where I kneel. I grab his shirt, pulling him into the blade that I press to his throat.

It brings me back to that day in the field—the last time I had a knife to Torryn's throat. When he'd promised that Drytas would not get away with it. All the while, he'd been manipulating me in court politics that I didn't understand.

This is familiar isn't it.

Torryn's voice echoes in my head, and I press the knife deeper. Shifting slightly, I try to shake his tone from my mind.

Drips of blood pool at the crease where my dagger kisses his throat. He swallows, and it bobs under the blade. Torryn smirks, eyes heavy lidded as he stares at my eyes, then my lips, then at the crowd watching us with bated breath.

"Did that strike a nerve?" he asks.

You can't win like this.

With one sudden shove and a moment of my hesitation, Torryn has me on my back. His foot stands atop the wrist holding my dagger. Staring up at Torryn, he raises both of our swords, crossing them at my neck.

"Do you yield, Lysta?"

Glaring at him through my brow, I grit my teeth as I try to shift him off me. Swiping my legs to kick at his arms. My arm is useless under his weight.

"Do you yield? I assume you would be used to it. Rolled right over for Drytas in the end. Ready to play house instead of continuing to fight."

Kill the fear, Lysta.

My anger reaches its climax, and like an explosion, my shield bursts outwards, flinging Torryn a few dozen feet. Wind sweeps away from the shield in a whirl-wind, rippling the sand and rattling the metal cage as it blows past the seats.

Breathing heavily, my chest heaves as I look around the arena that has frozen in silence. No one moves, speaks, or even breathes for a few beats.

Then every person roars. Standing, reinvigorated and ready to cheer as the battle takes an unexpected turn. Peering up at the viewing boxes perched around the arena, I can't help but wonder if they see me now.

Across the sand, Torryn pushes himself up onto one knee. Satisfaction gleams in his eyes as he beholds me. It hits me that this is what he wanted. For whatever reason Torryn justifies it, he wanted me to use my power today—in front of the capital and in front of the Crowns. This isn't about wanting to fight me. He's had plenty of opportunities to make a quick end of it.

This is about something more.

Our swords lay in the sand where the shield force flung them.

Torryn and I lock onto them at the same time.

When he rushes forward, running to reach our weapons that lay discarded, I make another choice. Summoning my shield, I fling out my hand. With it, Torryn is surrounded by a shield, encircling him like a dome.

Both hands pressed to the shield, Torryn leans forward, watching me. I stride toward him, leaning to grab both of our swords on my way.

Separated by the impenetrable barrier, Torryn, and I stand only a pace apart. Our gazes never waver.

"How dare you spin this as if I didn't come here for Falland? Like everything I've done so far hasn't been for the Untrialed." I pause, fury building. "I know it's a hard concept to grasp for someone who has always had the world at their feet. But until you have lived and struggled as someone from Falland"—I scoff —"don't you dare mock my efforts or motives. Because your power play will cost people their lives—it nearly cost mine."

I drop the shield that protects Torryn as much as it does me. Looking at the swords in my hand, Torryn stiffens as if bracing for a hit. And then he flinches . . . as I throw his sword in the sand at his feet.

"Now let's finish this farce you call war, because there's a real one waiting for me to make my move."

I gesture for him to stand, raising my sword, beckoning for him to fight me again. But his eyes shimmer with achievement, like he has just won the ultimate prize—but he makes no move for the weapon.

"I yield." His voice rings throughout the arena.

My heart skips as I stare at him in befuddlement. Jaw slack, eyes wide, and Torryn only nods to me in acknowledgment.

"I yield, to Lysta of Valor."

CHAPTER 39

War Hour changed the capital in the hours of its aftermath. People have no quarrel skirting the line between fear and respect, both kindred spirits in their own right, both cloaked in manipulative reverence.

Here, I've played every part in an eternal stage show, missing all but the cup for them to fling their coins into in appreciation for the entertainment. Apparently, I'm winning them over.

In the short trek from the arena to my room, I have been hailed by many passersby, applauded, patted on the back—even bowed to. Adrenaline pumping through my veins and exhausted from my increased power expenditure, I almost pass out when the first awe-stricken court member stops mid-walk to bow and step out of my way.

Completely thrown from the night-and-day change, I don't understand until Lady Ivianna catches me for a word. She praises my performance in the arena, making note that it's a rare few that could stand successfully against Lord Torryn. I'm certain to be missing something amid her apologies that the judgment hearing hadn't gone my way, anticipating the other shoe will drop.

Then she offers me citizenship in her court, and it all makes sense.

While before I was fruit of the poisonous tree, now I'm imbibed with opportunity and power. An asset to use as both threat and defense.

My assumption is only reinforced when Lord Nicaise and Lord Rhen extend the same platitudes and offers.

At the top of the staircase, overlooking the entry hall where Torryn, Ardis, and Sar stand ready to leave the capital, I can't help but wonder if that had been part of Torryn's plan, too.

I can see no advantage in Torryn's challenge to me during War Hour, nor in his defeat. And I use the "defeat" lightly, as I can't fathom the extent at which he must have held himself back. When I dropped that sword at his feet, I felt no more advantaged other than capable of stopping him from stabbing my torso.

Who knows what other powers Torryn possesses that he held back? Whether to keep them unknown or to let me win.

It all makes me think Torryn wanted me to end up victorious. He must have felt burdened by the guilt of the situation, that he just wanted another court to accept me.

But even if his words during the battle were meant to ignite me into a fiery audition for the Crowns, why do they sit so heavily in my chest?

Leaning on the railing, I still when Lord Gennady approaches the three. They talk for a moment, Lord Gennady nodding while sparing me a glance over his shoulder. My breath hitches at having been caught, but he moves on, shaking Torryn's hand before walking off.

Sar turns to Ardis and Torryn, grabbing each of their hands before turning toward me. When we lock eyes, she quirks her head and ascends the stairs and finding her way next to me. She says nothing. Daring me to be the one to break the silence.

"You're leaving," I state.

Is that it? Torryn didn't get what he wanted throughout all this, so he's leaving. And War Hour was what? His spectacular exit?

"Torryn is," Sar admits, her eyes trained on the two men hovering in the doorway. Despite her collected composure, I can still sense a waver in her tone when she adds, "and Ardis. Back to the Court of Self."

I nod stiffly, unsure of an appropriate response. Storming down the stairs and demanding answers from Torryn wouldn't impress anyone. I settle on the least telling question.

"You're not going with them?"

Sar looks at me then, her lip sticking out as she offers me a pitying shrug. "They have nothing left to do here—no other ways to help you from here. In fact, their presence will only make things harder for us." She nudges me with her shoulder for emphasis. "They'll work on stopping Drytas from the Court of Self. We will figure it out here. Together."

My heart nearly bursts. I offer her a quivering smile before nodding. It isn't hard to shove away any lingering suspicions of Sar. Even if everything they'd said about Torryn was true, Sar could only be accountable for so much. I'm too tired to keep pushing out allies when my enemies only seem to surge. Like the assassin that might still linger in the capital waiting for a second chance.

Turning to Torryn, I watch his exchange with Ardis with furrowed brows and a chewed lip. I'm not sure if I'll find out the answer to every question I have about Torryn. Perhaps he spent so much time being victim to the manipulations of court politics that he doesn't know how to help in any other way.

Torryn turns to meet my gaze as if able to sense it.

Whether he meant for it to happen or not, Torryn pushed me toward a realization during War Hour. I might have already been halfway there after talking to Lord Gennady, but Torryn's goading words cemented my choice.

I will not settle for peace at the cost of others' suffering.

Got some fight left after all?

Torryn asks in my mind. His head tilts as if asking from across the entry hall.

Blurring the lines between ally and enemy, Torryn can't be trusted with my life or the Untrialed's. But I can trust one thing—he wants to stop Drytas just as much as I do.

Enough to spare, I think back, hoping he'll hear the words.

At his smirk, I know he has.

Sar and Evander do not get along. An unexpected, unfortunate obstacle when trying to work together to make a plan. But after a few hours, they go a whole five minutes without yelling at each other.

The feud is obviously not just between Torryn and Evander but something deeper they wouldn't mention.

Every idea that Sar has is shot down by Evander. Too risky. Won't work. Will either end up getting us all killed or starting the next Trialed War for violating some protection in the treaty.

Evander's ideas are from the opposite side of the spectrum. Too safe. Not enough to truly fix anything. Sar has no problem telling him as much with a smirk on her face, which only fuels the next round of shouting. You can tell his hope is to come up with a plan that will try to resolve things without putting anyone in direct harm. But Drytas is already threatening war. Negotiating with him won't stop that now.

It all ends for the day when Sar throws her hands up in frustration. "You need to talk to him, Lysta. He's being utterly impossible. Does he want to actually help, or just sit there ruling out any of the ideas that might actually work?" Sar stomps off without an answer, leaving Evander and I tucked in the book stacks of the capital's library.

Evander leans against a bookshelf, staring me down when I whip around to look at him. Arms crossed, he smirks. I can feel the satisfaction rolling off him in waves. Hands on my hips, I give him a scolding glare, pursing my lips.

This is important. He needs to be taking this seriously. Regardless of any feud between him and Sar, he can't be picking a fight when our clock is winding down. With the judgment hearing out of the way, Lord Drytas has nothing standing in his way and then there will be nothing for us to do.

"Don't be mad at me," Evander says, trying his hardest to look repentant. He pushes off the bookcase, creeping forward. "I'm doing my best, but her ideas had a nine-out-of-ten chance of getting you killed." Evander backs me up until my shoulders press into the bookcase behind me.

I give him a warning look. Now is not the time for this. But as soon as his hands grip my hips, holding me to him, I can't help but fold into him. Dropping my forehead against his chest, I groan, "We talked about this."

Evander wraps his arms around me, leaning his chin to rest on the top of my head. "I thought we talked about this too— had it all figured out. You would be safe in Truth. You would be with me. I don't know what happened during War Hour, but you stopped treating that like an option."

I pull away from Evander, shoulders sagging, but he doesn't let go.

How many times will we have this conversation?

Looking to the side, I can't meet his eyes. Doesn't he know it hurts me, too? Every time that I have to tell him I'm not choosing him.

Evander chases my gaze, moving into my line of sight. "It is still an option, Lysta."

Tangling my fingers in the fabric of his shirt, I drop my head and inhale deeply. "Maybe playing it safe is how I got to this point. Back in Falland and here, once I got to the capital. If I'd taken a risk, maybe things would be different."

Evander's fingers slide under my chin, raising my head to look at him. A sad smile twists his lips. "But why does it have to be you? Why does the one who takes the risk and puts herself in danger have to be you?"

My heart clenches at the anguish that laces Evander's tone.

He doesn't know how much it means to me. He cares so deeply about what happens to me. Knowing that I have someone on my side, looking past the bigger picture. Not a pawn in a game or a weapon to be used—but a person to be protected and valued for more than my usefulness.

But it doesn't change what I need to do.

I smooth my palm over his chest until I can feel his heartbeat beneath my fingers, swallowing thickly. "Because I don't think anyone else will, and waiting around to find out will be a life sentence for so many Untrialed. Why is my life any more precious than any of theirs?"

Evander's jaw clenches at my words, looking down at me with a pained expression. "I've just found you."

Leaning up, I press a chaste kiss to his cheek, and his fingers tighten around my waist. "I need to do this."

Evander looks down, eyelids cinched shut, before looking at me with a new hardness in his glare. Pulling me to him, he sighs.

"Then, I better sharpen my sword, because *no one* will touch what is mine."

CHAPTER 40

Adrenaline ignites me like a match catching fire, and I burn with renewed purpose.

I have all the bones of a plan that could turn the table back on Lord Drytas. The details matter less when the most difficult part would be convincing the Crowns.

Evander said he would come with me to convince the Crowns after revealing they were all conveniently convened in a meeting. But I couldn't let my hope make him reckless. If my plan doesn't go over well, Evander should be free and clear of the fallout.

Gathered in the meeting room where they'd let Drytas sway them, I know exactly where to go. I'm not surprised when the same guards stand at the entrance, but they will not deter me.

My plan could work. I just need to get in there for them to hear it.

At the sight of me stalking toward them, dagger holstered visibly at my belt, the two guards tense. They exchange a look of fear, a world of difference from last time. Now, they have seen what I'm capable of in the arena. Now they know they can't keep me out.

Reaching for their swords, the surly guards march toward me, but I raise my shield. Creating a barrier tunnel connecting my path to the door and blocking out any interference.

I don't pay the guards any mind as they pound on the shield.

Standing in front of the last obstacle between me and the Crowns, I center myself with a long, shaky breath. If I follow through, I will no longer have the option to join the Court of Truth or any other.

Lord Gennady warned me, almost as if he knew being forced into inaction against Drytas would change everything—and it had. But now, I face the last step. If I make my way in there and tell them my plan, it will be the only option I have left.

Flexing my fingers at my sides, I clench my fists, curbing any remnants of the everlasting tremble. For this to work, I need the Crowns to be confident in my plan and abilities, meaning my anxiety dies here.

As I push open both doors, they swing with enough force to clang into the walls on either side.

Five crowned heads spin to look, shocked at the sudden interruption.

Upon recognition, Lord Bralas stands, the first to protest my intrusion into the meeting. "How dare you disrupt our meeting? This is a closed-door session."

Lord Gennady is the first to meet my eyes. He sits back in his chair, not seeming surprised by my appearance. When the corner of his lip turns upward in a discrete smile, I find my confidence knowing I have Lord Gennady's support.

The other Crowns join Lord Bralas's raised voice.

Lady Ivianna looks me up and down before adding, "You need to leave. This is no place for you."

Lord Rhen stands on the opposite side of the table from

Bralas. He turns to Gennady for an explanation, as if he is somehow a part of my plan. "You don't seem surprised at her presence, Lord Gennady. Is this your doing?"

Lord Gennady raises his hands, mouth curving into a frown as he shrugs at Lord Rhen. "I would never make such moves without the agreement of the other courts. I have nothing to do with this."

Lord Nicaise pushes away from the table to look out the door behind me. "Where are the guards? There's no way they voluntarily let her in."

Over the jumble of voices, I raise my own to be heard, keeping my tone firm. "I need you all to listen to me for five minutes. Just five minutes."

Lord Bralas strides to the door, muttering, "This is ridiculous."

Summoning my shield, I block the door, making it impossible for anyone to leave. Stepping to the side, I stand in Lord Bralas's way. "Just five minutes."

Lord Bralas chuffs an outraged laugh. "Or *what*?"

"Or nothing," I say with a tone of finality. "I will not harm you. I will not trap you here." I drop the shield, standing to the side to allow Lord Bralas to pass. "But you will sorely regret not listening to me if you walk out right now."

Before Lord Bralas can do just that, Lord Gennady clears his throat, tapping his finger on the table to draw our attention. "I do not see what harm five minutes could do."

At his words, three of the Crowns settle, quieting their arguments and sitting back in their seats. Lord Bralas stares me down, lips twitching.

Speaking just to Lord Bralas, I add quietly, "I would not waste your time, Lord Bralas."

He steps back, but does not regain his seat. Instead, choosing to lean over the table, hands gripping its edge.

"Lysta," Lord Gennady says, calling my attention. He gestures for me to stand at the head of the table.

"I know you believe the lies Lord Drytas has told you," I start, looking between the Crowns.

Lord Bralas groans. "This matter has already—"

"Shut it, Bralas," Lady Ivianna sneers. "I'd like to hear her speak freely. She never got the chance at the judgment hearing after all."

Lord Bralas quiets but glares at me with renewed intensity.

I shoot a look of thanks to Lady Ivianna, but her face is hard. *Get on with it, Lysta.*

"It is easy to let such accusations die at the dismissal of a lord. Especially when you have felt none of the impact nor fear any of the repercussions. But if anything I say is the truth, you have more reason to be alarmed than Drytas allows you to think."

The Crowns stare back at me in total silence. I can hear my heart pounding in my ears, and I take a deep breath before continuing. "If I'm telling the truth about what Lord Drytas has committed, and nothing is done, your Heirs won't have courts left to rule one day."

A startled look crosses their faces, and I know they are thinking of their children. Even Lord Nicaise, who is without offspring, draws a concerned face at my words.

"I have poured over every book in the capital's library, looking for the answer as to why Valor's Trial collapsed. It has never been heard of. But there is also no record of a lord breaking the consent requirement and forcing people to Trial."

I pause, waiting for the room to interrupt me once again, but they remain silent.

"Lord Drytas proclaimed right in front of me that if he could not build an army using his own Trial, he would take over the other courts, and Trial them there instead. He has no qualms about bringing war to your doorsteps."

Fists clenched at my side, I repeat what Lord Drytas had promised. A flicker of hope sparks in my chest at the pensive looks around the room.

"And if you don't think he would sacrifice the lives of your people to make it happen, know he sacrificed his own people as if they were a means to an end. Do you think he values your people over his own? No. All he values is power. At any cost."

The room is silent as the Crowns exchange a look between them. Even Lord Bralas, who had been beyond furious mere minutes ago, is understanding the gravity of my words.

Lord Nicaise is the first to break the silence. "Realize we cannot act on your word alone. Even if the truth of what you speak of is a threat to us all, we need some form of proof or evidence."

I nod rapidly, latching onto the chance to convince them. Stepping forward, I brace my hands on the table, gathering strength to tell them my plan.

A voice echoes in my head, warning me they will not listen.

"What if I could get you the proof you need?"

Five pairs of eyes watch me with an air of skepticism.

"How?" Lord Rhen asks, his gaze pinning me in place. "How could you possibly prove it?"

Standing up straight, I rub my sweaty palms on my pants before clasping my trembling fingers together. Steeling myself, I say it—my plan that could solve everything.

"Send representatives of each of your courts with me to Valor. I know the city better than anyone, and I can guide them. They can see for themselves the state of the Trial and the city."

Lord Bralas crosses his arms, finally taking a seat at the table among the other Crowns. "And if what you say is not true?

Our presence will only anger Lord Drytas, and we will have him to answer to. We'd be breaking the treaty."

It is then I get a glimpse of Lord Bralas I have yet to see so far. The angry force who endeavored to diminish me every chance he got is *scared*.

Looking to the empty seats on my right, reserved for Valor, I shift on my feet. Standing across from the people who hold my fate in their hands, I hold my breath before continuing. "If I'm lying, your people can hand me over to Drytas once we are there. You can pretend you changed your mind about my sentencing, and wished to deliver me to him to handle as he sees fit. Maybe you'll even win his favor."

Lord Gennady sits forward suddenly, eyes wide as he stares at me. "He would kill you for treason if we handed you over."

Giving the older man an upside-down smile, I shrug.

"Then it's fortunate for myself I am not lying."

Lady Ivianna taps her fingernails against the table in rapid succession, her face deep in concentration. "And who do you expect us to send? How do we know you won't bribe or threaten anyone we send into confirming whatever you say?"

I grimace, knowing the final part of my plan will likely be what sets off the growing tension.

"Send your Heirs. Who could you trust more to carry out such an important task?"

Before I can finish the sentence, they shake their heads, equally upset at the concept of sending their children on such a mission.

Leaning forward, I implore the Crowns to listen. "You've seen what I can do," I say, referencing the battle between Torryn and myself that exploded before them all. "And I know what your Heirs are capable of. I pity those who would step up against them."

I know I have said the right thing to convince them when

they exchange a look of solidarity. "And how do you expect to get into the city?"

I stifle the sense of victory blooming in my chest. "I have a way for us to arrive there quickly, and exactly where we need to be. But I will not be disclosing it until I know we are moving forward with the plan."

Even if Sar volunteered to use her power for the mission, there is no need to share the extent of her abilities when the plan is not guaranteed.

"You've thought of almost everything, it seems," Lord Gennady says.

I nod, swallowing the emotions rearing up now I have finally been heard. "I've been trying to figure out how to make you all believe me since I arrived. I foolishly believed if you liked me or I fit in, I could convince you. Turns out I just needed to be willing to go back to the place I escaped."

Lord Gennady looks at me with weary eyes at my words. He stands and the other Crowns follow his lead. "This is a decision we will need to discuss in private. Leave us, and we will summon you upon our decision."

I nod, holding back the abundance of gratitude surging in me.

CHAPTER 41

The hours between when I left the Crowns to deliberate and when they summon me back are torturous.

I sit with Sar and Evander in the library, replaying every sentence I'd uttered, every question they'd asked. Wondering if I pushed too hard or not hard enough and if I had forgotten an essential part of the plan. Preparing myself to either accept their decision or fight even harder.

Evander takes my hand under the table, rubbing the pads of his fingers across my knuckles. I try to hide my trembling, but he has already seen the physical depiction of my mental state.

Leaning toward me, Evander whispers, "Whichever way it goes, you've done everything you can."

His words aren't the source of comfort he thinks it is, but I appreciate the effort all the same. Sending him a half-hearted smile, I nod, pressing my other hand into my forehead.

I don't even know what my next step will be if they don't approve of my plan. Short of building my own army, there is nothing I can do to stand against Drytas on my own. Every chance I have of stopping him relies on the Crowns.

I'M NOT ENTIRELY TAKEN by surprise when the Crowns request Evander as well when they summon me back to the meeting room. Evander squeezes my hand before following the Guard sent to retrieve us.

When we arrive back at the meeting room, all the Heirs are present, which I hope is a good sign of their decision. Even Visha, while not directly an Heir, stands behind her uncle, watching our arrival. Lord Nicaise is turned around in his seat, speaking low to her as a startled expression crosses her face for mere seconds. When her eyes flick to mine, I realize he's likely telling her what the Crowns had been debating.

Shaking my head, I push out any thought of her. I could not let myself be pulled in by her theatrics or distractions today. There is too much at stake.

Evander leaves my side, casting a last glance at me before joining his father at the head of the table. A new tension rests on his shoulders as he stands beside Lord Gennady. The cool, collected mask of Truth's Heir falling across his face.

Murmurs echo across the table, the Heirs unaware as to the reason for their sudden summoning—and my own, for that matter.

"Everyone, take a seat, and we will get started," Lord Gennady announces, gesturing to both sides of the table.

I stay at the head of the table, not even wondering if the group would allow me to sit in the chairs reserved for Valor. For I am not a Crown, nor an Heir.

Lord Gennady starts, his voice commanding the attention of the room. "Lysta has given us reason to reexamine the accusations against Lord Drytas."

Some Heirs shift in their seat, leaning forward in interest. Neith catches my eye from his position further on the opposite side of the table but says nothing. Instead, he examines me as if I will give away what is going on.

"We have decided the risk of what Lysta's words being true means is too severe to leave the situation without looking into it further."

Bringing my hand up to cover my mouth, I stifle the sound of surprise threatening to burst out. My throat tightens, and I gulp, looking at the ceiling to blink away the mist clouding my eyes.

They believe me. Maybe not as much as I'd like but certainly more than I hoped. The Crowns are taking what I said and are endeavoring to find out more. No more pushing it off as the lies of a girl who has been seduced into saying the treasonous words. But as the words of someone who has some modicum of credibility.

I can't help but look to Evander with hopeful eyes. We have done it.

Evander's face is pinched, eyebrows drawn together as if scrutinizing every word coming out of his father's mouth. Looking at Lord Gennady as if he doesn't believe what he's just heard.

I can't help my small smile, glad my hand still covers my mouth.

Lord Gennady continues after he has let the information sink in. "Lysta has proposed a mission to the Crowns that allows us to confirm or negate the accusations. We cannot develop a course of action until the truth has been decided, but because of the potential danger of the mission, we agree it should be voluntary."

Several Crowns nod along to Lord Gennady's words, emphasizing their agreement. From opposite sides of the table, Neith and Visha share a conspiring look.

When no one protests his announcement, Lord Gennady

continues, his tone foreboding. "The plan would be for the Heirs to journey to the Court of Valor with Lysta. Each of you are well trained not only in your powers but in weaponry and combat. You would navigate the city undetected, observing not only the state of the court, but its people as well." Lord Gennady pauses, looking around the table once again. "The most important objective is locating Valor's Trial with Lysta's help and finding out if it is truly broken."

When Lord Gennady hesitates in his speech, Neith clears his throat.

"Apologies, Lord Gennady," Neith starts, but Gennady waves him on. "I'm sure this is not something approved by Lord Drytas, as that would be most difficult to believe. What if we are discovered while in Valor? I doubt our presence will be well received." Neith leans forward, pressing a finger along the length of his lips in a face of consternation.

I'm reminded of the possibility of Neith working with Lord Drytas. If he is, telling him this plan is a risk to us all, but not if we leave before he can make it to Falland.

Lord Gennady looks at me with a sad glimmer in his eyes, as if not willing to speak the part of the plan that would leave me to the wolves. He swallows, bending to prop both elbows on the table in front of him. "If—if you are discovered—"

Lord Bralas jumps in at Lord Gennady's hesitation. "If you are caught without being able to verify this information, Drytas will demand an explanation. You will tell him the Crowns have decided to allow him to deal with Lysta as he sees fit. And then you will leave her behind."

All the Heirs recoil, even Neith, at the declaration, obviously not having expected such an extreme answer. They share concerned looks across the table. Evander's eyes pierce me like a blade. As if his gaze will somehow carve the truth from my silence. I didn't tell him this part of my plan, knowing he would resist.

It's what must be done to get the Crowns to go with the plan.

"Is that understood?" Lord Bralas says, voice raising. When no one responds, he continues. "Lysta herself has proposed this plan and will accept the consequences should it fail."

Lord Gennady stands, leaning his weight on his cane as he peers down the table. "Knowing the uncertainty of this mission, all the Crowns have agreed it is up to each of the Heirs." Taking in a deep breath, he asks, "Does anyone have questions before we go around the table?"

The room is silent as we wait for someone to voice their concerns. I expect a similar third degree that I'd received from the Crowns upon first presenting the plan.

Neith is the one to start. He turns to his left, facing not only his father but also Lord Gennady. "What's the plan for getting into Valor?"

Lord Gennady nods in acknowledgment before swiveling his head to me. It takes a moment for every head at the table to follow his lead in a chain reaction until I am, once again, the center of attention.

I promised the Crowns that, if they agreed to move forward with my plan, I would tell them how we would get into Falland. But faced with telling Sar's secret, I hesitate.

Torryn had made it known on my first day to note how important keeping one's power a secret is. It's not only maintaining an advantage but protecting against weakness.

But Sar had been emphatic she wanted to do this, regardless of what Torryn or Ardis would think. Sar wanted to help me protect the Untrialed.

"Sar, of the Court of Self," I say, shooting a quick glance at Lord Bralas and Neith, "has volunteered to aid us. With her permission, I can tell you now she can produce portals for transport." I pause, letting the words sink in.

"How is that supposed to help?" Bralas asks, a sneer marring his features.

His disrespect of Sar makes me clench my fists under the table, nostrils flaring.

"My youngest son can do the exact same thing," Bralas admits smugly. "It's useful for traveling the length of the arena, but no more than that."

Lord Bralas is so eager to dismiss my plan. So quick to dismiss his daughter.

I struggle to conceal my attitude. "Sar can portal much further distances. On the day I arrived here, she portaled us from Lord Drytas's throne room, to just outside the Border Forest."

Jaws drop, and I wish deeply Sar was there to bask in their awe of her abilities. Lord Bralas's mouth snaps shut audibly, leaning back to stare blankly at the table in front of him.

Lord Gennady breaks the awed silence, a knowing smile creeping across his face. "We shall be grateful Miss Sarielle is with us then, and not against us."

Lord Bralas's face pales, and I let a smirk cross mine. Knowing the thoughts likely crossing through his mind, I can't help but shove Sar's excellence in his face.

"One might say she is one of the most powerful to be born to Wisdom. Wouldn't you agree, Lord Bralas?"

Neith narrows his eyes at me but turns for his father's reaction. Lord Bralas ignores my words, turning to Lord Gennady. "Shouldn't we be dealing with the matters at hand?"

Lord Gennady nods in his direction, letting Bralas shift the conversation away from his jilted daughter. "Can we have a show of hands from the Heirs?"

Bash stands, breaking the lingering silence. Looking at me,

he puts a hand on the hilt of his sword hanging at his waist. When he speaks, confident and assured, his words aim to lead the others as the oldest of the Heirs.

"I have found Lysta to be honorable in her time at the capital. I volunteer to join her on this mission."

Evander is quick to follow Bash, raising his hand, eyes locked onto mine. When the two nod to each other, a slow trickle of hands follows. Jona, from the Court of Will. Neith, from the Court of Wisdom, after a noticeable nudge from his father.

Turning to Lord Nicaise's wife, who sits as his Heir, I hold my breath to see if this will be a unanimous agreement.

Lord Nicaise stands, turning to address the table. "As you all know, my wife sits as Heir, as I have no children. But I request an exception be made in her being the representative who visits Valor, as she is not in a state to do so." He says this as he reaches to take his wife's hand.

Smiling back up at him, she circles her stomach with her other hand.

It takes a moment before the table breaks out into congratulations.

Lord Gennady moves to pat Lord Nicaise's shoulder firmly, grinning at them as if announcing his own child.

"What a great blessing, for the both of you," Lord Gennady says, as he sits back in his seat.

Lord Nicaise's eyes shine with pride as he gazes at his wife. "We thank you for your kind words." Clearing the sentiment from his voice, he sits up straighter. "We request my niece, Visha, be allowed to stand in her stead. She has trained with the Heirs since she became of age and is formidable in battle."

Looking around the table for protest, Lord Gennady nods when there is none. "I think we all agree with that, but does Visha volunteer willingly?"

Visha straightens behind her uncle at the room's sudden attention, obviously not surprised at the request being made. This must be what Nicaise told Visha at the start of the meeting.

Chin raised, Visha nods. "I would be honored, my lord."

"Then if there are no further questions or protests, I see no reason for delay. When do we leave, Lysta?" Lord Gennady asks.

The room's attention shifts to me once again. I fold my hands in front of me, trying to project confidence when I answer. "Tonight, my lord. It is when the Guard will be the least active."

It also leaves Drytas's spies, whether it be Neith or not, without time to get word to Drytas so that he can prepare, but the table in front of me does not need to know that.

Lord Gennady signals the end of the meeting. "Tonight, it is."

CHAPTER 42

The emptiness of the arena minutes before midnight is haunting. It lacks the stomping feet and the screaming crowd of War Hour yet ties my stomach in knots all the same. With the sun absent from the open top, the space is cloaked in shadows and darkness, lit with only the torches surrounding the battlefield.

Even with their dim glow, I can see Evander moving across the space between weapon racks, picking up supplies and letting them fall with a heavy clatter. His sword shines where the firelight hits the blade, making reflected spots flicker on the sand at his feet.

Stepping through the metal cage, the door creaks and groans as it swings open, announcing my arrival. He stiffens at the noise before glancing over his shoulder, relaxing at the sight of me. As I tread closer to him, he leans to grab a sword sharpener before bringing the metal chisel against the edges of his blade. "I'll do yours next if you'd like?" Evander asks without taking his gaze from the sword resting in his hands.

I murmur a word of thanks before making my way to the weapons rack. Scanning the blades and bows, daggers, and axes, I find the silver sword with the ivy hand guard. I bring the blade over to Evander, resting it against the barrel he sharpens his on.

Evander nods toward the dagger strapped to my outer thigh. "Might as well sharpen that one as well."

For once the blade sits proudly in its holster, not tucked away under clothes like it had in Falland nor dresses from here in the capital. Evander probably had not even realized I carried it with me until my fight with Torryn.

Unstrapping the blade, I twist it in my fingers as he scrapes against his sword with the chisel, the grating metal screeching. Walking up behind Evander, I lean toward him until my temple rests on the hard muscle of his shoulder. The smell of his leather chest plate drifts past me, and I can't help but breathe in the familiar scent.

Evander's shoulder moves when he murmurs, "You really want to go back there?"

Sighing, I pull away, knowing the comforting moment has passed.

His sword gleams as he sharpens it against the stone, his foot balanced on its surface as he draws it back and forth. When he examines its edge, he nods in satisfaction before sheathing the weapon at his hip.

"Of course I don't want to, Evander. If it was about what I wanted, then I would never make myself step foot in Falland again."

Evander turns to me with pleading eyes. "So, don't—don't go back. The Heirs are more than capable of carrying out the mission."

Evander curls a hand around the curve of my ear, pushing my hair away from my face. I raise my chin so that I stare down the bridge of my nose into his eyes.

"I know I am not a lord or a lady, Evander. I'm not an Heir

like you. But that doesn't change the fact that the people Drytas is weaponizing—they are *my* people, and I don't need a title or a crown to feel the same sense of duty for them as you do for your people."

A softness enters Evander's eyes, and, for a moment, I think he understands. Understands what I'm trying to say—what I feel. But then my hopes are dashed.

"I wish you would reconsider." He grips my upper arms, shaking me slightly.

Disappointment crashes into me, and I look away from his imploring eyes. Bringing one hand up to his chest, I can feel his heartbeat racing under my fingers. While I want his support—I do not need his permission.

"There's no chance of this mission being a success without me, Evander. I'm the only one who knows Falland. Without me, you'll run into a guard within the first thirty-seconds of being there. Not to mention trying to find the Trial."

I know his reaction is because he cares, which touches me more than I can ever explain to him. Having grown up in Falland, where self-preservation is such an ingrained trait in its people, I know having Evander care so obviously means a great deal. But I can't just walk away from this, and I can't have Evander questioning my ability to handle this mission once the other Heirs arrive.

"Hands off and two steps back, Evander."

Sar's voice echoes across the arena.

Evander's hands tighten for a moment, hesitating, before he lets me go. His head hangs between us, and I duck, trying to catch his gaze. When he turns away from me, keeping his back to me, I sigh. He grabs my sword before moving to sharpen it.

Turning to where Sar strides across the sand, I wave her off. "He's just worried about me, Sar. I'm fine. I promise."

Sar wrinkles her nose but relaxes as she comes to stand next to me. For someone who is not trained in combat like Evander, Sar has all the fight in her heart.

"Thank you for doing this," I mutter. "We wouldn't be able to pull this off without you, Sar."

How ironic that despite how much Torryn and Ardis fought to keep Sar safe by keeping her from the action that she is now running into it headfirst.

"I'll face the music when we get back, but it's worth it," Sar says with determination flickering in her eyes.

It isn't long after Sar's arrival that the Heirs trickle into the arena, faces drawn with determination.

Tonight will be about proving more than the truth, for the Heirs will prove themselves as well. Dressed in leather and metal, they're fit for battle, and I only hope our mission will not come to it.

Bash nods to me in greeting as he passes. Wearing a metal chest plate and wraps around his arms, a large amount of Bash's back is free. Likely left open so that he can summon his wings without obstruction. He approaches Evander, who has just finished sharpening my blade.

Pointing to the sharpener, Bash asks, "Mind if I take a turn with that?"

Jona slinks in behind Bash, covered nearly from head to toe in black. As he walks, he wraps black tape around his knuckles and fists. Two thin swords are crossed in holsters strapped to his back. The only color on his entire person are three strands that dangle from his wrist—braided bracelets like a child would make. One pink, yellow, and blue. He bows his head as he passes me before smiling at Bash and Evander over my shoulder.

Visha enters with her arms crossed, but her typical sneer missing from her face. The throwing daggers I've seen her fling with dangerous velocity are strapped to her belt and stowed away in the holsters of her vest. The silver of her weapons shine in contrast to the dark purple—almost black—garments she wears. A bow is strapped to her back with silver stemmed arrows collected in a leather quiver. Her curly hair is woven into tight braids gathering across one shoulder in a bigger knot.

She hovers near me, as if not sure whether she should acknowledge me or pass me by as the others did.

"I have no doubt you're telling the truth," Visha sneers. "I wouldn't be coming otherwise." She looks at the boys behind me. "Just don't get us all killed trying to prove it."

She stomps past me to join the others, patting Jona's shoulder, who sits crossed legged in the sand, meditating.

Neith is the last to arrive, a cocky grin plastered across his face. "Has everyone said their tear-filled goodbyes in case Valor over here plans to screw us over?" Neith jests with a poison laced tone.

Evander crosses his arms across the field before growling, "Cut it out, Neith. If you ever take one thing seriously in your life, Trials, let it be this."

I'm the first to step through the portal. One foot on sand while the other lands on the tiles of Drytas's throne room.

The space is cloaked in shadows. Even the sconces hung from the walls are out, not even an ember hinting at recent life. I didn't think the room could be any more ominous, but at night, when the black-and-white room is painted in further shades of gray, I change my mind.

When the only sound I can hear in the room is my breathing, I wave through the portal, gesturing for the others to follow. One by one, they step in, gazes examining the throne room.

"Why exactly are we entering through the throne room? Shouldn't we have started where it's a little less high pressure?" Jona asks.

Sar steps through the portal once all the Heirs have, and it blinks shut once she is clear of the opening. "Because I can only open a portal to where I've seen. Torryn was able to show me a glimpse of the throne room during his time here, so this is our only entry point."

Jona hums at Sar's answer, nodding in acceptance, but I send her a questioning look.

How had Torryn shown her the throne room?

"This is Valor. Huh," Neith says, walking further into the room. He comes to stand at the foot of Drytas's throne before turning to look at us. "It's nicer than the picture of poverty you painted for us."

I can't help but scoff at Neith's words. "I was choked midair by Drytas using his telekinesis about two paces to your right."

Neith steps away from the spot I point at in a comical way that makes Jona, Bash, and Visha chuckle. Sar and Evander just give me frowning glances at the morbid joke.

I shrug. "And as soon as you step out of the grand hall, you'll see the real Falland. Not this pride stroking building that Drytas hides himself away in." Brushing past Visha, I gesture to the city from the largest window.

Heavy breathing sounds behind me, and I turn to see Visha hunched over, hands braced on her knees.

Neith stands next to her, moving to rest a hand on her back. "Visha? What's wrong?" His eyes flicker to her.

When she looks up, her gaze meets mine, and there is a purple haze to her eyes. She's feeling someone's emotions, but whose?

As she takes in shuddering breaths, Neith moves to kneel in front of her, whispering, "Let go of it, V." Neith brushes her braids back over her shoulder before laying his hand on her neck, thumb rubbing circles into her skin. "Feel mine. I'm calm." When Visha's breathing slows and the panic leaves her eyes, Neith sags in relief. "See, everything is okay."

Visha nods tightly, pushing his hand off where it lingers on her arm. A frown passes over Neith's face before he wipes it away. "Who the hell is that freaked out?" Neith growls as he whips around to examine the rest of the group standing awkwardly to the side.

When no one answers, Neith turns to Visha, expecting an answer. She bites her cheek, staring Neith down before her eyes flick to me, but Neith catches it anyway.

He storms across the room until his reddening face is inches from my own. "Get over it and get it together. You're the only reason we are here in the first place."

"Back off, Neith," Sar warns, stepping toward us.

Narrowing my eyes, I push a hand into Neith's chest. "When you have to revisit where you were Trialed and tortured against your will, then—and only then—can you tell me to get over it." Shoving past him, I add, "Plus, I'm keeping it together. It's not my fault she can't handle what's in my head—"

"Shouldn't we get going?" Jona asks, voice monotone. "I'd like to get in and out of here as quickly as possible."

Standing next to the door, I listen for the sound of the Guard patrol but hear nothing. Taking a glance at the decorative clock tower that sits in the corner. Thirteen minutes after midnight. Keeping my ear tuned to the hall, I speak low.

"We just need to lie low here, so we can get a gauge of the guard's patrol."

CHAPTER 43

As the clock edges past quarter till one, my suspicions are confirmed.

I'd spent more than my fair share of days and nights memorizing the Guard's movement and patrol patterns. Every fifteen minutes, they pass the throne room—to the minute.

But crouched next to the door, ear pressed to the cool surface, I haven't heard a single rustle or whisper, yet we've been here closer to a half an hour.

The realization rings alarm bells in my head. I'd considered that Lord Drytas would likely change his security protocols following mine and Torryn's sudden departure from the Court of Valor. But my predictions had been along the lines of increased measures—not decreased.

Standing from my crouch position, I curse under my breath. When six heads whip around to look at me, the risk I've taken—that the Heirs have taken, nearly steals my composure.

Evander moves to me, breaking the silence. "What's wrong?"

Staying here is a dangerous waiting game, but roaming the

grand hall with no knowledge of the guards' movement is begging for trouble.

"The guard should have moved through this hall by now." Biting my lip, I debate what options we have. "We'll have to make our way blind."

There isn't the chorus of arguments that I expect. Looking between the Heirs, including Sar, I see no sign of protest on their faces. Visha's lips are pinched in a line, but she still gives me a tight nod—willing me forward with the plan.

Stepping into the hall, we file out in a line, flattening against the stone wall amongst the shadows. Every turn we come across, I tremble as I peer around the corner, praying no one will be waiting in the adjoining hall. All it takes is one guard to sound the alarm and then they would be on us before we knew what was happening.

Pressing forward, I follow my memory, pushing us closer to where the Trial's entrance had once stood.

Evander presses behind me, mouth near my ear as he whispers, "Are we getting close?"

"It's just around this next corner." Turning to look at everyone huddled against the wall, I ask, "Everyone still with us?"

Neith huffs impatiently, shoving past me. "I swear, we could have been in and out by now if—" He passes the corner, raising his sword, and Neith jumps, pulling at the weapon with his weight. "What the—something has my sword. You didn't say they could turn invisible."

"They can't!" I shout, my eyes wide as Neith struggles against the force fighting for his sword. I take a moment to realize that it's telekinesis he fights against.

"They're here." I jump into action. "The guard must be protecting the Trial."

Neith loses his grip on his sword, and it soars down the hall, leaving him without a weapon. I summon a shield, using it to block the hallway leading to the Trial as a rainstorm of arrows and swords pelt the space in front of Neith.

I slide to him on my knees, pulling my sword from its holster at my hip. I shove the blade into Neith's hand, struggling to do so while also maintaining the shield. When he tries to push it away, I snap, "You're better with a sword, and I can't hold my shield and fight with it anyway."

He nods, taking the weapon.

A dozen or so guards stand at attention at the entrance to the Trial hall. Each holds their hands in front of them, likely wielding the sword that hover slam against my shield. Two of them kneel, aiming arrows in our direction. When none of their attacks make it through the shield, they falter, summoning their weapons back to their persons.

"Why are they attacking?" Visha shouts from behind the wall.

I send her a withering glare. "Why do you thin—"

"Not the time for this!" Bash crouches, eyes leveling with my own. "Lower your shield, Lysta. We are more than capable of taking them on."

"Stay there!" I shout, keeping my head turned down the hall. I don't face Bash as I tell him my plan. All the guards can see is Neith and myself. They don't know that the five of them stand ready in the wings. "They don't know you are there. We can ambush them," I hiss, getting to my feet.

Weapons now in hand, the guards give up on their aerial attack, rushing toward us. Raising their swords high in the air, they give a loud cry before attacking my shield.

I stumble from the sudden force, each strike making my arms shake with the effort of holding up the barrier. It feels as if my muscles hold the weight and not my will.

Sweat drips down my brow, racing for my neck. Step by

step, I let myself be pushed backward, bringing my shield along with me. As the force field recedes, the guards push on, shouting in victory.

Following my lead, Neith, and I move away from the line until our backs press into the wall. Neith sends me an anxious look, struggling—not fighting back—but struggling to trust me with his life.

"Lysta," Evander warns.

I shake my head at him once, hoping he'll stop whatever he wants to do.

The guards pass the end of the hallway, stepping out into the open. I hold my breath, waiting for one of them to turn their heads a few inches to the right and catch sight of the rest of the team standing in the wings. But they never do, too focused on the two intruders trapped before them. I'm sure the bounty on my head is plenty of a distraction.

I watch, heart pounding, as Visha, Evander, and Jona slide into the hallway. Standing behind the guard with their weapons poised. Bash swoops above them, wings spread as he soars over the guards before landing beside Neith and I.

The guards startle at his sudden presence, following where he'd come from over their heads to find the others behind them. While they may have the numbers, we have them surrounded.

But this doesn't need to come to a fight. Our issues are with Drytas, not the people blindly following his rule. I had been the same not long enough ago.

"We mean you no harm. Let us pass through to the Trial, and we can resolve this without battle," I say confidently despite the tremble of my fingers.

The men grumble in front of us, and I can feel their ridicule as they glare at me menacingly. "We let you go, and we are as good as dead when Drytas gets back. It looks like we'll take our chances in battle."

My heart stutters in my chest, and my throat gets tight as I ask, "Gets back? Where is Drytas?"

The guards exchange a look but don't answer my question. With a roar, they charge, splitting up between sides. The sound of swords clashing echoes off the stone walls, followed by the grunts of effort and pain.

It's a dance of blood and steel, as both sides fight for the upper hand, but the guards don't stand a chance. Who knows how much training they have received, but it's obviously incomparable to the Heirs. The Heirs who have been preparing for war since their birth.

I can't help but flinch as Visha throws several daggers in rapid succession. Each landing deep in the chest of her target before they stumble to the ground. Her face is one of complete focus as she bends to pull each of the daggers from the prone bodies. But her eyes never leave the fight edging on around her, scanning for her next target.

Bash pumps his wings as he soars toward his victim, latching his arms around them as he lifts higher. The guard's feet kick in the air as they leave the ground but stop in an instant when Bash turns their head forcefully, breaking their neck.

Despite being the youngest of us at sixteen, Jona has no problem holding his own as he moves from one guard to the next. While his movements lack the fluidity and smoothness of the others, they certainly do not lack the precision as he cuts down his opponents with his dual swords.

My stomach rolls at the mangled body that slumps to the ground, but I'm distracted as I catch sight of Evander fighting a guard, sword to sword. Another guard edges behind him, and my eyes widen.

"Evander!" I shout his name, but it's drowned out by the sound of the fight. Raising my shield, I separate Evander from the attacker. Before I can be relieved, a battle cry echoes behind me, and I turn, flinching as a guard moves toward me, blade aimed for my torso.

Before I can even debate moving the shield to cover myself, a white wing moves between me and the guard. Bash.

Their actions are blocked from me, Bash's wings concealing their bodies. It is not until a sword pierces through the white feather wing, staining it a cherry red, that I spring into action.

Bash yells in anguish, folding his wings in as he kneels, but not getting rid of them entirely. When his wings close, I get a glimpse of the guard who'd tried to attack me. Bash's sword deep in his chest.

Bash took my hit, dealing out his own while protecting me.

Another guard rushes toward us, but I fling up my shield, separating Bash from any further threat. Kneeling in front of Bash, I hold my hands out, unsure of what to do with the blade protruding from his wing.

My hands shake as I lean forward to ask, "Bash, what do you want me to do?" He leans forward onto his hands, head hanging down as he mutters something ineligibly. "Bash, I can't hear you. What do you—"

"Take. It. Out." Bash grits the words out between clenched teeth.

"Are you sure? Can't you just get rid of your wings?"

"I would still have the injury, but somewhere else. My form shifts to create the wings."

"But—"

"Take it out!" Bash groans loudly in pain. Then again, softer. "Take it out. Take it out. Take it out."

Reaching up, I grab the hilt of the sword. When the blade jostles in my trembling hands, Bash groans, and I wince, sending him an apologetic look. Breathing in deeply through my nose, I pull the sword from his wing.

I toss the crimson stained blade to the side, and it clatters across the stone floor. Blood flows from the gaping wound in his wing, and I look for something to press to the wound.

"Here. Use this."

Evander stands behind me, holding out his jacket for me to take. His eyebrows are knitted together when he kneels next to Bash.

Bundling it up in my hands, I press the fabric into the wound, causing Bash to hiss out expletives in his pain.

It's only then that I realize the sound of the battle has stopped. There are no shouts, nor clanging of swords. The group gathers around us, sweaty and breathing ragged, but none of them harmed.

"He needs to be taken back to the healers, Lysta," Evander says in a low voice. "We should go. Before anymore guards show up."

I want to protest but bite my tongue instead. None of the Heirs have seen the Valor's Trial yet, nor any of the city. We haven't completed what we came here to accomplish. But how could I tell Bash, the man who saved my life, that our mission is more important than his life?

Staring at Bash, his face has paled significantly, a gaunt expression covering his face. Whether from the battle or from blood loss, I'm not sure.

I nod, acquiescing to Evander's suggestion. "Sar, can you take us back—"

"Hold up," Visha interrupts. "We haven't finished what we were meant to do here." She looks around at us all before crossing her arms across her chest. "We aren't leaving until we are done."

"But Bash—"

Sar steps forward to interrupt me. "What if I bring Bash

back first? Then you can finish what you need to here, and I'll come back for you."

I look to Evander, hoping he'll say we should do it. His face is tight, his lips turned down at the corners. When he doesn't speak up, I decide. "Do it. Come back as soon as you get him to a healer. We'll meet you in the throne room—now go!"

CHAPTER 44

When the Heirs stare at the rubble of the Court of Valor's Trial with abject horror, I expect to feel vindicated. After having been called a liar, a traitor, and a lord's whore—shouldn't it feel *just* to be proven right all along?

But as the gobsmacked Heirs fumble in disbelief at the broken Trial, all I can think about is Drytas's absence and its implications.

"Have—have you ever seen anything like it?" Jona asks with a shakiness to his voice. "I mean, I know they said it couldn't be Trialed, but it's truly broken."

Neith scuffs his feet in the shattered glass, kicking larger shards across the floor. Cursing under his breath, he squats to examine the carved fragments. Picking up a piece, he holds it up to one of the lit torches on the walls, letting the light shine through it. "The Crowns will freak when they realize what is possible. That *this* is possible."

"Where would Drytas have gone?" I mumble the question to myself, rubbing my forehead in frustration.

Neith shoots me an annoyed look. "You're gonna have to speak up a bit, Valor."

Raising my head to look at the group staring at me, I ask again with more sureness in my voice. "Where would Drytas have gone?" I pause, but no one answers. "We just left the capital, and he wasn't there. The guard let slip that he's not here in Falland. The only other place he would go—"

The Heirs exchange a look.

"There's a reason we weren't discovered by guards prior to reaching the Trial," I say with a growing sense of alarm. "They aren't *here*."

I don't want to say the words. Because as much as I wanted everyone to believe me that Lord Drytas planned to attack the other courts, I can't fathom it happening. If he is moving forward with his plan, that means time is up. The Untrialed are already at risk, along with every other court.

It means that I'm too late.

Visha finally says the words that hang over us. "He's going to attack the courts."

The only other things that the Heirs were meant to see were the Untrialed. I had planned to sneak them into the streets, hoping they would glimpse the oppression and mistreatment they face every day under Drytas's rule. But Drytas had been two steps ahead.

Standing, I gesture to the Trial. "Do you need to see anything else?" I ask, anger coating my tone. No one says anything but shakes their heads. "Good, because we need to get back to the capital. Now."

"Do we know where he would hit first?" Evander pants out as we jog through the halls toward the throne room.

While our entrance into the Court of Valor had been all about remaining undetected, our departure is anything but. Instead, we run like war chases us at our heels.

Every window we pass warns of how much of a head start Drytas had ahead of us. The sky is no longer a well of blackness, a combination of the night sky and the city's smog. Now the first cracks of light outline the horizon, forewarning the new day that has arrived.

"His original plan was to go for the Court of Virtue because they are closest, but I'm not sure if that is still his plan. He knows he exposed that part of his plan, so I don't think he'll continue with it now."

"How is it he decided to attack now?" Visha asks.

I scoff, looking at her from the corner of my eye. "You mean like I said he was planning to?"

"I'll make sure to applaud you for it later," Visha snarls sarcastically. "No, I mean why now? Out of all the times he could have attacked, how did he choose right when we were coming to discover his lies?"

I stumble mid-stride, coming to a sudden stop. Turning to Visha, I breathe heavily before asking, "Are you saying that—"

"I'm saying that he knew."

My heart feels as if someone is gripping it tightly, and I press a hand to my chest as if it will dissipate the feeling.

Visha continues, "I'm saying that someone warned him we were onto him, and he rounded up his people to attack while we were distracted."

Evander shakes his head emphatically. "There's no way. The only people that knew we were leaving were Crowns and Heirs. And that isn't enough time for anyone to get a message out. There's no way Lord Drytas could have mobilized an entire city in that time."

Visha and I exchange a look.

I think that's exactly what Drytas did. It's entirely likely that Drytas has been ready to attack on a moment's notice for weeks.

"Who knew about your plan before you brought it to the Crowns? You obviously told someone. Did you tell Lord Torryn?"

My gaze snaps to her. Shutting her down with one hard look. "I didn't tell him. The only ones who knew were Sar and Evander, who, if you didn't notice, were right here alongside us —fighting."

"I know about his little mind tricks. All it would take would be for you to even think about the plan in his presence, and he could find it if he was looking."

Visha's knowledge of Torryn's power takes me by surprise. When no one within the capital wall mentioned that power, I assumed it was not known.

I shake my head. "I didn't think of the plan until after Torryn had already left."

Evander chirps in, "So, then, Sar—"

"It's not her. She's risked too much by helping us, not to mention revealing a power that would have been more useful if kept secret." Turning to Visha, eyebrows knotted, I prod her. "Mind reading is from your court. I could have spoken to anyone who has Trialed in Virtue and not even known."

Visha's face darkens. "That doesn't mean it was someone of my court. Lord Nicaise lets practically anyone Trial in Virtue. It could be plenty of people."

"We can't prove who leaked. But it proves one thing. Drytas has been recruiting from the other courts. So, he may have more to his army than just members of the Guard and Untrialed."

～

Running the halls of the capital, I'm sure we look a sight to behold. Dried blood crusts on the weapons strapped to our body, mixing with sweat staining our clothes, making it look as if we are gravely injured.

At such an early hour in the morning, several staff members roam the halls. They doddle along, toting trays of food, and freshly cleaned linens as if today is like any other. Little do they know how much is about to change.

They would soon see a new kind of War Hour.

At the sight of the six of us barreling down the hall, they jump to the side and into open doorways with a shriek. Watching us with bulging eyes and pointed fingers. The Heirs that sprint past them in varying levels of dishevelment resemble no part of the trophies that had been paraded past them at the Peace Ball.

Gone were their fancy garments and luxurious jewelry. Gone were their charming smiles and hopeful words.

Today, any passerby witnessed the future of their courts. Warriors that are prepared to defend.

For all we know, Drytas has already launched a full-scale attack against one of the courts. Drytas could be standing behind his legion of Untrialed and guards alike, waiting as they fought their way into a court's center city. How long would it take to send word once the attacks begin?

My stomach knots at the thought of Drytas walking through a path of destruction, his crimson cape dragging along behind him.

Pushing in the doors of the meeting room where the Crowns await their Heirs, I feel the tension stifling the room. No one speaks when we enter, the Crowns watching us with bated breath.

Lady Ivianna stands, bringing a hand to cover her mouth.

"Bash. Where is Bash?" She asks, a growing horrified expression crossing her face.

Sar steps forward, raising a hand like one would calm a frightened animal. "Bash is fine. He got stabbed in the wing and was taken immediately to a healer. He's likely finding his way to you as we speak."

Lady Ivianna relaxes slightly, sitting back in her seat, but her face doesn't lose its pale sickly color.

Evander steps up to the table, clearing his throat. "Have any of you heard anything from your Trial cities in the hours since we've been gone?"

The Crowns look between themselves, each shaking their head before Lord Nicaise answers for them all verbally. "Nothing. Why? What happened in Valor?"

The Heirs relax, exchanging relieved looks. If the Crowns have not yet heard of anything brewing in their courts, it meant that there is still time. Drytas is not so far ahead of us as to ambush.

Visha nods, before adding, "Then hopefully we are not too late."

Lord Bralas stands suddenly, chair screeching backward. "Too late for what, girl?" Bralas growls out in question.

Neith steps forward, just barely moving in front of Visha. Sending a glare at his father, Neith tells the Crowns what had happened in Valor—what they had seen to be true. What I had said to be true.

They don't seem shocked by what happened. I can't help but wonder if they had doubted my allegations less than I thought. If it's the truth, it means they were willing to let Valor go on suffering if it meant not disrupting the status quo of their own courts.

"What's our plan of action?" Lord Nicaise asks, turning toward Lord Gennady.

Lord Bralas scoffs, looking at the table. "We? I don't know about the rest of you, but I'm headed back to my court immediately." He stands, pointing off in the distance. "If Drytas is targeting our courts, we should be there to defend them—to gather our people."

Lord Gennady stands, voice level compared to Lord Bralas's. "And what if each of us is not enough to defend against him? We are stronger together, so we must face him as such."

Lord Bralas leans forward across the table, hackles raised. "How do you suggest we defend all five courts at the same time?"

Without a moment of hesitation, I murmur, "Six," just loud enough to be heard.

The Crowns turn toward me with unsure expressions, as if in disbelief that I'd even spoken. Lord Rhen is the first to break the silence, leaning back slightly. "What was that?" he asks, tone grave.

I clear my throat, standing tall under the room's gaze. "It's six courts."

Lord Bralas's eye twitches as he stares at me, but I do not squirm under his gaze. I will no longer be bullied into submission.

When no one responds, I continue. "It's just as likely that the Court of Self is under attack."

Lord Bralas shakes his head. "We can barely figure out if we can defend our own courts, and you would have us defend him." Bralas moves to the door. "We are wasting time discussing this. I am leaving for Wisdom. Now."

"Wait, Bralas," Lord Gennady insists. "If we each check on our courts and return here if we find nothing amiss, then we can reinforce whatever court is being attacked."

"And risk *my* people?"

Leveling a glare in Lord Bralas's direction, Lord Gennady adds, "You will not be saying that if it is your court that is under siege."

This shuts Lord Bralas up.

"Trials, let it not be too late."

CHAPTER 45

Chaos unfolds as the five courts scramble to gather their people and head for their own borders. Riders were sent ahead on the fastest horses to warn of what may be coming. The Crowns and Heirs follow in guarded carriages, in a procession of guards and court members alike.

One court will be returning home to Drytas laying siege to their land, and they would need every able body to defend it.

Evander grips my hand tightly as we move for the carriage where his father waits to leave. "Will you do something for me?" He looks at our linked hands, rubbing his thumbs back and forth over my skin.

When he looks up at me, golden-brown locks almost falling into his eyes, my breath catches in my throat. It's moments like this that reminds me of the responsibility that weighs on Evander. As Heir—he has a court to protect and defend and people that rely on him.

Blinking softly at Evander, I nod, knowing that I will help him with anything in my power.

Evander brings a hand to my chin, and I don't flinch at the

contact. Instead, leaning forward into his warm touch. Anxiety swirls in the blue waters of Evander's eyes.

"When it's time for us all to go to where Drytas has attacked —stay here," Evander whispers in a soft voice.

My head recoils, eyes blinking rapidly at his request. Does he not think I'm capable of helping? I thought I showed my competency in our battle against the Guard—my shield could protect people, protect him.

Sensing my internal battle, Evander begs in a pained voice, "Please." He shakes his head as if refusing me. "I can't do what I need to if I'm worried about you. I need to give my court my full attention."

My heart cracks, splitting off at his words. Does he know what he is asking me to do? Or better yet—what he is asking me not to do? I've spent the last few weeks waiting on everyone else to come solve my problems for me, and now, when I'm ready to confront Drytas, he is asking me to stand down?

Lips pursing, I close off the argument that begs to be released. "If Drytas has his sights set on Truth, I will stay here. So that you can focus on your people. But anywhere else, and we hit the battlefield together. Okay?"

Evander pulls me in, hooking his arm around my neck, pressing my face into his chest. His lips graze my ear when he bends down, saying thank you over and over. Then he grabs my face in both hands, before swooping low to kiss me.

It's quick. A slight press of lips. Fleeting as if it never happened. But when Lord Gennady informs Evander it is time to go, Evander steps back reluctantly, his body rigid. It looks like he'll give in and kiss me for even a moment longer.

Rubbing his arm, I squeeze it. "Be careful."

Walking backward toward his father, Evander salutes me with one hand to his temple.

And as I watch him leave, prepared to defend his people

with his life, all I can think is that Evander will make a good lord one day.

I can think of no one better to be the future Crown ruling the Court of Truth.

~

"Do you suspect who betrayed us?" I ask Sar, twisting my fingers together anxiously from where I lay propped up on one of the couches in the living area.

Following the courts' departures, Sar and I retreat to the Court of Self's tower, hoping to catch a few moments of sleep. Sar had been confident, without any explanation, that there was no need to warn Torryn. She'd muttered some excuse about Drytas not being reckless enough to think he could Trial anyone successfully in the Court of Self.

Sar inhales deeply through her nose, biting her lip in contemplation. Turning on her side, she rests her head on her hand. "Whoever it was had something to gain by Drytas's plan, but anyone could have bargained for their safety from the upcoming war. Anyone who had an ear to what was going on could have seen what was coming. Not automatically a Crown or Heir, but they can't be ruled out either."

Pressing my fingers to my temples, I rub in circular motions, hoping it will chase away the doubts creeping in. "That would mean we've had someone in the court the entire time to do Drytas's bidding. We never had a chance of winning the vote during Drytas's judgment hearing."

A startling realization makes me gasp. I never told Sar about the assassin. Maybe she would know who could have Trialed at Valor or maybe who wielded a power that could turn off others'.

The words fall from my lips like a curse.

"The assassin."

Sar sits up like I've shocked her, whipping around to look at me. Her eyes are wide as they search my face. "What assassin, Lysta? I know nothing about an assassin."

Seeing the fear emanating off her, I stammer through a quick explanation.

"I'm fine, really. After the judgment hearing, I was upset and wandered out to the Border Forest. Someone followed me and tried to kill me. They could use telekinesis—Drytas's power from Valor. I tried to use my shield to protect me, but they also had the power to take mine away when I got close enough. I couldn't use it. I thought for a moment that it was Drytas, but he doesn't have that power, at least that I know—"

Sar wears a worried expression. "That's why you were hurt when you and Evander came back that night." I nod tightly. "You should have told us. Why didn't you?"

Sar's gaze pins me in place, and I avert mine. "Someone had just tried to kill me an hour after I was banished from my court. I didn't know who to trust. Can you blame me?"

She falls silent on the couch opposing mine. "I don't know of anybody having that power, Lysta. Which is far more worrisome than you probably realize." She curses before rolling to face away from me. "Let's just hope that your assassin didn't stay behind when the courts left to finish his job."

CHAPTER 46

When the screaming starts, I jolt awake, rolling off the edge of the couch onto the hard ground, fighting the pillows as if they are my attacker. All the breath is knocked from my lungs, and my heart races, pounding in my ears as I try to find my bearings. Forced from sleep's dark abyss that my exhaustion willingly succumbed to.

I flinch when bloodcurdling screams pierce through me. Not from my dreams but from the couch across from mine. Sitting up, I look over the table positioned between the couches for the redheaded girl who sleeps nearby.

Sar's share of blankets retrieved from the bedrooms have fallen to the floor in a slump. Her body lies trembling, her nails digging into the fabric of the cushion like a lifeline.

Rushing to wake Sar from whatever nightmare holds her captive, I trip over the blankets woven around my legs and land on my knees beside her. Upon closing the distance, I realize Sar is not asleep. Her eyes are wide open, pupils darting from left to right, a haunting sight. Reaching out to shake her awake, I shout, "Sar! Sar!"

She bolts upright, her eyes fixating off in the distance

behind me. She breathes heavily, a hand pressed to her chest. Tears form at the corners of her eyes as she looks around to collect herself.

Grabbing her hand in mine, I squeeze Sar's fingers tightly, trying to remind her of my presence. That she isn't alone.

My heart breaks as the warm, sunlike girl cries, and I pull her toward me. Wrapping my arms around her as she shakes. Soon after, her sobs soften and breathing evens out, but when it does, she turns to me with swollen red eyes.

"It's happening," Sar says. Her lip trembling as she takes in a shaky breath. "We need to go. We need to warn them. It's happening, or it will."

Furrowing my eyebrows at her, I lean back. "How do you know that, Sar?"

She looks at her fingers, not meeting my gaze. In a smaller voice, she answers back, "Because I could see it. It's one of my powers—I'm a seer." Inhaling a shuddering breath, she resolves herself, wiping away her tears with the back of her hand. "I get visions of what has happened, what is happening, and what is still to happen. They are usually just flashes, but I can't control them yet."

Leaning away, I appraise Sar, mind reeling from the recent development.

"You're Trialed . . . more than once . . . like Torryn."

She stares at me with wide eyes like the secret will be the final thing to force us apart. Sar hurries to explain, voice shaking. "No one knows. Except for Ardis and Torryn. Not even my . . . Lord Bralas. It would only give him a reason to use me, and I never plan on going back. It's why I didn't tell you—"

I wave off her apology. I don't blame her for not telling me. Weapons win battles, people win wars, but true power can start and end both. Knowing the before, during, and after—it must be terrifying.

"What did you see?" I ask, heart leaping in my chest.

Sar clears her throat. "Lord Drytas with an army of hundreds. Smoke surrounded them, buildings burned. But Drytas was shouting orders to attack." She shudders, closing her eyes slightly. "There were so many dead."

I leap to my feet, looking away from her. "What court was it, Sar? If you saw bodies, then you could see what colors they wore." Sar flinches when I turn toward her, scouring her face for the answer. "What court, Sar?"

She stands, reaching for me, and I suck in a harsh breath, realization knocking into me.

"It was Andolin, the Court of Truth's Trial city."

I stick out a firm hand, pushing away any attempt at comforting me. No. It's not over yet. We can still help them.

If she'd seen what is happening, we are too late. But if it's the future . . .

Looking toward the window, I examine the sky that has just started to speckle with the first stars of the night. The sun has just barely gone down as dark blue and purple hues still paint the horizon.

Turning to Sar, I grip her arms tightly. "What time of day was it in your vision?" At her confused expression, I rephrase, "Was the sun *still* in the sky?"

Sar's eyes widen, catching onto what I'm saying. Her eyes flick to the window. "It was dawn. So, you think that means we aren't too late? It hasn't happened yet."

Rubbing a hand across my face, I exhale deeply. "I think if war had started this morning, we would've known when we got back from Falland." I grab my jacket from where I'd tossed it, pulling it onto one arm in a rush. "We still have time."

Sar jumps into action like a flash, shoving her feet into her discarded boots. "I hope you're right. Trials, let us be right."

For all our sakes, I hope so too.

Every minute counts and Sar and I use each wisely. Changing into combat worthy clothes; reinforced leather and metal plates. Even now, as we break into the weapons storage of the arena, we do so swiftly.

Sar stands behind me as I search the sword mounted wall for my weapon of choice. The silver weapon blends in, making me grumble under my breath.

Sar hasn't stopped rambling, her anxiety rolling off her in waves. "The Heirs won't be back with word for a few more hours. By the time they make it back to the capital and head for Truth, it'll be too late."

We can't wait around for the Heirs, if they even show up. Lord Bralas had made it clear what his priority was before he left—his own court. And while it may be easy for the other Crowns to proclaim their loyalty when joined, doing so while safely stowed away in their own court is another thing entirely.

Glimpsing the ivy crown of my sword's hand guard, I reach for the blade that Neith had apparently abandoned for a different one before he left. "We need them to head straight there, and even then, it'll be cutting it close to dawn."

Sar mumbles to herself, pacing the enclosed space behind me. "Then waiting around for them to arrive is not an option. I'll have to portal to each court, one by one."

"Can you do that?"

Sar nods tightly as she tries to project confidence, but then she bites her lip and gives me a window into what she is feeling. "I've been to all the courts, so logistically I can. But I've never portaled that distance so many times without having a significant rest in between." At my worried glance, she hurries to insist, "Not that I can't do it. There always has to be the first time."

Everyone has their limits, and using her powers this way may ask too much of her. She could burn herself out by tapping into her power's reserves. And then what? Where would we be then? But I don't question her about it. She, more than anyone, knows the bounds of her power, not to mention her own limits.

I turn to Sar, a question I've been suppressing edging on the tip of my tongue. "Sar, what court—how did you convince someone to let you Trial? Unless it's from the Court of Self?"

A sad look passes behind Sar's blue eyes, and I instantly regret the question. Regret asking what could sap out all the life out of her smile. Just a fake curve of her lips.

Sar shakes her head. "No one. I convinced no one. I've Trialed four times, three of which successfully, and it was all in my birth court—Wisdom."

I send Sar an incredulous look. "The same Trial? Why would you Trial again in a court you've already passed? What would you gain?"

Sar hesitates, fiddling with the straps of her leather pads. "The way you solve the Trial—the way you beat it—determines what ability you gain."

I nod as Torryn said something similar when explaining my power to me back in Falland.

Sar continues, "And there are multiple ways to solve—"

I gasp when what she is trying to say breaks through. My eyes go wide with complete astonishment. My hand now hovers above my heart, feeling the beat race under my fingers. "You solved it in three different ways, so you have three different abilities?"

Sar gives me a half-hearted smile. "And I'm the only one to have done it. I started at first to just spite my father for not letting me train with Neith, but then it became more. So, I Trialed for every power the court had. Even an extra time to see if there were other ways."

Sar had given herself permission to be more than others allowed. I stare at her in awe. I want to know more. I want to ask how she'd known it was even possible—Trialing in multiple courts like Torryn had was a different thing than Trialing to complete a Trial.

But then I'm reminded of Evander and the Court of Truth.

"Well, if we all make it out of this, the Court of Truth will owe their lives to that power of yours."

Grabbing an extra dagger, I hand it to Sar, who accepts the blade gingerly. Letting her fix the weapon on her belt, I continue. "We don't even know if Lord Gennady and Evander know they are under attack yet. If Drytas doesn't launch his attack until dawn, they could think they are safe and not know what's coming."

Part of me wishes Evander had never left. But then I know his court and his father are better off with him at their side.

"If we go there first and something happens to us, then reinforcements will never come."

I go silent, hands fumbling over the weapons in front of me. After a beat, I add quietly, "Unless we don't both go." Peering over my shoulder, I flinch at Sar's disposition shift.

Sar's gaze hardens, her sky-blue eyes going stormy. "Not a chance." Her tone leaves no room for argument, but I push on anyway.

"We don't both need to go to the other courts—"

Sar cuts me off, waving her hand dismissively. "I said no, Lysta. I'm not sending you into a literal war zone."

"It isn't up to you, Sar."

She crosses her arms, raising an eyebrow as if to say it is.

I raise my chin, letting her see every ounce of stubbornness I'm ready to throw at her. "I can't portal. Which means I can't make my way to each of the courts by myself, but you can. Lord Gennady and Evander need every advantage they can get to win this, and that means they need to be warned. Every minute they can prepare before Drytas gets there may mean surviving until the other courts can arrive."

Sar frowns deeply, considering my words.

"You know I'm right." I add quietly. "Nobody can even come near me with my shield. I'll be fine."

Sar snorts. "Because you are known for your lack of enemies. For example, the assassin who can turn your power off real quick. And he won't be looking for Lord Gennady or Evander. He'll be looking for you."

My mind races. What do I do if Sar won't take me to Truth? There's no way I can get there in time, plus I would have no inkling of where I was going. I needed her to take me. It was the only option.

"I need you to trust me to do this, and it needs to happen now. You always talk about how Ardis and Torryn protect you, even when you don't need it. Right now, *I don't need it*, Sar."

And like that, I can see that I've broken through. Sar looks down at her feet, and when she looks back up, I have to hold down a cheer of victory. "As soon as I've reached all the courts, I'm going to Truth right after you." She shakes her head with wide eyes. "Trials, don't make me regret this, Lysta."

CHAPTER 47

Stepping through the portal to the Court of Truth is paralyzing.

Not from the awe of Sar's power, but from the contrast between peaceful night and devastating chaos. Screams echo all around me with no scrutable origin.

The bodies of guards line the floor—of the Court of Truth, from their navy uniforms. Their blood pools on the marble floor and runs like a river down the hall. It's smell overpowering my senses till I can taste it in my mouth.

Staggering against the wall, I press a tight fist to my mouth to ward off the urge to retch at the sight. So many dead. From both sides.

This shouldn't have happened yet. My mind races, searching for an answer or explanation. If Sar's vision was true, then Lord Drytas's army was a couple of hours from breaking through the gates. Then how were so many dead within the castle walls already?

A loud explosion jolts me into motion, breaking me from my trance. Head on a swivel, I creep down the hallway, peering into every room and window I pass. Fire lights my way from lit sconces and fallen torches that burn next to their holder's body. I consider taking one with me, but in the darkest hours before dawn, the light would only be a beacon guiding others to me.

BANG! BANG! BANG!

I freeze, molding myself into the corner of a door frame at the noise sounding from down the hall. It sounds again, ringing loud with purpose. It's a dull thud, like two solid forms hitting in succession.

Holding my breath, I lean forward to glimpse what unfolds a dozen paces away.

Two of Valor's guards stand in their gray uniforms, trimmed in Drytas's red. They stand on opposite sides of a solid stone column that hovers a few feet above the ground. Hands outstretched, they work together to pull the idol like a battering ram, slamming it with ground trembling force into a pair of closed doors. The door shakes and rumbles with each hit, cracking at the point of impact.

What could they want so desperately? My eyes drift to the crimson stain of blood that permeates the fabric of their sleeves and torso. It can't be anything good.

Can I take the two? Would my shield hold back the weight of the column if I became their next target?

I take one step back, planning to retreat down the hallway I've come when their next hit cracks through the door like the sound of lightning.

They'd made it through.

The two men grunt in victory, letting go of their battering ram with a resounding thud. Turning, I watch as one man sticks his hand through the newly made hole in the door, a chorus of screams echoing when he does so.

My face blanches in realization. People were in there.

Moving out into the hall, I dig down, bringing my shield to the surface. I've used my shield like this before—twice, in fact . . . by accident. Once against Lord Drytas and then against Torryn during War Hour.

When the shouts from behind the door surge in a mixed cry of panic and fear, I can feel the power at my fingertips. My shield blasts out in a perfect arc, slamming the two men into the wall. Disoriented and groaning in pain, the men struggle to stand from where they crumpled up upon landing. One's arm dangles awkwardly at his side—dislocated.

As they're distracted, I run up behind them, dagger removed from the sheathe at my thigh and in my hand at the ready. I launch myself at the injured guard, stabbing the dagger into the space beneath his arms. He freezes underneath me, coughing up blood, before slowly teetering to the ground. I stop myself from going down with him, but my knife remains lodged in the space above his ribs.

Spinning on my heel, my hand already grips the hilt of my sword, yanking it from its sheath. Before I can ready the weapon, the other guard knocks into me, locking an elbow around my throat. I kick and squirm, dangling as the guard summons his sword from where it had fallen when my shield hit him.

My hand follows his, using my shield to block him from retrieving his blade, but that can't save me from suffocating. Lungs begging for air, I slam my elbow into his torso, but he doesn't release my grip. Dots speckle across my vision.

Is this really how far I would get? One fight into battle, and I'm destined to lose?

In an instant, I'm dropped. I greedily gulp in air as my knees hit the marble floors. I turn around in time to see the guard get a sword through his chest.

The man who killed him. Severin. Lord Gennady's second hand and the Truthsayer.

His gaze is cold when it meets mine. I can only guess what

those eyes have seen in the last few hours. Severin holds out a leather gloved hand to pull me up. I hesitate at the vicious look in his eyes before taking his hand.

I regret it a second later.

Severin uses his grip on me to pull me close to his face. In his other hand is my dagger. He angles the blade under my chin, glowering down at me.

I could block the blade with my shield, but I pause, waiting for him to speak. I am not his enemy.

"Are you fighting for your court . . . or against it?" He snarls in my face.

I level a glance at the two dead men at our feet.

"Do you really need to ask?"

His grip tightens on me in warning, squeezing bruises into my flesh. I don't let the pain show on my face.

"Against Drytas."

Black eyes pierce into me, daring me to lie.

"And the rest of your court?" Severin asks.

"The Untrialed are innocent . . ." I start and Severin narrows his eyes. "If I cannot talk them down, I will not let them hurt other innocents."

Severin examines me for a moment before shoving me away from him. He holds out my dagger for me to take before leaning down and removing his sword from the fallen guard's body.

"You're not going to use your Truthsayer power to make sure I'm not lying?"

He flinches, sending me a scathing look before eyeing the length of the hall. "I must find Lord Gennady. If the attackers have made it this far into the castle, then I question his safety."

The words blurt from my mouth. "I'll come with you."

He starts to argue, but I cut him off. "I may need work on my offensive abilities, but you can't deny the usefulness of my shield."

Severin glares, before setting off at a brisk pace. "Stay quiet and stay behind me. And do not fall behind."

SHOUTING sounds ahead as Severin leads our search deep into the heart of the castle. Despite his confidence that the Court of Truth Trial is where Lord Gennady will be, Severin's face pales with every step, as terrified of what we'll find as much as what we won't.

His voice trembles when he explains how a small squad of Valor's guards, along with dozens of Untrialed, had been hidden within the fortress when they had arrived from the capital. That it wasn't until after Severin, Evander and Lord Gennady separated that the attack had started within.

Each thought that crosses through my mind ties to Evander. Where he could be, and if he's found his father. If he's safe, or bleeding out slowly out of my reach.

My every heartbeat thuds the syllables of his name, calling for him when my lips cannot.

The closer we get to the action unfolding ahead, the easier it is to identify the shouting voice—Belthan.

Drawing our weapons, Severin holds a finger to his lips as he creeps toward the end of the hall. Leaning in, I whisper the new information. "I know him. It's Lord Drytas's Head of the Guard. He can teleport."

Severin nods tightly before moving around the corner. Following behind, I prepare to throw up a shield at the first sign of danger.

Standing outside of the entrance to the Trial hall, Belthan grips the front of Lord Gennady's shirt, leaning the older man over the edge of a balcony.

Despite how close he is to death—how close he is to finding

out exactly how high up the balcony sits over the courtyard below, Lord Gennady wears not even a wrinkle of worry. When Belthan yells in his face, Lord Gennady speaks softly, his tone comforting.

"I can promise you. Valor is under no threat from my court or any other."

With Belthan's back to us, Severin edges toward the balcony, sword in hand. I hold my breath, heart racing.

Lord Gennady turns his head, eyes landing on Severin before moving to me. A frown settles across his face, and he shakes his head minimally.

Severin doesn't obey the silent order, moving closer, but Lord Gennady throws away any advantage of surprise we might have had.

"There's no need for that, Severin. This young gentleman was sent by mistake," Lord Gennady says in a calm voice.

Severin curses under his breath as Belthan whips around. At the sight of him, Belthan scrambles, holding Lord Gennady further over the edge. The crown on Lord Gennady's head falls at the steeper position, dropping off the balcony. I don't even hear it land.

"Back up!" Belthan yells, wide eyes flickering between Severin and his sword. "Back up, or I'll drop him!"

Severin growls, gesturing to Belthan with his sword. "You drop him, and you'll be dead before he hits the ground."

Stepping out from behind Severin, I hiss, "He'll drop him anyway."

Belthan's eyes ignite when he catches sight of me. A wicked smile spreads across his lips. "Lysta, you're so far from home."

Swallowing thickly, I shout back. "I could say the same about you, Belthan."

He shrugs, and Lord Gennady dips with the movement. "When Lord Drytas asks something . . . I answer!"

Moving to the opposite corner of the room, I try to draw Belthan's attention away from where Severin stands. Heart pounding in my ears, I pray that he can reach Belthan before it's too late.

"Is that why he's safely away from the fight?" I ask. "What is he having you do that he couldn't do himself?"

Belthan bristles at the accusation. "He's asked me to prove my loyalty—to my court. He's going to make me his *Heir*." He smirks when my eyes widen, continuing as he straightens with pride. "And all I have to do is eliminate the lord that threatens to breach our walls."

My brows furrow. Did Belthan believe that? From our interactions in Falland, I had assumed he was intertwined in Drytas's plans from the beginning, but now it seems he has been just as misled.

"Lord Drytas is using you, Belthan. No one is going to attack Falland. It was all a lie, a lie he used to make *us*," I gesture between him and I, "his citizens afraid to do anything against him."

Belthan falters, his smirk falling as he considers my words. "Lord Drytas is making us stronger. He knows what's coming, and I want to be on his side when it does."

Everything moves in slow motion, drawing out every agonizing second. Belthan shoves Lord Gennady, letting go of his grip on the front of his shirt. And as the Lord of Truth falls over the balcony's edge, Severin shouts, lunging forward. Belthan disappears in a blip, teleporting away before Severin can even touch him.

Severin and I both reach out for Lord Gennady as he disappears over the balcony wall.

I stand my ground, as he rushes to check over the ledge. Severin freezes, mouth agape as he looks down, to where Lord Gennady sits a few feet below, propped on a slab of my shield.

Severin's wide eyes find me, jaw hanging in bewilderment.

Struggling under the weight, my knees shake, and dark spots flicker across my vision. "Can you—can you grab him? I can't hold this for long."

As if struck by lightning, Severin jumps into action. Moving to straddle the stone wall, he leans down to grasp the neck of Lord Gennady's clothes, before yanking him back over the edge onto solid ground. They both slump, backs pressed to the balcony wall as they stare at me.

I release the shield, sinking to my knees in exhaustion. Adrenaline courses through me, and with no one to fight, it shakes my hands. Panting from exertion, the three of us exchange a look.

Once I've got my breath, I ask the question bouncing around in my head. "Evander?"

Lord Gennady's mouth tightens, shaking his head. "I went to head off anyone going for the Trial, but they were already inside. I haven't seen Evander since we arrived."

Dropping my head back, I curse at the ceiling.

SEVERIN BARRELS FORWARD, slamming his shoulder into the barricaded door leading to the Trial hall for the fifth time in a row. He stifles down a groan of pain at the impact, the only indication of his hurting being the way he winces when he pulls away.

"Severin, you stubborn mule. That will not work," Lord Gennady huffs as he eyes the door like it is his one true nemesis.

We can hear yelling on the other side, hinting that the Trial has been lost. Severin changes tactics, slightly winded from his failed brute force method of entry. Sliding his sword into the gap of the doors, he tries to pry the doors open.

After several failed attempts, I interrupt Severin, who looks ready to jump the window and walk the ledge to the door. "May I?" I ask, gesturing with a small disc of a shield held between my hands.

Severin glares at me through his brow before stepping aside reluctantly. Raising his sword next to me, Severin nods when ready to attack the first thing he sees once through the door.

My shield slams into the doors, breaking them off at the hinges until they topple outward. When the dust clears, six people stand on the other side—only two guards. From the other fours rugged appearance, I would assume Untrialed. My guess is only confirmed when I spot no Trial tattoos.

Severin is on the two guards before they can blink, slicing the first's throat before stabbing the second. Wiping the blood on his trousers, he heads for the Untrialed with danger promised in his eyes.

Without hesitating, I summon a shield, dividing Severin from the Untrialed. When he almost runs into it, he sends a warning look at me, teeth gritted as he orders, "Drop. The. Shield."

"No." Standing firm, I straighten under his glare. "They don't want to Trial here. They didn't ask to be brought here." I turn to the Untrialed who watch me with fear-filled eyes.

I remember being like that once. Quaking in my shoes at the presence of any Trialed person. Lumping them with how the Guard treated us. It wasn't that long ago though, even if it doesn't feel like it.

"Do you wish to Trial?"

They shake their heads, mumbling their denial. I look to Severin in triumph. Pointing a thumb toward the door, I gesture for them to leave. "Get out of here, then. Try to stay out of sight till this is over."

I don't acknowledge their awe-stricken faces as they pass

me, instead focusing on forming a shield in the doorway once they step past its threshold. Maybe getting rid of the door wasn't the smartest decision.

Crossing the room in a few quick strides, Severin grips my upper arm, pulling me toward him threateningly. "Stand in the way of me protecting my court again, and I will dispose of you. Understood?"

Without shrinking away, I snarl right back, "You protect yours. I'll protect what's left of mine."

Turning on my heel, I find Lord Gennady in front of the glass door to the Trial. A blue light shines through the engravings on the mirrored surface, humming slightly as if alive. A shiver scurries down my spine at its resemblance to the one in Valor. I move to stand next to him, remaining quiet for him to speak what is stewing in his mind.

"Someone's Trialing as we stand here," Lord Gennady says in a soft whisper. He presses a wrinkled hand to the smooth glass. "It wasn't enough."

I eye the door with a slack jaw. The reality of the situation creeping in. Who knows how long they had been Trialing people before we arrived to reclaim the Trial hall?

"What wasn't enough, Lord Gennady?" I murmur.

He bows his head. "I thought if they got to me first, that there would be more time before they got to the Trial—" he trails off.

My heart drops to my stomach. Mouth gaping as I examine the man who stands next to me. Without his crown, he seems much smaller—frail. "Are you saying—You didn't actually—" I can't bring myself to finish the sentence, but the look Lord Gennady gives me is all the answer I need.

He'd sacrificed himself. Giving himself to Valor's guards to stop people from being Trialed.

"Hardly anyone survives it," he whispers. "It's how I lost my wife—Evander's mother."

Glancing at Severin over my shoulder, he looks at me with a stone face, but even he can't hide the sorrow in his eyes.

My heart breaks for the lord whose purpose in life is to protect the very thing that stole his love from him too soon.

The moment is broken when the blue lights on the Trial door dim until the light is gone. Lord Gennady sighs, shaking his head before abandoning his place in front of the door.

The Court of Truth's Trial has claimed another life tonight.

CHAPTER 48

Bangs echo against my shield, and I stagger at the additional force. Sword held loosely in my hand, I turn to face the intruders with iron resolve.

How many could still be inside the walls?

With a quick glance outside, I estimate less than an hour till dawn arrives—and with it, Lord Drytas. That would be when holding the Trial would become impossible, not without Sar alerting the other courts.

It all comes down to if they make it in time.

The pounding sends goosebumps up my arms, but I stand firm, knees locked, waiting for them to break through.

When I look to who stands on the other side of the shield, I tense, ready to curse out whoever plans to step foot into the Trial hall. Who knows how many Untrialed they'd managed to Trial before we reclaimed the room? They wouldn't Trial another while we stand here.

But then I freeze, a sob of relief escaping my throat.

"Evander! Where have you been?" I shout, dropping my shield and running to him. "Why didn't you announce it was you? We would have let you in."

Evander's eyes go wide at the sight of me jogging over to him, wrapping my arms around his torso as relief floods my body. His arms wind around me in return, one hand settling over the back of my head.

Eyes wetting, I breathe in his scent, letting it flood my senses to comfort me. "When I didn't see you, and it was all Valor's Guard, I thought they had gotten to you—" My voice cracks on the words, but I shake my head.

Evander nuzzles his face into my hair, before murmuring into my hair, "You weren't supposed to be here."

I move to lean back in his arms, which only makes Evander tighten his hold on me, not letting me leave the crevice of his neck. "What do you mean? Of course I would be here if I can help."

"You promised you would stay in the capital," Evander says in a sad voice. "How did you get here so quickly?"

I had promised him before I knew he was in trouble.

When I tear myself from Evander's arms, I finally notice the figures standing in the doorway. Several Valor guards stand with their swords in hand, watching our interaction with amusement lit in their eyes.

Gasping, I grab Evander's arm, summoning my shield behind him. It splits the room once again, preventing the guards from advancing further into the Trial Hall.

"We can take them, Evander."

Evander's hand slides under my chin, forcing my gaze to his. "There's no need for that, Lysta."

I don't even process his words. Instead, focusing on how all at once my control of the shield slips away. I watch with horrified eyes as the barrier protecting us from the guards falls. Digging deep within myself, I try to bring the shield back with no result. When nothing happens, I look at Evander, and it's as if I can hear my heart shattering across the tile floor.

"What is going on?" I ask, backing away from him as if the answer will change the direction of what I know is happening. It makes little sense. Nothing makes sense anymore.

Evander approaches me slowly, blue eyes never leaving my own. "Step aside. Let things happen as they are going to." In a whisper meant for me, he continues, "I will explain this to you later. I promise." Evander reaches a hand out as if to touch my face.

Smacking it out of the way before his skin can touch mine, I retreat closer to Lord Gennady, who has not spoken since Evander entered the room. Out of his reach, I try again to summon my shield, begging for the familiar hum to zing through my body once again.

Abandoning the pointless pursuit, I unsheathe my sword, leveling it in the space between me and the man who had once made me feel safe. My eyes burn as hot, heavy tears escape and trail down my cheeks.

How had I not seen this?

If Evander has the power to take away powers, that means that day in the field. The assassin—it had been Evander.

A sob bursts from my mouth, and it feels like I can't breathe. The room suddenly feels too small. He is too close.

Out of the corner of my eye, Severin leverages himself in front of Lord Gennady, sword at the ready. Lord Gennady stares blankly at his son, disappointment clouding his expression . . . but not surprise.

"Talk to him," I cry out to Lord Gennady. "Why aren't you saying anything to him?"

"Evander has made his decision, Lysta."

"I decided?" Evander snarls at his father. "More like you decided for me."

It's as if a stranger has taken hold of Evander's body. Saying and doing things I never believed Evander would hours ago.

"Do you know *Lord Gennady's* power, Lysta?" Evander says, a crazed look in his eyes as he points his sword at his father. "What the Lord of Truth is capable of?"

"Don't blame—" Lord Gennady starts, but is cut off by Evander.

"He sees the truth. None of that lying nonsense like Severin here. He can see the truth in people. Who they are . . . who they can be. All before they truly even know themselves." Evander scoffs, shaking his head. "Imagine having your one parental figure—the person who's supposed to guide you in life—convinced that you'll burn his court to the ground one day. Punished for something that I might do as an adult when I was just a kid."

I don't know what words to say to fix what is breaking in front of me. Every word out of his mouth stabs through my heart, bleeding me slowly of anything I could have ever felt for him.

"Evander, you decide your own fate. Nothing someone else does gets to dictate your heart." My lip trembles as I stare into his eyes, begging for him to stop. "No one can do anything to change your heart."

For a fraction of a second, I think my words have broken through. His face softens as he looks at me and what I think might be regret crosses his face, but then his eyebrows knit together. "He plans to step down as Lord of Truth."

I look between them, trying to piece together what they aren't saying. "Isn't that what you want? I don't—"

Evander chuckles darkly. "No, Lysta. He plans on giving away the crown—not to me."

"You don't know that, Evander," Lord Gennady pleas from somewhere behind me. "I merely wanted the people to have a say. To vote on who would rule them. Who says that person couldn't have been you?"

"It's too late for that," Evander says as he storms toward his father. Sword raised, I cut off his path. He sighs, looking down before glancing at me. "Lysta, you know you can't beat me. Maybe you could have if you were able to use your powers, but there's no way you will win this. Don't make me fight you. You've been using that sword for a few weeks, if that."

"Then you shouldn't have betrayed me."

In a heartbeat, Evander sweeps forward, pushing his sword against mine, the blade scraping together. Unable to hold the weight, Evander knocks the sword from my hands, and it clatters across the floor. "Stay out of this, Lysta."

Moving for Lord Gennady once again, Severin steps in his path, raising his own sword. It happens in slow motion. A twist of blades. Some clever strikes. Whirling around on his knee, Severin aims a strike to Evander's lower torso that is blocked. Then Evander lands a hit that cuts diagonally across Severin's face from his taller position, and I gasp. Severin's head turns to the side from impact, and when he looks up again, a bloody gash travels across the right side of his chin, slanting up and over his nose and ending above his eyebrow.

Evander brings the hilt of his sword down over Severin's temple, and with a sickening crack, he crumbles, falling to the ground in a heap.

I don't have the time to react before a sharp blade presses to my throat. An arm wraps around my chest, pinning me to my attacker.

"Evander, cut it out with the dramatics. Drytas wants these two dead, and I can think of no better gift for him upon his arrival than their bodies at the gates."

Panic grips me, and I look to Evander out of instinct. His eyes meet mine, and I see the struggle locked inside him. His jaw clenches, the muscles there twitch with tension. He glances between the knife at my throat and Lord Gennady, who stands quietly, awaiting his end.

"Killing him wasn't a part of the deal," Evander grits out. He takes one cautionary step forward, away from Lord Gennady, watching the blade at my neck with extreme focus. "And I can as sure as Trial guarantee you she wasn't."

The man behind me grunts out, "That was when she wasn't supposed to be here. Drytas has been calling for her head since day one." He pauses, knife pressing harder to my throat. "That gonna be a problem for you?"

Evander glares at the guard with slitted eyes. "Not at all." Evander says cooly. "But I think I'd rather have that confirmed by Lord Drytas, and not some low level guard." He gestures to Lord Gennady. "Take him to Lord Drytas. I'll handle the girl."

My heart freezes. Is Evander really allowing for this to happen?

The guard passes me to Evander, moving for Lord Gennady, who stands docile, no fight left in him. In one swift moment, he turns, impaling Lord Gennady on his sword.

I scream, horror sweeping through me as the kind lord buckles, landing on his knees. My heartbeat races in my chest as the world around me goes silent. It's as if all I can hear is the blood rushing through my body.

Evander freezes, not moving—not breathing at the sight of his father. That is when I go feral. Screaming, clawing, fighting my way to Lord Gennady. Ripping free from Evander, I press my hands to Lord Gennady's wound, pressing tighter until more blood pools around my hands. Tears soak my face and blur my vision.

Lord Gennady's eyes glisten as he stares back at me. His gaze moves past me to his son.

I look to Evander, begging him silently to do something—anything.

Evander blinks rapidly. Watching as his father slumps to the ground in front of him. He clenches his hands, staring at the body, before turning to Lord Gennady's murderer with a darkened gaze.

"There a problem, Lord Evander?"

Evander shakes his head tightly, flinching at the title.

"Then grab her. Lord Drytas will be here soon."

The guard raises a hand, lifting Lord Gennady's body and I go after him, but Evander stops me. He wraps both arms around me, pinning my hands down. I go slack in his arms, letting him drag me to my death.

But instead of following the guard, he pulls me toward the Trial door. Juggling me in his arms, he brings one of my hands to the door, holding it there with his own.

"Come on, Lysta. Get it together," He whispers harshly in my ear.

"Hey! What are you doing?!" Someone shouts from the other side of the room.

Evander curses. "Trials, Lysta." He shakes me, gripping my face to make me look at him. "Do you consent to Trialing in the Court of Truth?"

When I say nothing, he slaps my face lightly, as if trying to will me into action.

"You die here, or you get a fighting chance in there, Lysta. So, answer me, do you consent?"

I can't process the implications of what he's doing, even less so than what he's already done. But I nod and the door cracks open.

He pulls it open, shoving me inside.

The last glimpse I get of the outside is Evander being grabbed by a guard. But his eyes never leave mine. And his ocean eyes are all I see when the door shuts, sealing me inside.

CHAPTER 49

Sitting against the Trial door, shivering uncontrollably, I try to wipe Lord Gennady's blood from my hands, but it has already dried. The bright red crusts against the pale skin of my palms, bunching under my nails as I try to scrape it away. I keep rubbing and rubbing, as if my blood-stained skin is the only thing keeping him from being alive.

Lord Gennady is dead, and I will soon join him, for I'm once again set to be Trialed. Trialed in the court with the highest death rate.

The tunnel rumbles in off-rhythm succession. Explosions from the attack on the Court of Truth that make me still, listening for the next. Stones crack off from the cave walls before dropping and breaking into several pieces. The pieces fall closer and closer, a fallen rock nudging against my boot, but I stare at them through tear-filled eyes.

My hand comes to rub at my chest, and I try to focus on each inhale and exhale.

Each rumble brings flashes of the dead I'd seen in the halls. People from both courts, Valor and Truth, dead because of not just Drytas, but Evander. Now his people, as well as my own, were being sacrificed like pawns for power moves. No one is fighting for *them*, and there's nothing I can do that will save either side.

With a shuddering breath, I stand on shaky legs. I may not be able to stop what has happened, what *is* happening, but I sure as Trial would not hide here while innocent people slaughter each other.

And that means facing Truth's Trial. Screw the odds.

THE SMELL of water engulfs me as I step closer to the gaping mouth of the tunnel. It's not the salty mixture that assaulted my senses when we first arrived at the capital, walking up the hill that bordered the ocean. Instead, it is a fresh smell, cool and earthy. The dewy humidity coats my face and skin.

A narrow stone walkway extends into a water-filled room. Only a foot in width, the stone catwalk stops in the center, standing high above the moat. High enough to be wary of but a manageable jump if necessary, even if I couldn't swim once in the water below.

Without leaving the entrance to the cavern, I peer at the cavern below. Barely able to see into the space from the lack of light, I squint through the darkness. The water is still, not a single ripple moving across the surface.

"I *know* you are there."

The shrill voice echoes through the cavern, sending shivers down my spine.

Where is the voice coming from? No one stands atop the walkaway, so my answer could only be down. Down in the depths of the dark water below.

"Who's there? Where are you?"

My voice reverberates, coming out louder than I had said the words, and I flinch at the volume.

"Questions . . . questions. Many to be answered, but not till you step out onto the bridge."

This was not like my Trial in Falland. Then I had the time to think. To see what lay ahead before I faced the Kadara. Time to decide before leaping into the Trial. Now I don't have that same opportunity.

Stepping forward, I struggle to peel my gaze away from my feet as I step onto the narrow path. With only inches on either side of me, I devote every part of my attention to not falling off this ledge.

When my body is clear of the entrance, the sound of scraping stone moves behind me. Whipping around, I rush forward as the opening seals; a stone door sliding out from within the wall.

"No!" I shout out as I try to push the door back open. As it thuds closed, a rush of light fills the cavern, torches on the surrounding walls burning above.

"There's no stopping once we've begun. No way back until we're done." The voice sings the words in a mocking tone.

I flinch away from the door when the small holes covering it click, seconds before spikes push out. The pointed rods are the length of an arrow, with razor edges around its entire surface.

I back away from the death trap door, stepping out onto the perilous-looking walkway. Frustrated, I clench my hands tightly. The cave suddenly feels much smaller than it had, and my chest tightens, each breath feeling more difficult than the last. The pressure of the Trial hitting me full force since entering the tunnel. I can't help anyone if I die before making it out.

Now with better lighting, I can see the water ripple, catching sight of a long black fish tail flicker around near the surface. I still can't see the bottom of the deep water.

What am I trapped in here *with*?

"What are you?" I croak out, my voice wavering noticeably.

A snicker of laughter chirps out.

"Ah, you don't want to come see for yourself? Don't be disrespectful now."

The water slaps against the rocky walls, swirling as *it* moves within the small pool. Inching forward, I creep the length of the path, heart pounding fearfully in my chest. When I'm a few feet from the end, I can see her. It.

Damp black hair clings to her face, which is concealed up to her eyes under water. I can't see the color of her eyes, only the whites of them that contrast with her grayish tone. It reminds me of being out in the cold too long during Falland's snow season, and my fingers and lips would tinge blue.

Her head creeps out of the water when she sees me, giving me a wide smile.

"Okay, I'm out here, aren't I?" I ask, gesturing with wide arms. "You said you'd tell me what you are."

Light shines in the creature's eyes as she cackles loudly, "Questions to be answered. I never said whose." Her smile taunts me as I glare over the edge at her. I'm about to yell when she continues. "But I shall answer so that you may Trial."

A long tail swirls beneath her as she swims to keep herself at the water's surface. It flicks beneath her smoothly. "I am a Calkli, distant relation of the siren family. We still desire to drag people to our depths, but we give you the chance to win your life." She giggles softly, bubbles erupting near her mouth. "Never saw the fun in singing songs, all the fun is in the fight."

When her words don't goad the desired reaction, her brows furrow tightly before continuing. "I'll ask three questions and then you'll answer. Only tell the truth, and you can ask me any question you'd like. We Calkli are all knowing, you see."

"I just have to tell the truth? What happens if I don't?"

"Lie to a Calkli, and you'll be drowned at sea . . . or here in these depths." She purrs out her words. "It would be nice to have a friend with me while I wait for my next visitor. There's been so many today the water almost isn't *deep* enough."

I slap a hand over my mouth to stifle the whimper that escapes. A wave of nausea hits me when I think of how many Untrialed have likely died here today.

"I can do that." I reply with a hint of anxiety leaking through. The Calkli notices but only gives me a haunting smile. She hums a low sound before whispering her question.

"Why did you and your sister grow up without parents?"

My eyes widen, and my mouth falls open at the mention of Cenna, stomach plummeting to the ground at my feet. My tongue suddenly feels too dry, sticking to my cheeks and teeth. How could she know—she claimed she is all knowing?

I thought when she said I would need to answer three questions, it would be a riddle to solve, or a test of my intelligence. But this is personal.

This would be a test of *me*.

There isn't a single question I wouldn't be able to tell the truth. Not a single secret I hold is worth my life. Through gritted teeth, I push out the words that I've been pushing down for a long time. "Our parents were forced into Trialing before I was old enough to remember."

The Calkli barks out a laugh, and my eyes flick to hers. The bright whites of her eyes are swallowed in black, leaving dark pools that surround her iris. "Lies drip from your poisonous tongue. Not off to a good start, are you?"

The stones under my feet crumble, and I feel the ground under my right foot give way. Losing balance, I fall backward, moving my way back as the crumbling rock follows me.

Backward until my back is pressed into the sharp blades. My heart races when I feel them pierce through the back of my shirt until they break the skin. I gasp, arching away from the pain. I try to move forward, give myself an inch between myself and the deadly objects, but the stone continues crumbling, until the heels of my feet hold my weight, and my toes hang out over the ledge.

The Calkli dodges the falling stones and circles the remaining ledge. Eyeing me as I grip the pointed objects to hold my balance. The cool trickle of blood seeps down the small of my back, collecting from the multiple entry wounds spanning my back. Even my hands sting from my grip on the sharp points, but falling now would end far worse for me.

Breathing heavily, I gasp for each breath of air greedily, the entirety of my lungs having been emptied. "What? That's the truth. It was the truth!" I yell to her, voice shaking. Flashes of their faces flicker through my mind, and I wince slightly, trying to shake the emotions.

"I know all, know more than you. I do not ask to learn but to bask in your answering."

Another image of them, whispering, yelling. From the day they were taken.

"Taken says that they wish to have stayed, but yours couldn't say that, could they?"

Her words feel like a sucker punch to the stomach. Of course they wanted to stay. They were my parents. We were their children.

A hazy memory is clawed from a place rooted deep in my mind. Clinging to Cenna's hand as we watch our parents marching up to the Trial hall. They'd "be back for us," they promised.

A cold air sweeps down my spine, and I stiffen.

We were their *children.*

Tears prickle at the corners of my eyes as I stare blankly at the Calkli flicking her tail almost jovially, as if in celebration of my pain.

I will not lose her game. I can't let her distract me.

"Who is to blame for the circumstances that befall you?" The Calkli grins widely as she asks.

This question was easier, not feeling like an attack, but more a prodding for information. My mind shifts between faces, anger swirling inside me. I could choose only one? Drytas could be blamed for almost everything that had happened. Even Torryn had his part to play, but now all I can see is Evander.

My heart clenches at the thought of him, but I shove it down. It's not like it had been love, but now it never would be.

"Evander." The name sounds like a threat as it leaves my lips.

The Calkli shrieks in happiness, "You can lie to yourself, but not to me. I know your mind better than thee."

As she speaks, I notice immediately her teeth lengthening. Sharpening. Until pointed, jagged teeth line the rows of her mouth, glinting dangerously at me when she smiles. With each question wrong, she is transforming into a nightmare of a creature.

The stone under my feet crumbles under me, and I scramble, back pressing further into the blade at my back. I yell in anguish as the tips bury deeper into the expanse of my skin, but no matter how far I push myself back, the bridge keeps crumbling until there's nothing left for me to stand.

I start to fall, screaming as I drop toward the murky water below. Grabbing onto the spikes, I try to hold myself up, feet kicking at the cave's walls to boost myself higher, but my hands are wet, and bloody from the spikes jagged edges. My fingers slip, and I fall backward into the water.

My head dunks below the glacial water's surface, and I have

to remember not to scream. Holding my breath as I scramble for the walls of the cave pool, kicking my legs in what is supposed to be my attempt at swimming.

Gasping, I break free from the water's dragging pull, shrieking when something hits my leg. The Calkli's tail whips away from me, visible from where it just cut through the water's surface.

My body shakes and trembles, fighting the chill that surrounds it. Holding onto the cave wall with a morsel of strength, I pray to the Trial. Begging for this not to be what ends me. Begging for the chance to finish what I've started.

The Calkli circles the pool, cackling as I fight to keep my head above water. "I remember Evander. He Trialed with me too, a tricky one he was. Nothing that he said was ever strictly a lie, but he always managed to say just enough of the truth that it didn't matter. I *so* hoped that he would join me down here."

Evander and his little white lies. *Yeah, I heard them too.* I feel like sneering at her, but I swallow the remark.

"If not him, then Drytas?" I ask, sputtering out water.

The Calkli bobs with the water that rises to her black filled eyes. She shakes her head with a quirk of her lips. "There are forces at play that even I dare not name."

That isn't an answer.

"Only one question left. You're keeping me on the edge of my seat here." The Calkli says, taunting me as she nears once again.

"Why you?" The Calkli asks with a crooked grin. "Why were you the one to set this war into motion? The Court of Valor's Trial breaking. A new war cresting on the horizon. You've saved lives and ended them with the same breath, so answer me this, and you will be free. Why was it you?"

I fumble for an answer, even if I've asked it myself a thousand times. Leaving Falland and everything that came after had been my decision. My choice. To fix things when no one else was.

But, like everyone else, I had been stuck in an endless cycle of hopelessness and fear. Not believing that things could change, so never trying to. Sticking it out to make it through every day.

The only reason that everything else happened is because of being forced to Trial. Which can't be blamed directly on Drytas, because he wasn't the reason I Trialed. Torryn was. And he had only stumbled upon me because I tried to save him—or at least the child he masqueraded as.

"Be-because I," I stutter, terrified of saying the wrong answer. "I tried to protect an innocent that I met by pure chance, and it's all I've been trying to do since."

I flinch backward, waiting for my fate.

The Calkli frowns at the admission, and I brace myself for the inevitable. At least I tried. Tried to make it out of here. Make it back. I wait for her hands to grab me and drag me under. But they never do.

The spikes in the door above me retract with a clinking noise, and the door rolls open. Just as the bridge had crumbled away, a staircase pushes out from the stone of the pool's walls.

Eyes wide with disbelief, I yank myself onto the bottom step, arms trembling under my weight.

The Calkli eyes me from the water below, glaring in annoyance. "If I didn't know that no one can speak about their Trial to those who haven't completed it, I would think you cheated. How else could there be two of you Trialing in the span of decades when I once could go centuries without another one of you?"

Two of us?

"Did I—Did I pass? It was the truth?" Excitement and

unbridled relief floods through me . . . until she answers in a bitter voice.

"It was a lie," the Calkli says, and my heart drops to my feet. Her tail gives an aggravated flick. "It just happens that it wasn't *your* lie. None of your lies were. I just needed *one real lie* from you, and you would have been mine." She bares her teeth at me. "But alas, not speaking the truth is not the same as lying."

I shake my head, raising my shoulders to my ears. Am I supposed to know what that means? The difference between my lie and another's?

The Calkli groans as she rolls over beneath the water. "You seek and say the truth, but others lie to you. They'll never lie to you again, and now your Trial is at its end."

I catalog the words for later, taking away only that I'm free —alive. The Calkli is a mind twisting demon, and it's obvious she takes pleasure in playing with the minds of her prey. I won't let her play with me any longer.

She mutters something under her breath that turns into bubbles as she sinks further into the water. It isn't until I see the flick of her tail at the surface of the water that I realize she's diving back into the depths away from me.

It is really over. I passed.

A prickling sensation moves up my arm, past my Trial tattoo from the Court of Valor, settling just above it. Beneath the scratches I'd received and Gennady's blood that lingered on my skin, the dark swirls raise to the surface, extending past my wrist now to include my forearm.

I don't let even a beat of hesitation pass before dragging myself up the stairs, and struggling to my feet. The bloody holes now scattered across my back side sting with each stretch of my skin as I move, but I won't risk being caught inside again.

I'm not done in the Court of Truth.

CHAPTER 50

I have no plan as I flee from Truth's Trial. Adrenaline surges through me, feeling like lightning powers every step, propelling me on. The divots that now pepper my back finally stop bleeding, allowing for my shirt to dry, now clinging to the wounds.

When I step out into the Trial hall, I expect a lot of things. I expect to be surrounded by guards, taken as soon as I move into sight. I expect Lord Drytas to be there, waiting for his chance to execute me if the Trial fails to. Evander would probably be there, too, but in what way I can't predict. I've lost any insight I thought I had into him.

But none of that happens.

The room is empty. Not a single person waits for me. Lord Gennady's body is gone from the room, the only evidence of having been there at all being the large red stain that stands out against the white tile floor. Severin is nowhere to be seen, and I can only assume he has been taken.

Dead or alive, is the question.

I try to put their fates out of my mind as I pick up my discarded sword and rush from the room.

Explosions echo in the distance, sounding off at random intervals. Each serving as my time counting down. The resounding booms bringing warnings of death like a clock striking twelve.

The sky outside is painted in the morning colors of dawn, and with it brings bloodshed and death. Jogging the halls, I peer out windows, searching for the chaos, but only find smoke and fire. The remains of what was the Court of Truth.

The castle's leveled ruins are the battleground of the ultimate War Hour, as men and women fight with every ounce of their strength. Fear etched in the faces of both sides as they each push their lines forward. Neither willing to yield.

This is not a feat of power and abilities. There are no hidden advantages, quick escapes, or deeper insights. No one can heal themselves if they are maimed. No one can predict how this will end. Each person feels the same struggle and pain and fear.

Drytas had made this a war of the Untrialed—Valor and Truth alike.

Instead, it is a storm of weapons. Arrows rain, hitting targets without warning. Swords clash against armor and shields.

My throat tightens at the bodies that litter the ground. Members of both sides who were slain. Angry tears leak from my eyes—there were more dead than those left alive.

In the distance, on the crest of a hill, stands Lord Drytas. The blood red color of his cape blowing in the wind like a flag, raised high above his people. His eyes feast on the battle before him, grinning maliciously as his people are forced to kill or be killed, all in the name of their lord's power-hungry rule.

Anger surges through me, just as blood pumps through my veins. Clenching my fists until my nails gouge into the skin of my palms, I shake my head in disgust.

The guard—the only people with any training or ability in

Falland stand in lines around Lord Drytas. Protecting him like a shield of bodies.

Coward.

Bringing the Untrialed had not been about increasing his number, or Trialing them to increase the court's power. Lord Drytas could not care less about the lives of those who were lost in his fight.

The Untrialed were brought here on a suicide mission.

My stomach rolls, knowing how easily I could have been one of the dead left to be trampled, sword still trapped in my ribs. Lord Drytas's plan falls into place in my head as I look between the two opposing sides.

There is no going home for the Untrialed—otherwise, the guards would fight right alongside them. Even if they survived here on the battlefield, Drytas would sacrifice them to Truth's Trial.

And Lord Gennady's guards? Is there an option for them to surrender? Or were they sentenced to die with their opponents? What would it mean for the citizens who lived in the city beyond the castle?

Standing at the frontline between the two courts, I'm torn between what to do. I don't have the energy in me left to fight, and even if I did—could I fight against my own, knowing they had little choice?

If the two sides knew the truth, would they continue fighting against each other?

The Court of Truth is only defending themselves from attack. It had been the decision of the Crowns to not convey the threat Lord Drytas posed until they could prove it credible, and instead it had left their people unprepared. These people who fought with every ounce of life they had left to give, likely didn't even know their lord was dead.

I could only assume the lies Lord Drytas had fed the people

of Valor, the Untrialed, to get them to fight for his selfish terrorism. Perhaps he hadn't deemed them worthy of an explanation, instead forcing them to battle under threat of their lives.

It all needed to stop.

I'm not a Crown or an Heir. I lack the training the other courts have received since birth. But I can't leave the saving to someone else anymore. No one is coming. If the other courts haven't arrived already, then they won't arrive in time. Not when only a hundred or so remained on either side.

Gathering every drop of energy in my reserves, I summon my shield. The exhaustion of my Trial weighs on me, but it cannot suffocate the fight I have left.

Raising my hands, I form the shield into a divide. Cutting off the fight that unravels closest to me. Two opponents step back at the shield separating them, looking at the other in shock. Reaching deep, I stretch the shield, pushing it to expand—reaching further down the frontline. A trickle of sweat beads at my forehead, feeling cool against the fire that burns under my skin.

As the shield makes its way further into the battlefront, more swords are lowered in astonishment at the barrier that protects them against their foe.

Too much of the war still rages on, beyond where my shield seemed to reach. With groans and clenched teeth, I push myself to the limit, feeling the ache in my muscles and bones. My head spins, vision blurring, as I push the shield to cross the entire battle line.

It's impossible to separate every Valor Untrialed from every Truth Untrialed, but I don't need to. The sound of the dying battle is audible. Swords thud dully on the shield, no longer scraping against their opponents' blades. The roar of battle seeps away as people turn to question the lull in fighting.

The stillness travels away from the shield in waves, as more and more of the battle comes to a screeching halt. Even Lord Drytas in the distance can see the change, as he angrily turns to the men around him.

There wouldn't be much time before he would be on us.

What did one say to people that have lost everything?

"No one has told you the truth," I bellow, my voice echoing across the frozen field.

The murmurs that had raced from neighbor to neighbor quiet, all turning to search for the voice that rings out. Those that stand closest to me pinpoint me as the speaker, turning to watch me with suspicious gazes.

Their watchful gazes stir doubt. Who am I to speak to them?

Resolving myself, I step forward, slowly walking toward where the shield starts. My knees shake, and I worry they will give out from weakness. I'm pushing myself too far. Stretching my power too much. If I'm not careful, I will burn myself out and then, if the fight resumes, I'll be defenseless.

"Your enemy does not stand opposite you. Your swords do not slay those who conspire against you." I shout the words as loud as my lungs will allow, my throat protesting as it cracks.

Following the gazes of their neighbors, more of the battle-front turns to follow me. When I stand in arm's reach of the shield, I focus on pushing it back. Each step I take, the shield shrinks back another foot.

"Valor!" I shout, gesturing to the people on the left of my shield. "I am one of your own. I too was Untrialed until Lord Drytas forced me to bend to his will, just like he does to you now." I hesitate, letting my words sink in. "Lord Drytas manipulates you—controls you. He is prepared to sacrifice you in exchange for power."

Pointing at Drytas from his perch on the hill, I shout at them with fervor.

"He is your enemy."

Turning to my right, I swallow. Staring down the people of the Court of Truth.

"Truth! You are fighting for your home and your fellow citizens against people who do not wish to take it from you."

When I reach where the shield separates the two sides, I hesitate. If I lower the shield now, and the battle reignites, I won't have the strength to raise it again. But even now I can feel the well of magic inside me emptying rapidly. I can only hold on for so much longer either way.

Looking between the two individuals, who only a minute ago were fighting each other for their life, I decide. Inching back the shield, I breathe a sigh of relief as both sides refrain from attacking one another. I continue my words, pushing the shield backward as I walk the line separating the battlefronts.

"Together, your numbers far exceed his. He cannot force you to do anything any longer."

When I reach the end of my shield, I pivot to see the two lines watching me with renewed fire in their eyes. Fire burning not in their fight against each other, but against their common enemy.

Turning to look for Drytas and the guard, I can see their masses moving down the hill toward us like a black wave crashing onto the green field. The two groups follow my gaze, landing on the sight of their true enemy.

Turning away from them, I wince as my brain splits, as if being cleaved by an ax. Using such a level of my power had been too much.

Worth it.

At least they would not go down blindly fighting. I would fight alongside them, but only against the real enemy.

"Lysta." A voice sounds from behind me, an Untrialed emerging from the crowd.

My stomach tightens, my eyes well with unshed tears at the sound of it. Turning around, my eyes land on his, and I can't stifle the whimper that escapes me.

Thoman.

CHAPTER 51

Overwhelmed by dizziness and exhaustion, I stumble forward, but Thoman rushes forward to catch me.

He smells like sweat and blood, and more unmentionable odors curdling my stomach. I cling to him anyway, wrapping my arms around him firmly as if at any moment he will disappear.

"You're alive. Trials, Lysta. I thought you were dead." His voice is thick with emotion as he squeezes me until it feels like I will bruise.

Hot tears stream from my eyes into my ears as I crane my head to look at him.

"I—I tried to stop him—Drytas," pulling away from Thoman, I examine him. "It's a long story, for another time if we get out of this alive."

"Don't say that," Thoman says forcefully, gesturing to the combined legion behind him. "Look at what you've already done. You saved us."

But I didn't. Maybe I would have if we'd gotten to Valor sooner, before Drytas could assemble his army. Maybe if I hadn't put so much faith in Evander, Drytas never would have escaped.

Giving Thoman my toughest look, I add, "Drytas has already taken too much from me. I don't think I could stand it if I lost you, too."

Did he know about Doireann?

Thoman frowns. He looks away, not meeting my gaze, before cursing under his breath. "I thought you knew—that maybe you'd seen her when you were in the grand hall—"

"It's okay, Thoman. I know about Doireann."

"Not Doireann." A broken expression crosses his face, but he shakes his head, grabbing my hands in his. "Before we moved on to Truth, we made camp a few miles away. It was all the Untrialed, the guards, and even the higher ups."

Thoman hesitates, reaching for me, but I yank out of his grip.

"Get to the point, Thoman."

"Cenna was there."

My ears ring as I try to focus on Thoman's words. It'd been so many years now since she'd left—left me. Looking around, I spin, searching the crowd. Praying that she is among one fighter who stands with me and not one of the dead bodies that cover the ground.

"Lysta, she's not here. Lysta!" Yanking my face to look at his, he makes me listen. "Cenna isn't an Untrialed anymore—"

That's right. She Trialed. Willingly. If she'd passed, she wouldn't be down here with the Untrialed. "A guard?" I ask, shaking my head in disbelief. "If she was a guard, I would have seen her, Thoman."

Thoman takes a deep breath before delivering the final blow.

"Lysta, Cenna is one of Drytas's generals. She's part of his counsel."

Shoving down the struggle that battles inside me, I turn to face the dawn of a new War Hour.

Lord Drytas's men barrel down the hill toward their new unified enemy; the Untrialed and what remains of the Truth's military. A renewed fight sparks in their eyes.

Stretching my hands out in front of me, I try to summon a sliver of my shield one last time. But nothing comes. The hum that sings through my blood is gone.

For a moment, I panic, twisting around to look for Evander. Only he could take my power away like this. But no matter how many faces I search, his is not one of them.

There is only one other explanation. My power burned out from stretching myself too thin. Now I can only fight. Fight as an Untrialed once more.

The distance shrinks between us and the army of guard, but their attack starts long before. In a storm of weapons, our swords raise, bows snap, as they lift everything we have and rain them down on us.

It'll be a quick battle. We are outnumbered. Outpowered.

A glow cascades over the field, haloing around us as if the sun were at our back. Turning, dead on my feet, I realize what would be our saving grace.

The white light radiates off a portal that cuts a hole in the space behind us. Sar stands on the other side of the portal, hair whipping around her as she expands the portal. Her mouth moves, but I can't hear her words.

When sound can reach her, I mouth the words, "Are they coming?"

She knows I mean the other courts—the ones who vowed to help whoever Drytas attacked.

Sar shakes her head.

I don't even have the energy to shout for everyone to go through the portal, but Thoman does it for me, screaming for a retreat. Waves of people hurry past me through the portal, watching in awed terror as they escape certain death.

Staring up at where Lord Drytas sits perched on his heel, I can't help but smirk. He'd thought we would die on this hill, protecting the Trial till we took our last breaths.

The Trial did not need protecting. It was the people.

He could have the Trial, and we'd see how much he could do with it when he had no people to Trial. Unless he wanted to start sacrificing his guard.

Backing up toward the portal, I turn to look through, making sure everyone has made it through. My heart clenches in my chest at who stands next to Sar.

Torryn.

His dark hair whips around his face, and like Sar he calls out to me. Mouth echoing words I can't hear. Face pinched in worry, his panicked eyes search me, and it is as if he can see what has happened. Maybe he's in my head and *can* see it.

The slice on my throat from the Trial hall when the guard had held a knife to my throat. The blood that stains my shirt red from the holes that now litter up and down my back. Maybe he can even see that I've lost control of my shield, burned out.

Staring at Drytas in the distance, his face is monstrous in his anger. Red, with veins popping out. He reaches toward one of his guards, pulling a dagger from their side. He throws it, using his telekinesis to slingshot it across the miles of the battlefield.

Aimed straight for me.

I move for the portal and just as I start to step through, I stumble, a fierce pain stabbing between my shoulder blades. Unable to hold myself up any longer. I fall through the portal into Torryn's arms, who catches me—calling my name repeatedly the whole time.

The world around me blurs as Torryn tilts my face toward his. "Lysta, talk to me," he urges. His voice is almost a low growl when he asks, "What happened to you?"

Dark spots flicker across my vision as I stare up at him. "You came," I mumble, trying to keep my eyes from closing for what feels like could be the last time.

He responds, but the words fall into the abyss that beckons me.

And then there is only darkness.

END of BOOK 1

AUTHOR'S NOTE
THANK YOU FOR READING!

Thank you so much for joining Lysta on her journey throughout *War Hour* and I hope you'll follow along for the rest of *The Broken Trials* series! Her story is just beginning!

Please consider leaving a review on Amazon or Goodreads. I can't explain how much they mean to us authors, and I could never thank you enough.

I'm beyond honored by your support.

WANT UPDATES ON THE SEQUEL TO WAR HOUR?

SIGN UP FOR THE MONTHLY NEWSLETTER TO GET UPDATES ON BOOK RELEASES, GIVEAWAYS, AND ARC OPPORTUNITIES.

NOT TO MENTION YOU'LL BE THE FIRST TO SEE EXCITING COVER REVEALS AND ART!

Acknowledgments

This book never would have seen the light of day (or reading lights for those pulling an all-nighter) if it weren't for the amazing people I'm surrounded by.

To my parents, Jeff and Linda, for never failing to let my dreams soar while also keeping me grounded. I'm proud of the daughter you raised and know all of the best parts of me—I inherited from you. I'm an ambitious dreamer and a business-minded woman, and hope to achieve heights that make you proud. Thank you for your excitement and support as I published this book, because it never would have happened without you.

To my sister, Katelynn, for finding all of the best books to read growing up and then passing them to your little sister to read. I remember you reading me your books back when we had sleepovers in your room, and I hope my niece, Juliet, will love books as much as we did.

To all of my family, grandparents, aunts and uncles, and cousins, thank you for being a part of my life, buying me books as a kid, and your overall support. My life has been brighter with you all in it.

To Jack, my first reader for every form this story has taken. Regardless of distance, time differences, and every other obstacle that could find us, you have supported this book, a reassuring voice when my doubts creep in. Thank you for saying this book was good, even when it was a first draft and absolutely terrible. Because eventually I made it here.

To my bestest of friends, Molly and Julianna, who have been my personal champions for every endeavor that I find myself pursuing. You are lifelong friends that I'm blessed to have found.

Just as in real life, I can't go five minutes without mentioning the light of my life—my dog, Aurora. No matter where I end up writing, whether it be my desk or the couch, you are never out of reach, and I treasure our cuddles and belly rub breaks. I imagine you are quite proud of your mom for finding a career aspiration that coincidentally keeps her at home with you all day.

Thank you to my beta readers, Kira, Taylor, Alyx, Abbie, Chelsea, Stephanie, Melissa, Megan, Nicole, Hailee, Badriyah and Brooke. You gave me the confidence that my book was a story people would want to read and that it actually made sense to someone other than me.

To my cover designer, Franziska Stern – Cover Dungeon Rabbit, thank you for the stunning cover. Scribubbles for my amazing under-the-dust-jacket cover art. Lazy Dragon Art for my scene illustrations. Cartography Bird for my amazing map. All of you made this book into something real and tangible and I can't thank you enough.

And to Booktok, Bookstagram—where I found a community that was excited for my book. Your support has meant everything. I would not be here without the likes, comments, and messages encouraging me.